RUSSIAN STYLE

glas

NEW RUSSIAN WRITING

8

Editors:
Natasha Perova (Moscow) & Dr. Arch Tait (UK)
Designed by Emma Ippolitova
On the back cover: a drawing by Dmitry Alexandrovich Prigov

> The photographs in this issue are from a series of 40 pictures by Laura Ilyina featuring modern Russian young people.

GLAS Publishers
Moscow 119517, P.O.Box 47, Russia
Tel./Fax: (095) 441 9157 E-mail: perova@glas.msk.su

UK address
for enquiries, subscriptions and payments:
GLAS, c/o Dept. of Russian Literature,
University of Birmingham, B15 2TT
Tel.: 021-414 6044 Fax: 021-414 5966
E-mail: a.l.tait@bham.ac.uk

North America
Sales and Editorial office, GLAS
c/o Zephyr Press, 13 Robinson Street, Somerville MA 02145
Tel: (617) 628-9726 Fax: (617) 776-8246
E-mail: edhogan@world.std.com

ISBN 5-7172-0023-4
US ISBN 0-939010-44-5

© Translation copyright, 1994 by GLAS
copyright reverts to translators upon publication

"GLAS has become almost disturbingly indispensable. The texts and voices out of Russia come through with formidable insistence. More now than ever before, precisely because hopes on their native ground are again precarious"—George Steiner

> Glas is published with the support of
> **SIGNALS INTERNATIONAL TRUST**
> for the promotion and preservation of Russian writing

Printed in Malta by Interprint Limited for Amon-Re Ltd.

Contents

Sigizmund Krziszanowsky *In the Pupil of the Eye* 12

Vladimir Makanin *The Safety-valve* 46

Sergei Task
S.O.B. 94 & *Four Knights Opening* 101

Nina Gabrielian
Happiness 118 & *The Studio Apartment* 122

Transfiguration:
Feminist Journal and Club in Russia 144

Ergali Ger *Electric Liza* 148

Dmitry Prigov *Poems, drawings, thoughts* 174

The Poet and Family Values: Mayakovsky and Lily Brik 186
The Last Emigre: Berberova and Khodasevich 190

THE FIRST GAY PUBLISHING HOUSE FLOURISHING 194
RUSSIA'S FIRST EROTIC PAPER PERSECUTED 204
Igor Yarkevich *The Provisional Government* 210

Centenaries: Mikhail ZOSCHENKO (1894-1958)
Isaac BABEL (1894-1941)
Mikhail Zoschenko *Youth Regained* 216
Babel as the Marquis de Sade of the Russian Revolution
by Igor Yarkevich 226

Alex Lamont Miller: In Memoriam
231

Grigory Kruzhkov *Where Unmagical People Came From* 234

About the authors 236

"LOVE RUSSIAN STYLE". The theme was suggested not primarily by the emerging erotic press in Russia, although that is represented here, nor by the uninhibited writings of the younger generation of Russian writers, some of whom we also present (Ergali Ger, Igor Yarkevich, Sergei Task), but by a story by the 1993 Booker Prize winner Vladimir Makanin about an unmarried woman who carries on an unsatisfactory relationship with a married man, then with two married men both of whom eventually abandon her. The detail of her slow-moving, tortuous love affair vividly characterises the hopeless and humiliating position of the unmarried woman in Russia, no matter how independent and uncomplaining she is trying to be.

There is a highly original treatment of the love theme by Sigizmund Krziszanovsky, a recently rediscovered author of the 1950s who didn't see a single line of his work published in his lifetime but who is now being extensively published all over the world as well as in Russia.

We are proud to present an interesting woman author, Nina Gabrielian, one of the editors of the first Russian feminist almanac *Transfiguration* and an activist in the fast developing feminist movement in Russia. Women are only just finding their voice, and outstanding women writers of the stature of Petrushevskaya or Tolstaya are still few and far between. Changes for the better in this area are nevertheless very obvious. In subsequent issues we hope increasingly to present new women authors speaking about their everyday experiences and sharing their views of the world.

The recognised leader of Russian post-modernism, Dmitry Prigov, is a man of many outstanding talents. He is represented here by his poems, drawings and, last but not least, his thoughts on the state of contemporary Russian culture.

This issue of *Glas* pays tribute to two great Russian writers of the 1920s whose centenaries fall this year: Mikhail Zoschenko (1894-1958) and Isaac Babel (1894-1941).

There are two essays, on Mayakovsky's love for Lily Brik, and on Nina Berberova's life with the poet Vladislav Khodasevich. Although *Glas* generally focuses on contemporary authors, we believe that the Silver Age of Russian literature is still so little known, and still holds so many surprises, that even for the Russian reader the work of those returned from the obscurity of past decades is refreshingly new. This is why we intend to continue acquainting our readers with rediscovered gems, as well as exciting new works by young authors.

— The Editors

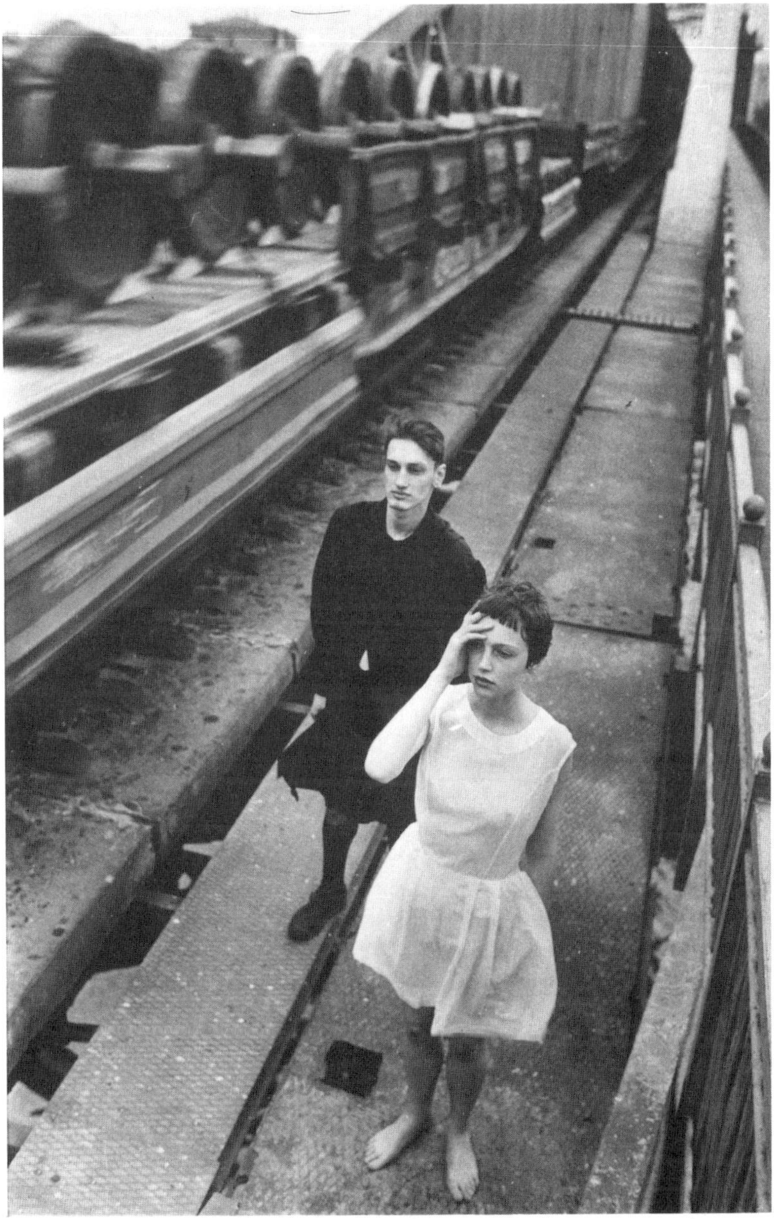

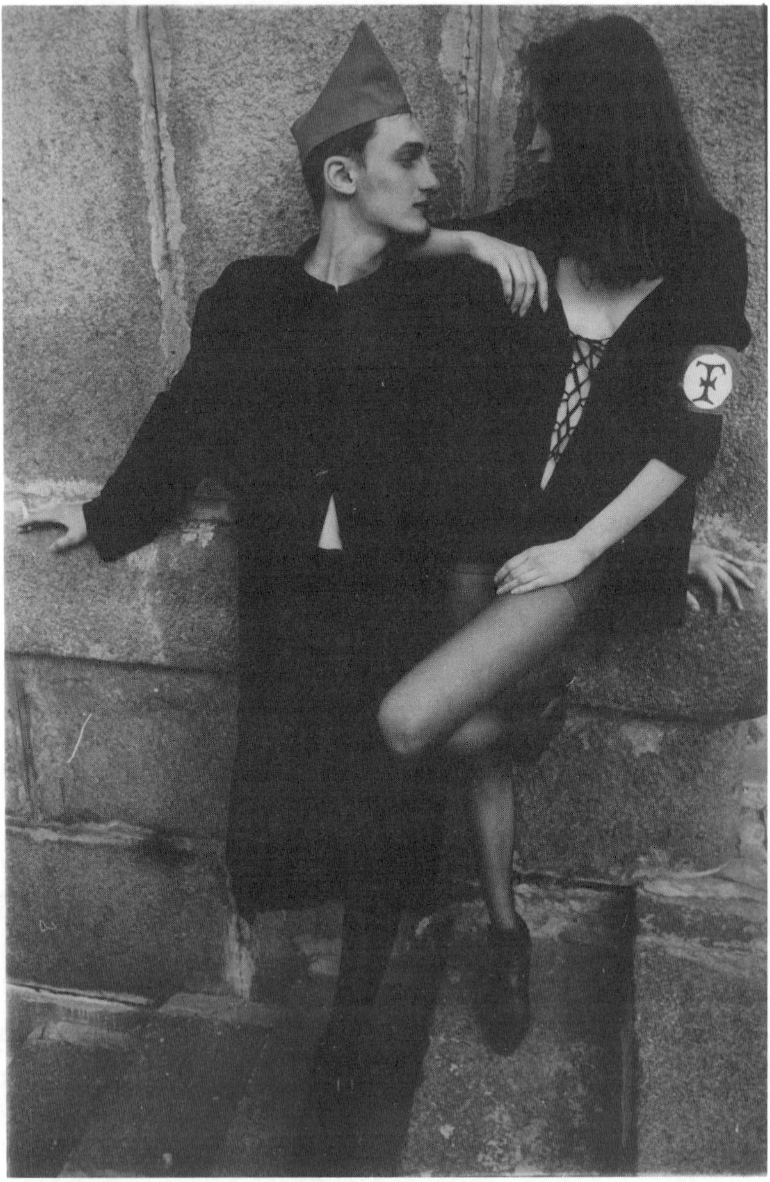

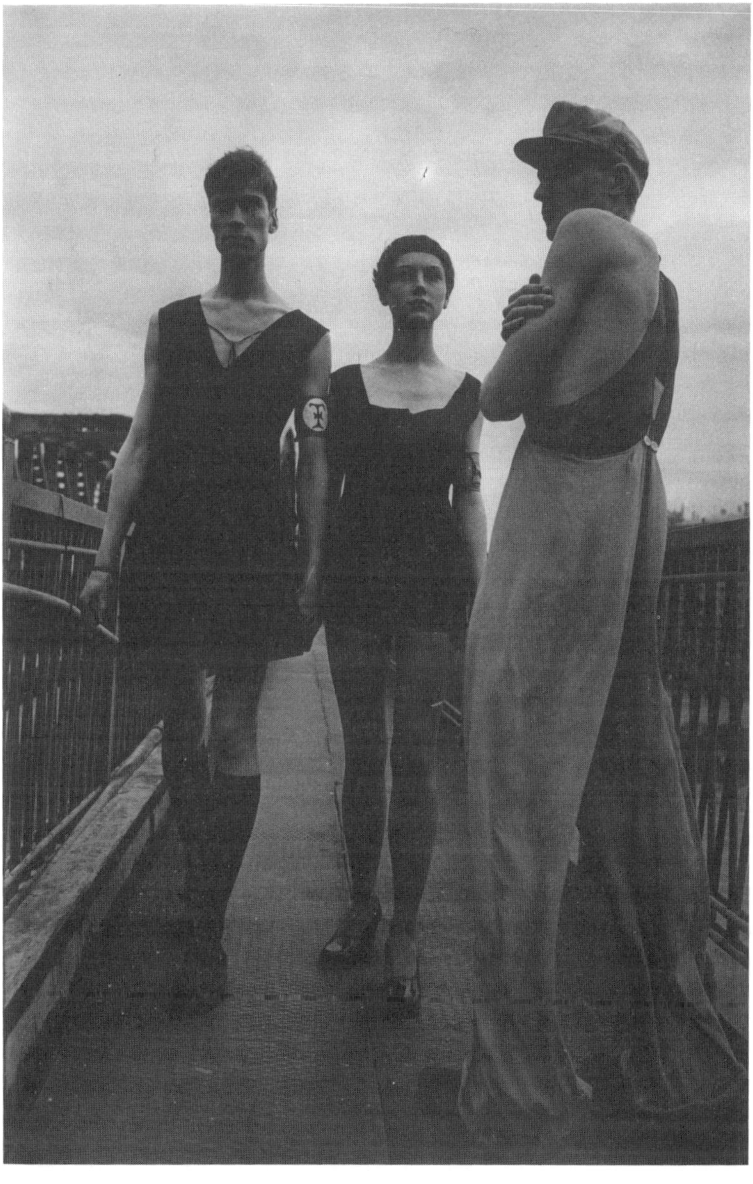

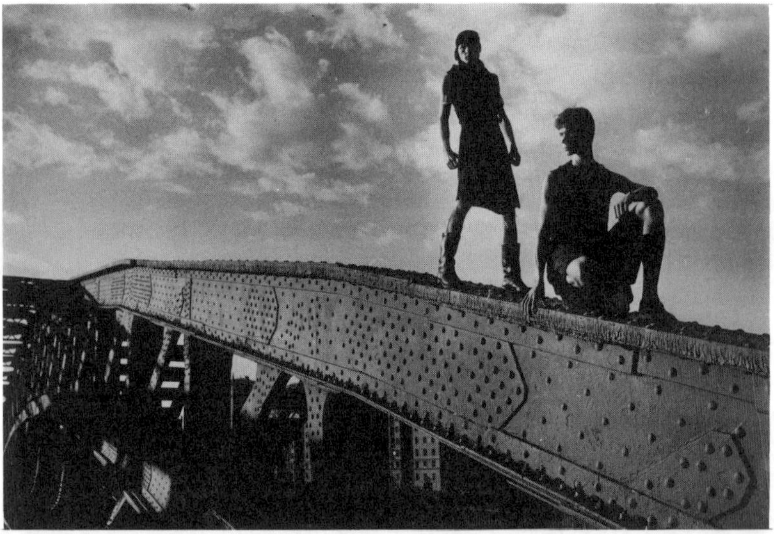

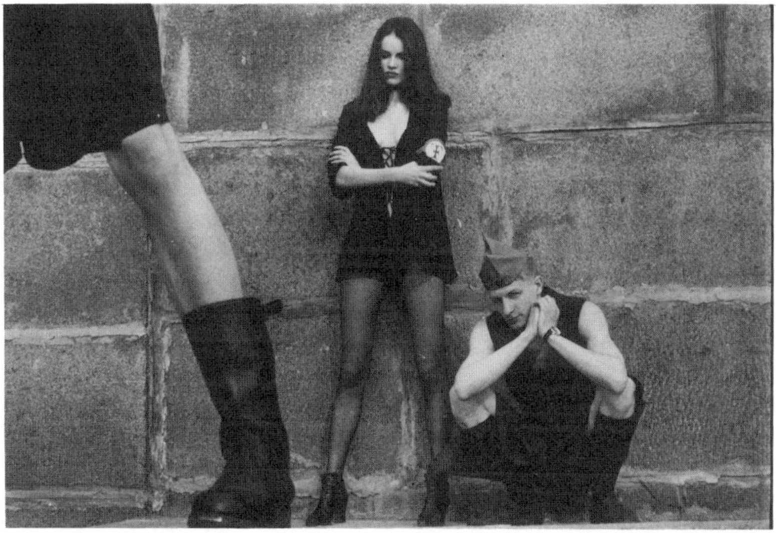

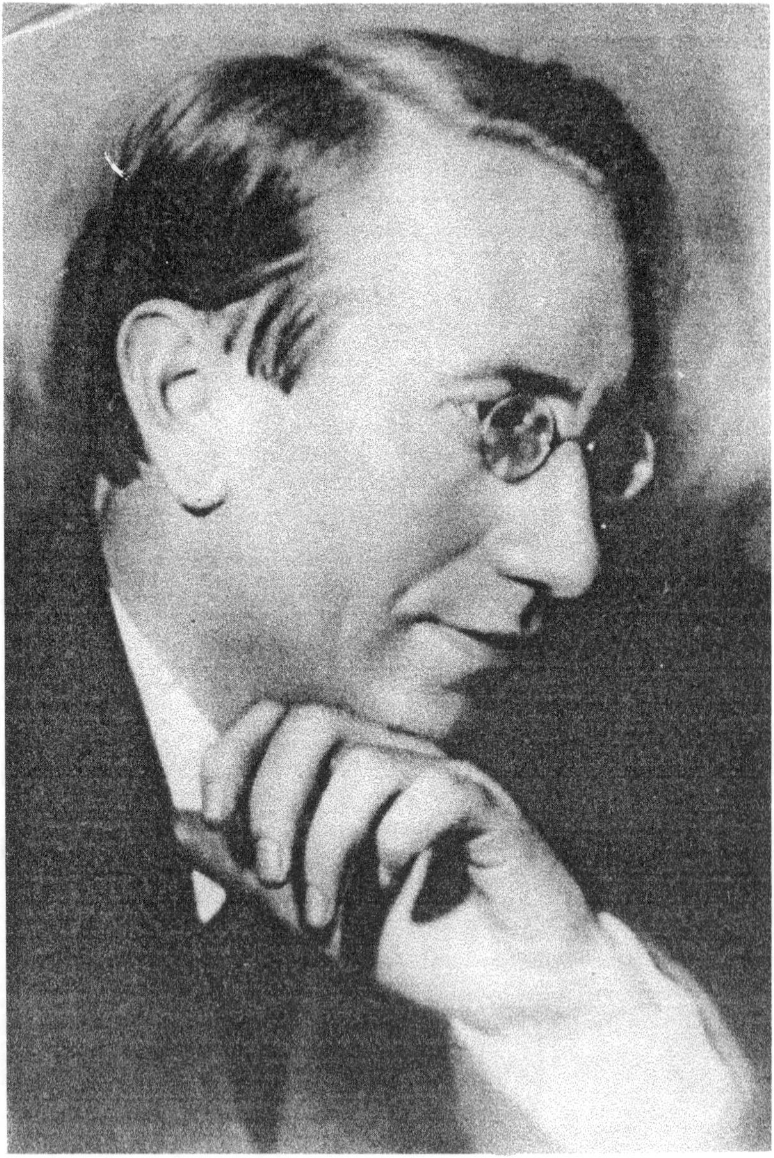

Sigizmund
KRZISZANOWSKY
In the Pupil of the Eye

1

Human love is a frightened thing, it keeps its eyes closed; it dives into the twilight, darts around darkened streets, speaks in whispers, hides behind curtains, puts out the light.

I'm not jealous of the sun. Let it do its peeping – so long as it stays put as I undo the clasps. Let it take a peek through the windows. It doesn't bother me.

Yes, I've always been of the opinion that midday is much better suited for love-making than midnight. The moon, on which so many enthusiastic interjections are wasted, is a night sun under a blue bourgeois lampshade; I just can't stand that. The story about a certain "yes" and its consequences – that's what this story is about – began in bright sunshine, by a window wide open to the daylight. It's not my fault that it happened to end between day and night, in the murky nastiness. It's the fault of the woman whose "yes" I'd waited for so long and so passionately.

But even before that "yes", certain events took place which it is essential to mention. One can claim that with love it's the eyes which, shall we say, run on ahead. That's understandable – they're more mobile and they know how to look right through you. While the lovers' bodies, by comparison with their eyes, are clumsy and huge and hide from one another behind the clothes, whilst even words somehow huddle and stumble on the lips, fearing to leap into the air, the eyes, running on ahead, are already giving themselves to each other.

Oh, how clearly I remember that bright day, shot through with an azure sky, when the pair of us standing at the window which was opened to the sun, simultaneously, as though by agreement, glanced... not out of the window, naturally, but at each other. And that was when the third person appeared: a tiny little fellow, his glance fixed on me from within her pupil, a miniaturized likeness of me, who'd already made his way there. I hadn't even yet dared to touch the edge of her dress, and he was already... I smiled and nodded to him. The little fellow nodded back politely. But the eyes turned away and we didn't meet again until that very "yes".

When it summoned me, that barely audible "yes", I didn't ask any more questions. Grabbing the wrists of the submissive arms, I saw

In the Pupil of the Eye

him prominent through the round window of the pupil, his excited face was getting nearer and nearer. For an instant, he was curtained by the eyelashes. Then he came into view again briefly and disappeared. His face, as I managed to notice, shone with joy and proud satisfaction: he was like a successful manager, busying himself assiduously with other people's affairs.

From then on, with every fresh meeting, before my lips sought out her lips, I would glance under the eyelashes of my beloved, seeking him out, that tiny fixer of love. He was invariably there on the dot, and however tiny the face of the little man in the pupil, I could always accurately work out his expression – sometimes it had a youthful cheerfulness, sometimes there was a hint of fatigue, sometimes it was peacefully contemplative.

One day, during a rendezvous, I was telling my girl friend about the little man who had penetrated her pupil and about my thoughts on him. To my surprise, my story was received coldly, even with slight hostility.

"What rubbish," and I saw how her pupils, with an instinctive shudder, shifted away from me. I took her head in my hands and tried by force to seek out the little man but, laughing, she lowered her eyelids.

"No, no," and it seemed to me that in her laughter there was no laughter at all.

Sometimes you get used to a trifle, you attribute some sense to it, you give it some philosophical significance – and lo and behold, that trifle raises its head and launches into an argument with what's important and real, shamelessly demanding an augmentation of its being, some elaboration. I'd already started to get used to the trivial little man from the pupil; it was convenient for me when I was telling some story or other to see that she was listening and so was he. Furthermore, into the normal course of our meetings there gradually entered a sort of game (lovers think up all kinds of such things) which consisted of the woman hiding the little man and me trying to find him; this was accompanied by a lot of laughter and kisses. And so one day (I still find it somehow rather difficult to think back about this)... one day, as we were putting our lips close together, I looked into her eyes and saw: the little man, peeping out from behind her eyelashes and nodding to me – his face was sad and he was on his guard – and then suddenly, sharply turning his back, with little mincing steps, he began to recede into the pupil.

"Well, go on, kiss her quickly," and the little man was shut in behind the eyelids.

"Come back!" I shouted and, forgetting myself, squeezed her shoulders with my fingers. In her alarm, the woman raised her eyes and from the depths of her expanding pupils there once again flashed before me the figure of the tiny me as he moved away.

To the alarmed questioning I remained silent, concealing my answer. I sat, looking to one side, and I knew the game was over.

2

For several days I didn't show up – neither to her, nor to other people. Then a letter found me. Inside a narrow cream-coloured envelope there were about a dozen question marks: had I gone away suddenly, was I ill? "Perhaps I was ill," I thought, reading over the spidery lines. I decided to go – immediately, without a moment's delay. But not far from the house where my girl friend lived, I sat down on a bench in the street and began to wait for the twilight. It was certainly cowardice, ridiculous cowardice; d'you see I was afraid, afraid of not seeing what I'd already not seen. You would think that the simplest thing to do in that case was right there to get my pupils to examine hers. No doubt, it was just an ordinary hallucination, a phantom pupil, and nothing else. But it was just that the very fact of carrying out the test looked to me like a sign of the real individual life of the little man in the pupil, that seemed to me a manifestation of an illness, a psychological jolt. The impossibility of that absurd trifle had to be rejected, so it seemed, in a completely logical way, without succumbing to the temptation of an experiment; for wouldn't a series of concrete actions, carried out for the sake of something insubstantial, bestow upon him a certain degree of reality? Of course, I was easily able to hide my own fear from myself. It seemed that I was sitting on the bench because the weather was fine, because I was tired, and because in the end the little man in the pupil was a good subject for a story, and so why not, right now, while at leisure, just think it over, even if only in general terms. Finally, the approaching evening let me into the house. In the dark

In the Pupil of the Eye

hall I heard a "Who's there?" It was her voice, but somehow slightly different — intended for someone else.

'There you are at last!"

We entered the room. Her hand, dimly pale through the twilight, stretched out to switch on the light.

"Don't bother."

I pulled her towards me. We loved each other blindly, soundlessly muffled in the murk of love. And that evening we didn't switch on the lights. I left with the feeling of one who has received a stay of execution.

There's no need to recount this in detail: the longer it goes on, the less interesting it gets. In fact, anyone could finish this chapter, anyone with a smooth gold ring on his finger. Our meetings, radically changing over from midday to midnight, became long drawn out, blind and sleepy, like night itself. Our love gradually turned into something civic, double-bedded, with a complicated inventory ranging from soft slippers to the chamber pot, inclusive. I went the whole way: yet the fear of encountering her pupils and seeing that they were empty, without me, woke me up every morning an hour before dawn. I would get up quietly and dress, trying not to disturb the sleep of my beloved, and then, carefully on tiptoe, I'd depart. At first these early disappearances seemed odd to her. Then it became part of the normal course of events. Thank you, man with ring on finger, I'll tell the rest myself. And each time, as I strode in the freezing urban dawn towards my place, at the other end of the city, I thought about the little man from the pupil. Gradually, as my musings continued, the thought of him ceased to frighten me: if earlier I had been alarmed by the prospect of his concrete existence and had thought about him with apprehension and suspicion, now the little man's non-existence made me sad. It was that very illusoriness and shadowiness.

"How many of these minute reflections do we scatter in other people's eyes," I would usually fantasize, as I made my way along the deserted silent streets, "and suppose I were to gather all those tiny, similar creatures nestling in all those strangers' pupils and form them into a whole little tribe of modified, miniaturized "I"s. Of course they exist, while I'm looking at them, but then so do I exist while someone, anyone is looking at me. If that person shuts his

15

eyes... what nonsense. But if it is nonsense, if I'm not somebody's vision but me in my own right, then the one who's in the pupil – well, he exists as well."

At this point, my sleepy thoughts would usually get muddled and I would have to disentangle them afresh.

"How odd! Why did he have to go away? And where to? Well, OK, fair enough if there was nothing at all in her pupils. What does that mean? What do I need that flicker of my facial likeness for? Isn't it all the same whether he's there or not? And how come that some little pupil person dares to meddle in my affairs, stage a phantom counter-existence and part one person from another?"

When I hit on that thought, I was ready to turn back and wake up my sleeping love and fetch out from under her eyelids the secret of whether he was there or not.

But, I'd never return before evening. Not only that, if there was a light in the room I'd turn my face away and not respond to caresses. No doubt I was morose and rude, until darkness put a blind over our eyes. Then I would boldly bring my face close to hers and ask her, again and again, did she love me? And the normal course of nocturnal events would take over.

3

On one such night I felt, through layers of sleep, how something unseen, clinging to one of the lashes of my left eyelid, was pulling the lash painfully downwards. I opened my eyes wide: something flashed past by my left eye, a little spot tumbling head over heels, and then it rolled down my cheek inside the helix, and in a whisper squeaked in my ear:

"Bloody hell! Like an empty flat – no-one's answering."

"What's that?" I said quietly, not being quite sure if I was awake, or whether it was one dream replacing another.

"First of all, not what, but who. And secondly, lay your ear down close to the pillow so that I can jump out. Nearer – a bit more. Fine."

At the edge of the pillow case, gleaming white in the grey air of the dawn, there sat the little man from the pupil. Leaning against the white threads, his head bent, he was breathing heavily like a traveller who has succeeded in making a long and difficult crossing.

There was sadness and concentration on his face. In his hands was a book, black with grey clasps.

"So you're not an illusion?" I shouted, looking the little man up and down with amazement.

"What a silly question," he interrupted me, "and don't make such a noise or you'll wake up that one, her. Put your ear closer. Right. I've got something important to tell you."

He stretched out his tired legs, settled himself more comfortably, and started in a whisper:

"There's no point in telling you about my pupil-warming party. We both remember all about that. I liked my new home. It seemed to me a comfortable and cheerful place, with its full complement of glassy reflections, the window in the round rainbow frame, the convex lenses neatly washed down with a tear, and the automatic blinds lowered at night – in a word, it was a comfortable flat. Well, OK, there was a long dark corridor stretching out behind, goodness knows where to, but I used to spend nearly all my time by the window, waiting for you to come. What was back there – behind me – didn't interest me. Sometimes it came about that one of the meeting you had arranged didn't take place. I'd walk up and down along the corridor, trying not to go too far away, so that at any moment I would be able to meet you. While this was happening, the day was fading beyond the round opening. "He's not coming," I thought. It got a bit boring and, not knowing what to do with myself, I decided to make my way to the end of the corridor. But, as I've already said, it was murky inside the pupil and after just a few steps I found myself in total darkness. My hand stretched out in front of me but found no support. I was already about to turn back when a low, muffled sound emitted from down there, from the depths of the narrow corridor, attracted my attention. I tried to listen in to it: it was like the long drawn out singing of several voices, voices off-key, but determinedly trying to hold a tune. I even thought that my ear could make out some individual words, then I couldn't make anything out.

This seemed an interesting phenomenon to me, but I decided that it would be more sensible to return to my former place in case the eyelid closing shut off the way back in the dark.

That wasn't the end of it. The next day, without even leaving my seat, I heard the voices behind my back once again. They were coming together in an appalling cacophonous hymn. The words were still difficult to pick out, but it was quite clear that it was an all-male choir. This circumstance saddened me and made me think. I needed to examine the passageway into the interior thoroughly. I won't say that I was particularly keen to undertake the search, with the risk of bumping into goodness knows what and losing the way back to the window and out to the world. For the next two or three days the phenomenon did not recur. "Perhaps I imagined it all," I thought, trying to calm myself down. But then once, right in the middle of the day, when the woman and I had each sat down at our window, waiting for the assignation, this peculiar sound reasserted itself and on this occasion with an unexpected clarity and force: an out of tune mishmash of words, long drawn out and tedious, repeating itself over and over again, assailed my ears and their meaning was such that I firmly resolved to make my way to the singers. I was gripped by curiosity and impatience, but I didn't want to go away without giving warning. We said goodbye: do you remember? Maybe it was a bit unexpected for you. And I quickly marched off into the pupil. It was absolutely quiet. The light which followed me for a long way down the cavernous passage gradually weakened and dimmed. Soon my footsteps rang out in total darkness. I walked on, catching on to the slippery walls of the ocular corridor, stopping every now and again to listen. Finally, from far away, a yellow, dead sort of light beckoned to me; no doubt the wandering lights of marsh gas give off the same kind of gloomy murky flame. Weariness and a dumb indifference seized me. "What am I looking for, what do I want from these catacombs?" I asked myself. "Why should I exchange the sun for this yellow, rotten gloom?" And perhaps I would have turned back once more but, at that instant, the singing which had started to fade from my memory rang out once more; now I could make out individual voices, disappearing out of the wild incantation:

> *Little man, little man,*
> *Come and play our catch-as-can*
> *If the mote is in the eye*
> *Come and join us bye-the-bye*
> *When your head's right in the noose,*
> *Then you'll know to not vamoose*

*Eeny, meeny, miny, mo
Odds or evens in you go!*

This nonsense drew me towards it like a fish to the hook. A circular opening met me as I walked forward, from which came the yellow light. Grabbing hold of the edge of the hole I put my head inside, down below from the void came the howl of a dozen throats. A yellow fluorescence blinded me. Peering in, I leaned over the gap but at that moment the sticky edges of the opening began to move apart and, with my hands grabbing helplessly at the air, I tumbled down. It didn't seem far to the bottom of the cave: I quickly got up on my elbows, sat down and looked around. My eyes, gradually growing accustomed to the light, began to pick out the surroundings. I was sitting as it were inside a glassy but not transparent bottle with pulsating walls, right in the centre of its convex bottom. Below me a glowing yellow spot was spreading out, around me a dozen human shapes, half hidden in the shadows, their heels to the light, their heads against the wall, were majestically reaching the climax of the refrain:

*Eeny, meeny, miny mo
Odds or evens in you go.*

My question "Where am I?" got lost in the roar. Looking for the exit, I tried to straighten up out of the hollow, but my very first step dragged me back, down the slope and, to general laughter and joyful roar, turning up my heels I sat down between two inhabitants of the well.

"It's getting a bit crowded in here," my neighbour on the left rumbled and turned to one side. But the one sitting on the right turned his face to me in a confidential manner: I would have described him as a University type, with an erudite bulbous forehead, thoughtful eyes, a sharp pointed beard and a carefully combed-over bald crown.

"Who are you? Where am I?"

"We're the ones who got here before you. The thing is, a woman's pupil is like any living-space. First they billet you there, then they eject you – and everybody ends up here. For example, I'm No.6 – this one to the left of us is No. 2. You're No. 12. As a matter of fact we don't sort ourselves out strictly according to number, but by our associations. Will that do, or do you want something still more popular? By the way, have you hurt yourself?"

"Against the wall?"

"No, against the sense?"

We remained silent for a moment.

"By the way, don't forget to register your being forgotten. Oh, these female pupils," he pulled at his beard, "the pupils which beckon you below the shelter of the lashes. Just think – such a wonderful entrance, all the sparkling colours of the rainbow and such a nasty dark bottom. Once I did this too..."

I interrupted him:

"Who registers you here?"

"Quagga."

"I've never heard such a name."

"Well, have you heard of telegony?"

"No."

"Hm. That's not so good, you won't know anything about Lord Morton's mare either."

"What's that got to do with it?"

"One thing at a time: there once was a mare. Sorry, first there was Lord Morton. His mare gave birth to a striped foal out of Quagga, while Morton out of Quagga gave birth to the theory of telegony. What it is is that whoever they mated the said mare with, her offspring was always striped, so to speak, in memory of Quagga, who was her first. From this one draws the conclusion that any female organism is irrevocably bound to her first lover and he continues to live as it were within future liaisons, immutably and indestructibly. The first inhabitant of the pupil, on the base of which you and I are presently to be found, in so far as chronology is in his favour, can claim the role of Quagga. I will say that I've more than once explained to him that this theory has long since been disproved by Mr Ewart, but the silly fool tries to dictate matters here, insisting that he's the ground and we're just lumps and all our attempts to repeat the unrepeatable..."

"Tell me," I ask him again, "this telegony, or whatever you call it, is it really disproved once and for all, or...?"

"I knew it," the University type smiled, "I've noticed for a long time that the higher the number, the greater the interest in the question – is love striped or not? But we'll come back to that. Can you hear? No.1's Calling you."

"Forgotten No.12 – come here!"

I stood up and, with my palms slipping along the wall, I went towards the sound. Stepping over the legs outstretched along the way, I noticed that the contours of the pupil-people stood out with different degrees of clarity: some of them so merged into the yellow fog of the nether regions that I involuntarily bumped into them, not noticing the faded, as it were, half-erased figures. Suddenly, two invisible but strongly-gripping hands grabbed me by the ankles.

"Please answer the questions."

I bent down so as to get a good look at the hands which were holding me as if in fetters, but it was impossible to see them. No.1 was clearly fading away to the colour of the air. The unseen fingers freed me and flicked open the covers of the book. This very book. Covered in signs, its pages rose and fell and rose again until a blank page fell open marked with my number.

The registration form involved dozens of questions. It began with one's date of entry, the basis on which entry was sought, the proposed length of stay (for this section there were three sub-paras: (a) eternally (b) until the grave (c) until something better turns up – please underline your preference. I seem to remember that the form concluded with a series of affectionate and diminutive names and your attitude to jealousy. Soon my page was filled. An invisible finger gently turned it over revealing more clean white sheets.

"Well, then," said Quagga, shutting the book. "Another new appointment. The book's getting filled up slowly. That's all, I won't keep you any more."

I returned to my former place between No.2 and No.6. No.6's pale beard jutted forward to meet me but, encountering silence, immediately hid in the shadows.

I sat for a long time, deep in thought about the clean unentered pages of the book of residence permits. A sudden noise returned me to the real world.

"No.11 come out into the middle," Quagga was shouting.

"No.11, No.11!" rang out from all sides.

"What's that?" I turned to my neighbour.

"It's the duty story," he explained. "It goes in numerical order: so next time it'll be your turn."

I didn't' have any reason for more detailed questioning, since the number who had been summoned was already scrambling up the mound that rose from the bottom. His heavy figure seemed at once somehow familiar. My predecessor, settling himself on the yellow spot, quietly looked around. Catching in his teeth the drooping string of his pince-nez, he thoughtfully chewed it, his flabby cheeks quivering:

"Right then!" It's funny to recall it but there once was a time when my sole aim, as with all of us, was somehow or other, by fair means or foul, to find my way through the pupil to our hostess. That's why we're all here. What now?"

He wound the string of his pince-nez round his finger, pulled the glass from his eye, and, screwing up his eye squeamishly, went on:

"A man-trap. Yes, sirree! But let's get down to business. The first encounter decided everything. I remember ours − that day she wore a black buttoned-up dress. And her face seemed somehow tightly buttoned up: her lips were primly sealed, her eyelids half-lowered. The cause of her melancholy is to the left of me. That's our revered No. 10. His story, which we heard last time, remains in everyone's mind. Because forgotten people don't forget. But at that time I had not had the pleasure of knowing him. That's to say that even then I guessed that not everything was all right in those pupils hiding behind the eyelashes and, indeed, when I finally managed to glance into the eyes of the woman, there was so much left-aloneness there that, because I was at that time on the lookout for suitable pupils, I immediately decided to take up residence in the empty property.

But how was that to be achieved? Each of us has his own way of getting into another's soul. Mine lies in the accumulation of little and mostly cheap good deeds: "Have you read this or that?" "No, but I'd like to"... and in the morning, the messenger brings her a book with uncut pages. The eyes which you require to penetrate encounter your respectful inscription and name under the cover. If she loses her hatpin, or the needle for cleaning the primus, make sure you remember all this rubbish accurately, so that at the very next encounter, grinning devotedly, you can take out of your waistcoat pocket a needle, a pin, an opera ticket, some pills and whatever else besides. Really, in actual fact, one probes into another person in tiny doses, with tiny, barely visible miniature men who, if they can be concentrated in sufficient numbers, will finally take over the other person's consciousness. And amongst all these, there's always one, just as pathetically small as the others, but if he goes away, all sense goes with him. Do you understand that? The whole atomic structure falls apart, immediately and irreparably, though you pupil-dwellers don't need to have that explained to you.

And so I put into action the system of small good deeds. All over the place, amidst the bits and pieces, books and pictures clinging to the walls of the room where our mistress lived, there began to appear the objects of my solicitude; her eyes had nowhere to turn from the miniature men who penetrated every nook and whispered my name from every cranny. I thought that, sooner or later, one or other of them would succeed in getting into her pupil. But, for the moment, the matter was moving forward only slowly: the woman's eyelids, as if carrying a huge weight, only rarely gave up, which for me as someone from the pupil, constituted a very difficult situation.

I remember how after the nth good turn, the woman said, smiling somewhere away to one side:

"I believe you're trying to put me under your spell. It's no good."

"Never mind," I replied humbly. "Once in mid-journey to the Crimea, I remember looking out of the window while the train was stopped and seeing a forlorn little brick house, rising up out of the yellow smudges of the fields. On the house was a board with the words *Patience Station*.

As I spoke to her, the woman's eyes opened slightly.

"So according to you, this is mid-journey. That's amusing."

I don't remember what stupid answer I gave, but I do remember that, having reached Patience Station, the train didn't move on for a long time. So that was when I decided to come to you for help, my dear predecessors. I didn't yet know who you were and how many of you there were, but I felt instinctively that the pupils were, so to speak, well lived in, that some Xs of the male sex were leaning over them, that their reflections... well, in a word, I decided, having dipped my spoon into the past, right to the very bottom, to mix it and stir things up again. If a woman has stopped loving one man and hasn't yet started to love another, then if that man has the slightest drop of common sense, he should work things out and not allow a moment of oblivion, until all possible approaches have been revealed.

I stirred my spoon more or less as follows: "Nobody loves people like me. I know that. The one you loved wasn't like me. That's right, isn't it? The one or the ones? Won't you say? Well, of course. Probably it was..." and with the dull conscientiousness of the worker who's been ordered to mix up the must, I continued to stir my questions around. At first I was answered by silences, then by half-words. I could see it: on the surface of her consciousness little bubbles began to swell up and burst, momentary flashes of the rainbow which had seemed forever buried in the past. Encouraged by this success, I carried on my stirring. Oh, yes, I know very well that one can't turn emotional stimuli upside down without disturbing the emotion itself. Images long unloved which I raised from the bottom immediately fell back again, into the darkness, but the sensation which was just on the point of being stirred into life and roused with the images wouldn't lie down and continued to stay up on the surface. The woman's eyes ever more frequently seemed to turn their gaze to meet the questions, and more than once I braced my knees, ready for the jump. But then my huge likeness, in whose pupil I was at the time, in its clumsiness and massiveness, let go one opportunity after another. At last the decisive day came. I, or we that is, found her at the window, her shoulders hunched with cold under the shawl.

"What's the matter with you?"

"Just a fever. Don't take any notice."

But the man who works by the small good turns method isn't allowed not to take any notice. I immediately made for the exit, and quarter of an hour later I was ordered to "turn away".

Tucked into the circulation of the minute hand, I heard the rustle of silk and the click of the knob: the thermometer was being erected in the expected place.

"Well, what does it say?"

"36.6."

Now came the moment when even my ridiculous bulk couldn't mistake the diagnosis. We moved closer to the woman.

"You don't know how to do it. Let me."

"Leave me alone."

"First you have to shake it. Like this. Then..."

In the Pupil of the Eye

"Don't you dare."

My eyes came closer to hers. I managed to jump. The woman's pupils were coated by that particular misty film which is the surest sign... Well, to cut a long story short, I misjudged my jump and got caught on the curve of one of her eyelashes, which was tossing from side to side like a branch in a storm. But I know what's what, and a few seconds later, squeezing through the pupil into the interior, short of breath and agitated, I heard behind me first the sound of kisses and then the clink of the thermometer falling to the floor. From the outside I was shut in by the eyelids. But I'm not curious. With the feeling of a duty performed, I sat down under the high vault, musing on the difficult and dangerous profession of being a pupil person. The future demonstrated that I was correct. Indeed, it turned out to be gloomier than my gloomiest expectations.

No. 11 fell silent as he sat, suspended morosely on the glittering eminence, and the forgotten ones started up their song again, first softly, then louder and louder they sang their strange hymn:

> *Little man, little man,*
> *Jack be nimble, Jack be quick.*
> *Odds you go...*

"What a rude beast," I summed it up as I met the questioning gaze of No. 6.

"He's one of the odds. They're all like that."

In amazement, I repeated the question.

"Well, yes. Haven't you noticed? I'm to one side of you, me No.6. To the other side are Nos. 2 and 4. So we, the even numbers, keep ourselves to ourselves, because, don't you see, all those odd numbers are all bullies and boors – just as if they'd been selected. So, for us quiet people of culture..."

"But how do you explain this?"

"How? Well, how shall I put it – no doubt the heart has its rhythms, it alternates moods of its own volition, it has its own dialectic of love, which exchanges thesis for antithesis, boors for peace-loving guys like us."

He chuckled cheerfully and winked at me. But I didn't feel like laughing. No. 6 also banished cheerfulness from his face.

"Look," he said, moving closer to me, "don't be hasty with your judgments – it is the audience that determines the speaker's style, you'll soon be convinced of that through your own experience. You can't deny No.11 some powers of observation. Let's put it this way: diminutive forms are used to express emotional expansiveness. As the intensity of expression diminishes, so the significance increases; after all, we use diminutive forms to denote those who are most important to us and it's not for nothing that in the old forms of our language dear and small are the same word. Yes, like No.11 I'm convinced that it's not the big people, the ones who shake us out of their pupil into another that they love, but us, the wandering little people who try to find a space in other people's eyes. And then if you remove the banal aspect from the theory of little good turns, No. 11 is right about this too. It means that to force the love-object to a state of loving you have to gain control of its so-called associative mass, indeed, love itself, speaking schematically, is no more, no less than a private instance of mutual associativeness.

"What is this all about?"

"It's this. In classifying our associations one way or another, the psychologists failed to see that imaginative links are either one-sided or mutual. Wait a moment," he hastened, seeing my gesture of impatience, "a minute of boredom and then it'll be interesting – you'll see. When you make someone fall in love with you, you unite not the idea and the image, not the image and the concept, but the image (of a person) and the emotion; he must bear in mind that this process is either from the emotions to the image, or from the image to the emotions. And until you can achieve, as you might say, a dual circuit... What – you don't understand? Well, think it over, I can't do your thinking for you. You want an example? I'll give you one. Example number one: emotions are already in place, but they aren't aimed, they aren't associated with any image. In the beginning, 'the soul was awaiting someone', there was aimless turbulence, a shot in the void, then that 'some' falls away of its own accord, and at the same time it's quite uncomplicated to enter into the vacant 'one'. Second example – that's when the image has to await the emotions. Here the growth of associative elements sometimes proceeds very slowly and with difficulty. Youthful affairs more often than not take the first route, those of one's second youth, the second. But the laws of association bring many concerns to those in love. When love is unremitting, it's essential that every time the so-called loved one enters the room the feeling of love towards that person should arise by association of ideas. By the same token, any sexual arousal, one would have thought, should immediately arouse the image of that same dreaded 'beloved person'. But in actual fact, feeling and image are generally linked in a one-sided fashion, like the currents in a cathode chain into which you plug a detector. In fact, the majority of liaisons are constructed on these one-sided half-loves. The first type of relationship is when the associative current runs only from the image to the emotion, but not in reverse: maximum betrayal, but great passion. Why? for God's sake, he doesn't understand anything – well, instead of the detector link, let's take the flow of blood through the heart. Every time, in striving to reach the other side, the blood opens up a valve; crossing to the other side it shuts off the valves and in that way it bars its own route. And that's how it is here – every meeting is passionate, indeed, every thought which enters the consciousness, in this case the image, brings with it a flood of passionate feeling. The blood, so to speak, opens valves for itself. But the emotion which arises in the absence of the bearer of the image is easily diverted along other paths: people of this type of loving are in love only when they meet the loved one, the image of the chosen one quickly finds the way to the sensation, but the sensation does not know the way to the chosen one. The blood, centering on the loving, closes off the heart valves of its own accord. You were yawning, I think. A nervous yawn? Very well, then. The second type of loving, as you may gather, leads to a small element of betrayal, but the passion is weak in consequence. The onset of hunger for love evokes in the consciousness – both during assignations and outside them – always the same image, but that image, if it was the first to enter the consciousness, does not bring emotions with it. This type of one-sided associativeness is very convenient for a continuous relationship which is family-centred and avoids catastrophes. But it is only the third example, the mutual association of ideas, when the image and the emotions are inseparable, which can give what I perhaps would agree to call love. No, whatever you might say, No. 11 knows where the corpse is buried, but he doesn't know how to dig it up. But as for me..."

"But why would one want to dig up old bones?" I burst out.

No. 6 sat without replying for about a minute. He looked like a man assiduously casting off the broken thread of his thoughts.

"Because where No. 11 came to a halt, is in fact the basic, most acute question for those who, like you and I, have landed up in this dark pit of the pupil, and... But anyway, all of us here are sick with a strange chronic colourlessness. Time slips away along us, like an india rubber along pencil lines. We're dying down like waves during a calm. As I grow ever more colourless, I shall soon cease to distinguish the nuances of my own thoughts. I'll lose my contours and fall away into nothingness. This isn't what annoys me, but the fact that with me will perish so many observations, scientific facts and formulations. If I could only get out of here, I'd show all those Freuds, Adlers and Meiers the real nature of oblivion. What could all those self-indulgent geniuses, collectors of slips of the tongue and slips of the pen, put up against the man who comes out of the black pit, the very name of which is oblivion? But that's hardly possible – it's easier to come back from the dead than from here. But it would be amusing. Because you know from my youth all my thoughts have been concentrated on the problem of oblivion. Encountering the problem was almost incidental. I was leafing through a book of someone's verses and suddenly:

> *Beyond the flight of the birds, the column of dust,*
> *The sun's circumference fades.*
> *If I've been forgotten,*
> *Then it's now, this very hour.*

Thinking over this handful of words, I never suspected that, taking up the thought, I would never let it go. It occurred to me then that imaginings are perpetually wandering from the conscious to the unconscious. But sometimes they go so far into the unconscious that they can't find a way back to the conscious. And I was interested in the question of how imagination declines: does it dim like slowly dying embers, or like a candle snuffed out by one breath, gradually, or at once, is the process long draw out and difficult or is it immediate? At first I agreed with the poet – the process of oblivion appeared to me like a slow build up to a sudden avalanche. Here it was, now it isn't any more. I recall using Ebbihaus's mnemonic rows to try to calculate the moment of disappearance, the point of its washing away, the collapse of whichever concept. Instantly, my attention was drawn to the question of forgotten emotions. This really is a most intriguing question. A certain woman meets 'n' times with some man, and each time both of them experience a certain arousal. But on the nth plus 1 meeting, shall we say, this woman comes to this man but the arousal doesn't happen. Of course, the certain man fakes it in all kinds of ways and, even when left on his own, meticulously examines his soul, trying to find again what he has lost. But it's all in vain: you can reconstruct the image of the woman you've left, but it's quite impossible to reconstruct the feeling once it has left you. You might say that the lizard has run away leaving its tail in your hands and so the association of the image with the emotion has disassociated itself. When I researched the cooling off process in which the thing dear to one becomes repellent, I could not help citing analogies: it became immediately obvious to me that there is some connection between the process of the cooling of passion and, let's say, the cooling off of a piece of ordinary sulphur. In extracting the calorific value from the sulphur, we transfer its crystals from one system to another; that's to say we force it to change its shape, to take another form, another appearance. In any case, this has already been the subject of enquiry: a chemical body, for instance phosphorus, as it gradually cools not only changes its crystalline formation, and its colour (from violet to red and from red to black) but at a certain point in the cooling process it loses all shape altogether, it decrystallizes, it becomes amorphous. Now, if only one could catch that moment of turning into formlessness. So if one can spot that instant when the gleaming carbon, which we call diamond, turns into ordinary coal which we avoid getting ourselves dirty on, then why can't we just catch that moment when "I am in love" transforms into...

But, even remaining within the realm of chemical formulae, it wasn't all that easy to do this. A crystal, before it loses its shape and its contours and becomes a formless, amorphous body, goes through the stage known as metastability, something halfway between form and formlessness. This analogy seemed to me convincing. Many people have relationships which are metastable, which occupy some middle ground between a thaw and boiling point. It's interesting, incidentally, that metastability gives the highest indicator of viscosity. One can take this analogy further. A white-hot body, if it is presented to itself, cools down naturally and continuously. It's the same with emotion. Just by altering its focus, just by piling on yet more fuel, you can keep it at the same level of heat. I do recall that at this point these analogies led me to a dead end from which there was no way back. But, in answering the question of the circumstances a cooling of the temperature turns a crystal into something amorphous, natural science gave me a kind of answer to the problem of the exact circumstances in which the process of natural emotional cooling, so to speak, turns diamond into coal, the loved into the indifferent, the formed into the formless. It seems that the crystal body, as it undergoes cooling, tries not to lose its shape but rather attempts to change but, since the speed of cooling exceeds the speed of recrystallization, that latter process cannot be completed, the particles which have been caught en route, from one shape to another, by the drop in temperature, stay where they are and the result is chilled and shapeless or, to move from the physical to the psychical – repellent and forgotten. In such circumstances, a sustained and lengthy relationship can only be explained in the following manner: it's a series of mutual betrayals between two people. Why are you astonished by this? That's exactly how it is. If one could only find one person who was completely faithful to the image of such and such a person, which had been engraved upon him like an inscription on a brass plate, then his love might last, well, let's say a couple of days, and even that's unlikely. For the real object of love is constantly changing, and loving you today is only possible by cheating on yesterday's love in favour of you. You know, if I were a writer I would try to write a fantastic story: my hero meets a young girl, you know, a charming young creature, in her seventeenth year. That's fine. Love. Sharing. Then children. Year in, year out. They love as they have always loved: deeply, satisfyingly, simply. Of course, he has asthma and she has wrinkles around the eyes and faded skin, but all that is familiar, habitual, it's their own. And suddenly the door opens and she comes in, but it's not her, or rather it's not how she was an hour or a day ago, but it's that 17-year-old girl as she used to be, the very one whom he swore to love eternally and unchangingly.

My hero is confused, perhaps even dumbfounded. The newcomer looks around at this ageing, unfamiliar life with incomprehension. She sees her children whom she didn't give birth to. She sees a paunchy, half-familiar man, casting frightened glances at the door to the next room. He's worried in case that other one emerges from there. "Yesterday you promised me," says the young creature, but the asthmatic wipes his brow in embarrassment. "Yesterday" was twenty years ago and he doesn't know what to do with his lady guest. And that instant he hears the footsteps of that other one, the same one as now, coming to the door. "You must go, she might catch you."

"Who?"

"Hurry up now."

But it's too late. The door opens and my hero, well, let's say... Maybe he woke up."

"Look here, No.6, this can't go on – from psychology to chemistry, from chemistry to literature. I don't see how you're going to get back from this point to your crystallization, whether it's images or whether it's phosphorus and coal."

"Well, I'm just getting back to the point. Listen: someone loves a certain A, but today's A becomes tomorrow's A_1 and next week's A_2. So it follows that in order to keep peace with a constantly recrystallizing being, you have to keep reconstructing the image, that's to say redirect your emotional sensation from one fancy to another, from one tussock to another, and so on... Cheating on A-primus with A-secundus and A... And if this series of infidelities is conditional upon the capacity for infidelity of the lovers and proceeds at the same speed as the replacement of the loved one, then everything is fine – and just as a man on the razzle doesn't realize as he covers a hundred paces that his body was about to fall a hundred times, but that on each occasion his muscles kept him on his feet just in time, so lovers, having spent many weeks, perhaps years with each other, never suspect that there were as many infidelities as meetings."

He finished with the air of a fashionable lecturer awaiting applause, but theorizing has the same effect on me as sleeping pills. After a moment's silence, No.6 got back on his hobby horse: different speeds, infidelity which can't keep up with the changes, changes which don't keep pace with the infidelities. My eyes closed and I fell into sleep. Even here, I was pursued by circling swarms of chemical formulae and algebraic symbols: with a fine, menacing buzzing they carried out their marital flight.

I don't know how long my sleep would have lasted if prods and voices hadn't woken me:

"Come out to the middle, No.12."

"Let's hear the new boy."

"No.12."

There was nothing for it. Pushed and urged on from right and left, I scrambled up on to the bright yellow mound. A dozen pairs of eyes, staring at me out of the darkness, were preparing to draw the secret of two people into themselves, to drag it off into their brains. And so I began my story. You know it. Let it pass. When I finished, they began to sing their strange hymn again. A dull gloom took hold of me by the temples and, rocking from side to side, empty and dead, I sang with the others:

> *When your head's right in the noose*
> *Then you'll know to not vamoose!*
> *Evens! in you go...*

Finally they let me return to my place. I crawled nimbly into the shadow. A slight shudder made my teeth chatter. I'd rarely felt worse. The little beard on the right nodded to me sympathetically and No.6 leaned over and whispered in my ear:

"Forget it. It's not worth it. You've said your piece and that's fine. I can see it got to you."

And his dry fingers squeezed my hand in a quick movement.

"Listen," I turned to No.6, "maybe that's how it is with all of us, me and the others, but what do you want from love? Why are you messing around here with the rest of us at the bottom of the pupil? After all, you've the soul of a librarian, you've enough bookmarks to keep you going, you could just live with them and your formulae, bury your head in the pages instead of poking your nose into other folk's business, getting involved where you're not wanted."

The lecturer lowered his head in embarrassment:

"Look, this happens to everyone... They say that even Falesius, as he walked along with his face pointing up to the stars, once fell into a well. Well, it's the same for me. I really didn't want to, but

In the Pupil of the Eye

if the pupils are there for the taking... In two words: I used to lecture to women students on psychology. Well, we went in for seminars, practicals, essays and all the rest of it. Naturally, the students used to come to me, sometimes to my home, asking for essay topics, information sources. And she was one of them − you know, our one. More than once she came. In those day I didn't yet know that for women science, like everything else, is always personalized. Questions, answers, and questions again. I won't say that she was particularly quick on the uptake. Once, explaining to her the logarithms of inflammation in Weber-Fechner's formula, I noticed that she wasn't listening. "Repeat it, please." She said nothing, smiling at something. "I don't understand why you come here at all," I suddenly exploded, and I think I banged the book against the table. Them she raised her eyes to me and I saw there were tears. I don't know what people do in these cases. I moved closer and was incautious enough to glance into her moist pupils. And that was that..."

No.6 waved his hand dismissively and fell silent.

And once again the yellow murk of the well closed over us. I ran my fingers over the glassy cylindrical enclosed walls and thought, is this to be my last dwelling place, has the present really been taken away from me for ever and with no prospect of return?

By this time No.1's turn had arrived. On top of the yellow spot there settled a black one. Beside him was his book (Quagga would not be parted from it).

"With the help of one intimate symptom," began the black spot, "it's possible to divide all women into four categories. To the first belong those women who, having presented themselves for an assignation, allow themselves to be undressed and dressed. In this type I would include many high-class courtesans and many women in general who know the art of turning their lovers into obedient slaves, on whom is laid the entire responsibility and all the feverish work of hooking and unhooking, doing up and undoing buttons which leap from the fingers. This first category, however, at the same time seems to play no part, she just shuts her eyes and allows it to happen. The second category are women whom you can undress, but who put their clothes back on themselves. At this point the man is sitting looking out of the window or at the wall, or smoking a cigarette. The third category is perhaps the most dangerous − they're the ones who themselves show you the way to the hooks and buttons, but who afterwards make you serve them lovingly in all the minutest and most touching details of their toilette. These are malicious flirts, lovers of dodgy conversations, experienced predators, in a word 'come hither' types. The fourth category undress and dress themselves whilst their partners wait with greater or lesser impatience. These are the run-of-the-mill prostitutes, fading spouses and goodness knows who else. Not let me ask you, in which category, my dear successor, do you place our mistress?"

The blot paused. And immediately from all sides, interrupting each other, came the cries:

"The first, of course."

"Of course not – the second."

"Come off it, the third."

And a hoarse bass voice, overriding the shouts, barked out:

"In the finalest category."

The black blob shook with silent laughter.

"I knew it. Opinions were bound to be divided. This book – the one I'm holding in my hand – knows a lot about many people. Of course it still has plenty of blank pages and we're not all in the collection. But sooner or later, there comes a time when the mistress's pupils will lose the capacity to attract and seduce. And, at that point, when I have written the last words on these pages, I shall get down to the compilation of a *Full and Systematic History of a Certain Attraction*, with the addition of a subject and alphabetical index. My categories are just the outline. They possess a methodological significance, as our No.6 would put it. The doors between one category and another – well, they're all open wide, there's nothing surprising about the fact that she's been through the lot of them.

You all know that with me she began to be a woman.

It was how many years ago?.. Anyway, the only thing that's important is that it did happen. We were introduced at some literary tea party: "Here is Miss... just up from the country – hope you'll be kind to her." Her unfashionable dress, which emphasized her youthful fragility, bore witness to this. I tried to catch her eye with mine, but no, with a flick of the eyelashes, they turned to one side.

After that we rattled our teaspoons in the cups and someone did a reading, mixing up the pages as they did so. The organizer of this piece of cultural boredom took me on one side and asked if I would escort the young lady from the country back to her place ("She's on her own, you know, it's night-time, she might get lost"). I remember that her coat had the loop torn off.

We left. It was pouring with rain. I called a cab and through the slanting whiplash of the rain we dived under the leather hood of the cab. She said something, but the cobbles were already clattering beneath us and I couldn't hear what she was saying. A turning, then another. I tentatively took her by the elbow; the girl was startled and tried to move away, but there was nowhere to move. The cobbles over which we were jumping jolted us towards each other with short nervous thumps. Somewhere here, just beside me, were her lips. I wanted to find out where exactly and bent forward and at that very second something very unusual happened. Thrust sharply forward, she ripped back the leather covering and leapt out of the moving cab. I can remember how I read in some novel about a similar device, but in the novels it is usually a man who does it and pouring rain doesn't usually enter into the situation. For a few moments I sat beside emptiness, completely discouraged and confused – just about the time I needed to wake the driver and stop his horse. The driver, seeing me jump out of the cab, took the thing the wrong way and yelled out about the fare – a few more seconds had been lost. Finally, I rushed forward along the damp pavement, trying to make out the silhouette of the fugitive in the darkness. The street lamps had gone out. I thought I had caught up with her at the crossroads. She turned round, the spark of a cigarette suddenly glowing between her teeth, and called out: "Let's go to bed." It was a woman of the streets. I rushed on. The crossroads was a muddle of streets – she was nowhere. Almost in despair, I set off at random across one of the streets and suddenly I practically fell over my fugitive. She was standing, frozen through and lashed by the rain, obviously completely confused by the network of streets and not knowing where to go. I won't recount our conversation: I've told it to you many times. My remorse was genuine: I kissed her wet fingers, begging her to forgive me and threatened to kneel down right in the puddle if she didn't stop being angry. We found the cab again and no matter how much the cobbles jolted me I sat through the whole journey quietly, trying to turn my shoulder away from hers. We were both frozen through and our teeth were chattering. As we said goodbye, I kissed her cold fingers once again and suddenly my companion burst out into a young and cheerful laugh. A couple of days later I called on her, bringing with me a heap of reassurances and some patent medicines. The latter came in handy. The poor girl was coughing and complaining of aches. I didn't have recourse to your remedy, No.11, at that stage it would have been... premature. The slightest carelessness could have destroyed the friendship that was developing. At that time there was rather more to me than this grey, faded blob. Sitting on the shuddering springs of the sofa, we would often chat till almost nightfall. The inexperienced girl knew neither the town, the world, nor me. The topics of our conversations seemed to veer from side to side, as though blown by the wind: sometimes I would carefully describe how to use a paraffin stove correctly, sometimes, muddling it up myself, I would set forth the premises of Kant's critique of pure reason. Snuggled into a corner of the sofa, her legs tucked under her, she would listen avidly, about the stove and about Kant equally, without taking her deep dark eyes off me. Yes, and there was another thing she didn't know about – herself. And so, during one of our conversations which lasted well on into the evening, I tried to explain to her about herself, I tried to open the clasps to the book which you see here, half filled and worn, in my hands. Yes, that evening we spoke about her future, about the encounters which awaited her, the involvements and the disappointments and fresh encounters. I deliberately tried to knock on the door of her future. Sometimes she would laugh, drily and abruptly, sometimes she would correct me, sometimes she would listen silently and without interruption. Once by chance (my cigarette had gone out, I guess) I struck a match and in its yellow light I saw that her face was different. It was older and more womanly, just as if indeed I had had a vision of it from the future. Blowing out the match, I threw myself further forward in time: first love, the first blows of life, the bitterness of partings, fresh attempts with the heart already left behind. Gabbling my words in haste, I was beginning to reach the years when feelings are whipped out and weary, when the fear of fading forces one to make haste and crumple up one happiness like waste paper, when curiosity gets the better of passion, when... at this point I struck another match and gazed eye to eye with amazement until I burned my finger. Yes, my

In the Pupil of the Eye

respected successors, if one could carry out my experiment correctly, a dozen matches would have shown me all the faces of which you have grasped the memory. But, ripping the box from my hand, she threw it aside. Our fingers intertwined and trembled, as though exposed to the cold pouring rain. Maybe I don't need to say anything more?"

And the blurred humanoid blob began slowly to descend.

"Well, what do you think of our Quagga?" No.6 was curious.

I remained impolitely silent.

"Hey, you look as if you were jealous. I must confess there was a time when Quagga's pretensions, all that boasting about being the first, annoyed even me. But you can't turn back the past. It's the Supreme Being. You have to come to terms with it and, anyway, when you think about it, what *is* jealousy?"

But I turned my back on the lecture and pretended to be asleep. Grumbling vaguely about badly-behaved people, No.6 relapsed into hurt silence.

At first I did pretend to sleep, but then I really fell asleep. I don't know how long this oblivion lasted: a sudden light which penetrated under my eyelids forced me to open my eyes. Around me was a phosphorescent blue. I propped myself up on my elbows, looking for the source of this strange light. To my great astonishment, I realized that the light was coming out of me. My body was surrounded by a phosphorescent halo, whose short rays disappeared several feet away. My very body became light and springy, as happens sometimes in dreams. All around were asleep. With one bound I leaped on to the hollow of the yellow blob and two sources of light, their rays crisscrossing filled the air with all the colours of the rainbow. Another effort and my light body, sliding in a crazy manner, began to clamber out along the vertical slope of the wall to the vault of the cave. The barely visible crack opened up and, with my hands grabbing its flexible edges, my viscous body easily broke through to the outside. In front of me stretched the low corridor which had beckoned me to the depths. Once before I had wandered its curves, bumping against the walls in the dark, but now the light, blue all around me, was pointing the way. Suddenly hope sprang up within me. I walked on, surrounded by my phosphorescent aura, back towards the exit out of the pupil. Spots of light and shapes slid along the walls overtaking me, but I had no time to make them out. My heart was in my throat when I finally made it to the round window of the pupil. I threw myself blindly forward and hurt myself against the lowered eyelid. The damned blind of skin blocked my exit. I wound myself up and began to beat against it with my fist, but the eyelid never so much as batted: it seemed as though the woman was fast asleep. Maddened, I started to beat against the barrier with my knees and shoulders, the eyelid quivered and at this point the light which had surrounded me began to fade and die. In confusion, I dashed back, fearing that I'd be left in complete darkness. The rays were drawn back into my body, and together with that, my weight returned. With leadening steps, panting from the run, I finally made it back to the opening into the vault of the cave; it stretched out obediently for me and I jumped down. My thoughts were swirling around, like sand in the wind: why had I come back, what force had turned me round again to the depths, from freedom to slavery, or perhaps this was all a ridiculous nightmare? But in that case why not... I crawled back to my place and began to pummel No.6's shoulder. He jumped up, rubbing his eyes, and faced a torrent of questions from me.

"Hang on! Hang on a minute, you say it was a dream?" he questioned me again, peering attentively at the last drooping sputterings of my burnt out halo. "Hm... I guess this really is a dream going on here and that dream, believe it or not, is you. Yes, yes, this has happened here with the others as well: her dreams sometimes wake us up and force us to wander about like lunatics, not knowing why or where. It's you she's dreaming about now, do you see? Wait a minute, you're still giving off a bit of light. Eh, it's gone out – that means she's finished her dream."

"Six," I whispered, grabbing his hand, "I can't take this any more. Let's make a dash for it."

But my neighbour shook his head:

"That's impossible."

"But why? I've just been there myself, at the entrance to the outside world. If it hadn't been for the eyelid..."

"It's impossible," repeated No.6. "First of all, who can guarantee you that, having got out of her eye, you'll find your master? Perhaps they've already split up, there's a lot of space and you... might get lost and perish. And secondly, there were other bold guys before you who tried to escape. They..."

"What about them?"

"Would you believe it, they came back."

"They came back?"

"Yes, you see the opening in the vault only opens for those who are being dreamt about and those who arrive there from the outside world. But the dreams lead us on a long rein, keeping us away from the waking world by means of the lowered eyelids and when we are done in the dreams they throw us back down to the depths. There remains a second possibility. Having waited for the moment when the crack in the vault opens to let in a newcomer, you can jump out – and then it's a matter of passageways through the caverns (you know them) and – freedom! You'd think it would be easy. But there's one detail which could rule the whole thing out."

"I don't understand that."

"Well, look, the moment when you break out you have to meet, head to head, shoulder to shoulder, with the new person who has jumped inside in your place. And here the temptation to look at your successor, if only for an instant, is so great... that, in a nutshell, if you lose a moment you lose your freedom: the opening closes and the fugitive, together with the newcomer, falls down right to the bottom. At any rate, that was what happened to all those who made the attempt. It's a matter, don't you see, of a psychological trap from which there's no escape."

I listened in silence, and the more the word "impossible" was repeated, the more my resolution grew.

I spent several hours, thinking over every detail of the plan. While this went on, it was the turn of No.2. My silent neighbour on the left made his way out into the yellow spot. For the first time I saw his colourless, squat, cheerless appearance. With an embarrassed cough, he began, stumbling slightly over his words:

"This was how it all came about. Once I received a letter – in one of those long envelopes. It smelt faintly of verbena. I opened it. There were these crooked spidery letters. I started reading: What was this all about?"

"Quiet," Quagga's voice suddenly rang out. "Stop the story. There up above, do you hear?"

Sigizmund Krziszanowsky

The story teller and the voices suddenly fell silent. At first there didn't seem to be anything. Then – was it imagination, or was it real? From far away above the vault there came a light and cautious step. Then it broke off. Then again. Then it fell silent.

"Can you hear?" No.6 whispered in my ear. "He's announced himself. He's on the move."

"Who?"

"No.13."

First quietly, so as not to frighten him, then louder and louder, we sang the hymn of the forgotten. Occasionally, at a sign from Quagga, we broke off the singing and listened. The footsteps seemed to be coming quite near and then suddenly they started to move away.

"Louder. Come on, louder!" shouted Quagga. "Draw him in, draw him in. You won't get away, old son, no, you won't."

And our hoarse, desperate voices rebounded from the slimy walls of our prison.

But it seemed as though No.13, hiding out there somewhere in the dark passages, was uncertain and blundering. Finally our strength ran out, Quagga allowed a break, and soon everyone around we was deep in sleep.

But I didn't allow weariness to overcome me. With my ear to the wall, I continued to listen in to the darkness.

At first everything was quiet, then, once again, there, above the vault, the approaching steps rang out. The opening began ever so slowly to move apart. Grabbing the slippery jutting out sections of the walls, I tried to make my way up, but immediately I lost my footing and fell, hitting myself on some hard object. It was the book of oblivion. Trying to move silently (suppose Quagga should suddenly awake) I opened its clasps and, using the hinges, I began quickly to pull myself up, from one protuberance to another, until my hand found itself holding on to the edge of the exit gap. Someone's head was pointing down at me but, screwing my eyes up with the effort, in one short burst I threw my body forward and out and charged forward without looking around. After my two wanderings around the labyrinth of the pupil, I was able somehow to find my way, even in the dark. Soon I encountered the first faint flickerings of light from under the half lowered eyelids. Forcing my way out, I jumped on to the pillow and marched off, fighting with gusts of breathing which met me.

"But what if it isn't, he isn't mine?" I thought, wavering between fear and hope. And when finally in the pre-morning light I began to make out my giant-size features, when I saw you after all those days apart, master, I swore never to leave you again and never to hang about strange pupils. By the way, that's not like me, but like you..."

The little pupil man fell silent and stood up, putting his black volume under his arm. The pink blotches of dawn were ambling by the windows. Somewhere in the distance, wheels clattered by. The woman's eyelashes gave a little flutter. The little man from the pupil turned to look at them apprehensively and again turned his tired little face towards we. He was awaiting instructions. "Let's do it your way," I smiled at him, and moved my eyes as close as I could to the little fellow. With one leap, he clambered up under my eyelids and stepped into me. But something, perhaps the sharp corner of the book which was sticking out from under his elbow, pricked me on the edge of my pupil and gave me a sharp pain in the brain. There was black before my eyes, I thought, for a moment... but no: the dawn turned from pink to black; around me was the black silent night. It was as though time, bending its paws, had crawled backwards. Slipping off the bed, I dressed hurriedly and quietly. I opened the door. There was the corridor, the turning, the door, another door and, fumbling my way along the wall, step by step, I made it to the outside. I was on the street. I walked on, straight, without turning off, not knowing where or why. Gradually, the air started to thin, setting free the contours of the houses. I looked round. A blue-to-pink second dawn was catching up with me.

Suddenly, somewhere up above, from the belfry, the bells stirred, clanking metal on metal. I raised my eyes. From the pediment of an old church, decorated in a triangle, an enormous eye was staring at me through the fog. The chill gripped me between the shoulder blades with a jab like the points of a pair of compasses. "Painted bricks." That was all it was. Untangling my footsteps from the fringes of the fog, I kept on repeating, "Painted bricks" – and that was all.

Out of the mist, through which rays of light were emerging, I came upon the familiar bench. Here I had waited – was it a long time ago

– for darkness to be my companion. Now the back of the seat was visible in the feeble light and damp from early morning dew.

I sat down on the damp edge and remembered. It was on this spot that, its outlines vaguely drawn, the idea of the story about the little man in the pupil had come to me. Now I had sufficient material to firm up the theme. And right here and now I began to consider, as I came to meet the approaching day, how I could tell people everything and tell them nothing. First of all, one must cross out the truth, who needs it? Then one had to depict the pain in sharper hues to the limits of the plot – yes, yes. Then just an old bit of the mundane, and on top, like veneer on paint, a spot of banality – you can't do without that. Finally, insert two or three bits of philosophy and – reader, you turn away, you want to shake off the lines out of the pupils – no, no, don't leave me on the long empty bench. Hold your palm in mine – like that – firmer, still firmer. I've been alone too long. And I won't tell anyone else, but I'll tell you: when all's said and done, why frighten children with the dark when you can use it to keep them quiet and get them to sleep?

1927

Translated by Michael Falchikov

Published in Russian in: Sigizmund Krziszanowsky, *Remembrance of the Future*. Edited and with an introduction by Vadim Perelmuter. Moscow, 1989

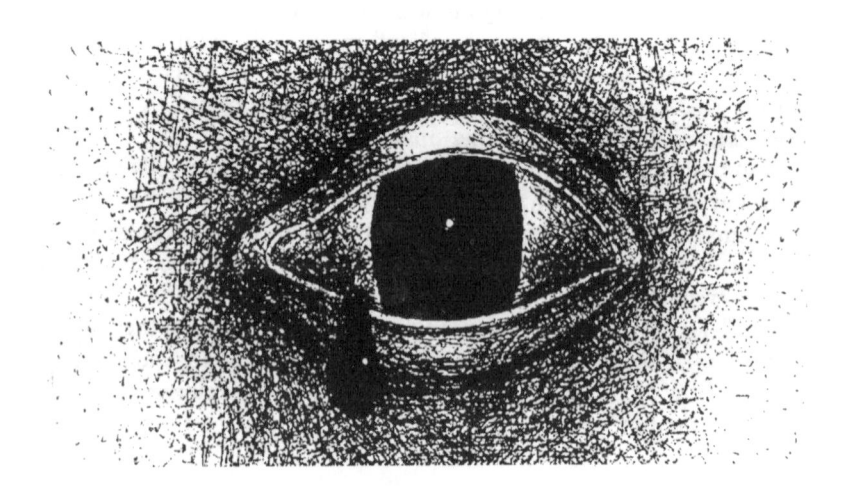

Readers International
Editors: Dorothy Connell and Sherman Carroll

8 Strathray Gardens, London NW3 4NY, UK
or
P.O. Box 959, Columbia LA 71418, USA

Readers International publishes world literature.
The very best. Year after year.
Readers International works like a magazine subscription.
Every other month you get a timely new book.
Subscribe to **Readers International**'s annual series
of six hard-cover volumes.
Many were banned at home or written in exile.
Readers International is committed
to publishing literature in danger.

RI's Russian titles:

- **Joseph Brodsky**, *To Urania*, translated into English in collaboration with the Nobel Laureate himself, a writer with "a formidable, sinuous command of English"—*Time*
- **Vladimir Sorokin**, *The Queue*, translated by Sally Laird. "Resembles Godot, but its humor is broader and nowhere so stark"—NY *Times Book Review*.

"With each new offering, RI becomes more impressive."
—*The Washington Post*

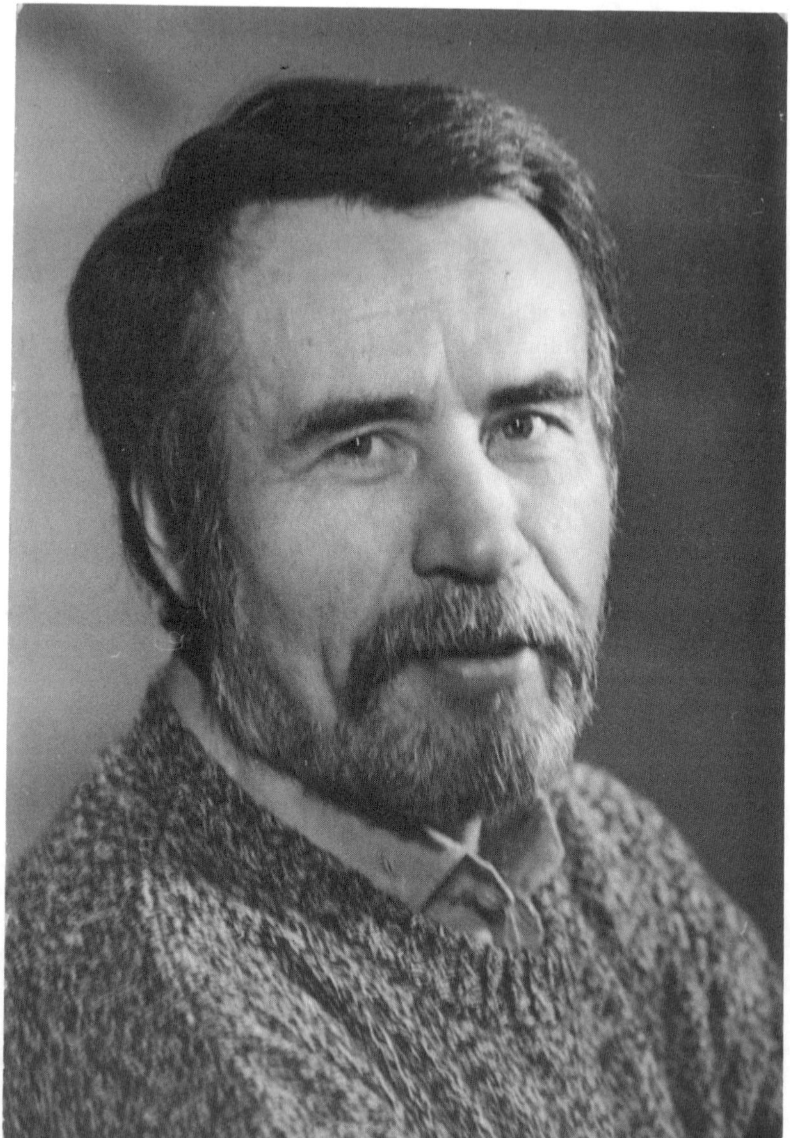

Vladimir
MAKANIN
The Safety-valve

1

There was nothing remarkable about the fact that Alevtina had a lover, a certain Pavel Mikhailov, who was just approaching forty. Perhaps he was a bit clumsy and inexperienced in love affairs, but on the other hand, given the way life flowed in a predictable fashion, for Mikhailov this was absolutely the right time for an affair – he had a wife, a nice flat, a good income and two sons already finishing school, one in his final year and the other the year below. "There's only a year between my sons," Mikhailov liked to repeat, seeing in this fact a certain significance and solidity. How Mikhailov managed to dodge between his family and his mistress is unclear, and it was difficult to believe that he could manage it, since, from the very first moment, you could tell that this was a man not well-versed in lying – with him it was awkward and unconvincing. "Mikhailov!" – he would be called to the phone amidst the hysterical screech of saws, fussy customers, workers milling around. Mikhailov would be gripped by fear: was it his kids or was it 'her'? So off he'd rush to his little nook where the phone was, and here one should note that, to outside appearances, he walked quietly, ponderously, but inside him he was all in a tearing hurry with the nervous twitch of people who tell lies incompetently and unconvincingly and, above all as befits their age, not very often. Alevtina and his children – these were the only things that worried Mikhailov at those moments when he was suddenly called to the phone, whereas at other times he was preoccupied with his work, his wife and his still living elderly mother.

Mikhailov was a man weighed down by responsibilities and by work and this gave a particular tinge to his love – the love of a busy man. He grafted away – an expression be often used – in a furniture factory which went by the official name of "Workshop for the manufacture of furniture – orders from organizations and the general public". Early in the morning, Mikhailov would arrive, invariably on time, and from first thing his clothing reeked of varnish and furniture-polish. But it wasn't as if he drank either of these substances like some of the labourers. A skilled man, his staid appearance and considerable bulk (he weighed more than 200 pounds) evoked repect, and sometimes a customer, or a young craftsman, or just one of the labourers from the workshop would ask interestedly:

The Safety-valve

"You wouldn't happen to be related to Mikhailov the hockey-player?"

"I am, as it happens," Mikhailov would reply with quiet modesty and when asked (even more respectfully, with a certain awe in the voice), "In what way?" he would answer, with the same quiet modesty "We're namesakes."

Of course, this was just a joke, and not a very good one at that, but still Mikhailov would repeat it from time to time, with the determination of a man who once, maybe, dreamed in his youth of fame and achievements, but did so no longer. He was now completely reconciled and knew his end and the outcome of his life in general terms. In any case, he had a little nook of an office where he could sit in private with his jolly little yellow telephone. His predecessor, who bravely stared life's storms and dangers in the face, used to spend long evenings there with the plump girls from Quality Control, and sometimes Mikhailov felt that the walls with the peacock wallpaper and the yellow telephone itself were looking at him expectantly, rather like intelligent lackeys, ever ready to be of service, waiting and watching. But of course they'd never get anything rash out of Mikhailov. A practical man, he didn't spend the day sitting in his office, but rather passed the time doing fairly simple designs to customers' orders and also basically observing how those designs were incarnated in the wood. Thus he would wander through the workshop, a tall, heavily-built man, sometimes letting out quiet jokes which fell flat.

Mikhailov had no grudges (or almost none) against fate or any expectations of personal success, not even in his youth. He graduated from a Building College, but instead of going off to build bridges over the Volga or sumptuous hotels on the Black Sea, he suddenly took a job at this little furniture factory. Some people would regard a furniture factory as depressingly prosaic. Others, rather smarter, would see it as an exceptionally subtle scheme ("A Moscow residence permit and a cushy job. That's a crafty move!") and only Mikhailov himself regarded the factory as just a factory. He lived by force of inertia. Perhaps he was spiritually sluggish in the way that some people are physically sluggish. Such people succeed in avoiding neither the good nor the bad, and if they're told it's to be the furniture factory, then the furniture factory it is. When something was suggested to Mikhailov, he'd agree. They promised to provide him with a flat in the course of the next three years and then they let him down. He went along with it once more. He just went on living his life quietly, believing what he'd been told that the factory had had some exceptional overspend that year on housing, and that even without that, the factory manager was utterly exhausted and that he, that is, the manager, suffered heartache at night from all his cares, so that he might even suffer a slight heart attack... And time passed.

Time passed and God, as is well known, looks after the simple soul. And so it suddenly came to pass that the furniture became fashionable and pricy and so the word *suddenly* was necessary once more and thus characteristic of Mikhailov, in the sense that only that word could change something in his life. The city, as it were, suddenly sprang into action after a long hibernation and people started coming from all over the place to see Mikhailov. They wanted imitation antiques. They wanted imitation art nouveau. They just wanted imitation comfort, they wanted everything. One man, he recalled, wanted lines of shelves where the lines would "intersect and then divide and then come together again" and he wanted it to give off light and for the whole thing to look like an airport ("What on earth?" "An airport, don't you see what I mean"). The cramped conditions of Moscow flats dictate the laws you have to fight for every square half-metre, and it seemed that Mikhailov found himself in that fight. He began to take an interest in his work and the money began to come in and one day Mikhailov suddenly noticed that he was living, eating and drinking far better than before. His flat looked better than before and his wife (this was amazing!) looked better and more attractive. A real lady, dressed with taste, and modest with it. And here the point must be made – and this Mikhailov bore in mind – a forty-year-old isn't a twenty-year-old and when it came to wives and womenfolk, a twenty-year-old wasn't for the likes of him. But Mikhailov himself looked better and it wasn't just a matter of how he dressed. He was experiencing a feeling akin to late fame and for a time this makes one younger and it gets easier to indulge in all kinds of twists and turns. When it rained, or just when the weather was damp, Mikhailov's voice would rumble in a lower register – a pleasant voice. So when they were getting acquainted, Alevtina (she was a poetess) asked him:

The Safety-valve

"You wouldn't happen to be related to the well-known bass, Mikhailov?"

"Yes, I am", replied Mikhailov with quiet modesty and when Alevtina (already with a certain respect in her voice) asked "In what way?" he again explained with quiet modesty, "We're namesakes", and *suddenly* for the first time, and – to run ahead – we can say for the last time, his joke went down well, though not all that well, or only relatively well, since poetesses are not much given to humour and tend to be patronizing.

Alevtina was long past twenty, she was thirty, actually thirty-one years of age: however, she was youthful-looking, with a large bosom and a reasonably pretty face – a young poetess, but if you wanted to know how she earned a crust, then it wasn't an easy crust and not all that sweet. Over the course of some ten years she had had three slim volumes of verse published, and now, as she waited for the fourth to come out, she did reviewing, or earned a bit extra giving poetry-readings in factory or local party recreation clubs or at festive occasions in student unions. Her pleasant appearances were apposite and in demand, although there was a price to pay: for instance, one Christmas she was asked at a club if, at the same time as reading her poems, or rather after reading her poems, she would mind dressing up as a Snow Maiden, since the girl they had engaged had just had to go off for an abortion and there was nobody to replace her. "Snow Maiden?" "Well, yes... I'd be really grateful, miss, if you'd read your poems and then just dash round by the Christmas tree. It's really simple!" And they told Alevtina that she'd get a special payment for leading the round dance, and of course this offended her. But later, Alevtina realized that there was no deliberate offence intended, that it was just a chance, even a farcical combination of circumstances, and that one should regard the whole thing humorously. So she came to the conclusion that poetesses should have a sense of humour. However, at holiday time and for a week after, Alevtina felt miserable and she wanted something to take her mind off it – like, for instance, going to a party – or suddenly imagining a well-used ski-track, snow and skiers in bright sweaters, laughing loudly. Alevtina tried to find a niche for herself in some empty-headed laughter, getting on the phone to all sorts of people, because as New Year approaches – typical of the winter holiday – the grey face of loneliness can quite suddenly obtrude and Alevtina knew this only too well. She'd no husband, no children, just a flat.

She had had a husband, he was a poet too, but a failed poet – somehow he hadn't been able to publish three slim volumes of verse, he hadn't even published once. He often cried and complained and then came out with the view that some planet, peopled by some extraterrestrials and as yet unknown to us was preventing publication of slim volumes. Alevtina thought that there was a different reason: instead of slogging away to make up for lack of talent, he developed a passion for fortified wine, to add to which he was something of a pretty boy and that decided it. He would disappear for several months at a time, living out his life somewhere, drinking, and he'd put in an appearance back home only when reliable rumours reached him of Alevtina's next little volume coming out – he'd come back for money. He would tell Alevtina that he loved here, that he'd thought things over, that he was tired, that he was starting a new life, but as soon as the money ran out, he ran out as a husband. He would vanish into the gap between the last lot of money and the next. So you could say that he would vanish into the gap between the current little volume and the next one, and that was indeed reminiscent of the cosmic fissure, or as it's now called, the black hole, into which, from time to time there appear interplanetary beings from distant civilizations who study us and then disappear again. It was typical of him not to look for a quarrel, and this too was like the interplanetary beings – he just disappeared without trace. And there was just the one postcard for New Year, that same New Year when Alevtina very nearly donned the Snow Maiden's costume. For some reason, the card was from the Crimea. "Darling, life isn't just crossing a field. Have a happy holiday." They had no children. They divorced, and now Alevtina Nesterova, a poetess and an attractive woman, was living on her own, in her own flat, and need one say that she was happy and that her old mother, in a village near Kursk, who in her ignorance still put up prayers for her in church, was absolutely wrong.

Pride often becomes an indispensable compensation in such situations, a pretty face and a large bosom is particularly pertinent, but above all – and this is important – Alevtina was proud of the fact that she earned her own living and depended on nobody: you might

The Safety-valve

say, it was one of those instances where a female on her own manages OK and doesn't cry on the nearest shoulder. Dignity, as always, has its reverse side: that sense of inner worth, basically a good thing, sometimes made Alevtina suddenly pretentious and over-familiar. It was as if she were always playing a role.

"Would you like some good poetry?", she'd ask, but not really ask, since she would start reading straight off. Fortunately she had a warm voice with a slight huskiness, and she read beautifully. She would separate the lines with a short, light, intimate pause, without naming the title or the author, and this was touching. This was where her good points, her tact, would show, because she would in no way drag her listeners into a high-flown discussion – she wouldn't ask you if you wanted to hear something from "Akhmatova's last anthology" (and you didn't even know there *was* a last anthology) – she didn't give you a hard time, she had complete trust in you, you were just a listener, the stream flowed simply and quietly a foot away from you and you could take it or leave it.

To return to external appearances, her pictures were hung all over the place, or sometimes just propped against the wall (mind your feet, dear) and the pinned-up black and white photos of the poets of the distant and not so distant past spoke softly to you and demonstrated that love knows no frontiers or, at any rate, doesn't want to. "I'll pull someone else's guy, if he's worth it," Alevtina was fond of saying above the din of the washing-machine to a girl-friend who was helping her to direct the hose with its jet of dirty water into the sink, "I'll pull the guy and get married, see if I don't." But really it was just words, for public consumption, merely play-acting. And it was just because of this pretentiousness and the persistent play-acting and the continuing uncertainty as to what lay ahead, that many people found Alevtina strange. And to Mikhailov, the practical man, who smelt of varnish and spent his days living the life of the furniture factory, the proud Alevtina at first just seemed crazy. And she, in turn, thought he had nothing to say for himself, almost as if he were mentally slow, and this of course in no way prevented their getting to know each other; this was a matter of mutual curiosity for them and was like a gradual recognition, like the stripping away of the outer skin and the gradual revelation of the white heart of the onion.

2

The poetess wasn't at all frightened off by the fact that he was a "furniture man": she had a sort of general leaning towards simplicity and she liked it when a person knew his job and that, whatever job that might be, he had not just drifted into it and was highly regarded. She tried with enthusiasm, and sometimes without – that's to say with effort – to make it so that Mikhailov liked being with her. And she showed understanding of her own efforts: she tried to be "just a nice woman", tried to get him to rest from fuss and bother and vain attempts and to see that he didn't torment himself with his fate, for example, or his wife, or whatever else men torment themselves with – men, who don't understand the simple truth that you can't reach above yourself and that, in the end, playing with life, like playing with women, ends up as neither one thing nor the other. Men don't want to know about that, but let the poor chaps at least get a taste of it. She wanted Mikhailov to be her friend and here one shouldn't make this word seem any worse than it is. There were times – for instance, once, when she was jolting along in a bus and, on the back seat, an old lady, exhausted, surrounded by bags, with eyes dimmed, was suddenly caught in the pinkish rays of the setting sun, like a little angel, or the incarnation of serene old age – then, for instance, Alevtina thought she loved him.

At other times he was too much for her. Alevtina might be thinking about a quiet evening, about what a nice mug Mikhailov had and about the love that had suddenly settled on her in that jolly bus: this thought, as it became more tenuous, gradually resolved itself into a long drawn-out mood, a tenderness towards everything and everybody, and it would be at this point that Mikhailov would suddenly cut right across all that by saying (or grumbling) that Alevtina was one thing, but his family was something else. Alevtina snorted; it wasn't that she was offended that his family took first place (so what, who cares about first or second!) but it was just that way of emphasizing their importance. "Look at the snow outside the window," said Alevtina, cherishing the mood, but it was as if he didn't hear (sometimes he was a bit dim) and then he went back to the same old thing:

"You can find love often, but you can't often find a family."

The Safety-valve

"Well, you took it on. Anyway, I've heard you can have more than one family." Alevtina was trying to be funny.

"That depends on the person."

Mikhailov spoke dully and ponderously, even somehow menacingly and was quite prepared, after such oppressive words, to sit there unsociably for a whole hour. The poor fellow was suffering: ever since Alevtina had announced a new acquaintance, a brilliant, handsome and somewhat bored mathematician, Yuri Strepetov, Mikhailov had began to speak about his family in a particularly gloomy way, as though threatening or demonstrating to Alevtina that, well, yes, he had more important things to do in life after all, and perhaps he wouldn't be coming to see her any more and would just disappear. But he didn't disappear. It was the same old story: a guy might be prepared to lose a woman, or even to throw her out, but no way would he cede her to someone else. And Strepetov also wasn't going to disappear – and Strepetov was handsome and clever and, all in all, Alevtina fancied him, you couldn't deny that. And one day Alevtina came to understand that a triangle had formed and that the attraction and counter-attraction from one angle to another was manifesting itself almost on the forgotten classical model. (Oh, Lord, why dost thou tempt me?) So, having agonized about it for a couple of evenings, Alevtina felt it was time to send off those nice idiots in different directions. it was time she pulled herself together, sorted out her life and set off on the straight and narrow. And she'd have to do it herself, you couldn't expect anything of the guys, guys weren't capable of anything these days.

"I'll have to decide," she said to herself. And of course, she rather liked the fact of having to decide.

But here was something to hesitate over: thinking in general terms and dispassionately, then of course she felt closer to Strepetov, he was physically more attractive and he was a rather finer judge of poetry – mathematicians and poets were the same – but an old friend is worth two, and Alevtina found herself repeating this old saw more and more often. She felt sorry for Mikhailov. Mikhailov was kind and sensitive and had done a fair bit for her, especially when it came to furniture and it would be cruel to give him his marching orders just because a good-looking fellow had appeared on the horizon. Good-lookers appear and disappear, that's the way it is, but an old friend is an old friend, and whatever else, women know how to appreciate that.... But on the other hand, if Alevtina were to suppress, let's say, the voice and call of her heart and, as a result, Strepetov were to disappear and Mikhailov to stay, you still couldn't expect gratitude from him. One could easily imagine Alevtina coming to regret this.

"We'll all disappear," Mikhailov would mutter sternly and gloomily in response to this, and he wouldn't even turn out to be very good at responding to Alevtina's generosity. He was a bear after all, and bears go where the honey is.

But now for Mikhailov's hesitations. The furniture workshop had emptied, it was the end of the day, but still Mikhailov didn't know whether to go home that evening or to Alevtina's. He folded things up, locked something away in a drawer and finally heard his inner voice: home... and the thought of Alevtina became a small and insignificant thought and even if it was something he wanted, it came with a certain sense of his new firmness.

"I'm off," he said to the girl at reception.

"Goodbye, Mr. Mikhailov."

"Goodbye." Mikhailov walked along the street, pleased as he sought to convince himself of the rightness of the decision he had taken. However, having finally convinced himself, he suddenly realized as he embraced the unexpected: he wasn't walking home, he was going to Alevtina's. He couldn't even pinpoint the moment at which he had decided to go to her, and had he even decided. He had just discovered that he was on the metro, sitting in the front carriage, swaying to the rhythm of the train in motion on his way to her. And then it suddenly came to him as he remembered that his wife had sprung a slight temperature that morning. Maybe she was ill and the weight of this, not much in itself, having fallen on him unexpectedly, began to feel very heavy and, swearing at his own spinelessness (what a wimp he was), Mikhailov leapt out of the carriage and breaking into a run, clutching his bulging briefcase to his side, he crossed over to the other side of the platform.

And so he was home.

"Well, how are things?" he asked, screwing up his eyes to one side. He was out of breath.

"Not too bad," answered his sick wife, and that "not too bad" cast Mikhailov down. Some people can live with divided feelings easily,

The Safety-valve

or maybe just craftily. They just get on with their lives – and good luck to them – but one would think that everyone had already guessed how much he was suffering. For example, some workers had taken a coffee-table and a settee to Alevtina's out of the factory (he had been walking on the other side of the van while they were loading up and had overheard their chat). "Mikhailov's got a bird in Khimki – she sucks him dry." "A bit of all right?" "Not bad. I wouldn't turn her down." And this snotty-nosed laddy had come out with such awful stuff that Mikhailov had wanted to yell at him, give him a right dressing-down, tear him off a strip, and to hell with people would start talking.

His wife was preparing the supper, her hands were numb, but she was carrying out her everyday female duties conscientiously and not without a certain concealed reproach. A sick wife was a different person, quiet and tearful. She was afraid she might die. Leaning over the stove top and poking in the frying-pan with a knife, she wept:

"You know I've got nothing in this life, only our boys..." And an hour later, her temperature went up to over 100. She went to bed and again cried in a wary sort of way, but again her words were very much to the point:

"Dear, please don't marry again."

Her face was flaming red.

"If I die, look after the boys." His wife was lying, looking up at the white ceiling. As with all sick people, her words were aimed at nothing specific, she was completely detached and alienated, away into a landscape of her own. Mikhailov squeezed her hand gently. He realized that his wife wasn't going to die, but fear had already touched and pricked him – the imprint of some kind of secret terror which is implanted in every one of us from childhood.

And it was at that point that she rang. From the other room (having shut the door firmly behind him) Mikhailov was explaining in a muffled voice that he couldn't come now, his wife was ill.

"Yes, yes," Alevtina whispered sympathetically, "when I particularly need you, your wife's ill."

And she hung up with a sigh.

Mikhailov smoked a cigarette in the kitchen and then strode heavily through to the children. They had broken off their homework and come out of their room and were standing there, his fine slender sons. Their faces bore the same traces of terror at their mother's being ill. There they stood, faces uplifted towards their father, as though laying bare their souls. They waited.

"Lads," he said, clearing his throat. "Drop your homework for the time being." They were silent. It was already after eight in the evening.

"Drop your homework for the time being and go to your mum. I've got to go out."

He gave no explanations. They were used to understanding and trusting him and did what they are told. They weren't yet of the age for hail-fellow-well-met kind of jokes. They said nothing, just nodded, yes, OK. First the younger nodded and went off towards his mother's room, followed by the elder.

"I'll just finish this one exercise, dad. Two lines."

"Finish it off then."

And, needless to say, Alevtina wasn't at home.

He paid off the taxi-driver and now an out of breath Mikhailov was climbing up to her floor and forcefully, nervously, ringing the doorbell. Maybe she was asleep? Then he went down and looked up from the street at her dark windows. He knew which were her windows and she wasn't sleeping — she just wasn't there. Mikhailov realized this, but still couldn't avoid a short burst of jealousy. He was embarrassed and ashamed at himself, a big, solid, pudgy man pressing his face up to the keyhole and then, looking round furtively, he kneeled down on the dirty floor of the landing putting his ear close to the keyhole, absorbing that emptiness which lay behind the door and hoping for some kind of noise or creak from within.

He hailed a taxi, grunting with every step, running across the road and then back, in the fussy, pathetic manner of a stout forty-year-old, whom everyone would take to be fifty. He was in a hurry, he could have done without a taxi, but he wanted to have a smoke in the cab (one of life's pleasures which he had only recently discovered) and as he smoked and seemingly looked out of the window of the speeding cab, he was peering into a kind of cloying and wearisome emptiness within himself. And so he smoked as he rode in the taxi to a cheap self-service cafe near a certain publishing house. He arrived (having smoked two cigarettes) and roamed among the tables and the slightly drunk people, staring, his eyes seeking

The Safety-valve

out the familiar dark little head with its close-cropped hair, a nervous, timorous female head. But Alevtina wasn't there. So he went to the Writers' Club which wasn't far away (two places where she was most often to be found: "I must meet people. I must get on and do things," she'd say). But he wasn't allowed in. At the door there stood the manager, full of his own self-importance, and Mikhailov had to wait while the man dashed off somewhere with a frenzied shout and only then, downcast and pathetic, with an embarrassed giggle, he handed over a rouble note to an old woman with a moustache who had replaced the manager. But there was no sign of Alevtina.

There was still her friend, the basketball player, at whose place they'd been recently (the only time Mikhailov and Alevtina had been out to a social gathering). Mikhailov didn't like going anywhere, he preferred Alevtina's nice little flat in Khimki and liked to spend long evenings just sitting there, quietly and uninterruptedly. But here he was on his way to the basketball player, and by now this was just desperation and like a last attempt, if only to draw a line under the whole thing. But in fact Alevtina was there. There was a tobacco fog, the smoke rose in layers, and the little dark head turned sharply and energetically, arguing with someone in the smoke that was bluish and red from the table lamp. They were a small, cheerful group of people – the basketball player and his wife, mostly thirty-year olds and even younger – lean tall, a little coterie, bound together by their talk round the table and their youth. There was much banter and glances thrown in the direction of Mikhailov as he dragged himself along, entering with the guilty smile of the uninvited. They were looking at him as people do on such occasions at a fifty-year-old creep, damaged by life, already with a little belly and grown-up children, yet who was "still keen". He was now sitting there, nodding in agreement and putting up with the jokes and all this not even for a woman, but just so that he could sit there, basking in their youth and giggling at the anecdotes and then perhaps, as the curtain was about to go down, he might grab a bit for himself. The drink had just run out and someone was being sent out to a late-night shop. "Hang on, hang on," Mikhailov got his oar in hastily, a childish smile spreading over his features. "Let me give you something for this. Here you are." He was fiddling with his wallet, not knowing how much to hand over and feeling that people were looking at him.

"Yes, he's well off! Take some more off him!" Alevtina shouted, making it clear to the company that he was worth something. Some young whippersnapper neatly snatched 10 roubles from him (grabbing the note, he waved it lightly round in his hand – would more be forthcoming? And he took some more) and sped off to the shop. There was general laughter. Everyone had the same feeling, that the evening was still going on and that its conclusion was pushed further into the distance to an indefinite point, from the moment when the door slammed and Victor, programmed in advance, plunged purposefully into the bustle of the Moscow twilight, with the crumpled red bundle of the two banknotes he'd grabbed bursting into flame and burning his palm as he was impelled onwards. Victor would manage all right... Catching the moment, Mikhailov whispered to Alevtina: "Shall we go to your place?", but she shook her closely-cropped head. "No, we won't, it's not at all bad here, let's stay for a bit." But the noise and the company round the table wasn't to Mikhailov's taste. They wanted to dance and romp around, that was understandable, but he wanted to be with Alevtina at her place and that was also understandable. Having established that she was planning to stay there until late, he got up and went away quietly, without a backward glance, without saying goodbye, realizing that no-one would miss him either now or when Victor returned and that the best he could hope for was that someone would ask Alevtina: "Where's that fellow of yours, the guy who didn't make it in his youth – has he gone back to his faithful old wife?"

He returned home chastened but with an unpleasant aftertaste. The evening which he had projected to be with Alevtina was lost and he only had a couple of such evenings a month. After work the next day and the day after he had to make calls to customers and so wouldn't have time to go to Alevtina's. And then came Saturday and Sunday. With a sick wife, he would have to put aside several evenings on the trot for his family. Such was life... He was back home. Dead tired and overcome on the stairs by shortness of breath, feeling the constriction of guilt in his heart, he sat down beside his wife. She hadn't changed and was lying as she had been. Trying not to breathe his casual glass of vodka over her, Mikhailov kissed her on the forehead and whispered:

"Here I am... I'm back. See, I've done all I had to and got back."

The Safety-valve

The children were preparing for sleep. The elder was already in bed and the younger, just in his shorts (how thin he was), was standing in the doorway yawning (he'd waited a long time) watching his father sitting by his mother.

But even if he had one of his more successful days and found Alevtina in, an "evening" didn't emerge straight away and out of nothing. For a start, Alevtina was driven to distraction by his silence or by his correct, though tediously positive reasoning.

"Mikhailov, you're a good guy, but a bit dull."

He said nothing.

"You're boring, Mikhailov," said Alevtina in challenging fashion, expecting a reaction.

"I'm not boring. I'm old."

"I couldn't give a toss about why you're boring – I know it all by heart: you're old, you're hard of hearing, you've got a family, you're out of puff, you're a put-upon furniture hack. By the way, yesterday Duzhkin (an artist) really went to town criticizing your furniture..."

This was a reference to some furniture which Mikhailov had made for Alevtina.

"He said you were a genius in your own way – a genius of cautiously militant philistinism."

"That's my work you're talking about."

"OK, don't take offence."

He didn't take offence: touchy people are those with time on their hands and Mikhailov didn't have time on his hands. Letting out an evening yawn, he listened without interest to how all these Duzhkins and Konoplevs whose opinion she valued sent his furniture up.

But gradually the evening came into its own – the conversation between the man and the woman became softer and more intimate and so to speak more of the twilight, there was mutual contact... On some of these occasions, it's true, bed took over. Alevtina would say: "All right, then. I feel in fighting mood tonight," and, with a smile, she would throw herself at him and fix on him. This got Mikhailov a little worried: it was clear what was queried, but each time it seemed to him a bit of a task to overcome the space between the armchair and the bed – the problem was his fear of his own awkward movements. As a rule, they would spend a lot of time chatting, unwinding as it were – two grown-up people. Alevtina would make coffee and talk about her childhood or her mother who was still milking cows in the village near Kursk. Alevtina had a favourite topic – how for a long time everyone at school thought her plain. Or suddenly she would ask whether Mikhailov would like to hear some poetry, sometimes these were 'fresh' poems. "You don't understand, Mikhailov, how important a listener is, even to the most minor poet – in fact for a minor poet it's even more important." "Why shouldn't I understand?" Mikhailov would smile a kindly smile. "Understand or not, you're going to have to listen today," she would laugh. And so she would read:

> *I love! And loss there is no more!*
> *I love! And all on earth's within my grasp!*
> *Tell me, my love, tell me my dear...*

She was always loving somebody in her poems and, thank God, Mikhailov had acquired the knowledge that this loved one of hers wasn't him, or another, or a third, but generally speaking as it were, a non-living person. Sometimes he had slender hands, sometimes blue eyes. Sometimes he seemed to be healthily swarthy ("My Gypsy, my little tousle-haired one!") but of course the main thing was the refrain:

> *You were sad, I was cunning*
> *And autumn gave us joy...*

On one such evening, or rather as one such evening was just taking off, there appeared Yuri Strepetov, blond with finely-chiselled features. Strictly speaking, Strepetov appeared with a friend, but despite the novelty of them both, he was the one who she seemed to have marked out for herself. Strepetov sat there for the whole evening, talking intelligently and nervously. He was pale, exhausted and handsome. "Who's this fallen angel who's come down to us?" asked Mikhailov in a low voice. He was cautious, even perhaps alarmed. Mikhailov had gone into the kitchen to speak to Alevtina who was making coffee for them all. She wasn't cross – she laughed, even complimented him.

"You're observant, Mikhailov. You really have learned some subtle responses in my house – don't you feel that?"

The Safety-valve

"I do try."

"And you're a little bit jealous?"

"Get away..."

And just at that point, Strepetov came into the kitchen (he was bored, fed up with looking at all the etchings on display). He said with a smile:

"On your own?"

And with the smile on his face, he began to walk the tiny kitchen ($4 \times 2m^2$) from corner to corner and this measured tread separated Mikhailov and Alevtina diagonally. From opposite corners they exchanged glances. And Strepetov spoke:

"The coffee smells good. I like to smell it. And I like to smell new-mown hay." So he continued walking without raising his head or looking at them. This degree of self-absorption looked rather ridiculous in the small crowded kitchen. Mikhailov weighed him up calmly and coolly. "What a prat." But then he weighed up something else. "He's a good-looker, the bastard." And although Alevtina's eyes were on him – Mikhailov – rather than the newcomer, Mikhailov felt that in those moments something new had started up and that he, Mikhailov, wouldn't alas, be able to avoid this new element, but could only hope to come to terms with it.

What started up was this. A more or less continuous sitting in a threesome. Other guests were rare and on the whole not favoured with the eye of the hostess – they came and went – but those two stayed – Mikhailov and Strepetov, or perhaps Strepetov and Mikhailov, or to be more accurate, whoever sat out the other, and the most depressing thing for Mikhailov was that the sitting along with and the sitting out always fell on the evenings he'd planned and it was obvious that this was no coincidence. He would ring her to fix things up, confirm them all over again (sometimes deliberately), he would postpone visits to customers, tell lies at home and finally arrive and right away, as though arriving to a timetable, along would come Strepetov. Sometimes Strepetov was already there, as if ready for him in advance. There the three of them would sit, drinking a little wine, or more often coffee, absentmindedly leafing through poetry anthologies and conversing in a desultory fashion. Playing the game of being the unwanted third party is simple, but demands a certain caution. Alevtina, therefore, changed her style. She insisted, practically forced them to listen to tapes of some well-known concerts. Both she and Strepetov seemed willing to put up with it, and sat and listened, but Mikhailov liked neither piano nor harpsichord – especially harpsichord. He made no attempt to be devious, or hide his dislike. You couldn't like what you didn't like. But it was as though they were trying to starve him out. He could feel how intolerably his brain was being dulled by these monotonous, albeit melodious no issues. Mikhailov's features were unbearably distorted by annoyance and the desire to yawn, and when there was a mirror opposite he could see that his face was losing any semblance of humanity. They would leave together and walk to the metro, both of them inhibited, both with briefcases. It was as though they'd both come off duty. Or, if Strepetov had come by car, he would give Mikhailov a lift as far as his route would allow him. Mikhailov still managed to be on his own with her occasionally and from these few "occasionallys" he would occasionally stay at Alevtina's till morning. But he had not the slightest assurance that the same thing didn't happen with Strepetov. The game, if game it was, was long drawn out. Alevtina was capricious, unpredictable, self-willed in the best sense of the words – and there is a positive connotation to such words, a hint of an independent attitude to life, an "It's my business".

"Don't keep asking me, Mikhailov, that's enough questioning, you're always talking nowadays: just be silently jealous."

"I still want to know."

"Why?"

"Well, just that it's always better to know than not know."

"I'm not sure about that. And how will you pay me back for knowing about it? Come on! Just suppose in exchange I asked you to turn yourself inside out. Suppose I wanted to force my way right into the depths of your soul?"

On another occasion she spoke with tears in her eyes and unfeigned pain. She wept:

"Leave me alone, can't you just leave me alone... When you're dealing with a woman, you have to stamp on her – right?"

Her eyes dried, but then she started to cry again and the second batch of tears made her look ugly and quite pathetic:

"Leave me alone! I don't want my life to be an open book to you all the time. I don't! I don't!"

The Safety-valve

And then one day, Mikhailov stopped questioning her altogether, he just dried up and faded inside and, to make thing worse, the endless harpsichord recording made him dry up and fade outside. And then he was much quieter and much more docile as he sat opposite Strepetov. They both sat and behaved themselves, like cultured males of the species, controlled in all aspects and not importunate, for whom the word of the woman is law and her words towards the end of the evening were usually as follows:

"Right, lads, that's it. Time for tonight's shuteye." And the forty-year old "lads" would stand up. If it wasn't summer, they would put on their coats and peaceably without pushing or shoving, retrieve their briefcases. In the hallway, Alevtina would kiss them both on the cheek, with obvious pleasure, squeezing them generously in farewell with her magnificent lofty bosom, which moved under her sweater when she flung her arms round them in a parting embrace. She wished them a "good-tonight", with a smile of sincerity. Cunningly, tenderly, she had another couple of words for them in parting:

"Mind you don't come to blows with each other."

And of course, the hostility towards the mathematician grew in Mikhailov: he had his own car, he was a handsome devil, and seemed to have no end of free time, and of course he wasn't short of women. But as for Mikhailov, for whom Alevtina was a rare gift that had landed in his lap, going to her nowadays was like going to the most hopeless place where you could be dismissed with a snap of the fingers, if not today, then tomorrow. Of course, this might not happen, she could still be nice to him, but... Mikhailov would arrive home unsatisfied and not knowing what to expect. Nothing was said. "What's the matter with you?" his wife would ask: it was already late, the boys were asleep and his yawning wife would be watching a documentary on TV about the natural beauty of Siberia. Yawning, she would inform him that a customer had phoned.

"What about?" Mikhailov would press her.

"He wanted some kitchen cupboards."

Mikhailov thought this over — yes, he should be getting on with this, the man had been waiting for a long time.

"They wanted them done Finnish-style."

"That's their business what they want." Mikhailov didn't indulge customers' whims, be insisted on his own way. And the less he indulged them, the more they praised him and the more tangibly they rewarded him, that's what they were like. His wife went on again about the customers (without tearing herself away from the TV), but Mikhailov didn't answer – all of him was *there*, with her, with Alevtina, and yet perhaps not with her even. Right now, he was on his own, and distanced in that great depth of loneliness which only a beloved woman can bestow when she is not there beside you.

The idea to send his sons to the university came to Mikhailov on the very day when he and Alevtina were visiting Zagorsk monastery (she loved looking at churches) and when they were strolling through the little streets and alleyways. They attended an evening service, there was singing and it wasn't at all bad, or at any rate less of a torment than harpsichord music. As they walked round, looking and listening, all the while this passing thought kept growing in Mikhailov. By nightfall they were dead on their feet, and, as they tried to find somewhere to spend the night there in Zagorsk, the possibility presented itself of an awful shabby hotel. The walls were grey, the room was dingy. The food was tasteless and the only thing to cheer about was lovely hot tea. Alevtina was greatly out of sorts: had the mathematician been with them, he would have taken them back in his car – it would have been a better idea, of course, to have gone in a threesome – at the age of thirty it was nice to sleep at home, sod any romantic stuff... And it was sleeting. The snow was falling, mixed with rain and striking the windowsill with a flabby sort of sound, like lumps of semolina.

"I know what I don't want in my old age," Alevtina conveyed this gloomily. "And that's to die in a hotel like this one."

And she went on grumbling:

"What a hole."

And again:

"What dreary walls."

The walls were indeed dilapidated. The wallpaper was hanging down in strips. The bedding was clean, but the bed itself gave off such a whiff of shabbiness, of lonely old people and poverty, that the cleanliness of the linen only underlined the shabbiness. Mikhailov noticed none, or hardly any, of this. He was completely wrapped up in his own thoughts, his idea filled him up to the brim. He pictured his two sons on a bright day (what sunshine!) climbing up the steps to the tall building of the university with its spire, the younger with his exercise books tucked under his arm. They stopped, or rather they had met on those steps during a break between lectures, and the elder was explaining: "My lecture finishes at two. Shall we have lunch together?" "OK" "Don't be late, mind" – and they both laughed). Unable to resist the happy picture, Mikhailov suddenly spoke and it was as though a draught of air emerged from him:

"That's good." He pulled himself together and saw the dim hotel room and Alevtina undressing and with a grimace of annoyance folding her skirt over a chair. Mikhailov tried to cover up the enthusiastic expression which had escaped from him:

"I think it's OK here. I like it."

Alevtina snorted:

"D'you know, Mikhailov, you're a happy man."

"What?" He didn't see the irony.

"You're happy. Whatever you put in your mouth turns to honey." She was wondering whether to undress completely, she liked sleeping in the nude. She hesitated, fighting against temptation, took another look at the whiteness of the sheets – and eventually lay down in her slip. Mikhailov lay down too. The walls of the hotel once again very easily gave way in his consciousness to the shining steps leading up to the university – his sons were standing there, side by side, talking, and from above the yellow sun rays slanted powerfully down on them. Mikhailov thought that after this little scene he didn't need anything more – he had a family, his children were on their feet and indeed Mikhailov had lived out his life productively – even love had come to him in the twilight of his years. What more could he want?

And so, finally, to Strepetov's doubts: he was vain, proud and arrogant and naturally with this unfortunate combination of traits, he suffered acutely from the slightest trifle... The extraordinary fact that Alevtina didn't prefer him straightaway (it had to be straightaway, immediately!) to some smelly Mikhailov who gave off an odour of varnish, of course upset him seriously. To comprehend Alevtina's duality was quite beyond the mathematician Strepetov ("What choice is there? What's there to discuss, my dear?") To him, Mikhailov was a rather dim and slow-moving "furniture-man", a fixer, a minor boss with a belly; maybe he had a soul, perhaps even some spiritual depths, but that was just by the by, it came from nature, from the deep valleys, from his peasant grandfather, not from his own depths. And, of course, first and foremost, Mikhailov annoyed him with his habit of sitting down wearily and proprietorially, laying his elbows on the table, as though everyone around had been drinking tea all day while he'd been ploughing the fields round the clock and now he was entitled to his plate of pork and cabbage soup. What a dope!

Rivalry – and especially a humiliating rivalry – was something Strepetov couldn't stand at all; he knew he was attractive to women, and this knowledge either immediately attained its goal, or else equally instantaneously led to his backing off from "a fight over a female". Of course, he could play for high stakes – he could introduce Alevtina into his circle of mathematicians, she'd be out of her mind with excitement, she'd wanted this for ages. He could get her to come to one of his lectures, or just bring her along. He could even take her with him to Paris to the next symposium as his secretary. That was a possibility and what woman would be able to resist a two-week stay in Montmartre? Strepetov hesitated. He could do all this, of course, but it all seemed a bit shameful, a bit pathetic, it was a clear and unequivocal admission that he couldn't compete with the furniture-man on equal terms and was forced to take a gamble on what he could offer in the way of fame and the social whirl. That was embarrassing, and on top of that – and here Strepetov acknowledged this to himself all the way – there was no certainty that all this heavy artillery would really help and blast away through. He was forced to concede that, after Paris in the misty autumn, he might still find the furniture-man right back there at Alevtina's with the first snowfall of winter. And it seemed as though that's how it really would be, and that would be intolerable, and what a scar it would leave behind.

"Anyway, what's the point?" Strepetov grimaced. Yet again, he said to himself that Alevtina was stupid and capricious and not very sensible about people and in general very prone to falling for lofty words, like an untutored primitive whose whole life has been untutored and primitive and who has only just the other day become aware of heaven, beauty and God. She was one of those, just down from the trees, who starts to shout and make a lot of noise, thinking that, until now, no-one else has conceived of the existence of heaven, beauty and God.

Suddenly, he experienced jealousy. He was at the wheel of his car and he'd left them there together: he was on his way home and he was jealous about Alevtina in the most elementary fashion, jealous and increasingly angry.

3

Mikhailov and Alevtina had got together straightaway and rather precipitately, though perhaps it was rather that it was precipitate for Mikhailov. Perhaps concluding that it had all happened rather hastily for him and seeking to justify the haste, Alevtina said, on their very first evening:

"It's like this with me. If I suddenly fancy a guy, then I don't try to hold back."

She explained this further:

"I'm a free woman on my own. I'm not married, but I still want some loving, too, don't I?" And again, it was obvious from her eyes that nothing improper lay behind these words, just her particular, personal, female search justified by her loneliness.

"Of course you do," Mikhailov nodded in agreement. "Of course..."

Visiting Alevtina was convenient – it was on the metro, he had the time, but it wasn't a case just of time and metro. Mikhailov had said that he was married with children, and already this was a matter of trust, it never entered his head that Alevtina had an eye on him, that she was angling for something from him, wanting to tie him down somehow – it was just a matter of come if you want to, suit yourself.

"It's great at your place," he once said to her as his lips latched on to a cup of coffee. "I'd never have imagined it could be so wonderful. You know, I used to be scared of you at first, I'm scared of women anyway."

"I know," laughed Alevtina, "I know everything."

Alevtina's openness and transparent nature almost carried him away. She had a girl-friend who was also nice, but she much more resembled an entrapper of men, a husband-hunter. Somehow her eyes were always enticing him, she was too much of a woman, too obviously a single mother. And there were male friends too. Alevtina would be talking one-to-one with Mikhailov and, breaking off, would say to the other fellow on the telephone, without leaving the room, all out in the open: "I couldn't make it. I was busy. I'm a woman, my dear, forgive me." And all this without in any way speeding up or slowing down the natural rhythm of her life and without, of course, flushing or fussing. It was exactly that quality of not offending you and not frightening the other that Mikhailov found so hard to resist.

"You certainly know how to handle us," he once said to Alevtina when someone else arrived by coincidence – someone who came, sat around, drank coffee and then went away, encouraged, convinced that Mikhailov was just some fat guy, in no way involved. Indeed, the fool went away triumphant, although Alevtina had behaved quite equably towards him and had not offended or humiliated Mikhailov in his presence with a single word – and of course without the old story that Mikhailov was a relative from Leningrad and that the poor chap had nowhere to stay the night.

"Handle you, do I?" – she didn't like the rather crude word.

"It's just the way I say it. For God's sake, don't take offence." Mikhailov was backing off straight away, but at the same time smiling at her knowingly, with a look that said, "You and I are clever people, all the more reason for seeing each other and being friends." Mikhailov was having his little joke.

He joked quite often these days, looking down on her life, as it were, from above and laughing, so to speak, like an adult at a little girl playing, but even as he joked he didn't notice how he was being drawn into her life. One time, Mikhailov went to Alevtina's solely in order to hear about how and why she had finished with her piss artist of a husband (the previous time she hadn't finished the story, she'd been interrupted, but it was all intriguing). On another occasion, he very much wanted to hear about her girl-friend with the enticing eyes, on yet another occasion he hadn't any reason at all, it was just that it was a tedious evening, he hadn't anywhere to go, and he could always get home rather later.

Once a month – that clearly was too rare, unreasonably so; once a week was perhaps a bit too often. Mikhailov weighed this up and

The Safety-valve

limited himself to twice a month, or three times at the most – he was a busy man, a family man, he barely had the time and he was a man literally pulled in all directions by his customers ("Could you please do us a little cupboard and a dividing wall? We'll see you at eight – you couldn't manage during the day?" He couldn't manage during the day, he had to be in the workshop). Therefore twice a month seemed dependable and frequent enough, until one day Alevtina said to him:

"So, I won't be seeing my lover again in April. It's to be May, then?" and she looked at him with a smile, and there was no offence, or if there were, then it was concealed. But the fact that she had guessed at what was going on and, as it were, done so with indifference, bothered Mikhailov. Alevtina was looking at him with a smile and a certain regret that he was so busy and so tired out like all ordinary people and she even forgave him that ordinariness. This bothered Mikhailov, so he turned up at her place that week, and again, and yet again, and discovered all over again how wonderful it was to be there. And when on one occasion, Alevtina had an unknown male guest, obviously someone new, Mikhailov suddenly experienced the pleasure of being a long-time resident of this cosy place. It was an ample feeling and Mikhailov behaved like a long-term resident – he asked for coffee, he walked up and down, he rummaged familiarly in the bookshelves, as one who knew his way around. At this point he realized that, to a certain extent, he was living in this flat (a regular, you know, old chap), he had his own favourite books of poetry, his own coffee cup, and the armchair in which he sat most often had in its way become *his*. This armchair seemed to Mikhailov much more comfortable and better placed than the other two – from the mirror, part of the entrance-hall was visible, so you could see who was coming and how they arrived. And even his feelings towards Alevtina – and at the strait they were only moderate – stopped being no more than a little blast of warmth, a little piece of his life, because her living-space itself, and the spatial disposition of objects – the armchair, the books, the coffee-cup, became that bit of warmth, that little piece of his life. And the new guy who appeared was Strepetov, or rather a new guy suddenly appeared and disappeared in a flash and a second new guy – that was Strepetov, the mathematician.

Mikhailov suddenly saw that now was not his turn or his time and that Strepetov was being drawn into this life of hers, Strepetov was coming, Strepetov was phoning. And it seemed, too, as though the mathematician was also getting used to things imperceptibly and that he too was starting to look down jokingly from above on Alevtina's life and perhaps limiting himself too and starting to think in terms of twice a month. As to the mutual convergence of their feelings, there could be no doubt. Alevtina was reading her poems during a trip through the Crimea – there was a whole company of them working there, singers, poets, humorists. And the mathematician was on holiday in the Crimea. Mikhailov could fill in the rest of the picture for himself. And he pictured, too, their first evening. Completing this picture, Mikhailov found that a mathematician wasn't too bad an idea and a lot letter than one of those humorists writers from that same crew, or a compere for example (a very persistent and annoying character, who would have borrowed fivers off Mikhailov, or casually demolished a bottle – "let's put one away, quickly, old chap", words that were intended to suggest that he had an expansive nature, unlike Mikhailov). A mathematician wasn't the worst idea, at least there wouldn't be any fights.

Now, Alevtina appeared in a new light – and not in the best light, as with any person seeking a choice. She did things openly. She didn't just get to know him, fall in love, then get disappointed and give him the push – she directed the whole process, she pulled the strings, she clicked the needles, she knitted it all together, like her great-grandmother used to knit socks for her grandson. "Not today, Mikhailov, I'm tired." "I'll just come for a little while," Mikhailov would assure her. "No, no, I've someone coming to see me today – that mathematician," she would explain frankly and simply over the telephone, putting off her evening with Mikhailov for at least a week. But there was nothing to be done. He was being squeezed out quite simply and, so as not to cause pain, quite unceremoniously. Alevtina was knitting the affair together, putting her own conclusion to it and causing pain herself, without waiting for the other person suddenly to disappear and cause her pain.

Mikhailov tried to change things, he would phone more often or else arrive without phoning and without warning ("I was just passing by and thought I'd drop in") but this only led to his being forced out even more unceremoniously. Alevtina would get cross: "Look, Mikhailov, you've got a bit too used to this, remember your place."

"I was just passing and thought I'd..."

"Drop it".

"If you don't believe me, I'll tell you – I was going from Paveletsky station to one of my customers, he lives..."

"Mikhailov, we're grown-up people!" Alevtina was annoyed. She had always received him kindly. She read him poems, she made him nice coffee. She was honestly and genuinely fond of him and she had let him indulge in full measure in what must be described as a difficult emotional situation. And that was enough. If she weren't to drop him tomorrow, then he would drop her, wasn't that how things always turned out? Both of them maintained a highly-charged silence and perhaps for the first time saw and understood each other clearly – indeed understanding begins at the very moment, that acute point in a relationship when one party feels nothing and the other feels pain.

"So that's how things are," said Mikhailov, without any meaning whatsoever and he went on repeating this, trying as far as possible to hide within himself and behind his own sense of caution. "So that's how things are..."

Alevtina was pummelling his shoulder, but her voice was certainly not gentle.

"Head up, Mikhailov. Nothing special's happened, if it still hurts, we're still alive."

"That's really wise."

"Well, whatever you wish. I don't write very wise poetry, but I'm quite sensible as a person."

She kissed him on the cheek and added more gently:

"OK, Mikhailov, off home now."

"Are you expecting someone?"

"Maybe yes, maybe no, it's got nothing to do with you."

"Let it be then."

"There's a clever boy."

He departed. He'd been given the push, that was obvious, and another thing was more or less obvious. He'd had a smack in the face, and a big one, and now he had to be grateful for the lesson and go off, disappear, as it were, with some homework to do. That's how things usually turn out, he wasn't the first. One derived something from the experience and then one would set off again on life's path and hasten to find some place where one could use the experience, calling one's pain and everything connected with it, one's past. But the nub of it was that for Mikhailov it wasn't just a matter of Alevtina, not just an experience and not at all in the past — it was love, or nearly love, and moreover it had come about just as the curtain was about to go down on his life (Mikhailov was forty, and one of those who considered that at forty the curtain was about to descend). Therefore, Mikhailov would go away, but not completely.

First, he did actually disappear, he wasn't around. But a couple of weeks after (Alevtina had once asked him to do this) he sent some workmen up to her place with a very elegant wall-cupboard. The bill, of course, was attached — he was sorry, but he wasn't going to give away anything for free and there was also a note, saying that he had done what she'd asked and so on, sorry it was a bit on the expensive side (in fact the price had been knocked down for such an excellent saleable item). Alevtina phoned afterwards — just thanks and nothing more. But nothing less, either. Mikhailov was business-like and dry as he told her (not that she'd in any way invited him round) that right now he was very, very busy:

"I can't drop round."

"There's a clever boy," retorted Alevtina, not without irony. And again, she made no move to ask him round and waited to see what he would say, now that she had driven him into a corner.

And this is what he said:

"Look, would you like a kitchen cupboard? We've just started producing them. They're very handy and right up to date."

And for another couple of weeks, he kept away and didn't phone. When the kitchen cupboard arrived, she phoned him:

"Mikhailov, you really are pressing your furniture on me. Why is it so cheap?"

"That's the price. It's not standard quality wood."

"Don't give me that."

"As you wish," he laughed. "You can order your furniture from another place." At this point he had to introduce an extraneous topic. "Yesterday, on TV, they ran that old film 'The Building Site'. You didn't happen to see it? There was an actor who looked like me."

"He was probably better looking than you", Alevtina didn't mince her words.

"Yes, he was," Mikhailov readily agreed and readily laughed.

"And did he stay silent for hours, like you?"

"Yes, he did. He stayed dumb all the time," Mikhailov laughed. "To be honest, it was rather a dumb film."

And once again, he neither called nor phoned. Once he did actually call round, but not, so to speak, in a personal capacity, but rather just as an acquaintance and in the capacity of a furniture-man, much in demand by the mistress of the house. Of course, Strepetov was there. But Mikhailov wasn't bothered by Strepetov – he was calm and businesslike and clearly had no pretensions. He enquired about her health, looked around without fuss to see how the new furniture had settled in – and it had settled in excellently (if anyone was familiar with the interior of the flat, it was Mikhailov) – and then he departed, leaving the two of them alone and having spent less than ten minutes there. Then Alevtina was taken to hospital with appendicitis.

Mikhailov visited her, brought her apples and oranges, though no more than anyone else (and others indeed came, bearing fruit) and the only thing he did was to make an appointment with the consultant in charge of the ward, as a result of which the consultant operated on Alevtina himself, since she was one of those timorous people who didn't want to be operated on by those nice young medical students. Mikhailov didn't spend time standing under the hospital windows and he didn't try to bribe his way past the nurses with chocolates, just to have a chat with Alevtina in the ward. Nor did he try to force confidences out of her – he did no more than would any person on good terms with her, and no less either. And when Alevtina was finally discharged from hospital, she invited him round. She was semi-recumbent, not having fully recovered, and they were alone together. Mikhailov brewed up coffee for both of them and now he was pouring out the hot, strong-tasting liquid into the cups and, as she watched his leisurely movements, just dropping her head back on the pillow, Alevtina delivered herself of one of those portentous statements:

"You know, Mikhailov, you're a real friend." The words came out too baldly and the baldness detracted from their authenticity, but the essence ('You're a real friend, Mikhailov') remained without any passionate protestation.

He remained silent, and Alevtina scrutinized him, as one scrutinizes a person who returns after a long absence. She derived pleasure from looking at people as it were afresh and marvelling afresh. After illness, all sorts of things give pleasure. People drink in sensations like wine. Alevtina blushed deeply.

"I'm very fond of you as a human being, Mikhailov, and you know it's not at all the way I loved you before." Alevtina was slightly embarrassed. She'd really said too much already, but though she realized this, he hadn't yet noticed.

"I'm glad," he replied.

She was looking for the right word.

"I love you, but, let's put it this way, I really don't want to go to bed with you. I don't want anything like that." Alevtina's smile was timid and apologetic, and the words came out sharper. "You're not offended?"

"No."

"Honestly?"

"Honestly."

"Mikhailov, you're a treasure."

Silently, he brewed up some more coffee and they drank it. When Mikhailov was leaving Alevtina shouted at him to stay — she just wanted to read him a bit of poetry.

"I'm still very weak. I won't be able to read much, but it'll still be poetry."

She read poems that he had once praised. And he praised them again — and left, and in leaving he, as it were, finally took away with him everything he had always wanted to take away. Poetry was a way of saying thank you, but that might be altogether too short-lived, and when each time the poems lost some significance and that sense of being a gift in return, Alevtina began to fall into a state akin to dependency on Mikhailov. She did not know this as yet, but he knew it very well.

It was at this very point that there began that sitting opposite one another with cups of coffee in their hands. Both of them, Strepetov and Mikhailov, had been, so to speak, accepted and allowed in and this no doubt somewhat disturbed Alevtina's customary forward

The Safety-valve

planning of her life, but she managed to put up with this unpredictable element. So time passed and Strepetov still chuckled, like a long-standing guest, but this was beginning to change, since he was patently nervous. But Mikhailov continued with his quiet, modest, unassuming insinuation: the state of 'you do it for me, I'll do it for you' is not so complex, but then comes the point when it crosses over imperceptibly into a state of dependency. One of Alevtina's guests, some hanger-on, broke her tape-recorder − it was the merest trifle! − and in a telephone conversation, Mikhailov remembered this trifle and said to her:

"Listen, it just so happens that one of my customers is a TV and electrical engineer. Should I send him to you?"

"Mikhailov, that's a bit much."

"Dear, don't worry. He's up to his ears in debt to me. He'll be glad to be able to repay some bit of it."

"Thanks, Mikhailov."

"But don't even think about offering him money for his work," laughed Mikhailov.

He actually didn't have such a customer at that point, he'd lied, but he was laughing. He dug around in his address-book and he did find, well, not an engineer, but a TV technician (the same thing), someone who really could repair TVs and other domestic appliances and who really was in Mikhailov's debt and, to cut a long story short, within three days Alevtina's tape-recorder was in fine shape, he'd changed the brushes and cleaned and oiled the motor all in one go, and at the same time brought two tapes with the latest recordings as a gift. Alevtina was kind of complaining that she hadn't the recent subscription edition of Maupassant. She was willing to pay three times over for it, but where could she find such a thing. (She used often to complain about things without any specific aim, as women often do − and she would do it to Strepetov and Mikhailov and numerous other acquaintances as well.) Without letting anything slip, Mikhailov rummaged again in his well-thumbed address-book the next day and, within the week, Maupassant was on Alevtina's table. Of course, it was for money and without the pressure and the burden of being an expensive present, but nevertheless Alevtina hadn't had to run around searching − the man came to see her himself and sold her the volume cheaply. It would have been quite easy for Mikhailov to have bought the volume himself and perhaps make her a present of it, but he was anxious not to place her under any obligation. Of course, he was insinuating himself, but he was doing so with a light touch and at a distance and spreading his largesse around subtly, perceiving with some foresight that free gifts are oppressive and that recipients of such gifts don't feel comfortable about it and sooner or later long to free themselves from the spider's web. And Alevtina valued this lack of a sense of obligation.

One time, after they had made love and in an exhausted state (she had just got over the flu) Alevtina said to him:

"You're awfully sweet, Mikhailov."

He was embarrassed. He was always embarrassed by her praise, realizing that he was neither witty nor handsome and a long way off being a Strepetov, just an ordinary fellow with a certain business flair, honed in a furniture workshop. He pulled up the sheet (he was embarrassed by his large, fat body) and Alevtina noticed this at once, interrupted his movement and laughed as she pulled a corner of the sheet onto herself:

"Don't be shy – you're nice, nice, nice and I love you." And she added "You've a nice body."

"It's you that has the nice body."

"What did you say?"

"You heard me..."

"No, say it again. Fancy squeezing a compliment like that out of a silent type like you. After that, I wouldn't care if I was looked on as a plain Jane for the rest of my life!" Laughing, she got up, naked and happy and went into the kitchen to make some strong tea for the two of them.

And feeling returned: that was remarkable, but even more remarkable was the way in which it returned – first of all concealed presents and favours which required no commitment. That was just a move, a fairly well-directed and well thought-out move, one of the levers by which Mikhailov raised his status in the eyes of Alevtina. But very soon, Mikhailov came to the realization of the joy of giving. That was love. This feeling has been rising to the surface almost from the time of the cavemen, it is akin to the worship of women and thus, suddenly, an ordinary, harassed guy called Mikhailov recognized and discovered that feeling in himself, though he had never previously been aware of it. Well, of course, he knew it from films, but he had considered all this present-giving as just as example of the adaptability of the male mind, an ability to attract a woman and hold on to her. He was amazed as he listened to himself. Was the feeling as triumphant and as pure as it had seemed? This was the time when he made that wonderful one-legged table for Alevtina (it was his idea, he drew the sketches and the model and meticulously followed through its making) and this was the start of the period when all the workers at the factory gossiped all over the place about how some dame was sucking Mikhailov dry. Mikhailov couldn't give a toss – he didn't notice the flak. But he did notice something else – Strepetov had lost.

And so came the evening when Strepetov was sitting there for the last time and it came to one of the final moments – the mathematician stood up and announced that it was time for him to go home.

"I'll just have another cup ot coffee," this was Mikhailov.

"So will I," Alevtina took him up.

But Strepetov, so clever and so undervalued, stood up and left. Descending the stairs, in a fit of temper, he kept on saying:

"The dummy's won, the dummy's won... How come?"

Mikhailov overheard this. The mathematician had left his scarf behind. He departed too quickly and in too strained a mood, and of course he'd forgotten it, so Alevtina sent Mikhailov after him telling him to "catch him up and give it to him". Mikhailov took the scarf, with Alevtina smiling down on him ("I'll be waiting for you, love, come back, love") and, his heavy body quivering, he leapt down the stairs to catch up with Strepetov and that's where he overheard the word "dummy" – he couldn't quite make out what was being said, but the meaning was clear, as was the man's bitterness. He was already at the exit door, when Mikhailov caught up with him and handed him the scarf.

"Oh, thanks," said Strepetov and went away. And Mikhailov went back upstairs.

4

At certain moments the rather dull, but, you could say, crafty Mikhailov appeared to him in a sympathetic light. He was a human being after all and he led a dog's life. At any rate, Strepetov didn't feel the kind of hostility to Mikhailov which every now and again pulls at the heart strings when you think that someone is with the same woman, that's to say your woman and you know that he knows about you, and both of you know, indeed all three of you know or at any rate think you know...

"You seem to lead a pretty knackering existence," Strepetov had once said to Mikhailov (while Alevtina was banging out her artifacts on a typewriter).

"Yes, I'm knackered..."

"And here's the only place you can relax?" Mikhailov gave a laugh and didn't answer, as though he were concealing something.

"What are you guys on about?" asked Alevtina, momentarily distracted.

"About someone," laughed Strepetov. He had involuntarily used conciliatory words to Mikhailov, but having spoken, he instantly put the brakes on, not wanting to step over the boundaries too much. It was a momentary sympathy — no more than momentary — whilst the sitting each other out continued and even intensified during that period, until the crafty Mikhailov somehow or other saw off Strepetov decisively.

It was a strange feeling, all the same, if feeling it was and a strange love, if love it was, thought Strepetov to himself. After his lecture, he hurried off to the Research Institute where he gave consultations every day. He hastened, driving fast, always short of time, then he spent an hour and a half at the Computer Centre, then it was back to the University, and only then could he go.... but where to? The trouble was that Strepetov couldn't find his safety-valve in some bar and not only because it was boring and because he would invariably find himself sitting beside some noisy, worldly-wise fellow on a business-trip from out of town, who knew everything about life and the cost of living. Not because he might find himself (even more wearisome) next to some tedious snob from the intelligentsia, some Petersburg-type lush, whom one could only put up with if one drank oneself stupid, only Strepetov didn't have the necessary constitution of a horse. He wasn't very keen on company anyway. He wouldn't even have visited Alevtina if there'd been people there, even if that took the form of a peaceful celebration of the flesh — some people might find that restful, he didn't. A safety-valve was when you were in control, a safety-valve was for you alone, but not in isolation, one needed Alevtina and poetry-reading and coffee and a kind of loving...

And so, on a day like this – and days were much alike – Strepetov turned up at Alevtina's. He really did turn up, without having had time to think about just turning up for a minute and having a look to see how *they* were getting on and maybe having a drink of coffee, all this before even the humble and timely thought of such a capitulation had had time to develop. As though by habit, Strepetov concealed his car keys and wearily made his way up the stairs to her. It was just another evening – the time for the safety-valve. The crafty Mikhailov, needless to say, was there and, needless to say, was beloved and bathed in caresses.

"Look who's come, I've almost forgotten his name," shouted Alevtina. And it was only at that point that Strepetov fully understood where he was and whom he was visiting.

"Yup... We could get to know each other all over again. Long time no see," said the furniture-man in his slow, ponderous, jokey manner.

"Want a coffee?" Alevtina sought out the cup with the stork for Strepetov, filled it up and laughed: "What an age since you've been! Must be four months, mustn't it?"

Strepetov was plunged into gloom by his visit. "I shouldn't have come," he thought. Annoyance and vanity usually stopped him going back to women. He had gone back to garrulous women, to plain women, to "cheats", even to avaricious women, but never to those who, in his own eyes, or those of other people, had made him seem insubstantial and a loser – and that was what he was here. That was something new for him. Feebly, he turned over in his mind a few long-standing, prepared phrases with which he could seize back the initiative. The phrases which he had thought up in isolation had seemed witty, but here they were too generalized and lifeless and reminded him of those great flashes of recognition in dreams which, on waking in the morning, appear striking only in their colourless banality.

"I'd better be off," said Strepetov.

"Let's have another coffee and we'll take off together," Mikhailov suggested. He didn't need to wait for the furniture-man; this was stupid, even ignominious, all that was required was one tiny show of willpower, just enough to say, "I'd better be off" – even to say it calmly and with dignity. But this very slight fresh possibility having presented itself, he sat down again and remained seated, as though his backside had stuck to the chair.

And there was nothing remarkable about the fact that, after coffee, they both went down the stairs together. Strepetov went first, Mikhailov following him.

"Get in," Strepetov got him into the car. He would probably give the furniture-man a lift to the metro, like he used to.

For a long time, they drove without speaking. Strepetov was experiencing a lingering feeling of humiliation and here he had to give Mikhailov credit for his tact, since the together man had not directed a single word at his shameful return to the woman.

"I shouldn't have come," Strepetov burst out.

There was a pause. Mikhailov was silent for a while, then he spoke:

"Why shouldn't you have come? Maybe it was just the right moment". Here (for the first time) Strepetov had not yet paid attention to the 'maybe' which had slipped out. It seemed like an introductory phrase and a make-weight to smooth things over. But immediately afterwards Mikhailov allowed himself to repeat the word and said something which was most unexpected:

"I might be splitting with Alevtina. Splitting for good."

"Have you gone off her?"

"No, but I've had enough."

"But why?"

"I've got to think of the kids... I've got difficult times ahead, complex situations, I only want to think of the kids now."

He was wanting to say something else, but stayed silent, at least for the moment. But Strepetov was silent too. Then Mikhailov started to speak again:

"Getting into the University and into the Maths Faculty isn't easy, I know that. Couldn't you recommend somebody who'd coach my son?"

One confidence deserves another. Strepetov answered:

"I'll think about it."

"You wouldn't be taking a gamble with my son." Mikhailov spoke deliberately. "He's a very good student, but one has to insure oneself against any emergency."

The Safety-valve

"Yes, one has to. I'll think about it."

Mikhailov had already got out of the car. He stood there, his big body leaning forward, thanking him for the lift.

"Let's meet and talk about it. When are you going to be at Alevtina's?" This confused Strepetov, but he didn't want his confusion to be noticed:

"I don't know. Maybe Thursday... But maybe I won't be going to see her any more anyway."

If Mikhailov was leaving, then he would stick to that. That dumb fellow didn't waste any words, and if his words weren't absolutely clear, then they were just interim words, not fully articulated, but still not vain words. Strepetov caught the faintest nuance which suggested to him that Alevtina didn't know about the words which had been spoken in the car and therefore that she didn't know that Mikhailov was leaving her: it had all blossomed behind her back. But the game, if indeed it was a game, was one Strepetov didn't know and he didn't want to make a false move. When Thursday came, he arrived, but he was going to be restrained. He had come, but he would be uncommunicative.

Strepetov found it a lot easier and simpler when it turned out that Alevtina wasn't at home. Mikhailov opened the door to him and said "Come in" but Alevtina wasn't there.

She'd gone to the TV studios. She'd been invited to read her poems and of course this was all very sudden for her, and very delightful and of course a great honour – she was due back in about three hours, Mikhailov said, she'd only just left. She was on Channel 4 at 9.30. "So let's listen to her on the TV!" Mikhailov's broad face was gleaming – he was genuinely pleased for her.

"When all's said and done, it's real publicity for Alya. She's really made it. It'll help get her book out quicker."

"I'll say!" Strepetov rejoined. "I'm glad for her too..."

Perhaps Strepetov really was glad, but he was confused rather more. He was wondering whether that conversation in the car had really taken place, he hadn't imagined it, that's to say, not the conversation itself, but the sense, the significance of it – had that been so? Or had it been some kind of psychological disguise, some self-deception? Strepetov lit up hastily. Restraining his voice and his feelings, he wanted to sit it out, take a back seat, but almost immediately he couldn't stand it any more and let out a trial balloon:

"We were going to talk about that matter of yours."

"Yes," Mikhailov nodded in agreement. "In a minute..."

The silence gathered a little faster and a little denser than Strepetov would have liked.

Then Mikhailov decided to come clean and straight out with it:

"I'd like you to give my son some coaching yourself, Yuri, do you get it?"

"Of course."

"And do what's needed to get him through his entrance tests."

"If he really is an outstanding student, I can do it."

"He's very good."

Now the two of them felt that things were both easier and more difficult. The main problem had been defined and understood, but all the details lay ahead and there would have to be some plain, ordinary human conversation to firm it all up, and that could not be avoided, and now it was time to go ahead.

"I've another son."

"Will he be going to university too?"

"Yes, but not yet. He's in his next to last year at school. So in a year's time."

At this point, Strepetov couldn't help looking Mikhailov in the eye: what a guy... For a second, he weighed things up, as one would a price. One summer for the entrance exams was OK, but for the next summer, he wanted plenty of freedom and peace, he wanted to go off somewhere, to escape. Two years on the trot in the heat of the city was no joke, but the very fact of its not being a joke (and Strepetov understood this now) added a firmness and a durability to their agreement.

"You want a lot, don't you?" he suddenly laughed.

"Not that much." Mikhailov was serious. "You won't find it all that difficult: my second son's very bright as well."

"I hope you've only got two sons."

"Just the two." Mikhailov's face finally displayed a half-smile, the first during the entire conversation. Strepetov was pouring out the cognac, he took his glass and Mikhailov moved his thin, elegant hands, freezing for an instant on the dark crimson surface of the table, as though on display. "My sons have got hands like that," Mikhailov observed to himself and then be suddenly spoke again:

"I'd like my children to be good mathematicians and for them to be rather like you."

"Are you serious?"

"Absolutely. Give you my word."

"Men don't usually throw around compliments like that."

They fell silent, and this time their silence resembled a final outcome, a line drawn under their bargain.

Mikhailov was quite unable to communicate to her the chronological detail that this was to be 'our last evening together, my love'. Of course, the words had been prepared, but his tongue wouldn't go round them. But he couldn't get out of it, so he was on the point of saying those words.

"Come on, Mikhailov, why are you so boring?"

She was pestering him:

"Don't be boring. Don't be old. Don't be a pain in the neck. Wouldn't you like a glass of something?"

Alevtina was recounting everything in a rush. A week had passed, only a week and already she was getting a response to her appearance on TV, people were writing her letters. ("And what letters! What naivety, Mikhailov, but then what purity — but do you know what letters from ordinary people are like?"). She was instantaneously overjoyed and Mikhailov interspersed some meaningless words and thought that this unbridled enthusiasm should be cut short, if only by the first harsh move.

But then the telephone rang, and with almost the same ardour and passion, Alevtina threw herself at the machine (she adored the phone) and now that Mikhailov no longer had the harsh opening move, he had a moment to reflect. The merest moment, but he managed it, so that when Alevtina, hand over the receiver told him in a half-whisper:

"It's the basketball-player and his wife. They're wanting to come round," he nodded:

"Tell them to come."

"Why?"

Alevtina continued to speak into the phone, but Mikhailov was preoccupied by the not particularly brilliant novelty of the idea that to leave her was one thing, but to leave with someone's help was simpler and easier. And it was entirely possible that he night manage to take offence at that windbag the basketball-player — the fellow would be bound to have a go at him a couple of times, for instance, about his (Mikhailov's) furniture. It wouldn't be at all bad to set up an insult and then go off; slamming the door would be even better, and then he could do the rest over the phone at a distance and it would be much easier at a distance. Or maybe Alevtina herself would ask for trouble, perhaps by saying the wrong thing, or saying it in the wrong way (in company she was never averse to having a little dig at Mikhailov) — or maybe it would be the basketball-player's wife, a sharp-tongued woman with a barb. Mikhailov didn't know how his being insulted and his departure would turn out, but he knew very well that it would be much more difficult to achieve all this in isolation.

"Why are you so silent?"

"Eh?" he replied, as though from another room.

"You're awfully talkative today, my dear."

"Huh."

And so he kept his silence. He was nervous.

"When are they coming?" he enquired.

"They're not." Alevtina laughed. "Well, stuff them, they're bores. I told them I was busy."

She was laughing at the prospect of the whole evening and night before them. ("Just the two of us, my dear, we're not expecting anyone, and we can just flop down and relax.") Mikhailov nodded hastily — "Yes, yes," said he, "the evening and the night and the two of us". He was frightened by her intuition, by that subtle feminine feel for things, if she managed to guess before he could tell her, then he wouldn't be able to tell her, he just wouldn't.

"Yes, yes, just the two of us will be better," he hastened to agree. "Of course it will."

Encouraged by his gentle words, Alevtina didn't guess. Indeed, she suddenly began hastening matters. As always, she put on soft music, put the lights out, all but one, and all this in a speedy, impetuous way and then with a giggle she disappeared into the bathroom, leaving Mikhailov face to face with a simple fact looming over him. He heard the splash of water. Mikhailov sat in the semi-darkness, with the muffled music, fully dressed and completely incapable of moving from the spot where he was rooted. Soon Alevtina was sitting next to him in her nightdress, aroused, her eyes like big black cherries.

"What's the matter with you? Are you going to sleep in your jacket? Or have you got carbuncles?" She was laughing at him, but he said nothing.

"Come on then – off to the bathroom! Mikhailov!"

She didn't understand, couldn't grasp what was happening – and how could she? She was kissing him, her head, from her close-cropped hair. She whispered:

"You know, I'm really turned on tonight. I don't think I've felt like this since I was young – I'm awfully fond of you..."

And then she whispered again:

"Don't you feel like it? Not really?"

Mikhailov didn't have to dissemble, there was complete accord between what he thought and what he said, and in measured tones be explained that, yes, he didn't particularly feel like it, maybe he was just tired, worn out.

"Getting a bit past it?" she mocked him gently.

"Maybe I am a bit past it."

Alevtina nimbly divested him of his jacket, let him have a quiet minute on his own with his exhaustion and then got going again ("didn't I get some lovely letters today!"), she tore open his shirt at the collar and pulled it off in one thrust over his head ("come on, love, you don't expect me to take your trousers off – I guess I'd have to pull off your shoes first") and thus Mikhailov, half pulled along, half pleaded with, found himself in the bathroom, standing under the shower with the water, a bit on the cold side, pouring down onto him. OK, this would be the last night. And Mikhailov caught himself thinking that he wouldn't bother now to regulate the water – let it stay as it was.

They were in bed and she was whispering to him:

"But not right away, OK? I feel like a chat."

Going along with her mood, Mikhailov felt that after the shower he just didn't want to move, he wanted to grow heavy and seize up in immobility.

She continued her whispering:

"Only, don't think I've gone off my head from the poetry and the letters on TV — well, there's a bit of that, but on the whole I don't give a toss about it. I like being with you."

And she suddenly burst into tears:

"I've got nobody but you."

Mikhailov was used to her exaggerations, but it still made him feel bundled up and warmed through. However, thinking over her pretty speeches, he saw himself from the outside in this semi-darkness of lovers; a big, bulky man, his body crumpled into the bed, his hands lying, or rather resting on his capacious stomach. His face bore the hard, practical lines of the storekeeper and his overall appearance was crowned by the hair, flopping across from the cap he wore and from the day's bustle. All this had taken place in someone who had once been a thin, anaemic lad, who had eaten sparingly and whose dream had been to own a sledge with iron runners. His childhood stirred into life and Mikhailov was suddenly scared at the thought that he loved Alevtina and that perhaps he had never loved anybody but her and that he had had a long life.

"Don't cry," he said to her.

"Can't one have a little cry?" Alevtina's response was suddenly cheerful and from somewhere to one side. And only now did things start to get going between them — and continued — and went on some more — and then finally Alevtina brought it all to an end, with a kiss — of gratitude. She sat up, as was her wont, pushed her feet into slippers and in a relaxed way, as though she were walking slowly through a forest, went to the kitchen to put on coffee. The gas hissed, Alevtina's voice came across, slightly distorted by the night, the distance away and by her lengthy whispering prior to that: "There's some apples. Shall I bring them along?" "OK." As he lay there, his eyes went round the darkened walls. The bedside light had long since been switched off and as he cast his eyes around, he pronounced the words deliberately, trying to find out how they would sound in the past tense: "I once had a woman who lived here." He wanted to muster up some courage from these harsh words, but immediately fell silent and retreated before the pain and the truth that were approaching.

They moved their cups carefully in the darkness, removing them from their mouths and bringing them back up again.

"It's wonderful that we're together (she swallowed at this point), it feels as though we've been together for a hundred years."

And then she went on (swallow, swallow, swallow):

"I thought at first, well, he's not a bad guy, but it's time to pension him off."

And again:

"Because I don't like attachments. That rotten little husband of mine sucked so much blood out of me that I wasn't able to live close to anybody and that's why I wanted to get rid of you. Do you remember?"

"Yes, I do."

"I'd just about decided. And then somehow you just happened to come back. Wasn't that funny?"

She wouldn't stop talking, but it was kindly:

"After all, I don't need much. I don't need anyone else."

"Yes," he said.

"The years will roll by, summers and winters, one after the other, and we'll grow old quietly, won't we?"

Realizing clearly that it was inappropriate, rude and even to some extent untrue, he said:

"You've slept with an awful lot of men."

"Me?"

"Well, not me." As he spoke, he was amazed at his own words – they had been prepared in advance, and now they found the right moment to come out. And what he said next didn't surprise him any longer, this had also been prepared in advance and duly followed on:

"Where have you put those papers of mine? I might forget them in the morning."

"What?"

"My papers."

He got up, barefoot, decisive and in a meaningful manner he shuttled across to her desk. In the darkness, he banged into a chair and swore. He fussed around at the desk, looking for his customers' receipts and invoices – once before he had left them by chance at Alevtina's and of course he would have to get hold of them now. He found them. He knew the flat intimately. He hid the papers in the maw of his briefcase and in the dark of the night the harsh, long-drawn out noise he made with them was like the clash of metal. Then he went back to bed. He was ready for an explanation and waited for what was going to happen, but nothing did.

"You poor love. Are you jealous? Don't be daft..."

He slowly closed his eyes, he couldn't reach her inner feelings. She seemed to be lowering over him, stroking his temples and whispering from somewhere above:

"The years will roll by, winter following winter – I like you most of all in the winter, I don't know why – the years will roll by and we'll grow old."

He wasn't sure if he had slept – but he supposed he must have done for an hour, or an hour and a half or so. Beyond the window was a grey, early light – there was no dawn.

He arose. "Go back to sleep," he said to Alevtina when, with a certain movement of her body and the barely perceptible anxiety of a sleeping person she asked, without opening her eyes, what was happening now and when will you come again, dear... He made no answer to that, but said:

"Go back to sleep – I'll do the needful myself. There's no need for you to get up."

He ate his breakfast dully. He was sleepy and shattered and he'd said nothing to Alevtina.

He went back into the room to get his briefcase and gather up his cigarettes. He lit up, but didn't leave immediately (the room called him back) and so he delayed by the window. At his back he felt Alevtina's eyes upon him: she had the blanket pulled up to her chin, right up to her lips in fact, but her sleepy eyes were still looking at him. It seemed as though something had touched her to the quick – it had got to her, creeping up on her, just as though the outcome of the past year and a half were creeping up on her by degrees as she slept. So she looked at him – and why not?

Mikhailov was also looking – but out of the window, finishing his cigarette. He was looking out with a sudden pang of emotion – there was the open field, the gully, the two raised construction cranes and the unfinished foundations of an apartment block. Now he was looking at all this as on the day of a hasty departure, striving to take it all in, to absorb this bit of the earth, where he wasn't ever likely to return to or set foot on again, because life is short and the cares and the flow of life and the coaches of the metro would rock him and bear him on, like a fragment of wood. Mikhailov dressed and went out. The smooth hum of the lift (he plunged the button in and everything flowed and bore him along) reminded Mikhailov that one way or another, life flows on.

5

Three or four times the telephone rang, but by now it was as if it wasn't Alevtina, but a kind of transient link for erasing his memory:

"I can't, I'm busy, very very busy."

"You can't, or you don't want to?" she would weep and of course lay on a bout of telephonic hysteria, or suddenly call him an old fat hog and say that she was fed up to the back teeth with him. Sometimes it helps to prick and to wound and a man angry or affronted may return to his former girlfriend to answer the charges or to justify himself, not realizing that to arrive is, after all, to come back. But Mikhailov didn't do this. There was a hiatus. Then there were three or four fresh calls, but he was on his guard — his wife, Vera, took the call and with semi-professional venom replied to Miss Nesterova that Mikhailov wasn't there (that was the first call), that he was out of town (that was the second) and that he was at his work — was there any message *if it was a work matter*? The calls ceased and that was the end. Mikhailov knew, or thought he knew that Alevtina had taken a step back and was now getting used to and attaching herself to Strepetov, as once she had done to him. So that was the end, though for some time yet Alevtina occurred in his everyday thoughts (out of inertia, but also out of necessity to be on guard) and then her face, her appearance and her whole image vanished beyond the line of the horizon into what is called a variety of things, but most often called the past and her image thus occupied a position which clearly belonged in the past.

On one such day there took place the long-awaited and therefore brief telephone conversation with Strepetov. They came to an agreement as to time and place. The older son's coaching would begin that very week.

"I've been making some enquiries. Because you've got a PhD, I'll pay you a double rate."

"What, you were going to pay me money as well?" In Strepetov's voice there was both amusement and irony.
"But of course."
"Well, well..."
And that summer, Mikhailov's son passed his university entrance exams easily, even brilliantly.

Translated by Michael Falchikov

European Bookseller
an independent bi-monthly magazine
Edited by Eva Skelley
information bridge between East and West

ESSENTIAL NEW INFORMATION SOURCE ON BOOK PUBLISHING ACROSS EUROPE. CONTAINS BOOK TRADE NEWS, TRENDS AND DEVELOPMENTS, COMPANY PROFILES, BESTSELLER LISTS, MAJOR REVIEWS, BIBLIOGRAPHICAL LISTINGS AND DIRECTORIES.

The European Bookseller is intended for publishers, booksellers, literary agents, librarians.

The **European Bookseller** has launched the **European database** of forthcoming titles, an indispensable tool for marketing and rights sales worldwide.

Write or fax for information to European Bookseller,
3, Queen Square, London WC1N 3AR, UK
tel:44 71 837 1357, fax:44 71 837 7004

BIRMINGHAM SLAVONIC MONOGRAPHS

A series of scholarly studies in the Slavonic and East European field. The following titles are available:

Rosemary Quested, *The Russo-Chinese Bank: A Multi-National Financial Base of Tsarism in China*, vi + 65pp., 1977, L5.00.
Lesley Milne, *The Master and Margarita: A Comedy of Victory*, iv + 55pp., 1977, L5.00.
C.J.G. Turner, *Pechorin: An Essay on Lermontov's* A Hero of our Time, v + 72pp., reprinted 1988, L7.00.
Evelyn J. Harden, *The Murder of Griboedov: New Materials*, viii + 96pp., 1979, L8.00.
G.G. Corbett, *Predicate Agreement in Russian*, xiii + 113pp., 1979, L9.00.
Amanda J. Metcalf, *Evgenii Shvarts and his Fairy-Tales for Adults*, v + 101pp., 1979, L9.00.
Daphne M. West, *Mandelstam*: The Egyptian Stamp, v + 154pp., 1980, L10.00.
A.G. Cross, *The Tale of the Russian Daughter and her Suffocated Lover*, viii + 55pp., 1982, L5.00.
Cynthia Marsh, *M.A. Voloshin: Artist-Poet. A Study of the Synaesthetic Aspects of his Poetry*, xii + 160pp., 2 colour and 6 black and white plates, 1983, L12.00.
A.L. Tait, *Lunacharsky: Poet of the Revolution*, v + 116pp., 1984, L9.00.
Anthony Hippisley, *The Poetic Style of Simeon Polotsky*, viii + 96pp., 1985, L8.00.
Michael Molnar, *Body of Words: A Reading of Belyi's* Kotik Letaev, viii + 58pp., 1987, L5.00.
C.D. Luck, *The Field of Honour: An Analysis of Babel's* Na pole chesti, v + 84pp., 1987, L8.00.
Marie Gilroy, *Lermontov's Ironic Vision*, x + 82pp., 1989, L8.00.
Richard Peace, *Oblomov: A Critical Examination of Goncharov's Novel*, viii + 87pp., 1991, L9.00.
Katy Simmons, *Plays for the Period of Stagnation: Lyudmila Petrushevskaya and the Theatre of the Absurd*, iv + 35pp., 1992, L5.00.
C.J.G. Turner, *Time and Temporal Structure in Chekhov*, viii + 113pp., 1994. L12.00.

Forthcoming titles:
Lina Bernstein, *Gogol's Last Book: Selected Passages from a Correspondence with Friends*
Nina Allan, *Madness, Death and Disease in the Fiction of Vladimir Nabokov*
David Wells, *Akhmatova and Pushkin: The Pushkin Context of Akhmatova's Poetry*
Advance orders for these titles may be placed now.

Prices shown are for direct orders from the Department and include postage within the U.K. Please make cheques payable to "The University of Birmingham".

Orders from outside the United Kingdom: send no money, but await our invoice.

Please address orders and enquiries to:
Birmingham Slavonic Monographs
Department of Russian Literature
The University of Birmingham
B15 2TT UK

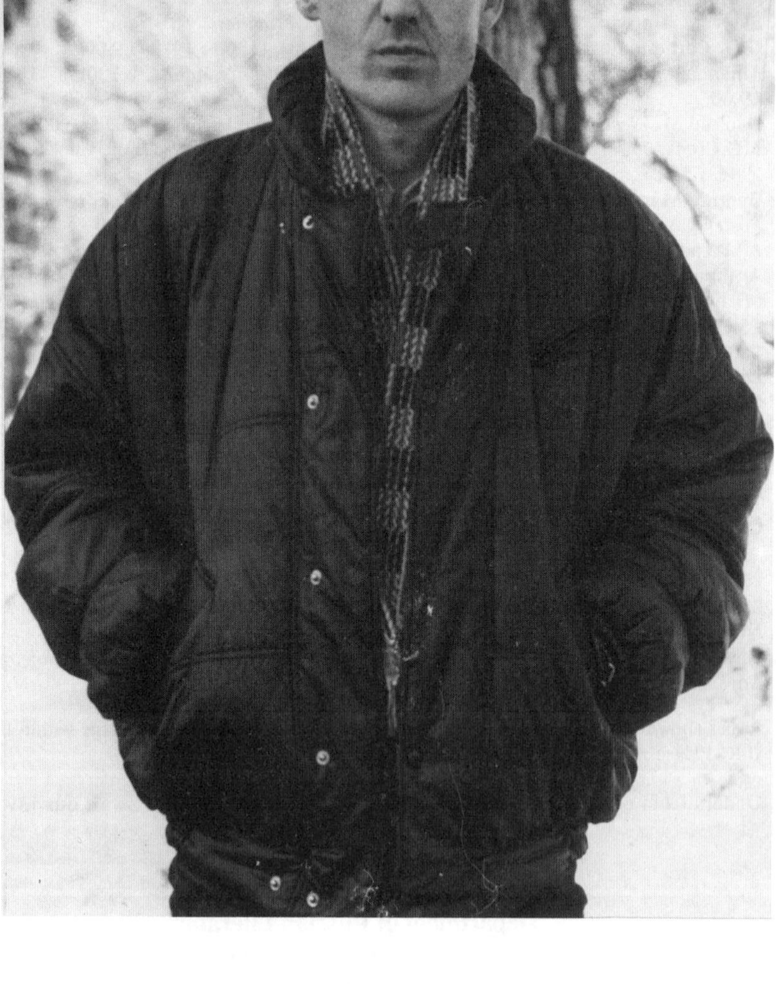

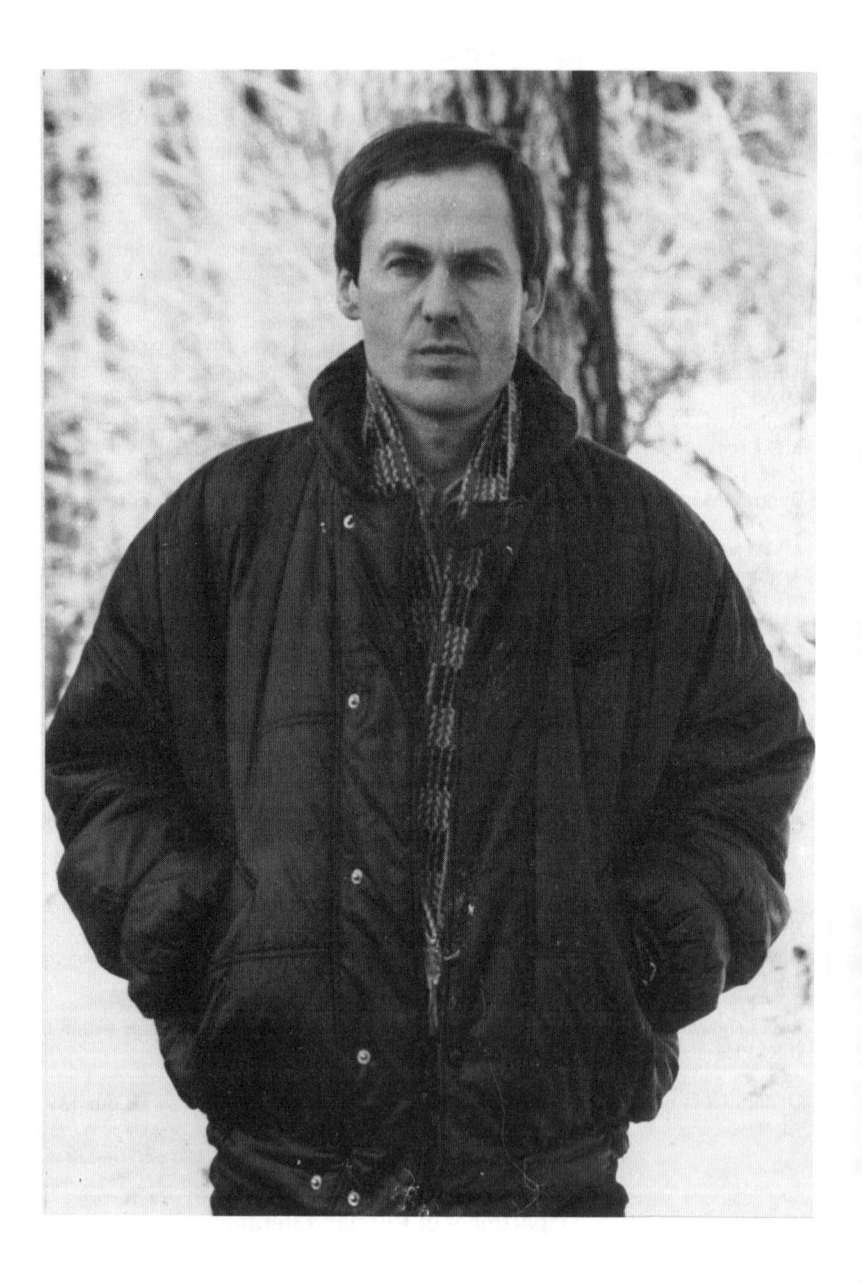

Sergei
TASK

S. O. B.
Four Knights Opening

Sergei Task

S.O.B.

No, girls, there's something about him. He's got that face... What face? The usual. Nose, lips, eyes, chin. Bingo, a jerk in a million. Green as a worm in a faint. But that body! Yeah, not so bad. Take him? Why the hell not? But hey, I've got dibs next! There you go, you nincompoops. Get a look at what he's wearing. What did you expect from a fatherless child? You want jeans? He's got 'em. All his button-downs are fitted. Fitted! Handstitched, can't you see? So what?... T-shirts, this, that, a windbreaker with a zipper, as good as anyone's. And those shoes, by the way, are Yugoslavian, I noticed, and the sneakers – he's just making a play for your sympathy. Simple, yeah, a regular son of a gun. "'Tis a gift to be simple... "Hold on, Ninka, you were going to say... I was going to say that he's a little box with a secret. For instance, why doesn't he ever look anyone in the eye, huh? Why's he looking into the wild blue yonder when he's supposed to be looking at you? Next time his blue yonder ought to give him a clue about how you spell *monogamous* – one word or with a hyphen. Go on! What – he really didn't know? What do you care, he's got the bod, who needs a brain. All right you, now you know. No, but still? What? Ninka said he's a little box with a secret. What secret? *That* secret. Him? I bet... hey Mr. Big Stuff... Well now, I can tell you a story that'll make your eyes pop out! So? We all got together at Svetka's, remember? Let's say I do... Remember, when things started gettin' crazy and he went out on the balcony? Go on. Okay, Yulka, spell it out for our comrade here. Here's how it was... I go out on the balcony. What'd you skip out for? I say, Let's go for a spin, I say. And he says, I don't play your games. What games do you play? I ask. And he smiles, What games? And you know, he runs his finger down my neck like you do when you're checking a table for dust... Well, was it very dusty? Oh ho! Aren't we witty now. Ninka, lay off. Well, what then? Then I walked around in a scarf for a whole week. Exactly, girls, I was telling Svetka too, look, I say, Yulka is working in the Beryozka ensemble. But I don't get it, what's with

S. O. B.

the scarf? I'd like to see how you'd look with a mark like that – an honest-to-God hickey. Get out of here, Yulka! That's from a finger? What, you don't believe it? Ninka, she doesn't believe it. I saw it myself, girls, as red as red can be. At first I thought the same as you, that, I'm laughing, who laid that on you? And she says, I'll lay one on him, yeah, I'll lay one on him he won't forget! Hey, what kind of guy is he? A real worm. Not much to look at first off. I'm telling you, a jerk in a million. And not much going on up *here* – always mumbles at the blackboard – eh, mm, um... Remember how we all split after our last class to see that American mystery movie and he didn't go! My head's pounding, he says, I'm going to go sleep it off. So what's your point? My point is that after the film one of us saw him in the subway. So what? Listen, what I mean is, he doesn't give: a damn about anything. Westerns, classes, dances, anything. He didn't go to the art museum, and he refused to go on the field trip too. What a drag – that's it, Drag Man. It's a fact. Okay, Svetka, you don't have to give him back, I'll make a present of him. Only Svetka, be sure to wash your neck or he'll start checking it for dust... Never mind, I'll let her have my scarf. A muffler! Even better. Ha ha ha... Well? Better... Ha ha ha... This could go on all night. Oy, I have to pick up Pavlik! I have to run too. Bye girls. Ninka, don't forget tomorrow. What we talked about. Give me a call tonight. What? Call me-e-e!...

The alarm clock, your nastiest enemy, awakens with the punctuality of a country rooster. Seven o'clock. Judging by the sound, the steel rooster's neck has been slightly wrung. Its muffled call makes no impression on you, though. If the alarm clock is half-alive, then you're a corpse. You only sleep like that if exhaustion's been accumulating inside you for weeks. Finally, a few mighty blows on the wall, something's starting to happen: the springs creak, the blanket humps a bit. And here you are sitting up on the bed at last and sending thought signals to your lower extremities, which will have to grope for your slippers, which is about the equivalent of finding a needle in a haystack. Oh well, go to the bathroom barefoot. You put the kettle on the nearest burner and you burn your fingers as usual, and that, thank God, brings you around. It's revolting to look in the mirror, so you keep your washing ritual to a minimum. You're in a hurry anyway. Today you absolutely cannot be late; you're expecting someone from community ed. What do we have here for breakfast? Bread-sticks, mm-hmm, the last bit of sausage, some weak tea. And then five lumps of sugar – to restore your strength after yesterday. Sipping burning tea from your mug, you suddenly stiffen, staring at a single point. The rumble of a distant tram shakes you out of it. And now you see that you're hopelessly late, you scramble, stick your briefcase under your arm (don't forget to tape up that frayed handle) and plow out of your shared apartment, your half-asleep co-inhabitants – five adults, one high-strung little girl who dreams of travel and who when asked what she's going to be answers "Zigmund and Ganzelka," and also a rusty old pussycat misnamed Tom as a baby – curse you roundly without ever waking up. Skidding down from the fourth floor like a top, you spit down the stairwell as usual and attempt – in vain, naturally – to reach the bottom before the spit splashes on the Dutch tile. You'll fly the whole way to school, the length of two old Moscow lanes, whose astonishing curves are a credit to the arcane fantasy of their seventeenth-century builders, taking one big jump and braking before the next so you don't step on a crack. Only one thing can tear you away from this highly intellectual game. Then you speed up, trying as you go to summon up a portrait of that stranger, so that when you overtake her you can ascertain how right or wrong your sketch is. You run into the school-yard with the bell. You hesitate at the classroom door, already envisioning how you'll push it open, your guilty: "May I? Today I..." And the class will crash-hang amiably, rejoicing that you're late again and someone won his bet, reveling in their own invincibility, and then, with a doomed sigh, you push the door open and say: "May I? Today I..." and the class amiably... And so forth. You walk to your desk, trying not to look at anyone, and at the same time you can't help but notice the tight sweater on Yulechka Luntz, and Svetka's new hairdo, and... But they're already calling you to the board, and the chalk is crumbling in your fingers, and someone is motioning to you from the back rows, but what's he saying? – you can't make it out. All right, what's the deal here, time to unfurl the white flag. You sit there as boring as a blank pad, but your internal clock is running, racing, less and less time remains until the start of the show, your show. Only please, no idle talk... Talkers, atten-

S. O. B.

tion! Left face! Narrow hips, straight spine, jangling charm bracelet. And what size cup do we have here? Oh well, not much. But those legs – a kangaroo! Houndstooth mini, barely to cover. Shoulderblades temptingly shadowed under a white turtleneck. Cropped hair that collects in the back in a barely perceptible hollow. Sixteen, seventeen if you push it. Heal fast, you can tell right away. Tries to pass for naive. Voila! She's speeding up for the trolley. Runs like a boy, too, no flailing legs, no flying heels. Gone. Set sail. Home, to Australia. Just give a whistle and I'll be there. Now here's something completely different. Slutty strut, freckle face. Aren't we all decked out! Cotton frock slit to the waist, red polka dots on the bottom, navy top, lace inset tease across your breasts, puff sleeves – how chic. Auburn hair. Center part. Light brown curls in back. And the breasts, the breasts, just like Yulka's. Only this one's shape is nobler. If I could just have a quiet moment with you, my beauty, in some dark entryway... but what's the best approach? She's an ocean liner, and who am I? A skiff bobbing over the waves right at her waterline. Better move on to that hick over there. Fire. Volcano. Country and western. See-through gauze with loose ties flapping over her breasts, a long wraparound wham-bam-thank-you-ma'am skirt, cork-wedge sandals. Maybe a little low-slung, but the rest is perfect. I speed up, only three or four meters separate us. Now I'm going to put my left hand on her hip, and cover her pointy breast with my right so that my middle finger slips... Sensing my touch, the hick turns around and I see – holy, holy, holy – an honest-to-God flounder flattened by her humdrum life – two miserable leeches for kids, a shrew of a mother-in-law, a cheating husband who buys her off with his lady friends' secondhand clothes. So much for your volcano. Great bods, I tell you, they're like jubilee rubles – engraved on one side, nice to the touch, but turn 'em over and they're flat as a pancake. Here's the subway. Going down the escalator I ogle the sex kittens coming up. No need to be shy here. They can dish out a kilo of contempt and in a second it's over. On the chilly platform I take up my usual post, by the third column, where I have a terrific view of the entire area. Sacred moments draw nigh. I'm standing behind the column, merging with its gray marble, an invisible being, a cyclops. I'm one omniscient eye now which, like the beam of a searchlight, rifles through the crowd expelled from the train for a soothing figure, a

Sergei Task

pretty little face, and then it switches to full power – so it's you, is it? Well, let's see what we have here. An utterly incomparable gratification: grab, undress, fondle, squeeze. No one can deprive me of this private pleasure. This is my time. I'm the boss here. If you could see your Drag Man now, master of this underworld kingdom. With a single glance I command – this one – and she's mine. Head-spinning color, a kaleidoscope of naked arms and necks, a carnival of bright beads and stupid earrings, the muffled tapping of clogs, the horsy clip-clop of metal hooves. And the smells! Air electrified by the confused scent of perfume and skin. Intoxicating, ravishing smell. Around me chaos, movement, fragments of words bouncing off reverberating walls, rustling dresses, frills, flounces, tanned necks, creamy pink, an almost edible little knee flashing from under a mini, a pleat, a gather, ruffles, cutouts, sashes dancing on butts to the beat of feet, hands flying up, patting hairdos on the way, artificially lengthened eyes of new-age Cleopatras, ankles, calves, hips showing through thin cloth, a precision bikini line, the pout of a coed late for her date, the breath poured out by a haughty blonde, the sly look of a cute hairdresser aimed suddenly at me from a velvet ambush – it's more than words can tell! And then, having sucked the nectar dry from that blossom, I board the train. All this so far is merely a prelude, a preliminary etude, to fire up the imagination; the train itself is an almost mystic ritual, shamanism. Now I'll set my magnetic capabilities in motion. Don't think I'm making it easy on myself, no allowances made. I've got only two and a half minutes or so, the time it takes for the train to fly from one station to the next. I check out the train like an experienced horse-thief and make an instantaneous choice. There she is, a little round-shouldered, red-headed, so wrapped up in her mystery she doesn't even notice that the squished tomato in the string bag of the lady pressed up against her is drooling on her two hundred – ruble denim dress. From that moment on the people around me cease to exist. As do the few meters that separate me and the redhead. I press up behind her, I stroke her coarse hair, rake my fingers through it; my other hand glides over her hip, feels the roundness of her stomach, clambers up to the left breast, my God, I can feel her warmth in my palm and a birthmark just down from the nipple, I can hear the beat of her heart, it's so strong it seems to be throwing my hand off, and now I close

S. O. B.

my eyes, I don't need to look at my chosen one, her image is stamped in gold inside my eyelids, I whisper, my beloved, my saffron mushroom, I stroke her, and kiss her, inhaling the almost sickly sweet aroma of her expensive perfume, and I already know by heart how the depression under her protruding collarbone smells, and I can call each little hole in her lace bra by name, with the tips of my fingers I read, like a blind man, the innermost curves of her pliant body, I comprehend that body like my own property, although what do I have to do with it, there is no me, I've already dissolved in her, I breathe through her pores, I catch the draft through the slit in her dress, and I'm about to lose it – but how can I in front of people? – when I need to scratch one particular place where an escaped elastic (I meant to mend that yesterday!) has cut into my skin. The train is slowing down, we're coming into the station, and so my time is running out, but even with eyes closed I can well see my saffron mushroom looking at me with dilated pupils, crumpling her forgotten mystery against the bag of tomatoes, her chest heaving. Not without effort I pry my lids open and... meet the unblinking gaze of green eyes, and of course, I can't hold back, I never can, and save myself by running through the incredibly necessary opened doors. End of experiment. After that there'll be other trains, other directions, so that I'll quickly forget where the next train is speeding me, and naturally, my choices change – young and older, skinny and ones with some meat on them, as they say, ones who kick in with half a turn and ones cold as subway marble, but it doesn't matter – I'm going to conquer them in the numbered minutes of the train's run. But what's the point if I know I'm going to give it up when, eventually, it's time to open my eyes and slam into the stare of someone who may already have agreed to everything. Take last Wednesday. The train was coming into Kashirskaya station, I was standing – not in my dreams, no! – next to this hippie, we weren't looking at each other, but she was already won over, she wanted it as much as I did, I knew it, our hands nervously squeezing the metal bar moved closer and closer, slowly, irrepressibly, they weren't more than half a hand apart now, I was like a taut string, well then, well, here, now, put your sweaty palm over that little fist and she's yours, and you're hers, and that's the end to the inhuman torment that's been tearing at me as long as I can remember and that's developed this astonishing gift in me – but there was the station, and I never did manage to relocate my hand half a hand to the left, and when the doors opened, the girl cast a desperately appealing and at the same time contemptuous look at me and then stepped out onto the platform. The train shuddered, floated off, and she was still standing on the platform and looking at me strange-like. Even today – this was getting on toward ten, time to get a move on home – something absolutely wild happened. An elegant lady of about forty, the wife of some very successful wheeler dealer, turned out to be highly receptive. I didn't even have to close my eyes. It only took a minute to get her going. And then, squinting slightly so that from the side it looked as if I were dozing off, then when I could observe her without interference through a web of lashes (my favorite trick), I pressed her to me with one hand and with the other unzipped her tweed skirt. I was a little hasty, and as a result the only – brass – button, which had been hanging on by a thread, popped off, as if it were alive, onto the floor, and hid under someone's sole. I slipped two fingers under silky cloth and then... then... My head was spinning, I thought I was going to faint. In my opinion she was near to fainting as well. I'd never gone that far before... But here she was already moving toward the exit, holding her skirt up with her hand and covering it up with a "Beryozka" package just in case, and suddenly through the clang of the doors her voice floated into my consciousness, three letters, uttered evilly, jerkily: "S. O. B.!" It seemed like there was an extra sound... "oo"... yes, yes, "oo", a very raw, dank sound, as if it had come from under ground, where moisture beads on the walls and the ceiling is covered with a foul mold. She must have screamed out: "You S. O. B.!" But then the doors slammed closed, and I was rocked backward.

You go home through emptied back streets lit by infrequent streetlights. Your temples pounding, the noises of the subway swirling in your ears. Lord, how much can I take? A month, maybe, maybe five. Not years, for sure. After magically dissolving in someone else, in a woman, your own flesh is defiant again, shameful. Your brain is splitting. To hell with everything. Home. Take a bath, free yourself... if only... if only... How filthy can you get. And this one still at her sewing machine. Mom, you again! We go out of our way for him, and what does he do in return? Did I ask?! You purposely sew one after another so that you can reproach me later. Purposely! M-m-m. Do we have any aspirin? Doesn't hear. When she needs to she hears everything. You should sleep with that Singer of yours! Oh well, my feet aren't throbbing so much, and my head's let up a little. Now for a bath. Why deny yourself this little weakness after all.

He raised himself heavily from the bed, and grabbing a Western magazine with an ad for summer fashions from the year before last, he went to the bathroom. The latch clicked, a powerful stream pounded from the faucet. If at that dim hour of the full moon a fallen angel flying over the upturned earth were to fly in the open door to the kitchen and, scratching the faded wallpaper with its sharp wing, rustle down the narrow hallway past the bathroom, the angel would shudder to hear through the foaming of the water a repressed, beastly groan.

1979

Translated by Marian Schwarts

Four Knights Opening

If life could be described in algebraic equations, with love and hate, passion and reason, ingenuousness and perfidy balancing each other out perfectly, then the story I want to tell you would be totally apropos, whereas at present it risks being relegated to the ranks of the merely curious, although I do hope this will make it none the worse – maybe even better – for what if not the curious can spice up the watery puree of the everyday. Of course, among my readers there are vegetarians as well, who prefer lenten verses and unseasoned novels, but these I would beg in advance not to trouble themselves and refer them to the literary disciples of Bragg.

Last fall I spent ten days in Abkhazia, at a small resort, in the home of a Greek woman I know, where besides me there were two other Muscovites, a young couple with a toddler from Leningrad, a

Lithuanian woman with her granddaughter, and a big noisy family from I think Donetsk. I felt like part of a happening going on in that cramped yard, on the patch of ground between the well, the makeshift kitchen, and the hen-house. Here, under an awning entwined with grapevines, stood a long table – the main prop and, simultaneously, the logical center of the improvisation played day in and day out, with variations, without pause or cease, with only a brief intermission of three or four hours, the hours when all cats are gray. The first, even before dawn, to cast his vote was the toddler behind the thin veneer screen that demonstrated yet again the conventional nature of the barrier artificially erected between Muscovites and Leningraders. Directly under the window of my small room in the half-basement where, in addition to me, two other devotees of sea bathing gladly took shelter, a stray mutt yelped irritably as he relived his proletarian origins with particular intensity in his dreams. The door to the annex opposite slammed – the miner dynasty was beginning its pilgrimage to holy places. Then a light blazed on in the kitchen: Grisha's wife, for whom all the sounds of the world had been drowned out once and for all in the howl of the giant pterodactyls that had chosen the Adler airport, put the coffeepot on the burner. A little later Grisha would get up and prime the well pump – an act of mercy (not for his wife, for us): maybe today we wouldn't hear their children, a girl and a boy, youthful terrorists with imaginations, carry out their next military sortie bombarding the peaceable nursery. Sudden animation in the hen-house could mean just one thing: the chicken god, whose superiority the rooster himself reluctantly acknowledged, had come out into the yard. I'll say! He was carrying a pail of choice millet mixed with something that doesn't have a name, and if it does, then an abstruse one, Latin, for the man runs a pharmacy, and his name is Fyodor, and he's married to Grisha's younger sister, who, as every chick knows, is expecting a child, otherwise why would the sewing machine be buzzing day in and out – Sofia is sewing a layette, that's quite obvious. But if Sofia doesn't get up soon, then her other sister, Olga – she's the one who invited me to visit – she, I hear through my slumber, will have completely taken over in the kitchen. Meanwhile the nice Leningraders' fed toddler is stirring up trouble with the disgruntled mutt, who is at his wits' end in the morning trying to figure out where he buried his sugar bone the night before. The miner dynasty amicably begins their ablution rite. In the annex, the six-year-old cutie is lisping something in Lithuanian. Car horns – that's Olga's parents, whose appearance the lightly sleeping grandmother blesses from the upper terrace, returning from a wedding.

That is how – more or less – the prologue to the day's action was played out, usually in several open areas, but primarily in the yard, and more specifically at the long table under the awning, to the cackling of hens, the buzzing of the above-mentioned sewing machine, and the unobtrusive muttering of the two televisions, one color and one black and white, that stood in front of the kitchen, one on top of the other, and fell silent long after midnight. But if I experienced the prologue somewhat vicariously, then the subsequent peripeteiae unfolded with my direct participation. I immediately became virtually the central, albeit passive, figure – because I was a guest and, consequently, the ideal repository for food in the eyes of three women. Soon, though, my role expanded somewhat. I suspect that, willingly or not, I had come under attack from Grisha, who had given the grandmother an earful about how I wrote for Moscow magazines, whereas the only actual publication I could claim was a want ad in the classifieds ("Prepared to publish a story, 25 pages, in any magazine. No offers for foreign issues please....") and how through me they could all go down in History. The cult of the printed word is obviously so highly developed among Abkhazian Greeks that I wasn't even all that surprised when two days later the yard filled with visitors. Neighbors came to get my help writing a letter to a minister suggesting that the therapeutic mud baths finally be built next to their house, on the site of a perpetual puddle whose curative properties had been enjoyed by local inhabitants from time immemorial; under cover of night I was approached by a fussy man wearing an elastic headband who implored me in a theatrical whisper to inform certain authorities about the criminal activities of the local mafia, who secretly, in the foothills, behind a solid fence with an "M" on it, were testing explosive devices so powerful they made his skull crack; a shepherd came down from the mountains to stir up a case against a large flock of sheep that had refused to yield "hot" wool. I was sitting at the dining table, under the awning, which bent under its heavy load of grapevines, among steaming polenta, and lavash, and roast chickens, amid big bottles and small, huddled over petitions, complaints, and proposals. I'm not exaggerating: never before had I worked so intensively. The main thing was that never before had I tested myself in so many different genres at one time.

The grandmother took an active part in my work. This expressed itself in her recounting for each petitioner, in his presence, all there was to know about him, starting with the petty theft in his bare-belly past and ending with the escapades in his jeans present, and with such knowledge of the affair, moreover, that one could only guess what role she herself had played in this, shall we say, chamber play. She unrolled each compromising scroll with frightful thoroughness, and woe to whoever tried to make changes or clarifications in that list. For some reason the story has stuck in my memory about some distant relative who at his daughter's wedding put the gifts of money in a canvas bag and made sure to write down the exact sum and name of the giver so that he couldn't be caught unawares later by the organs of taxation.

So once when, I remember, I had just finished composing for a nervous young man a petition to the police to issue him a new passport or, at least, insert a page in the old, for the young man dreamed of marrying, and it turned out there was nowhere to note this seminal event in his life other than under "Military Service" since the preceding one, "Family Status," had been thickly tattooed by various registries in the country and there was no more space, on that quiet Sunday afternoon, yes, Sunday, because it was on Sundays that the clans joined in battle, the two branches of the Onufriadi family tree, which during the week would have no part of one another over the six-foot fence that separated their adjacent lots, a stone fence festooned with the yellow flowers of hate, and so on one such quiet Sunday, when the morning battles had abated and someone was getting first aid and often second aid immediately after from the chicken god, who, which in this case is more important, was also the head pharmacist, and until the evening skirmishes, for another two or three hours, in that pause when, exhausted by the midday heat, the fowl fell silent in the dusty branches of the persimmon and the very air breathed love and forgiveness, the grandmother asked me to bring her her book from the bedroom. I climbed to the upper terrace, walked through the living room with the real stucco molding, through

Four Knights Opening

the sisters' room, where a week's worth of panties was exhibited on the columns of their Akai sound system, and down a small hall past a hank of cans of Greek olives – a kind of Hellenic flourish that successfully enlivened the interior – and finally found myself in the grandmother's bedroom. Here reigned cleanliness and barracks-like order. I easily located the right book on the shelf and was already getting ready to leave when my eye fell on chess figures set out on the nightstand in the niche. I took a step closer to size up the position. The next move would checkmate White. But if... I moved a white pawn to h4.... Still checkmate, just two moves later. I restored it to its previous position and left the bedroom.

The grandmother was giving the nervous groom tea, but as soon as I handed her the dog-eared, coverless volume, she forgot all about her guest. She carefully took the well-read book, opened it at random, and began reading to herself, turning several pages at a time due to her obvious agitation. The silence was getting heavy; even the spool on the sewing machine whirred in fits and starts. The nervous groom undertook a concealed maneuver in the direction of the far corner of the table, having forgotten all about his ill-starred passport. Suddenly the grandmother tore herself away from the book and, aiming the bulging pupils in her sunken eye sockets at the groom, uttered, either her own words or citing from memory: "In passionate love perfect happiness consists not so much in intimacy as in the last step toward it." The groom stiffened. The sewing machine fell silent. Even the hen-house experienced some confusion, or so it seemed to me. The grandmother sighed heavily and once again gave herself over to reading. Sofia, with exactly the same sigh, which was streaked not only with understanding but with tacit approval for the grandmother's hidden thoughts, turned the wheel on her Singer. A few minutes later the grandmother laid the book down on her knees, and her face became pensive.

"He's right," she said quietly. "A proud woman is most vexed by petty, inconsequential people, and she vents that vexation on noble souls." Distractedly, the grandmother straightened a folded under corner of the oilcloth. "Out of pride a woman is capable of marrying her idiot neighbor just to sting the idol of her heart that much more. Yes, yes, an idiot!" she repeated, convinced, turning for some reason toward the groom, who under her gaze progressed to a new stage – petrification.

"What kind of match is it you have set up in your room?" I tried to steer the conversation into a calmer channel. Sofia's eyes blazed in my direction, but I didn't understand the signal and continued with the undue familiarity of a companion to the grandmother: "To tell the truth, in that situation I wouldn't risk playing White."

"Or Black," followed the scathing rebuke.

I bit my tongue.

"Perhaps I should go, yes?" the groom interjected, and he leaned all the way across the table for his passport.

No one stopped him.

"That's enough layette sewing already," said the grandmother as soon as she had shut the iron gate behind the visitor. "You'd think you were a hen hatching a dozen eggs. You ought to be sitting with your husband – look at the black eye Fyodor's got, and they're probably just about to start in again."

Sofia stood up abruptly, inasmuch as her eight-month belly permitted, and went into the big house. The grandmother and I were left to ourselves.

"Don't be offended at me, old lady that I am. When I think about that I'm not myself. Look, there's a gleam in your eye! All right, since that's the case, then listen. There you are looking at me, at my hands with their dark spots, and you're thinking – don't interrupt – and you're thinking the old lady is worse than a mortal sin. But do you know what I was called in my youth? Yelena the Beautiful. That's my photograph up there – take a look, take a look. Kostas stole a gold bracelet from his own mother – just to prove that he was prepared to do anything for me. And I wiped my feet on him... and a year later we were wed. Funny, yes? After that, Niko often came to see us. He came and sat – one hour, two, and then left without saying a word. My Kostas felt, if he wants to sit let him sit, Niko may have been only his cousin, but they were family, they grew from a single tree. For me it was hell. I was even happy when they sat down at the chessboard, well, I thought, even so, that made it all easier. Easier! But to see him nearly every blessed day?! True, he never started in with me about anything at all, I'm not going to lie. Even on my name day, when he brought me this very hook, Stendhal, he didn't say anything, only when they left to play and I opened up to the bookmark and there it was underlined... just a minute" – she

Four Knights Opening

skimmed the dog-eared volume – "here: 'The sole medicine for jealousy consists, perhaps, in very close observation of the rival's happiness.' Yes...." She paused. "You know, I don't understand anything about chess, but once my husband, pleased with a victory over poor Niko (he almost always beat him), began to demonstrate certain moves to me on the board, I listened closely and toward the end asked: 'Then why did he lose to you?' My husband laughed for a long time and then said: 'He lost and he's going to keep on losing. Because he's as stubborn as a bull. I move a pawn and he moves a pawn, I move a bishop and he moves a bishop. ' 'Can't you do that?' 'Yes! You can do anything! But I have my pace, you have to understand that! I have my pace!' Of course, I didn't understand anything, and he called me a fool and vowed never to talk about chess to me again." Only now did the grandmother notice the flies crawling brazenly over the jar of fig jam – for five years already she had been trying unsuccessfully to get it past her insatiable grandchildren and feed it to her great-grandchildren, a la the classic scene in the city park where the sharp sparrows steal the best crumbs out from under the noses of the pigeons for whom those crumbs were intended. The grandmother shooed the flies away and covered the jar with a plastic lid. "But he did" – she slowed down, as if checking her own memory – "he did speak to me about chess one more time. It was right before the war, five or six years must have passed."

"You mean to say that all those years they continued sparring over the chessboard?"

"You can imagine. When Kostas was hospitalized with suspected jaundice in the winter of '39, Niko's sister – you've seen her – at his request brought my dear husband messages to the hospital for two weeks. Only afterward did we realize that the only thing in those fat bundles was his next move."

"Yelena Kharlampiyevna," I reminded her, "you said that your husband spoke with you about chess one other time."

"Yes. After the match that remains on the board today. It was their last match." The grandmother's spine suddenly unbent, her eyes flashed, and for a moment I saw before me that same Yelena, Yelena the Beautiful, for whose sake it was no sin to take a gold bracelet from your mother. "He lost that time."

"Who? Niko?"

"My husband," she said almost indifferently, but, strangely, in her tone I sensed a note of triumph. "It was that rare instance when he lost. And how he lost!"

"Yes, it's a clever trap" I agreed.

"I'm not talking about any trap." The grandmother smiled. "They were playing, as people put it then, for stakes.'"

"You mean for money?"

"Not necessarily. For money, for a hunting rifle, for just about anything. The Onufriadis are a wealthy family."

"So what did your husband lose that time?" I asked, smiling in turn. "A cow?"

"Me," she said simply.

"Who?" I didn't understand.

"Me," she repeated.

I made an attempt to inflate a new smile, as if to say that we too are capable of recognizing a successful joke, but I don't think anything came of it.

"My husband also decided that Niko was joking," the grandmother continued as if nothing were amiss. "But he was so sure of himself that he accepted that audacious, that insulting bet. Afterward, trying to vindicate himself to me, he swore that he'd never even considered the thought of defeat. He knew Niko's passion for copying his moves so he settled on the four knights opening – you see, I'm not such a fool anymore, I've learned something – he settled on it as entailing no risk. They'd already come across this opening, and Kostas as White had always checkmated Niko. I don't know whether it's true, but that's how my husband explained it to me later."

"So what happened?"

"No one knows. He was like a crazy man afterward. Shouting, tearing his hair. He wanted to kill me, himself, him. He'd even convinced himself that I'd set the whole thing up."

"But maybe Niko" – I stopped short, looking for the word – "maybe he didn't play completely above board?"

"You mean he cheated? the grandmother clarified brutally. "Niko would never have done that!" For the first time she seemed to raise her voice, though she immediately took herself in hand. "Do you really think that my husband didn't check each move a hundred times? He sat over that devil's board until dark."

"And didn't find a mistake?"

"No."

I stole a look at the grandmother — old, completely gray, all in black, which made her seem almost incorporeal — and I couldn't ask the question that was on the tip of my tongue.

"I know what you want to ask. You want to ask whether my husband kept his bet? This is how I'd answer: he was too weak to send me off to something like that. He sprawled at my feet, hugging his gun, but when I got up from bed in the middle of the night and started dressing, he pretended to be asleep."

She fell silent, and so did I, even the two hens circled each other silently in mortal combat over a watermelon rind.

"But Niko, he didn't pretend," the grandmother continued. "No, he was not one for pretending. He was waiting for me.... He was waiting to spurn me. Imagine! Niko turned me out! But my husband never found about that, you understand, and before dawn they set out for White Cliffs. Have you been there?"

Yes, I had. The day I arrived the Leningraders took me with them to White Cliffs, which turned out to be stone cankers like dripped candle wax, right by the sea, about a half-hour's brisk walk. White Cliffs... a beautiful spot, no denying it... only desolate, especially that early.

"So I don't have to explain how far it is from here. But I heard it. A milky fog had just begun to disperse outside my window when I heard two shots, almost simultaneously."

I was expecting more, but the grandmother rose heavily from the bench and started clearing the dirty dishes.

"That's all?" burst out of me. I could tell how incredibly naive that sounded. Like a child who hears a sad story and expresses his objection to the cruel ending.

The grandmother shrugged her shoulders in reply.

"Help me clear the dishes away from sin," was all she said. "They'll be starting soon." She craned her neck as if she were expecting a heavenly sign: lightning was about to strike the earth, like a golden staff, and then they could start.

And suddenly I realized! It was over her, over the grandmother, that they came together every Sunday! Of course! For forty-five years two branches of the Onufriadi family — grandfathers, fathers, and now even sons — bloodied each other over a once beautiful woman, each side hoping to vindicate, albeit half a century too late, their original claims, and nothing was more important for either than this. It meant restoring the original earthly order, when love was equivalent to itself and did not require adjustments for the size of a dowry or parental ties, when higher justice meant higher justice, only that and nothing more, when it was hardly appropriate to argue in the spirit of the modern thesis of the "survival of the fittest," and even if these latter-day Achilles and Patroclus — just as bellicose, just as naive — proved nothing to each other before the Second Coming, even so, every week they tried to demonstrate beyond a doubt to this proud old woman — and with her all mankind — the triumph of the spirit over pitiful matter.

"Have you gone deaf!" The grandmother was practically shoving plates into my face. "Why feed you men! Here, take these to the kitchen, dear."

I took the pile of sauce-encrusted dishes, chicken bones crunching between them, from her hands. When I had ferried everything to the kitchen, I was ordered to take Stendhal back. In the grandmother's bedroom I made a space for myself on the sagging couch, in a lap between two broken springs, and buried myself in the book. I should say that the book was pretty heavily penciled. One sentence was circled in red: "For a girl it is a much greater violation of her modesty to lie down in bed with a man whom she has seen twice in her life after saying a few words in Latin in a church than to be forced to yield to a man she has adored for two years." Lord, that's about them! was my first thought. And my second was that she hadn't circled that in red, he had! I hurried, afraid they would call me, the courier, back. I turned the well-worn, dog-eared pages, snatching certain bits at random, and suddenly a shock ran through me: I had reread a sentence three times, not believing my own eyes, but right then I heard steps on the terrace, and I started like a thief caught committing a crime, slipped Stendhal into a slit on the shelf, and left quickly.

On the terrace Grisha, dressed, had sprawled out to sleep. Evidently the mosquitoes had finally eaten him up in his room.

Right before the sun set they "joined" once more. From my small room in the half-basement I heard little Niko, the legendary Niko's grand-nephew, invoke Christ the Savior to witness his opponent

Four Knights Opening

breaking the unwritten laws of fisticuffs; I heard Andrei Konstantinovich, Kostas' son, who had graciously opened the doors of his home to me, a stranger, loudly triumph after his crowning blow to the jaw; I heard them all. All but the grandmother's voice, but I didn't doubt one whit that during those sacred minutes she, as always, was sitting in her wicker chair on the upper terrace and from on high, like Pallas Athena, observing with interest the battle's progress. To the feeble support of my lamp, which the flies had turned into a candled quail's egg, I hastened to write down the astonishing tale. The grandmother, I felt, had omitted something important. But what? Maybe she didn't know herself. Didn't know? But what about the sentence from Stendhal? Couldn't that sentence, in fact, have escaped her notice, even though it was underlined? And that opening... four knights... why did it trouble me so? Her husband, she said, had found no mistake, had checked each move a hundred times and hadn't found... Actually though, why should I believe her husband? Niko's win was no accident, that's clear, the stakes were too high for that, and that meant... Here the thread of my reasoning broke time after time. I had to go out and rewrite the position, that's what. And play it out from there. Granted, with my chess erudition I wasn't going to play it out very far. No matter. I'd go back to Moscow and sort it out there. Yes, I honestly admit, I was quite obsessed by then, and when an idea gets hold of me, I can hang the moon in ribbons.

I apologize in advance for rattling off how imperceptibly those last days by the sea passed for me, how I took the grandmother's tkemali home with me, and, oh yes, her divine fig jam, how I didn't have a return ticket and Grisha's wife Tanya got me an "overflow" flight, favor for favor, after all I'd written a letter to Aeroflot for the girls on duty in which I wrote something histrionic about how they were going deaf on the airstrip and weren't even getting any extra compensation for it. Not that all this was unimportant, but right now, this minute, I, like you too, reader, doubtless, am already there, in Moscow, where, one would like to believe, the solution to this bizarre story awaits us.

The day after I flew into Moscow, on Tuesday, I called the Central Chess Club and was distressed to hear that the library was only open evenings. In order to make the time pass more quickly, I saw a trashy movie, ate lunch twice – on grounds of nerves (and was still hungry) – and roamed the city. By four o'clock on the button I was at the cozy building on Gogol Boulevard. In the library they gave me literature on the theory of openings, a box of wooden chess pieces, and a folding board. In less than an hour I had found what I was looking for. Quite agitated, I played out the fatal match that had ended in two shots. It turned out that in 1936 the newspaper *Evening Moscow* had chosen this opening for a match with its readers. Up to the eleventh move Black copied White's moves exactly. Further continuation of this symmetry quickly threatened the readers with checkmate, so on White's eleventh move Qd2 they moved the bishop to f3, taking the knight. But that didn't save them either and on the twentieth move they conceded defeat.

Did Niko Onufriadi know about this curious match? I don't think I would be wrong if I answered in the affirmative. But after all, he, Niko, had won with Black! Yes, won ... after losing many times, knowingly following the false lead pursued by *Evening Moscow's* readers. Yes, over and over again, he lost to his cousin and rival, laying the groundwork for the principal match of his life. And when the decisive moment came, he played the eleventh move in a new way – he moved to check with his knight to f3. Lulled by easy victories, suspecting nothing, his rival made his following moves essentially under his dictate. On the fourteenth move Niko modestly moved his king to the corner of the board... and White was trapped! After Kt:f6 followed Rd8. Mate! A belated attempt to open a "window" to the white king also, as I had been convinced even then, in the grandmother's bedroom, led to mate. Well well! Kostas' eyes must have popped out of his head. I wouldn't have been surprised if he'd had a stroke.

You ask: what makes me think Niko had to have known about that match? And if he did, then what devil made him play giveaway with his rival for so long? Stop! Why don't we ask ourselves *how* long? If my memory serves me well, between Kostas' first and last attempts to familiarize his wife with the ancient game five or six years passed, the last one of these, shall we say, pre-duel conversations taking place right before the war. Consequently... Don't rush, this requires absolute precision. I set out for the public library and in the card file under "Stendhal, Henri Beyle," I looked for the same volume from the fifteen-volume collected works he'd given to Yelena the Beautiful. The 1935 edition! Good for you, old woman, everything checks out − six years. So that's when this maniac got the idea for his fantastic plan! I'm talking about that sentence in Stendhal that so astonished me.

So, it was then, in '35, that Niko was frequenting his cousin's house. I don't think he had a precise plan of action at first. I think he got the idea of adopting "mirror" chess as his ally from the comment in *Evening Moscow*. An ingenious idea, by the way. How else, I ask you, could you program your rival for the desired result? Oh, I didn't believe in those countless losses of his from the very beginning! Anyone beautiful Yelena had loved for fifty years was worth her weight in gold. She did love him, she did! "He was so pleased with his victory over poor Niko," she let drop. That word, "poor," cost her dearly. The sly dog, he had let himself be eaten so often in this game of cat and mouse that toward the end he risked losing the ways of the hunter. Even more amazing, though, was his long-suffering patience. To come to the house of someone who belongs to another every day for six years and, without giving yourself away, lose to a conceited fool time and again − you'll agree, not everyone is capable of that. I figured in my head: in six years they must have played about fifteen hundred matches. The openings varied, naturally, however by all accounts up to a specific moment he always mirrored the moves of his opponent, passing it off as his aberration, or "stubbornness," as Kostas assumed, but in actual fact by degrees accustoming the latter to the idea that he would go on like that forever. In this sea of matches the four knights opening must have come up more than once (after all, Kostas himself admitted as much!), but, amazingly, Niko passed up his chance over and over again. He had no right to take the risk! And he suggested his astonishing bet, of course, not *before* the start of their decisive match but *after*, when their knights, White and Black, were rushing at each other, foaming at the mouth, and everything became immediately clear, and both weapons shot soundlessly, so that a little later, at dawn, the echo could reverberate at White Cliffs. But then why, we ask ourselves, having born his cross and reached the threshold of bliss, didn't he take that last step? That riddle, I'm afraid, is beyond me.

My story is drawing to a close. I'm looking back over the first pages and I can't shake a certain ambivalence: if the main, love-chess, *sujet* has been written more or less straightforwardly and convincingly, then everything leading up to it seems to fall short: a strange intonation creeps into the description of the household arrangement, sentences are at times heavy and airless, the humor, as they say, of the Evil One. What's to be done? Art imitating life never rings true.

I cannot part with my reader on this sad note. The match has been played, the pieces are returning to their starting positions. What are we to do? I roamed aimlessly in the rain and thought about my beautiful Greek lady. I also felt like sacrificing something for her, if not my life then... then... I went to Kuznetsky Bridge Street, scouted around among the black market dealers, and the next day had in hand, for a mere 500 percent markup, a paperback of ambiguous color with an equally ambiguous sketch depicting either a breaking adipose heart or a time bomb toward which the foxfire of passion was inexorably stealing up a safety fuse. It was Stendhal. I sent the grandmother the book, having inserted a bookmark. She would open Stendhal and surely turn immediately to the sentence underlined in red: "A woman can be won, like a chess match."

1986

Having come to a full stop, I surveyed the field of battle one last time. Suddenly a shock ran through me. What blindness! All it took for White to escape checkmate was to play: 15. Rfc1 Rg8+ 16. Kf1 Bg2+ 17. Ke1. Kostas *could* have saved himself! My poor hero – your dream nearly burst, like a balloon. But the story has already been written. I'm happy I gave you this illusion, albeit at the expense of my own mistake.

Translated by Marian Schwartz

SOGLASIE PUBLISHERS

Georgi Ivanov, Complete Works in three volumes.
Hard cover with dust jacket.

For the centenary of the poet's birth

Georgi Ivanov (1894-1958), a major poet of the "Silver Age", has been little known in his home country, until quite recently, but was hailed by the Russian emigration as their greatest poet. His complete works include much previously unpublished poetry and prose, and have been supplied with detailed notes and introductions. Careful textological work has been done by literary scholars who followed instructions contained in Ivanov's will.

Vol. One: 656 pages. Poems and translations.
Vol. Two: 480 pages. "Disintegration of the Atom", the notorious poem in prose, and the novel "The Third Rome"
Vol. Three: 720 pages. "Petersburg Winters", "Chinese Shadows", memoirs, criticism.

Ludmila Saraskina. DOSTOYEVSKY'S GREAT LOVE

Apollinaria Suslova: biography in documents and letters
700 pages, hard cover with dust jacket, richly illustrated with archival photographs, some of them published for the first time.

Apollinaria Suslova, Dostoyevsky's long-time lover, was a striking personality who was loved by many outstanding men of her age and later married the great philosopher Vassily Rozanov. She served as the prototype for many of Dostoyevsky's heroines.

Ludmila Saraskina, a famous Dostoyevsky scholar, has discovered 40 previously unpublished letters by Suslova and 20 new letters to her, including Rozanov's letters.
This impressive volume is the first fundamental biography of a woman who made an impact on the literary life of her age and herself was a writer of considerable merit.

SOGLASIE ALSO PUBLISHES A LITERARY MONTHLY SOGLASIE.
Address: 113054 Moscow, 28 Bakhrushin St
tel: (095) 235 1556/235 1352 fax: (095) 235 1526

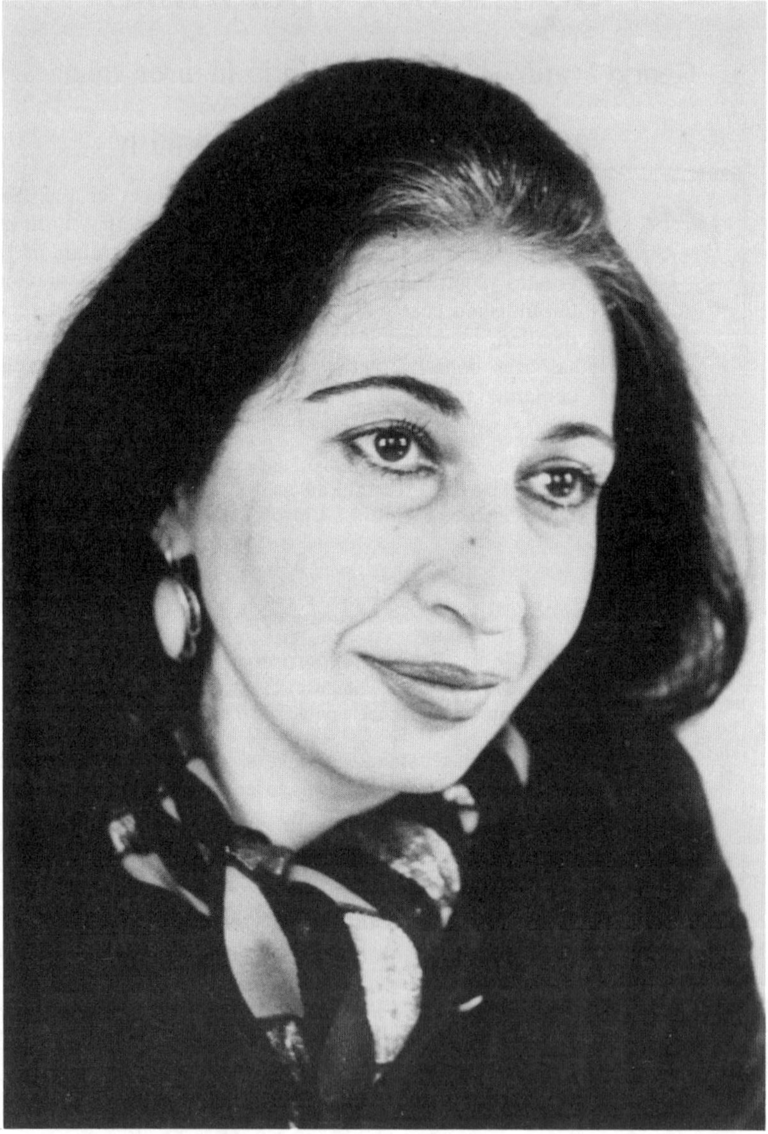

Nina
GABRIELIAN

The Studio Apartment
Happiness

Happiness

"Oh, God!" she sighed. "Oh, God!" and burst into tears.

"What's the matter? What is it, darling?" he said, tenderly stroking her hair and gently pressing her close, close to his beautiful body.

She didn't answer, she saw in his eyes that he understood perfectly well what was the matter. She continued her voluptuous weeping. Then she seized his hand and began kissing it.

He smiled and kissed her wet, shining eyes.

He soon drifted off to sleep, holding her close and responding in his sleep to her slightest movement. She was uncomfortable lying that way. She was no longer used to sleeping next to a man, her arm had gone numb, but she was afraid to move, afraid that she would scare away the miracle that had occurred. He breathed silently, and the pulse in his neck throbbed softly, but she already knew how frenzied this beautiful male body could be.

Her body was beautiful, too. She had always known that she had a beautiful body. Even when her former husband used to say that her legs were too short. But she knew that he said that to get back at her for his failure as a man. He also said she was not his type, that he liked long-legged redheads. She felt her hatred rise and was about to open her mouth to ask when he would finally gather his strength – his powerful male strength – and pound the nail into the wall, so that he could hang on it the precious gift that his loving mother had given them for a wedding present. How much she must have loved her son to give him for his wedding this amazing print, that must have cost all of three rubles!

She had even begun to utter this phrase, but caught herself in time, remembering that he would undoubtedly answer by talking about her father, who was so filled with love for his daughter that he called her all the time – at least once every two months. No, she was no longer as stupid as she had been in the first months of her marriage, she would not give her husband the chance to catch her out, tease her out from the depths of her private world, and tie her, like a goat to a peg, to some stupid phrase. Especially now, fifteen years after their divorce.

The sleeping man breathed quietly and in his sleep tenderly and firmly pressed her body, her beautiful body, close to his. Her very beautiful body.

...She was eating strawberries sprinkled with sugar, oozing a thick juice. The strawberries had the taste of happiness and freedom, because she had passed all of her eigth-grade exams with flying colors, and in three days she and her mother would be in the Crimia. And she would lie on the hot bronze sand, and her body, separated from the world by only her new red bathing suit, that they were so lucky to get at the Moskva department store, would absorb the red-hot currents of this ancient, dark part of the South, and would itself become the color of old bronze.

...And then she would enter the green sea and swim forever, chasing away schools of hook-nosed seahorses. When she reached the red buoy she would turn over on her back and lose track of the divide between sea and sky, between herself and all of this.

...Then her father came into the room and, looking in disgust at her adolescent knees poking out from under her short nightgown, asked why she had again hung her panties and bra in the bathroom where everyone could see them. Couldn't she find some other place to dry them? And she felt how disgusting her body was.

The sleeping man trembled and opened his eyes a bit. But she gathered all her will power and looked her father right in the eye in such a way that, muttering something unintelligible, he disappeared into thin air.

"Go back to sleep" she told the sleeping man, "Sleep". And carefully laying his head on her shoulder, began to rock him quietly. The sleeping man hugged her trustingly and, smacking his lips like a child, fell even deeper into sleep. She was suddenly seized by a desire to look at her legs. But she controlled herself and whispered again, "Sleep."

She herself could not fall asleep, because her mother came into the room, took her by the hand and led her into the kitchen. There, closing the door tightly after her, her mother nervously adjusted the white bow in her hair, and, looking around fearfully, asked in a loud whisper if she felt any pain in her lower abdomen. No, she answered in surprise, she didn't feel anything like that. You will soon, answered her mother. A lot of pain. An awful lot. And every month. That's the way it is, said her mother.

And then she screwed her courage up to ask where babies come from. "Ssssh!" said her mother. "Your father will hear." And then she blushed furiously and explained hastily that a woman has a hmmm, well, in general, and a man has to tear it. And this hurts a lot. And the worst thing in a woman's life is the memory of her wedding night.

She laughed at her mother's words for it wasn't just the first — memories of the second and the twenty-second nights were not all that pleasant, either. She shook her head. Harder and harder. To shake out of it the thing that had already begun to spread through her body, threatening to mutilate it once again. No, she would not allow it. She would never again allow them — her father, her former husband, her mother — to paralyze her body's ability to become bronze, long-legged and happy.

The body of the sleeping man embraced her, giving off a dark, acrid heat. She tensed her nostrils and began to drink in this heat. She drank it in until she was filled with it, until there were no empty spaces left in her being where the past could creep in. Not the smallest hole.

And only then did she allow herself to fall asleep. She slept, trustingly throwing her head back in the darkness, protected by this dark male scent that wrapped softly around her — the smell of love, of happiness and security.

And in her dream the sleeping man came up to her once again and offered her a movie ticket. He smiled slyly, just like he had a few hours ago, and said what a shame it was that his friend had fallen ill. That was why he could give her a ticket. It would be just too bad if such pretty girls couldn't get into the movies. He had noticed them, he said, when they were still in line, and he knew right away that they would not be able to get tickets. He had bought his yesterday. For himself and for his friend. And then his friend had to go and get sick. So, if they wanted... But, unfortunately, there was only one ticket. Let the girls themselves decide which of them would go. And since in her dream she already knew what would happen, that it wasn't just a simple ticket, she behaved quite differently than

Happiness

she did in real life. She didn't bother to put on an act, to insist that her friend take the ticket, knowing full well that her friend would persuade her to accept it in the end. No, she didn't refuse, she just held out her hand and took the lucky ticket.

And then the cup of tea in her hand shook and fell slowly to the floor. And he laughed and said that it was good luck when dishes break, and that she had beautiful hands. And then she saw that her body was also beautiful. It was lying on a white sheet, and it was already naked and tanned. And she was that body, stretched out and trembling beneath his kisses, and at the same time she was in another corner of the room, in front of the mirror, watching in it what was happening behind her back.

But since the cup continued to fall slowly from her hands, she could not get a look at the faces of the two people in the mirror, one of whom was she herself. And she tried to get a good look at them, and the tension was a torment, sweet and growing. Then it became unbearable, and she understood that she would now, finally, experience something she had never been able to, not with her husband nor with other men.

And she became frightened. Frightened of her husband. Actually, she was afraid she would remember his pitiful face, so ashamed. And then she would ruin it, again. She ground her teeth and moaned. Loudly. Even more loudly. Tears streamed down her face, and through her tears she gave a mental push to the cup, falling all too slowly. The cup crashed down, hit the floor, and, freed from its overfull contents, smashed into a million shining sharp pieces that flew in different directions...

She lay, liberated, empty, happy, and she cried, burying her face in his shoulder, not answering his tender "what's the matter" because she could tell by his voice that he knew perfectly well what was the matter.

And then morning came. Sunday morning, and they drank tea in the sunny kitchen. And he laughed and told her how he had tricked his professor at a university exam. All he did was look him straight in the eye and begin to answer a different question than the one on the test card, the only question he knew the answer to. And he spoke in such an animated tone that the professor was taken in.

Then he said that she looked wonderful for thirty-five, and how nice it was that she had her own apartment. Then he got ready to leave, and, kissing her tenderly, said that she owed him fifty dollars. She laughed at his joke. But he continued to insist. She laughed even louder and kept laughing until she realized that it wasn't a joke. Then she told him he was a scoundrel. He smiled. She began to choke. He smiled even wider. She got fifty dollars out of the sideboard and gave it to him. He thanked her affectionately, and, scratching some numbers on a piece of paper, said that when she wanted to see him again she could call this number. She answered that she hated him.

She cried for an entire day, sitting in front of the mirror and tearing at her face. Then for a week she couldn't face anyone. Two months later she called him.

Translated by Jean MacKenzie

The Studio Apartment

It's as if I were standing in the hall of our old Lenin Avenue flat, and someone's telling me that my friend has come. Before I turn to see which friend, she jumps on my back and sits astride me. I dash to the mirror to try to shake her off so I can see her reflection. A quiet snap behind my back – and her head, having traveled a quarter circle, comes to rest at my right elbow. The face in the mirror is MINE! My face, bright purple, with glowing red lips. She giggles, jumps off my back, and kisses me on the lips. I scream and slap her across the face...

I am lying in semi-darkness, my eyes wide open, my heart stuck in my throat beating a mad tattoo. The bedside clock shows eight – morning? evening? I have no idea. I know only one thing for sure. My apartment has once again got the better of me.

I was ready to love it. Right from the start, the day I moved in. It was empty, with ugly grey wallpaper and brown streaks on the ceiling. I got my courage up, and, temporarily overcoming my old fear of the service sector, went to an interior-decorating firm. Two

The Studio Apartment

months later, three men in grey appeared, and worked a miracle. My studio apartment was softly glowing with wallpaper in creamy yellow, and window sills of a snowy white. It had furniture now – the sofa, coffee table and television my friends gave me, and the wardrobe, bookcase, kitchen table, chairs and fridge I got for myself. We didn't need anything else, my apartment and I, especially since we had only two walls along which we could line the furniture. The others were taken up by two huge windows which gave off a transparent grey coldness. But I managed to arrange the furniture so that a delightful yellow dominated the place.

When the first symptoms appeared, I paid no attention. All my favorite Chinese cups broke – not all at once, of course. If they all had broken at once, I'd have seen something was wrong. But they broke so naturally, one by one, at long intervals, when I was washing the dishes that had built up in the kitchen sink for several days, that it never occurred to me there was something wrong. The dust appeared later. And then – Jerry came. I wonder which came first. Possibly, they came together. Oh no, the dust was first.

I saw it when I was getting ready for my housewarming and my twenty-third birthday – two parties at once. I tripped over the leg of the kitchen table I was carrying into the other room, and fell. It was then I saw the dust – three fluffy grey balls making little movements under the sofa. I lay flat on my stomach, trying to recollect when and where I had seen them before. Finally, I remembered.

I am fifteen, and sitting in a wicker chair in Leah's neat little garden in Parnu, Estonia. Above me is the dazzling leaden-blue Baltic sky, bathed in sunlight after a long rainy spell. Some steps away, a tiny furry ball is trembling in the dewy grass – a sharp-nosed mouse with a long pink tail. I make a stealthy step, then another, but the mouse doesn't run away. It merely sits, shaking all over. From under its bristling fur, red drops are falling, one after another. Something inside me begins to shake, too.

"'Timsy! Quite a big boy!" I hear a surprised and triumphant voice behind my back. It's Leah.

I turn around, but there's no Timsy to be seen.

"Timsy darling," Leah warbles. "Puss-puss-puss! Time for your milk. See, Sonya," she turns to me, "he's a big boy now, he can –"

"– Kill!" I retort.

123

"Would you like the whole place crawling with mice?" Her fine brows make an indignant arch over her eyes.

I swept my studio. Jerry appeared the next day. I don't remember which of my friends brought him to my house. Jerry was forty years old; his massive head with its hooked nose and green eyes was attached right to his stumpy trunk. No neck to speak of. He immediately made a pass.

He edged into my kitchen in a funny way, as I was making tea. "Listen, Sonya, would you sit for a moment? We've got to get properly acquainted." And he sat astride my kitchen stool, and moved it closer.

"Know what, I'm a night watchman" – this with a searching look at me.

"Nice to meet you," I mumbled as I backed away from him and his stool. "You shocked?" he whispered as the six legs – his own two and the stool's four – resumed their motion.

"Not in the least. It's very interesting," I blushed.

"Conformists!" he growled as he adjusted the flimsy stool under his bulky form. "Most people are lousy conformists, while I am free from the community. I have two advanced degrees, by the way. I don't want anyone to manipulate my brain. Where do you work? Lenin Library? I see. Freedom's a burden. It's sweet to be dependent and manipulated."

"But I'm a translator. I specialize in museums."

"No matter," he said with an enigmatic stare. "Want me to read my essays to you? Here's one, On the Death Urge," and he produced, God knows from where, a fat grey folder with pink trimmings.

"Where's that tea of yours?" an indignant wail came from the room.

"Maybe some other time " I said, excusing myself.

"Sure, sure, some other time," he enthused.

My studio seemed to scare away all my lovers, actual and potential. Surprisingly, it was always glad to see Jerry – possibly because he would never be my lover, however hard he tried to get into my bed; or because he liked it the way it was. We always spruced ourselves up, my studio and I, when we were having guests. But for him we did nothing special. And he was still excited about everything.

"What a nice robe! Awfully becoming," – he whispered as he

The Studio Apartment

tugged at the sleeve of my threadbare dark red flannel. (My other robe, an expensive affair from a good store, lies unworn in the wardrobe, stored away with two French bras and five Lebanese panties for the hypothetical day I need such nice things.) "Dark red's your colour. Know what? You're like an Egyptian fresco. Ah, that's it! Don't stir! God, I go crazy when I see your face! Especially this little spot," and Jerry contoured my lips with his stumpy finger.

I winced and pushed his hand away.

"You're nuts!" he flared up. "I have already told you that it's my manner to touch people I feel a psychological affinity with. It's all so natural. Don't you see that eroticism is the basis of all human relations? Even between children and parents or between friends. I have it all in an essay, Volcanic Eruptions as Manifestations of the Planetary Orgasm. I'll read it to you. I gave a pan-erotic explanation to the Pompeian tragedy in it," and another mouse-grey folder with pink tail-strings appeared in his hands out of nowhere, from which he extracted the rustling white innards with a flourish.

I listened to his reading, wincing at the gusto with which he uttered "orgasm," his catchword. I didn't notice that his stool had again begun to move, and became aware of it only when he had seriously invaded my personal space. I jerked back sharply and hit the wall. My apartment and Jerry must have been plotting against me – the wall pushed me back. Jerry leaned forward quickly and glued his mouth onto mine.

I pushed him back, screaming, "You fool!"

The grey folder landed on the floor, its pink tails jerking.

"Crazy woman," Jerry replied in surprise.

I had been ready to love my studio! I liked it at once, the day I moved in after my divorce. It was my fourth home. I hardly remember the first. We moved in when I was three. As Mum and Dad told me later, it was a room nine square meters in a communal apartment we shared with ten other families. I don't remember any of them. The only things that stuck in my memory were my red knitted dress with yellow pompon trimmings at the neck, and a man in grey – he sat on a chair in the centre of the room in the dead of night, staring at me.

We later moved into a separate apartment on Lenin Avenue. One room was big and yellow, the other small and red. I liked the yellow one, and was afraid of the red. Mum and Dad lived in the yellow, with its new pretty furniture. They often threw parties there. I was confined to the red, where I spent only the nights – during the day they forced me to go to kindergarten. My red nursery detested me and amused itself with little practical jokes at night. Sometimes it would slam something against my quilt, or turn the flowers on the carpet into nasty winking eyes or leering mouths. With the years, we grew to tolerate each other, my room and I, with only occasional sudden bursts of antagonism. But even so, right up until my wedding day I preferred the yellow room.

It was a sunny room – not just because its window faced south – the red's did, too. No, it was something else. Maybe it was the yellow wallpaper, or the blue cut glass pitcher, or the china Pushkin bust, dazzling white against the black piano. But what did it matter, after all? What mattered was that the room and I loved each other. Not that I didn't love my parents, but that was a matter-of-fact attachment, with nothing of the miracle about it.

Besides, Mum and Dad were dreadful nuisances. Whenever we kids played hide-and-seek in the yard, I was told not to hide in the basement and attic, and was the first to be discovered in the shrubbery, to peals of mocking laughter. These were trifles, annoying but of little importance. What mattered was that Mum and Dad were shattering my love affair with the yellow room. Oh, the rare occasions we were alone together! Whenever others were present, it poured its love on them in equal portions. But there were happy hours I arranged by sheer deception – for instance, by seizing the slippery tip of the thermometer and shaking the silvery mercury up to at least 38 degrees.

Even though I was a big girl and knew that a Young Pioneer was supposed to be an exemplary child, the temptation to be alone with the yellow room proved stronger than civic duty.

I lay in bed in my red room, with a tragic expression, listening with a perverse glee as the doctor said to my flustered mother:

"She's a big girl. Go to your office, she'll be O.K. Nothing to cry about! She has a sore throat, that's all. (Of course I did! I had gorged myself on snow the day before.) She'll spend a nice week in bed, with her books, and back to school. Eager to get back to school, Sonya?"

The Studio Apartment

"Sure," I whispered, my face mournful.

"Be patient. Just don't forget to take your antibiotics the first thing in the morning. And Mamma'll wrap you in mustard plasters in the evening. Okay?"

"Okay," I whispered, giving an assiduous sneeze. (You won't catch me eating these antibiotics of yours! As to mustard plasters, I'd have to put up with them — love demands sacrifices.)

Alone, at last! I put on my slippers, and dashed to the yellow room to build a house — a forbidden game, God knows why. I made it from the sofa cushions. It was a tiny house, but mine, and no one else's. It was on an uninhabited island that I was to settle. I began by planting flowers — artificial ones that Mum got for New Year's would do fine. I stuck them in the parquet cracks, and got back into my cushion house to admire my blossoming solitude — green, white, purple and, most important, yellow!

There was not a single yellow spot in my husband's home; there were two rooms — one grey, the other green. And there was my mother-in-law, to top it all off. Not that it came as a surprise. I had seen his apartment and his mother when we were engaged, and knew we were to have the grey room, and she the green. The unpleasant surprise came later, when I learned that my husband was a closet drunk. I divorced him a year later and moved into my studio, immediately changing its grey wallpaper to yellow.

Six months later, Mum and Dad moved into a new apartment in Izmailovo, a drab three-room affair. That was the end of our Lenin Avenue period.

...It's as if I were asleep, and aware that I'm asleep, and suddenly remember that I haven't locked the door. I know I must get up and lock it, but I can't. Something is pressing my chest to the bed. I turn onto my stomach, crawl down, and out into the hall, snake-fashion, my stomach always pressed to the floor. The door's ajar. I stretch out, trying to get it — and find myself in bed again. I know I've got to wash my face before I close the door. Again I'm crawling, now to the bathroom. I snatch at the bath brim and pull myself up to get my face into the water — luckily, the bath is full. I wake up the moment my face touches the water, but the instant I'm lifting my head the front door bangs, a hand squeezes my nape and pushes my head down. Kicking, suffocating, I suddenly feel I'm free!

I sit up in bed, switch on the side lamp and tiptoe to the hall. The door is safely locked.

We never put on airs, my studio and I, with Jerry around. Other guests were different. In just an hour and a half we removed all traces of our former lives, we were new and shining and ready for a miracle. The miracle was sure to happen and change our lives. Maybe it would ebb today, or, at worst, in the very near future. So we couldn't let this miracle catch us with our hair down – unprepared, unprettified, unadorned.

The apartment was first. Last week's dirty dishes were washed, fluffy grey balls swept from under the sofa, and skirts and sweaters confined to the wardrobe. My turn came next. I took my vantage point at the kitchen table, arranged my cosmetics on it, and took a close look at myself in my compact mirror. With a fine film of powder on it, the tiny thing offered a more flattering picture than the large one in the bathroom. Looking in the inside wardrobe mirror was still worse – it ruined my mood for hours. It offered the worst face I had – I had many, you see. I liked some, and detested others.

I learned that I had more than one face when I was nine. Sveta and I were making soap bubbles in my bathroom – hard to find a more interesting pastime, because bubbles emerge out of nothing, or almost nothing. You have to stick the tube in a jar of soapy water, then take it out and begin to blow cautiously into the dry end. Then out of the empty tube comes a pearly, iridescent ball, bloating till it tears off from the tube and floats in the air to hit against the tile wall the next instant, and burst.

These births out of nothing and disappearances into nothing fascinated us so much that we came to ourselves only when the soapy water was all gone. Then I had a brainstorm.

"Let's turn into soap bubbles," I suggested.

"How?" she wondered.

"Like this." I inhaled as deeply as I could, pressed my lips, and bloated my cheeks, my eyes glued to the mirror. My face grew big and red, the eyes narrowed into slits, and the nose grew long and pointed, reaching my upper lip. Sveta looked spellbound, then gave a short laugh and inhaled, too. Her skin got a bluish tinge, and her green eyes bulged. We made mooing noises as we stared in the mirror, at the two monsters which had been lying hidden inside us.

Sveta's was the first to go. Mine resisted for a moment or two – and was gone, too. The faces that looked at us from the mirror were not quite the same as before. There was something new and sinister about them, defying words. They shook a little as if there were something moving inside, trying to get out.

"Now, let's play skeletons," said Sveta and drew her cheeks in, pressing them with her jaws.

"Let's," I agreed, and sucked my cheeks in.

Two new monsters, with no cheeks and lips, were floating in the mirror, winking at us.

For almost a week after that, whenever I met Sveta I felt peculiar awkwardness, something akin to shame. I think she felt the same. After that we never again tried to let loose the monsters inside us – at least not together.

I see now that with the bathroom escapade, we breached the smooth wall of the universe's defenses, built to keep us from the true picture of the world, so that we could not guess that its three-dimensional solidity was but a colorful screen hiding its perfidious, flowing, all-corroding anonymity. I'll never know why the screen tore in my bathroom, of all places, to reveal to a little nine-year-old girl the terrifying multitude of her identities. I think it was by mere chance – because I soon forgot, only to have it rise to the surface now.

"Know what?" Jerry said after another abortive attempt to touch my cheek with his finger. "Your face is quite different without makeup – so sweet and nice."

"So sallow," I joined in, echoing his intonation.

"No, you're quite pretty – but different. Defenseless. I would love to kiss you when you're like this."

"Oh would you?"

"Why do you resist me? Don't, my little one," he said in a coaxing voice as his hooknosed face trembled and shook dangerously, coming closer to me and growing alarmingly.

Something inside me began to tremble unpleasantly. The air between my upturned face and Jerry's descending profile became more and more compressed, began to vibrate, and suddenly burst with a vicious crack. I saw through the hole the leaden Baltic sky, the dewy grass, and a tiny, bleeding fluffy ball in it, and heard Leah's shrill voice: "Would you like the place to be crawling with mice?"

Shocked, Jerry jerked back. Leah and the mouse were gone the same instance.

"Lord, the face you had!" he whispered.

"What was it?" I asked, hoarsely.

"A hellcat's."

How it played up to anyone who came in, that apartment! No one except me knew what a talent it had for mimicry. With Jerry, it took on the air of the modest abode of a lonely, intellectual, underappreciated lady (for a long time I thought that that was its true nature), with a vague eroticism in the air, crammed with books, even the kitchen where I usually received him. (Now I see that this absence of adornment was just another of its weapons. It allowed the place to reveal another of its many faces.)

When Victor broke into our life, it tried to look cosy, and even got inexpensive tan curtains to conceal the absence of two walls.

...It's as if everyone were gone at long last. I put slippers on my bare feet and dash out of my red room to the yellow to build my cushion cabin. I must be quick before Mum comes back — she's sure to pull it down. I hurry, but the roof doesn't hold on the soft thick walls. At last! I arrange the paper flowers around, jump in and, breathing heavily, enjoy my blossoming solitude. It's green, white, purple and, even better, yellow. Suddenly, I realize that I haven't locked the front door. I crawl out of my cabin and out into the hall, always on my belly, careful not to touch the paper flowers — I know the main danger is in these flowers. When I'm about to reach the hall, my right hand gives a sharp jerk, against my will, snatches a lavender flower, begins to rip it apart. Here, the front door gives a bang, a hand snatches me by the scruff of my neck and drags me to the sofa where, sticking my head inside my house, begins to push it under water. Blowing bubbles with my nose and mouth I kick and shake the house apart. The soft walls give way, the roof falls on my head — free at last!

I loved Victor dreadfully. I can hardly remember what it was that so drew me to him. I think it was his neck. Yes, that was it. His neck radiated strength and confidence, so unlike my ex-husband's skinny one. A low-pitched, mellow voice came out of that neck. Now that I see things better in retrospect, I discern the mysterious link between my invisible desire to stroke his neck and the absence of two walls in my studio. I suspect my desire was born long before the moment

The Studio Apartment

the door burst open to the room where we, the employees of the Lenin Library Information Centre, were sitting, and a tall, muscular male appeared, saying in a beautiful voice: "Mornin', ladies. Can you give me a little help with my thesis?"

It was then I saw his neck – a thick but graceful column rising out of his unbuttoned collar to support a salt-and-pepper head of hair. I wanted to touch this neck the moment I saw it. This was a familiar desire, though no other neck had ever excited me like this before. Now I know it was my apartment's suggestion. But I had not been aware of it before. I don't think I ever had desires of my own – or the apartment strangled them to impose its own desires on me, and I mistook them for my own, the fool that I was. Otherwise, the fact that I bought a divan soon after I met Victor defies explanation. I never use it. My sofa's good enough to sleep on, and kitchen stools are fine to sit on. But my apartment wanted a divan, and used a plausible pretext to get one.

I tidied it up some days before our date. At first, I mistook the thing for a cobweb, but a closer look revealed a network of fine cracks in the wallpaper. Grey, the original colour of my apartment, was penetrating through these cracks, and I wanted to pick at them with my nails. This desire was so strong I felt pins-and-needles in my hand. There was only one way to fight it – by getting a divan to cover this temptation, these narrow cracks leading to a different identity for my home.

I had felt something similar when I was a child. Sveta and I used to have a fine time on the old, squeaky carousel in our yard – a wooden circle with a steel column in the middle, and steel bars to connect the column to the edges of the circle. You had to stand with one leg on the wooden circle, and hold tight to the bars while pushing off with the other leg. Then the carousel with an aged screech would begin to turn, slowly at first, then faster and faster. Once Sveta and I got it going so fast that my leg slipped off the wooden circle, and, taking off into the air I began to go round and round. I felt that my body was dissolving in the air. Everything was gone but my hands clinging to the bars, and a shrill voice, screaming. It might not even have been my voice – it could have been Sveta's, or even the wind rushing by in the opposite direction. All of a sudden, I felt my body again, stretched on the ground in its crumpled pink dress. A huge red flower was blossoming on my leg, giving me such pain that

Sveta's face looked green to me. Then I became dizzy again, and came to my senses only in my red-room bed. "Now we'll save your leg, little lady," a thick voice said, and a spray of transparent liquid touched my thigh. The flower on my leg began to foam, to hiss, and then it began to devour my leg. But then they dressed the wound quickly and the pain died down. Several days later, I felt pins-and-needles in my right palm. I scratched it with the fingers of the left – no use. I saw what my right hand wanted. When I stayed alone at home, I removed the bandage and picked at my flower, now wrinkled and brown. It blossomed scarlet again under my nails, but the pain was weak and pleasurable now. It brought back the feeling of flight on the old merry-go-round.

But after that I never flew again. So when Victor stood up from my new divan, pushed the coffee table aside, made a resolute step to the kitchen stool I was siting on and embraced me, I was frightened at first. I felt my body was vibrating and dissolving in the air. I had never felt like that with my husband. To stop trembling, I put my arms around his neck – and the floor shook under me. Then the ceiling came down on me. My soul left my body, floated up to the ceiling, went through it – and I died.

"What a face you've had!" Victor whispered.

"What d'you mean?" I brought out as my soul was getting back into my body.

"You had a face like a fresco."

"I'm not a fresco. A live woman, honest."

"What d'you mean?" he asked, in his turn.

"I'm a woman of flesh and blood, not a fresco. But only a few people know it. Think I'm crazy? It's my manner of joking."

"I have a perfect sense of humour," he said moving aside.

"No offense."

"None taken. I like you dreadfully. You're small and defenseless."

"Me-e-e? Defenseless? The idea!"

"All women are defenseless before men. Weaker body, soul – and brain."

"Body O.K., but what makes you think a female brain is weaker than a man's?"

"See, you women have never done anything worthwhile in art or science."

The Studio Apartment

"How about Tsvetayeva, or Akhmatova — to say nothing of Madame Curie?"

"Did you get me here to lecture on history, or what? We really don't have that much time. I'm expected at home. I can offer you a much better pastime than discourses on women's lib."

"Like what?"

"Guess. I think you like it. What's this? You blushing? Never thought you were so shy. Charming!" And he embraced me again.

I trembled all over.

"You're crying?" he asked, astonished.

"I love you so," I sobbed.

"Hush, darling," his mellow voice enveloped me as he stroked my head.

... And it's as if I were in a big room with white tiled walls, like in a bathroom, but it is a housing office, where I was to get an official certificate confirming that we had rented a country house in Skylarks nine years ago. I needed it urgently. Tomorrow would be too late. Two doors opened into the hall, and I knew everything depended on my choice. My intuition was drawing me right, but I knew it was a trap. So I pushed the door to my left to see a large well-lit room with several polished desks, an official at each, with a small crowd of applicants in front.

"Sorry, sir," I addressed a grey-haired gentleman at one. He gave me a cheerful glance, but said nothing. "Would you please tell me —" I started again. "You are absolutely right, madam," he interrupted. "But I haven't explained my business yet," I brought out while he was already talking to others.

"Excuse me, madam," I said to an elderly lady in a pink dress patterned in big cornflowers. She lifted her kinky grey head from her papers and gave me a gloating look, drawling: "Didn't your parents tell you not to play hide-and-seek in the basement!" — and I saw it was the schoolmistress I had had in the sixth grade. "I have a college degree already, don't you know?" I even stepped back. "I know, dear, but the principal has abolished all degrees. So where's your apron?" And her plump form emerged from behind her desk. I shot past her, back into the hall, and pushed the other door open. He was standing in the room, his arms stretched out to me. "Didn't you see at once you were to enter here?" he said in a tenor voice. "I'm waiting. Come,

we'll make love " *I was drawn to him. My whole body screamed, "Yes, darling!" "Come,"* he repeated, *his strong neck tense. But my teacher was standing at the opposite wall, and he had just said the same to her, as I could tell by her maudlin countenance. "How could he?" I said to myself, knowing all the time that he could and that she could not see me, and that when it started I would not know that she was feeling the same thing at the same time as I was.*

"Come, love," he called again, and I clung to him with a moan.

I wonder which it was – whether my dreams foretold that Victor would leave me soon, or he left me because I had such dreams. Not that I ever told him about my dreams. He didn't know about the cracked wallpaper, either – the divan covered it. But he must have had a subconscious awareness of them.

I hate this uncertainty more than anything else. It frightens me more than darkness did when I was a child. I think I was afraid of it because I didn't know what to be afraid of in the dark. I can drive away the fear of something particular – not the fear of obscure, shapeless things. If only Victor had said we had to part because he didn't love me any longer, or hated to be an adulterer – anything, however painful it might be – I'd have overcome the blow. But there was no blow. There was a suffocating fog like the one I saw in my yard once when I was a little girl. White and solid, it enveloped the house entrance. I saw it out of the window, but when I ran into the yard, it receded to the sandpit, and I ran to get it. I wanted to wallow in this fog, but when I got to the sandpit, it had receded in two directions. Now it was far in front, and back at the door out of which I had just run. It was like that again now.

A month after we first met, Victor disappeared for a whole week. Or maybe it had started earlier and I was overlooking the dangerous symptoms. I had enough to do keeping my studio tidy – trying to prevent it from throwing my skirts and sweaters about, from storing my dirty dishes in the kitchen sink, and keeping the fridge full for the day Victor came.

My studio repaid my attentions with the soft yellow glow of its walls, the dazzling white of its window sills – it seemed to grow bigger, in fact. It was trying to prove we were happy, the two of us, on our own, and a man was the last thing we needed. But I was miserable with no Victor around. Sure, I had at least one desire entirely my own. The apartment could not stifle this one. On the contrary, it felt the power of my desire, which overturned its value scale and destroyed the hierarchy it had imposed on everything it contained. The books lost their primacy and came under the jurisdiction of the new divan, conspicuous in its imposing nakedness, I hated to recline in divans, so I brought a stool from the kitchen, sat on it across the coffee table, and talked to the divan.

"Know what," I said to it, "back at college, I wrote an essay on Copenhagen structuralism, a very interesting linguistic trend. Universalism's fascinating. Just look, the category of case is intrinsic in all languages, even when it seems absent. It is simply latent. I think we can't find a better proof that a proto-language existed, don't you see?"

I must have been saying the wrong things. After my lectures, the divan looked even more conspicuously naked. So I changed the subject to tell it about women's contribution to the arts. I went as far as the Silver Age, and saw the air in my studio was growing even more forbidding. I couldn't see the cracked wallpaper behind the divan, but I was aware of the oppressive greyness penetrating through it – my studio's original greyness. The phone rang, and the air at once became sweet and yellow.

"Hullo," I screamed.

"What're you screaming for?" said the surprised receiver in Jerry's voice. "Just finished another essay, 'Erotica as Death's Superconductor'. I think I'll read it to you now."

"Right now, over the phone?"

"Why not?" said the receiver in a flat voice. "In fact, I meant to drop in. I miss you," it added tenderly.

"I'm not well," I mumbled.

"Then you shouldn't be alone. What do you need? Aspirins? A painkiller? Want me to wrap you in mustard plaster?" He got excited at the idea.

"No!" I screamed in flight.

"O.K., I'll come right over."

I changed the subject with amazing agility.

"That essay of yours, what is it about?"

"You and me. I see it now, why you're treating me this way. It isn't my fault, or yours. There's a third person between us."

I heaved a sigh of relief. I was tired after this week of wandering alone in the fog of guesses and psychological analysis, vainly trying to catch it in my palm, and sculpt it into a definite shape. Here was Jerry, with his analytical mind – the best man to explain Victor's conduct to me. I was not cruel enough to talk about it myself. But if he knew he knew. So much the better.

"What do you mean?" I cried impatiently.

"It was only a random guess at first, but now, alas, I know it."

"How did you guess?"

"I can't explain it in two words. I better come and read you the whole thing."

I hesitated. Too great was the temptation to understand it all in a matter of an hour. But then, Victor might ring within that hour while Jerry was on his way, and explain it better than any essay would do. But what if he didn't? I'd be alone again in this evasive fog.

"See, Jerry, I like to be alone when I'm not feeling well, but I'd like the gist of your essay."

"All right," he gave in with a sigh of disappointment. "See," his voice dropped to a whisper, "I've long noticed something was wrong with you. You seem not your own self. I'm afraid for you. Don't panic, baby – I think death is after you. He's the third person I meant."

"Wha-at?"

"Easy, darling. You're not the one he's looking for. It's me he's after, through you. The thing is –"

"The thing is that such tricks don't work with me, you blackmailer!" I shouted.

"Can't you see my psychological mould requires –"

"It requires sponging on others!" I screamed at the top of my voice, and threw the receiver down.

There was no getting away from Jerry. The phone rang again.

"Well?" I asked ominously.

"Hello," Victor said merrily. "Wanted to drop in the other day. Took the ring line in the metro – and suddenly saw I was back in the station I started with. So I got out and went home. Can I come now?"

"All right," I said with feigned indifference, and added, God

The Studio Apartment

knows why, "Press the bell button as hard you can. Something's wrong with it."

"What do I want with the button? I'll force the door!"

I put down the receiver, swept the fluffy grey balls from under the sofa, and dashed to the kitchen to make up my face. I quickly painted the features he liked most – the long-eyed Egyptian visage, changed into my best underwear and posh new negligee, and took up my observation post at the kitchen window. A taxi came half an hour later, and a giant red-coated blonde emerged. Five minutes later, a little old gentleman trotted by in his yellow shoes and grey coat. The bell rang as I was wiping the television. I cast a quick glance in the bathroom mirror on my way, and liked what I saw. I ran to the door and threw it open – it was the guy next door.

The stench of long-unwashed flesh swept over me as he stepped into the hall. "Hullo, Sonya," he brought out. "Listen, I'm ill, and not a kopeck for my medicine. A fiver'd do."

"Three's enough," I snapped, diagnosing his disease by his shaking hands. Four hours later, I realised Victor wasn't coming. It was sheer torture to cry with no compassionate soul around, so I went to the bathroom to cry before my mirror, which kindly reflected my Egyptian face with mascara running in dark streaks off my almond eyes.

Now I know my apartment chased Victor away so it could get complete control over me. I didn't know it then, and thought it was just a misunderstanding. I thoroughly weighed all the pros and cons, and did something I had always thought indecent – I phoned his office. I knew he was often held up there until late at night. He sounded embarrassed.

"Ah, it's you! Here I am, drudging away – lots of things to do. Ill? No, no, I'm O.K. Call a bit later."

The fog was seething out of the receiver, and would not take a definite shape. I tried to seize it with my palm.

"Listen, you have no obligation to me, none at all. I want you to know that. If you don't want me, just say so. I'm not going to throw a scene or anything, and I'll never call you again. But I've got to know where we are."

"We're right here," the fog burst out of the receiver in a thick cloud.

"I mean it!"

"So do I. I'll call you later. I promise. Ah, Mary, it's all right. I'm finishing. Just a few lines left."

"Victor, I know you are alone in the room!"

"This chair, please. Just a moment. I'll call you later. Understood?"

"Are you talking to me?"

"Sure. Bye."

Now the receiver splashed same busy signals in my face. I put it down, but the fog would not lift. It nested inside me, and stuck in my throat, stopping my breath. A few days later it began to break up, as the fog travelled down into my chest, hurting my nipples.

... It's as if I were standing alone in the kitchen of our old Lenin Avenue flat, and have to get to the yellow room, which I can reach only through the garbage chute. I open it, hold my nose, and stick my head down. The noodles! The noodles I dumped down during lunch, when Mum wasn't around, stick to my cheek. I jerk my head up – but it has become wedged in. I can only crawl down, so I do, trembling in disgust. I'm standing in the kitchen, watching my shoulders and chest disappear in the chute, then my kicking legs in their new shiny shoes. I heave a sigh of relief, and run into the yellow room.

The fog that came out of the phone receiver and got down into my breasts through my throat was getting more solid with every passing day. The pain was worse and worse, and the rest of the fog in my throat made me sick.

Here we are, Mum and I, in my doctor's reception room. God knows why, the doctor has the face of Nurse Lydia. I'll be having my tonsils removed.

"Will it hurt?" I ask Mum.

"Not a bit!" the doctor says indignantly as she gets hold of my head with her right arm and nestles it in the bent left one.

"Should she have anaesthetics?" Mum asks in an ingratiating little voice.

"Why, this is simple surgery! She doesn't even have to lie down," the doctor snaps as she sticks a hairy fist down my throat.

"I wonder why Lydia has a hand like a man's," I'm thinking.

The doctor snatches at something in my throat, and tears it off. I scream with the pain, biting at her hairy paw.

The Studio Apartment

Soon I saw that the fog had at last acquired a shape inside me – a shape quite undesirable for a woman in my position, with no husband. I still hoped it was a mistake, but this hope was more ephemeral than the fog in me.

Fog outside, fog around, fog inside – too much really. So I saw a specialist to find out which fog was the more tangible. It was the inside one – seven weeks old.

So the something that had entered me without my will had an age. That was all it had – it had no sex yet, no features – nothing. I wondered what to do about this indefinite thing which desired, for some unknown reason, to become part of me. It had taken me unawares. I had never gone through anything like this when I was married. My mother-in-law made me see a doctor, and he said I had a disorder of some kind or other. Now I saw medical science knew no more about these matters than I knew why Victor had left me.

Peculiar things were happening to my body. It swelled more with every passing day. The something that had stolen into my flesh was not merely using it as temporary home but was adjusting it to some mysterious needs, of which the main one was living space. The things it was doing to me resembled what I had been doing to my studio – only I was agoraphobic, and my foggy lodger, claustrophobic. This little something, or rather, nothing, was painstakingly rebuilding its temporary dwelling in the dark recesses of my body. All the medical books told me that it had no lungs yet, but it was breathing, and blowing me up like a soap bubble. Not that you could see my bulging belly. It would show about two months later, so now I was the only one to know that I was no longer myself but a bubble bloated with a little stranger's breath. Funny as it may seem, this ephemeral feeling had something pleasurable about it, distantly recalling my crazy flight on the carousel.

It's as if my little girl were ill. They say there's only one way to save her – by burying her for the night with her face wrapped in chloroformed cotton wool. I'm afraid she won't survive this night, but they say it's an old, well-tested folk treatment, and they all went through it when they were kids. This argument persuades me, and they wrap her little face in cotton wool, and her tiny body in a cloth. They're deceiving me! "Unwrap her, quick!" I cry, but they show me a paper, saying I've just signed this contract of my own accord to assume the whole responsibility for the outcome of their experiment. They carry my baby away, her feet dangling in their red knitted booties.

My secret was making me burst. I had to share it with someone. With whom? I didn't trust anyone enough. The only person to share it with without any risk of inviting unwelcome confidences in return, was myself. My handbag mirror was too small to keep me company, so I went to the bathroom to talk to the mirror there. The face in it was tense and waiting.

"Well," I snapped. "Satisfied?! Here's love for you."

The face in the mirror made a tearful grimace.

"Cry now! That's all you can do," I mocked.

She had pulled herself together, and was contemplating me with hatred. It frightened me — a quarrel was the last thing I wanted.

"Easy, darling," I brought out. "What are we going to do?"

A quarter of an hour later, I left my bathroom in a much better state — not because I liked my choice but because I had made a choice at all.

Now I had to implement my decision. I had a college friend seven years older than I was, with two kids and considerable experience in such matters. So I phoned her and described my problem, after I was subjected to a torrent of reproach for keeping so long out of touch.

"How on earth did you get yourself pregnant?" she sounded really astonished.

"It somehow never occurred to me I could," I sighed. "Does it hurt?" "It does — in a regular hospital, but I have a friend who has a nurse friend. She'll do it all, for a sum."

...It's as if I were washing up in my kitchen. Victor enters all of a sudden, wearing a posh grey suit I've never seen on him. He quietly comes up from behind and embraces me. The floor is shaking under my feet, and I drop the cup I'm washing. With a happy sob, I lean into his strong arms.

A week later, I was struggling upstairs, my sweaty palms clutching at the bannister, every step a little whimper. Surprisingly, a disembowelled body was much harder to lift to my third floor than a body bloated with fog. Void was heavy. It trembled, clawing on me from within, eager to flow out as tears. But I hated to waste it on this deserted staircase, and could only afford an occasional whimper.

I made it to my door at last, unlocked it, and dashed to the bathroom for a good cry. The void that entered me this morning in the clinic burst out at last.

"They've cheated me!" I screamed to my reflection, which jerked its head and made faces amid peals of squeaky laughter. "Played a trick on me!" I was shouting. "They took my money and didn't give me any anesthetic!"

The face in the mirror turned purple, with slit eyes under swollen lids. I couldn't stand the sight anymore, and dragged myself to the other room. The void kept trembling inside me, anxious to pour out in words. I dialled my friend's number. She sounded enthusiastic.

"You home already? You'd be laid up for three days in that stinky hospital without my connections."

"They've cheated me," I said in a dull voice.

The void that had filled me during the surgery was getting stronger and more demanding. The bathroom mirror talks got longer and longer, but they weren't enough. The void needed a formidable sacrifice, so I allowed Jerry to come almost every day. We sat in the kitchen, with all the four gas burners in a merry blaze, lounging in the warmth and our intellectual refinement.

"I adore antiquity, I see the world as the Hellenes did," Jerry moaned.

"I don't. Greeks were too perfect, to my liking. Look at their statues – not a single blemish to them! Theirs is the perfection of death. Any progress is impossible at this level of finite perfection. I think their culture died because it was too good to be true. They had nowhere to go. I prefer Egypt."

"Right! Egypt, with its impassioned mutual attraction of life and death, this huge mystery play of sensuousness in its perpetuum mobile! If I believed in reincarnation, I'd say you were an Egyptian priestess of love and death."

My void thoroughly enjoyed this last sentence. I turned to look out the twilit window. It was snowing. My companion slipped out of the bathroom, invisible to Jerry, went through the glass, clung to it on the outside, and stared at us with her preternatural Egyptian eyes.

"O Lord, how lovely," Jerry sighed as he stretched his hands about the gas stove. "Yea, lovely," I echoed.

We were really enjoying it, the four of us – me, Jerry, my companion and my void.

At night, when I had no Jerry and no bygone eras to feed my void on, it devoured the substance oozing from the wallpaper cracks, however solidly my divan covered them.

Just think that I was ready to love it, this poor, drab apartment – all scarred by its previous life. I offered it a chance to forget what it had been before I changed the oppressive grey of its remembrances to yellow, the best color under the sun. Why did it repulse me, with my love? Why this recurring grey, oozing into the room through its barely discernible cracks?

...It's as if I were alone at last! I put on my slippers and dash out of the red room and into the yellow. The dinner table is in its center, I don't know why – right under the chandelier shining with all its eight bulbs. My pediatrician is standing at the table in a long oilcloth apron, dismembering a huge pig carcass, her apron and hairy arms crimson. She spots me before I slip out, and whispers: "Wait in the surgery. I'll call."

"But I'm O.K. I've been taking my antibiotics."

"Don't tell lies, little girl. You want this place to crawl with mice?"

"But I sweep the floor every day."

"And you are afraid of a little operation? A big girl like you!"

"Will you give me pain-killers?"

"It won't hurt a bit. Go now."

And she snatches at her carving knife again.

...They are showing me a paper, saying it's a contract I've signed to assume all responsibility for their experiment. I try to prove it's a misunderstanding – they've got it all wrong, I never signed it! But they say my sixth grade principal has confirmed the authenticity of my signature, and if I persist, they will disclose that I've run out of soapy water and don't have anything to make bubbles of.

...A fluffy grey ball was jerking under my bed, and I gazed at it, squatting. I couldn't sleep with these dust balls under the bed – the spot they liked most. This was the largest I'd ever seen. It fascinated me. I touched it with my palm, and it clung to it. I clenched my fingers, rose, took it to the bathroom, and drowned it in the toilet. Then I went back to bed.

The Studio Apartment

...A huge yellow sun was floating above the meadow, and I laughed and ran to catch the sun. I made leaps, suspended in the air for some moments, then landed, made another jump, and ran in the sweet, resilient air.

...I scream, and they pay no attention. They have wrapped my little girl so tight that only her feet in their red booties are showing. I implore the principal to tell them that though I was untidy in class, I always did fine in math. She gives a reluctant nod, and it makes them hesitate. Here, Jerry comes in to tell them he is my lover and that his ex-wife will confirm it because she has always admired him as a sex partner. I'm merely shy and can't admit it, because Egyptian frescoes are afraid of mice scratching at their stucco. This testifies to the authenticity of my signature. They give a triumphant laugh, and carry my baby off.

...Victor is squeezing through the crowd, in his posh grey suit, away from me – and I can't call out because I'm wearing my old wine-red bathrobe, and I can't put on the new one because I'll have to open the wardrobe to get it, and see the face I detest in its mirror, and it will show even through a thick layer of powder.

...Now I'm walking along the Lenin Library basement corridor, empty, with thick humming yellow pipes along the walls, and locked steel doors at long intervals. The door I need isn't here. I know the one I need will be open and will lead into the room where I'll get some papers my boss wants. The humming suddenly stops in the pipes, and I understand that I've missed my door. I turn back and push at every one. One door opens, I bow and enter.

It's empty but for a kitchen stool on bare cement floor, with Jerry astride it. "O Lord, how lovely," he says, his hands uplifted, then moves to me with the stool. "No!" I scream. "Yes," he groans lustily as a small grey spider dashes from under his right foot. I jerk back, leaning against the locked door. "Fresco, my fresco, come!" he mutters deliriously. His hooknosed face grows bigger and bigger, covered in grey pallor. I give a sob, rush at him and drum my fists against his hateful, ratlike face, growing ever paler with terror and amazement.

Translated by Tatyana Butkova and Jean MacKenzie

Published in Russian in *A Mile of Death, a collection of three women writers,* L.Fomenko, N.Gabrielyan, E. Allaverdons. Tver, 1992

Russia's First Feminist Journal

It is called *Transfiguration* and its first issue marked the beginning of the feminist movement in Russia. Published by the feminist club of the same name it looks at the problems caused by the disrupted harmony of the sexes in the modern world.

The first attempts at introducing order on planet Earth were undertaken by women back in pre-historic times. Matriarchy was eventually replaced by patriarchy, which is seen today as the historical failure of the female order. But patriarchy gained only a "Pyrrhic victory" which brought in its wake bloody wars, ecological problems, and neglect of culture. Isn't it time to start looking for a balance of male and female forces, for a harmony of the sexes?

Women are descended not just from Eve (femininity) but from Sofia (wisdom) as well. In her essay "Sofia's Spirit Descending Prior to Creation" Natalia Krymova shows that sex, personified by Eve, was only the second distinctive feature of women, the first being the sign of wisdom, or Sofia, which appeared even before the division of the sexes and which was bestowed on the woman at the moment of creation. This Sofia principle was later suppressed in women. Whereas the biological tragedy of the woman is not the end of the world, the Sofia principle can very well bring this end about. "The world deprived of femininity will soon become as hell," says Vladimir Mikushevich in his essay "The Swan Song of the New Being".

The first issue of the journal reviews the key works of Western feminism, and carries an essay by Dr. Tatyana Klimenkova, the ideologist of the feminist club *Transfiguration*. Much attention is paid to the development of feminism in Russia which is seen as an interpretation of the world from the woman's point of view. The literary section contains stories dwelling on all aspects of female nature. There is an intelligent and perceptive article on women's literature by Nina Gabrielian, and poetry by Nadezhda Maltseva and Olga Koltsova.

The first issue of *Transfiguration* has been compiled and edited by the writer Olga Tatarinova, the second issue by the writer Nina Gabrielian whose stories you will find in this issue of *Glas*.

Irina Kurskaya

Pelevin's talent for the fantastic and the grotesque and his sparkling expressiveness put him in the forefront of Russian literature.

Index on Censorship

Trained as a cosmonaut for the Soviet space programme, the hero of Victor Pelevin's novel *Omon Ra* – his name combines the Russian word for special police force and the Ancient Egyptian sun god – finds that his mission to the moon develops unexpectedly, and builds to a bizarre conclusion. Presented with *The Yellow Arrow*, a remarkable short fictional portrayal of a country in turmoil, it reveals the talent of a major new Russian writer.

ISBN 1 899414 00 2

From good bookshops, or directly from Harborn Publishing 58 Harbord Street London SW6 6PL

UK £ 6.99 net

One of the most exciting of Russia's young writers.
Daily Telegraph

Victor Pelevin
Omon Ra
with the novella *The Yellow Arrow*

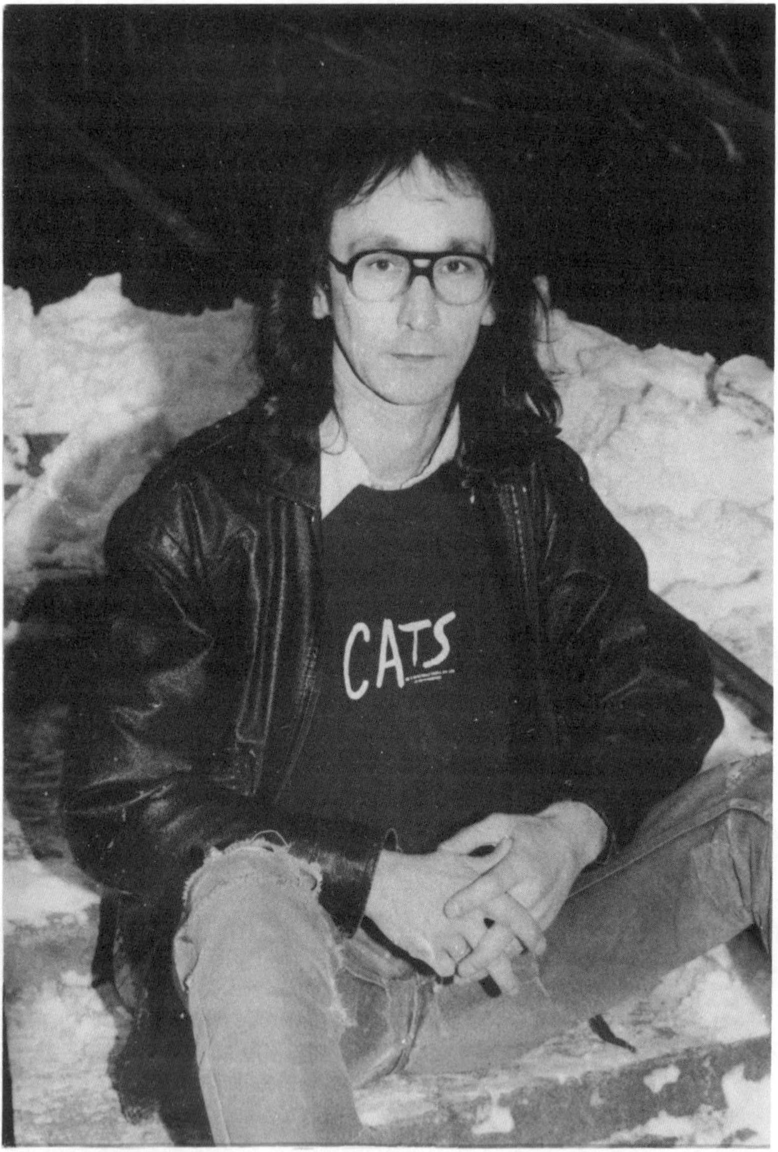
CATS

Ergali GER
Electric Liza

Ergali Ger

1

When I was seventeen I used to go around in narrow technicolour patched Wranglers, looking like a grasshopper or a late-hatching chick. I lived on S... Boulevard in Moscow, in a fifth floor flat above the then famous basement cafe called the "Squirrel". It was famous for its clientele who used to gather around a huge electric samovar, which sat enthroned like a Buddha on a low table in the corner. It was self-service – you paid three kopeks for the first cup, and after that you could sit there the whole day drinking free fragrant tea and measuring the hours by the police patrol which would appear in the doorway of the basement at a quarter to every hour. Any casual visitor would always want to come back, the police being no exception: people treated it as their home, and for cafes in this country that was pretty unusual, and, naturally frowned on. Dilapidated ancients, one-track-mindedly gibbering on about economics or the Book of Job, shuffled from table to table; adolescent dopeheads shocked and horrified the provincials; long-haired hippies read English paperbacks or deloused each other, while polite clean-cut gays, who would give anything in the world for a heart-to-heart talk or a fresh marzipan roll, pined away quietly.

Now everything was different: the hippies had gone – they were replaced by deranged, short-legged punks. The marzipan rolls had gone too, as well as the garrets, where we shared unsterilized needles, – and I was now living not above the "Squirrel", but above the dry-cleaners it had been turned into five years ago. Either it was too cosy for us and had a corrupting influence on our ability to cope properly with all the trials and tribulations of the Great Cause which the country was fighting for, or it was simply considered unprofitable, no one knows. No one was told anything, as you'd imagine, and in such cases there was no one you could ask, and no one to explain to that as far as we were concerned with our youth and the nearest wine shop the "Squirrel" was entirely viable. Such things as that are dealt with here impersonally and quietly, as if of their own accord, according to the logic of their own development, as it happens in nature, – the "Squirrel" brought about its own demise, and was transformed into a dry-cleaners' as a diaphanous butterfly becomes a caterpillar.

That summer I finished school and was deeply distressed about the need to do something about it, for the sake of my parents, such as write a magnum opus or simply enroll in a college. I chose the latter which I still regret to this day.

That summer my parents had gone off to the country, leaving me to "study in town", and I "studied" with all the unspent ardour of youth. I'd get up at half past eleven or thereabouts, wake up my equally assiduous friends, then we'd take back our empties to the Palashev Market (which isn't there any more either), and go on to have breakfast at the "Squirrel" – sometimes I'd wake up alone and sometimes with Tanya Gushchina, the star of my youth, or else wake up Christ knows where: but it made no difference – in the morning all roads led to the "Squirrel", and from there everyone would crawl in all directions like crabs. Once into the mixer you could end up almost anywhere, even in Leningrad, or in some high class country house. Or even in the local nick. And Tanya Gushchina, the star of my youth, once woke up in Togo a married woman, or rather one of the "wives" of a local official in a department dealing with culture and cooperation. But obviously things like that were well out of the ordinary; more often we'd hang around aimlessly in the "Squirrel", frozen in expectation of a miracle to save us from boredom and the stagnation of existence. You could even say the whole of my youth, and not just mine, was the stubborn expectation of a miracle. Of course these happened at times, but somehow they weren't the right sort – with us body triumphed with amazing regularity over mind, so that in the idealistic fog of our world views was silhouetted the hairy snout of reality – a daunting sight, it must be said, not at all miraculous, as I have realized after the passing of so many years. The things that happened to me were all like the events which the following story is based on: in it, as you will see, there is nothing miraculous, apart from the fact that it all really happened, and passed along with my youth.

2

I sat in the "Squirrel", suffering from acute financial insufficiency, and half listened to a discourse on the similarity between the short story as a literary genre and the sexual act – the author of this extraordinary discovery was Voldemar, a handsome man with painted eyelashes, – when I noticed that someone was looking at us in open amazement: I followed this gaze and caught a smile, which gleamed in that basement like a gold fish in muddy water. She was standing impatiently in the queue for cakes at the counter, looking curiously from side to side and doing the traditional acquaintance dance, only no one had as yet managed to take up the challenge. A little hippy bag (or a large purse, I wondered?) was dangling round her bronzed neck. And no one had yet managed to take in her bag either, although the cafe's atmosphere had become noticeably electrified: in her pale blue eyes, indeed in all her vigorous appearance there could be felt something very encouraging – provincial friendliness, visible flamboyance, a great readiness for energetic exchange with her external environment – I sensed her electricity in myself, because I got up and went to the counter like an electrician going out on a call.

"Hi, how are you for cash?"

"Okay thanks, I'll make it home somehow," she retorted eagerly. "Do you always count other people's money?"

"No," I lied. "Only sometimes. Not when I want to get to know someone. Only when I want some breakfast. But this is just an amazing coincidence. I desperately want to have breakfast with you: just the two of us, intimacy and trust, not to mention the breaking of bread. The joint partaking of food brings people closer together, like any other physiological act. I'm afraid I haven't got any money. I'd wait till I had some, only you might be in an advanced state of starvation by then..."

And this went on for about three minutes. To break the ice.

"And what about your friend, doesn't he offer you joint acts?" she asked, having listened politely to my entire spiel.

"You like him?"

"Not a lot actually," she admitted, then looked suspiciously at me: "what about you?"

"Well actually we have problems..." I admitted. "He's a serious kind of bloke, and he calls me a womanizer."

"Dear, dear, dear..." she twittered reproachfully, softening. "Well yes, of course it must be difficult for you to find a common language..."

But then we found a common language very quickly. She wanted to look like a grown-up city girl, and it must be said, she didn't make a bad job of it, she really tried, although of course she hadn't a clue about city style – and thank God she hadn't; there was none of that anaemia, boredom or bitchiness, instead there was a lively and daring provincial girl, quivering beneath her grown-up's dress, through which two very girlish breasts poked like columbines. I wanted to touch them, they drew me like electricity attracts a naked wire, but I restrained myself; we still hadn't crossed that rubicon by the time we got to the front of the queue.

Her name was Liza, it was a name that suited her, it too had something electric about it. She had finished her ninth year at school and had been with her sister, who was a boring old maid, on holiday in the Crimea. Now she was on her way home to Novogrudok (wherever that was) while her sister was going to Minsk to work on the student building project organized by her teacher training college. So they were just passing through Moscow, and that evening they'd be on the train and it would be bye-bye big city, bye-bye happy holidays in the sun away from mum and dad! It's good that she got clear of her sister, who was still languishing in the queue to the Pushkin Museum, queueing up for culture, while she managed to make four mistakes in the name Hemingway... I wondered how old she was, fifteen? Oh, sixteen...

"Are you hard-up or something?" she asked with a curiosity that could have been either genuine or feigned, when I'd eaten my half of the sandwiches and she her half of the cakes. We looked each other in the eye, swapped plates and burst out laughing. At the next table, meanwhile, Voldemar was taking great pains not to pay us any attention. I said no, I wasn't hard-up, on the contrary, I was well-provided for and wealthy, otherwise why would I be treating myself to breakfast? – poor people are proud, whereas I was comfortable and carefree, that was the in thing nowadays, didn't she know? – Liza listened as I chewed my sandwiches and told her I lived in this very house, on the fifth floor. I had some great music, my parents were away at the dacha, all you could ask for, it was just that all my weekly pocket money had gone, gone and not come back.

"You're not just carefree, you're cynical too," said Liza. "What do you mean 'all you could ask for?'"

I replied that I meant "that" too, but not only that; some girls wouldn't mind a couple of days in a house overlooking the Kremlin, trying out a different kind of life, after all that's the sort of thing they like, girls, and personally I didn't see anything wrong with that. Liza smiled. Slowly but surely we breakfasted and found a common language, then went walking in the side-streets near the Arbat – she had to see the Arbat, in those days I loved walking down the Arbat with the girls I loved, and in those days I loved any girl who I could get down to the Arbat – that was the kind of place it was. The side-streets were empty and hot, and Liza in her smart blue dress fluttered along the grey asphalt like a Chinese butterfly. We had a glass of champagne in the "Adriatica" cafe, which was also quiet and empty except for two small negroes, embassy chauffeurs, pretending to be rich foreigners, and it was there I kissed Liza on the ear – she had a milky, exquisitely fashioned ear, and as she burbled on and told porkies about the social life in the Crimea, I kissed her and thought, how lovely that tender, tiny, warm, radiant and very erogenous ear was, how well it defined a woman and how basically good it was. These and other thoughts I spoke aloud and capped them with an invitation to lunch at my place. Liza was both astonished and amused:

"But a certain person was complaining he had no bread at home and that he hadn't eaten for three days, if I'm not mistaken."

"We don't live by bread alone," I replied. "We'll get some meat and greens, and a couple of bottles of champagne or white wine, preferably the latter, and then you can play the hospitable Moscow housewife, young, beautiful and successful," I added, seeing her quizzical expression.

This was a somewhat delicate moment. I explained that a party such as this wouldn't work out any more expensive than a decent lunch for one in any Moscow cafe. And it wasn't just that the hand of the giver for Christ's sake I fancy you and I don't want to seem like some alphonse in front of you (– I hope at least you know what an alphonse is? – there you are, you see, you really aren't that stupid and let's not talk about that meat.)

"I'm an alphonse not because I let women pay to have lunch, although in that respect I've no prejudices – I'm an alphonse because I take more than I give in love, and why that is I don't know. It's probably because I'm so receptive to beauty, goodness and soulfulness – other people's beauty, other people's goodness, other people's soulfulness. God knows..."

"That must be the champagne talking," I added.

"In that sense I'm an alphonse too," said Liza. "So don't upset yourself."

She shook the contents of her bag onto the table, counted her money, and said she accepted the invitation to be my guest, wetnurse and housekeeper and that we had four hours and fifteen rubles to do everything in and with.

With limits like these and a girl like this it would have been a crime not to fit everything in. I had no doubt that the task we had set ourselves would be carried out worthily.

3

Meat and potatoes were cooking in the kitchen, and in my room – my parents had been sensible enough to lock theirs – in my room with its view of the Moscow boulevard fading into the bluish Parisian smog sang Elton John, anachronistically sweet, and Bulgarian tomatoes, laced with salt, pepper and onions, mingled their juices with sour cream. I sat alone on a sofa drinking Riesling. Liza had just rushed to the shower – she said she was too hot – but before that we had been kissing in the kitchen and on the sofa, and now I was completely overcome. It was time to take the initiative, I drank Riesling and prepared to do so, I even went into the kitchen and turned down the heat under the saucepan. So, I thought, going back into the sitting room and sitting on the sofa... Liza was splashing under the shower, and I saw her quite clearly, splashing naked, carefully drawing a soapy channel round her breasts and washing her supple athletic body. All the girls in Novogrudok loved gymnastics. So...

"There's someone's dressing gown here, can I put it on?" Liza shouted from the bathroom, and I shouted back that she could, surprised by her effrontery and cosmopolitan bravado – she was pretty self-confident for a sixteen-year-old from Novogrudok.

"This is an improvement!" she said, coming out barefoot in my mother's dressing gown, happy and refreshed. "How's the meat?"

"Yours is fine." I replied. "As for what's in the kitchen, it started to burn so I turned the heat down."

"Ugggh... you should be ashamed of yourself."

She put out her leg and bared it almost all the way up. My heart missed a beat and I threw up my arms in shame: I couldn't have thought of anything more coarse and ridiculous than the word "meat". It was a slender, finely shaped leg, more mature and substantial than the body itself; suddenly I realized that this girl had only just begun to develop her beauty, and that genuine beauty would not come to her for a long time yet – only perhaps when some of her zest for life had died down, and that this would be a magnificent beauty, capable of manipulating men and breaking their hearts, and it would be a vengeful beauty, aware of its own value and able to apply itself, – all this flashed before my eyes, together with the bare leg, and the next moment Liza was already sitting in my lap accepting my apologies, and we drank Riesling, and I felt her body, the only trouble was that mum's dressing gown put me off a little. Good old dressing gown, it didn't arouse me in the slightest, just the opposite in fact, and I tried to explain this to Liza, basing my arguments on the absence of an Oedipus complex – she didn't know what that was, but the rational essence of my garbled explanations got across to her effectively.

"I can't take it off, because there's nothing underneath it," she admitted, slipping off my lap onto the sofa, but I followed her there whispering something passionate to her, then I was no longer saying anything – at last. Liza thrust herself at me like a little leech, this wasn't very sexy but showed her exuberant feelings. We found what we were looking for, rapid, well-placed kisses at breakneck speed and slow, full, penetrating ones – a company of tiny drummers started playing in my head, and we were on our way. Her breasts turned out to be small, firm and extraordinarily sensitive, they emitted an exciting and inimitably tender smell, more than could be said for mum's dressing gown; however, the dressing gown slipped open very easily. My hand roamed the paths of the brave and reckless, then daringly penetrated the gentle, hidden depth of her cherished inner self and Liza sighed, trembled, squirmed beneath my touch like a lizard, completely tangled in the remainder of mum's dressing gown, which was finally tossed into the middle of the room. My own clothes, meanwhile, I ripped from my body like a diving suit. Liza turned me over onto her – there was no point in our playing love games, that wasn't what we were about – and I sank in Liza like a fly in a cowpat: I sank in, floundered, pealed like a bell on victory day, then roared like a rocket, exploded like a rocket, and either from the force of the explosion or from the recoil I was thrown up on the shore. Then I came to, but remained immersed.

Then it happened all over again.

Then we drank wine and had a good time.

We'll spare the reader the details here, so as not to lead him or her into temptation. We just had a good time; our weightless bodies hung beneath the ceiling, clumsy and ruffled like worn-out overalls, while our souls got up to all sorts of mischief and teased around playfully, and were happy that they'd found each other, and were grateful to each other for the idle ease with which we got on, for the delicate twinkling and quivering of the air, for the bliss of freedom from our own shells. We had already recognized each other in the cafe, we immediately singled each other out for our lightheartedness, sincerity, our thirst for life, ability to make a chance banal meeting into fireworks, a salvo with all guns blazing, like two ships meeting on the open sea, – and we loved each other: the passion and the thrill matured in tenderness and mischief, our unearthly bodies ran with earthly juices and slumped down onto the crushed, long-suffering sofa.

There wasn't a whiff of that female post-coital languor from her – only of wine; just wine, just a feverish young body and a tiny, tiny hint of mum's deodorant which I think must have been in the bathroom.

4

On the low heat, the meat didn't so much cook as shrivel up, and we unsuccessfully tried to cut it. Then everything went dark and gloomy and things started happening at a crazy pace: four hours flashed past, and our time was up.

"Have I forgotten anything?" asked Liza, looking hastily around the room. "I'd have liked to leave something here, so I could come back."

I wanted to advise her to leave a kopek, or preferably a ruble, like the tourists do, but instead I said:

"You left a part of yourself here, you'll come back."

We kissed, like for the last time, as if outside the door of the room our kisses wouldn't be the same.

"Stay here," I said. "Don't be a fool, Liza, to hell with your sister."

"You're crazy! She'll ring mum!" she shouted in panic. "Let's go, she'll make such a hullabaloo and turn the whole of Moscow upside down!"

We left hurriedly, caught a taxi and raced to the Byelorussia Station, gaping, a bit dazed, at the bustling evening streets.

"What street is this?" asked Liza as we drove down Gorky Street. I told her.

"Great..." she sighed in disappointment, "now I've seen Moscow."

"You can see it on the telly."

"Let's try this..." She thought for a moment, and her deep blue eyes became distant and intense. "Let's say you're in my class at school, your name's Volodya Smirnov, you're in Moscow with your parents and you're staying with relatives... No, she won't believe it, the cow, no way! Or what about this: we met last summer in Artek, I really was there last summer, and tomorrow we're having a reunion of the Artek crowd, etc. etc., isn't that a brilliant idea? I'll stay the night with a girlfriend and go home after the reunion. What d'you think? The girlfriend doesn't mind! Oh yes, and remember your name is Alex, we wrote to each other after Artek. Got it?"

I nodded. We leapt out of the taxi, ran to the waiting room and found her sister, who was loping across the room on her hind legs like a brontosaurus, not knowing who to pounce on. Liza loomed up before her like a candle, and the sister laid into her with reproaches. Liza got the message, and I too, that the holiday was over, because with her sister everything was clear from the very beginning: she was a bitch through and through, a hysterical and unruly schoolma'am – a brontosaurus would have been easier to deal with. I wouldn't have described her as ugly, just the opposite in fact – her face was nice, but white as chalk and unendearing, and she was clumsy and bulky, and her dress was provincial, as was her expression. It only took Liza to mention our reunion for her sister's mascara to run, and she started waving her arms, talking about mum, God, the venereal clinic, and uttering typical provincial phrases like 'don't even think of it', 'over my dead body', 'not on your life'. Liza smiled at me painfully from afar. There was no going back. I went up, introduced myself, explained how much time and effort we'd spent preparing for the reunion, what we hoped to achieve by this undertaking, traditionally carried out under the aegis of the All-Union Board of Scout Troops, of which I was honoured to be a member, rebuked Liza for her frivolousness ("yes, yes, she's very frivolous, deary me..."), – for her criminal frivolity, I added, because there is no other way to describe her unwillingness to maintain links with us, the Artek people, the great hope for the future – such links should be appreciated from an early age, don't you agree? – today they are the Artek people, tomorrow they will graduate from privileged colleges, and then... Her sister nodded, spellbound and fascinated.

"Enough playing the fool," I concluded. "Tomorrow the whole crowd will be at the reunion. You haven't shown up for a whole year – now come and show yourself at last and after that write to us every month, okay?"

Liza nodded shamefully.

"But I can't just abandon her in Moscow!" howled Zhenya (that's what this anachronism's name was), coming out of her trance.

Her expression became lost and tearful, as she pondered, then she exclaimed again that she couldn't, no way, and then she was off, sobbing, gesticulating wildly and utterly terrorizing poor Liza. I decided that Zhenya must be unhappy in life, because she was unfree, she was a captive and a stubborn mule, that even if she wanted to she couldn't turn away from her set path, a bit like an armored train or that same brontosaurus again...

Ten minutes later we had Liza's suitcase out of the left luggage and were standing on the platform by the carriage.

"To hell with it all, just jump out of the train at the first stop and come back," I whispered, finding the appropriate moment.

"And what if she sends off a telegram to mum?"

The train moved off; Zhenya squealed; we looked each other in the eye – it was obvious there was absolutely nothing we could do about it, – we sighed to each other, Liza got into the train and slipped away from me.

"Love to mum!" shouted Zhenya, and Liza was gone. We wandered down the platform to the waiting room.

"Well that's a weight off my shoulders!" said Zhenya more cheerfully, and I said nothing, even nodded, by now I was feeling sick and indifferent.

Zhenya, on the other hand, came to life, there was even a spring in her step – she didn't even seem about to pounce on anyone anymore – clearly being in charge of Liza didn't come easily to her. She asked me respectfully to help her get a ticket to Minsk. I went into the waiting room, feeling the silk banners of the All-Union Scout Troop hovering behind me, and we spent two hours queueing for tickets and conversing pleasantly about Moscow museums before finding out that there were no places on today's train, and on tomorrow's only side bunks in second class. Zhenya panicked, gasped and fussed around in front of the ticket window, while I struggled to overcome the temptation to make a run for it as she was hovering with her back to me (and screaming at the booking clerk with her front); finally we got a ticket for the next day and went to try to bribe the carriage attendants on all the Minsk trains. Zhenya hung around my neck like the burden of my sinful past. I looked on her with concern and growing astonishment: I couldn't work out how Liza's sister could have made room for such a reservoir of tears, but if her entire volume had been nothing but them, they would have dried up in the space of one hour; in fact she spent two hours non-stop watering the platforms, and a third was fast approaching.

"Right then, Zhenya," I said after we'd seen off yet another train to Minsk. "First of all stop crying. Can you just listen to me for a moment?"

"Yes," Zhenya sobbed, nodding.

"Good. Now just go to the toilet, tidy yourself up and come out again acting normally. After all you are a normal person basically, aren't you? Good. Now's the time to check this bold hypothesis. Then I'll take you for a walk around Moscow, because these attendants shy away from you as if you were a foreigner. You're not a foreigner, by any chance? Okay I believe you. And you can stay the night at my place, and have supper there too."

"No I most certainly cannot!" prattled Zhenya, and I let her set her face against it, because deep down I felt empty and indifferent. I would have gladly sent this burdensome creature with her smeared mascara to hell. Her idiocy was enough to have spoiled my day. Even outside she carried on whimpering, although she had cheered up noticeably. We took a trolleybus to Pushkin Square, then walked down Tverskoy Boulevard. I maintained a stubborn silence, even though I realized how unpleasant this was for my companion – but both she and my own gallantry were difficult to bear. This silence meant that Zhenya had to talk whether she liked it or not – this turned out to be a good thing, because her own chatter acted on her like a tranquilizer.

It was about ten in the evening, – a time of twilight, when the freshness of the air and the warmth from the stonework heated up during the day were equally pleasant and both the sleepy calm of the back-streets and the smart crowds emerging from theatre exits, and the roar of car engines, moving into gear as the traffic lights went green, – everything was somehow especially exciting and meaningful. We walked down boulevards. Zhenya was still a little tense, but talked a lot and looked keenly from side to side, taking stock of what for her was a different world. I half listened to her, occasionally stealing a glance at her, trying to understand her life or see Liza in her features. There was no trace of Liza at all, in fact there was just an ordinary face, to be more precise the face of a girl about two years older than me, with the same dreams as every other girl has, modified by the provincial teacher training college and the Moscow twilight.

So we arrived at my place, successfully weathered yet another attack of doubts and went up to the fifth floor.

"Where are your parents?" Zhenya whispered as she crept into the room.

I said they'd gone, that they'd been working for two years in the Soviet sector of Atlantis, so she could talk and behave normally.

"And all that time you've been living on your own?" asked Zhenya with both surprise and pity.

"Yes," I answered, also surprised. "So what?"

"Oh, nothing. I didn't mean..." She suddenly decided to get all confused and blush. "It's just very odd... A young man on his own... I'd probably have been scared to come here if I'd known."

She had actually succeeded in getting on my nerves.

"Oh for heaven's sake, Zhenya," I said angrily. "Just think about it: if you wanted to you could fend me off no problem, wouldn't you agree? I'm not sure which one of us is in the greatest danger. So let's not flatter each other, and let's make some supper."

This seemed to bring her to her senses. We spent the rest of the evening peacefully: desiccated meat – the food of the single young man – made Zhenya go all motherly, and after supper she cleaned up the kitchen and then the sitting room. I didn't stop her. Then we drank tea and listened to music. It was about midnight by the time Zhenya, after painful hesitation, made a superhuman effort and asked what the sleeping arrangements would be. I said there was one camp bed and one sofa available. Then I made up the sofa with clean sheets, and put up the camp bed. We spent some time discussing the intricacies of etiquette: who should sleep on the camp bed? the guest or the host? – after I had convinced Zhenya, she went off to the bathroom and I put my own sheets on the camp bed.

"Shall I switch the music off?" I asked when Zhenya returned.

"No it's all right, I don't mind it," she replied with an excitement I would describe as panicky. I said goodnight and went out.

In those days I had a habit of sitting in the bathroom reading; now I read in other isolated places but in my youth, when my heart was not so sensitive to physical exertion, I'd spend hours splashing around in the bath, reading LITERATURE and preening my steamy body. The only trouble was it was bad to smoke in the bath, the air was very damp. And I remember how that time I got in, hoping to while away an hour or two – I never went to bed before two – and at the same time wash off that hot but eventful day. My body still remembered Liza and smelt of her; I got into the bath and the hot water washed off all the smells. I said goodbye to Liza and immersed myself in my book. I can't remember what I was reading, but I remember that very soon there was a knock on the door and Zhenya's anxious voice said:

"You're wanted on the phone..."

"Tell them I'm coming..."

I quickly dried myself, put on some underpants and went into the room. I caught Zhenya diving into bed: she was wearing white panties and a white bra. It was my mate Foma, and of course the first thing he asked me was who answered the phone: Foma was as nosy as a woman. Then he said he was somewhere or other with someone or other and they were drinking and thought, why not call on me; I said no very gently, citing the lateness of the hour, Foma grunted and wished me and my charming, he hoped, stranger, who had dragged me to the phone from God knows where, a good night. I left this tactlessness on his conscience, put down the phone, put the music off and turned out the light. Zhenya was curled up on the sofa like a mouse, and she didn't even seem to be breathing. I got into the camp bed. The springs creaked, then all was quiet. Very quiet.

5

It was then that something like a game of giveaway began. Neither of us could sleep, we sighed and tossed in our beds, and the air in the room got noticeably thicker, like a viscous sickly-sweet liqueur dripping into a cup of thick coffee. Absurd erotic and even, hmmm, pornographic scenes flashed past me in that thickening air, and I didn't even try to work out how from having completely ignored my guest I had stooped to such intense and concentrated attention to her – it was all the fault of the summer night, these things happen when you're young.

Zhenya sighed and tossed on the sofa, then all was quiet again, except for the odd car far down below us outside.

So there, I said to myself, she wants it too.

She wants it too: to get up, to run her pretty plump hand through her tangled hair and call you, but she'll never do it because she's afraid and inhibited, she's never lived of her own free will and probably never wanted a free will, and if you don't help her it'll always be that way: life on the straight and narrow, slavery is the highest virtue, and tonight's agenda will be: sighs until morning, then dull sleep and a joyless awakening – she won't forgive you if you don't help her today, now, she'll never forgive you, so stop lounging around and get up.

Get up and go to her.

Still there? So you don't want her, otherwise you'd have got up ages ago, sat by her on the edge of the sofa and ever so quietly and tenderly called to her: "hey, baby, baby..." and she'd snuffle away to herself, pretending to sleep, because she's a slave, because she's afraid and ashamed of herself, and then you'd slip between the sheets, you dirty bastard, and feel the trembling of her hot body, longing for you, and only then, when there was already contact, when her ripe breasts burst like baby hares out of her bodice, and her thighs clung together magnetically, only at this point would she pretend that she'd only just become aroused... No, I seriously want her, I know what I want, everything's under control, but I don't want to take the initiative, I want her to, because I had Liza, Liza-electro-Liza, whom this little schoolma'am sent off to vegetate in Novogrudok, and lay down in her place, and may I be damned if I don't expose her hypocrisy to the end, to the very end, to the final and absolute end... Suddenly I sensed that something had changed on the sofa – there came a pleading, passionate whisper, an incoherent summoning, I caught in this whisper, measured like breakers, a single piercing phrase: COME TO ME DARLING come to me darling COME TO ME DARLING come to me darling... I couldn't tell whether these words were real or simply a figment of my imagination – I looked distrustfully into the darkness, my eyes had already got used to it, and now, I thought, I could distinguish the features of her body under the blanket, all the hillocks, folds and pits of her bed, whose whiteness softly and ghost-like percolated through the darkness – and something unfathomable, like a column of smoke, wafted in the lilac air over the sofa. It was her arm: Zhenya's agile, bare, dancing arm. COME TO ME DARLING come to me darling COME TO ME DARLING... Her arm quivered like seaweed, beckoned and called, tantalized with its entrancing passes, full of languor, passion and serpentine exquisiteness; holding my breath, I followed this magic dance, then feeling like a tiny hypnotized hummingbird, drew back the blanket, got up, swayed and went over to the sofa...

Zhenya was asleep, with the blanket wrapped up to her ears, her whisper, it transpired, was just light even breathing. I stood stupidly over her for a minute and headed for the toilet.

"Well there you go, mate..." I reproached my bird-brained member, whose caprices had caused all the confusion. The guilty party shrivelled and hung there morosely. Cockroaches warming themselves on the pipes wriggled their antennae in fright.

We answered nature's call, then I wandered back to the folding bed and plumped myself down with the firm – no, you guessed wrong – the firm intention of surrendering to a decent, thorough sleep. Take a leaf out of Zhenya's book, I said to myself, yawning luxuriously – and at that moment there came, like an echo, a sigh from the sofa. Zhenya threw off her blanket and followed in my footsteps to the toilet.

She came back and got almost too calmly onto the sofa, and I nearly fell asleep completely I was so annoyed and humiliated. Again her breathing turned into a whisper, again her fierce, passionate appeal drew every cell of my shameless organism towards the sofa, but I didn't believe this nonsense, I was falling asleep. The young schoolma'am, tired from running around museums and station platforms, was sleeping like an angel, having put her faith in the decency of a single scout leader, and so he should stop somersaulting in his couch like a pancake in a frying pan − so said the narrator, and I agreed, though I didn't believe it in my heart, but time was passing, and Zhenya's even breathing was more convincing than my argumentative dreams. As I fell asleep I continued to listen avidly to her breathing, and she'd obviously decided that I'd dosed off: there on the sofa, some kind of movement started, soft rustling sounds alternated with the smacking of lips, and her breathing now quickened, now ceased altogether, now became loud and passionate. Zhenya had really let herself go, the sofa creaked and groaned beneath her, and she tossed from side to side so wildly that I followed the demonic raving of her passions with some trepidation. Then she sat up and started swaying from side to side like a pendulum, tucking both hands underneath her; I was afraid to move, and frighten her out of this charming girly game, though my conscience was awakening and I couldn't just cold-bloodedly watch her suffer. You like it when things just fall into your lap, I reproached myself later; but now it's your move. I lurched forward, woke up and stared perplexedly into the darkness; all was quiet. Zhenya was dozing peacefully; outside a broken-down car was crawling along the boulevard, and my foolish heart thumped wildly.

I dozed off again, and almost at once Zhenya slid off the sofa. I got up too, and we crawled towards each other over the carpet, making sure each of us crawled an equal distance, then we sized each other up and roared at each other like beasts. This nonsense was put paid to by a genuine sound from the sofa; Zhenya took off her bra, stuffed it under the pillow and turned over. But by now I couldn't believe anything, especially as there was more movement from the sofa, only this time there were four arms at work − I looked to find both sisters, Zhenya and Liza, on the sofa. This was nothing surprising. This amazing twosome could have done acrobatics or synchronized swimming, judging by the number of daredevil tricks they'd introduced into their lesbian games – while I admired their coordination, it was difficult to determine whether it was sport or art. I dreamed that I was lying on the camp-bed pretending to be asleep while the girls aroused each other and looked lustfully in my direction; no, you're too harsh on these warm tender pink creatures, you've been trying their patience too long; they must have thought the same – we shared common thoughts, like water in communicating vessels – because they had frozen there on the sofa, upset by my lack of concern, and the blanket which had covered them fell picturesquely to the floor... suddenly it dawned on me in a flash that the sound of the falling blanket was coming not from my dream but from outside, from the actual night – I opened my eyes and saw the impossible: Zhenya's blanket had fallen on the floor and Zhenya herself was lying there before me in all her glory, in nothing but her knickers, like a huge birthday cake... This seemed like just another dream or hallucination. I realized I'd have to get up, otherwise she'd be offended and freeze up, but my body literally grew into that wretched camp bed – no, there was definitely something wrong here; finally I made one last desperate effort – and woke up again.

The clock said half past two. I sat up, leant back against the book case and considered my options. Zhenya was by all appearances asleep. For me, you must realize, the only chance of getting some sleep was to get a definite, unambiguous, direct and rude refusal out of her. Well, of course I knew that's how things would turn out. There was no getting away from humiliation in the situation we were in. It was by day that she was the stupid cow and I the chief of staff, but now she was a woman, Galia, the earth Mother, and she would lie there stretched out on the sofa and wait for you to stop faffing about and descend on her, and she'd wonder whether it was really you she wanted or just cucumbers and honey... I had to stop dithering. I sat and dithered.

"Are you still awake?" sighed Zhenya.
"Yes," I replied mistrustfully.
"Are you thinking about something?"
"Yes."

"What?"

"You. And why aren't you asleep?"

(Zhenya sighed, then sat up and pressed her blanket to her chest): I can't sleep... you groan and fidget... I thought maybe you'd got sick..."

"Oh, Zhenya!" I said sadly. "I must have really got sick if I'm lying here and thinking of you. Touch my forehead..." I moved over to the sofa and bent over Zhenya, she wanted to touch my forehead with her hand but I protested:

"You won't feel anything with your hand, you must use your lips," and unexpectedly even for myself kissed her on her sleepy, coagulated lips. "That's the only cure," I added, kissing her again, then muttered something else incomprehensible but convincing, you understand, because Zhenya sighed, wound her thick hot hands round my neck and descended on me. I, meanwhile, was cold as ice...

"DARLING..." she whispered. "COME TO ME DARLING..."

6

And as things turned out, I got confused. In other words I suffered a spectacular defeat. Zhenya turned out to be too languid a woman for me, her ripe, hot breasts proved unbearably succulent, and her womb ran with hot honey – basically, no sooner had I entered her than I exited again; my erotic dreams had been too much for me. Zhenya's loud, languid moans lacerated my eardrums – these moans were a plea, this was a living being groaning and pleading for help, and I, to my great shame, was powerless to do anything.

"Hang on Zhenya," I muttered, "hang on. It's gonna be all right, but I must take a breath first. Be patient, Zhenya..."

Zhenya groaned, then turned her affections and passions toward the revitalizing of my manhood, and then there was a ring at the door. Then a second. Zhenya recoiled with another groan and feverishly, with a kind of frightened howl, began to look for her knickers in the remains of the bedclothes – I wondered deliriously whether or not to open it, and that stupid howling of hers obviously decided me.

"Listen, Zhenya, get a grip on yourself. Do you really think..."

The doorbell rang again. "It's one of my mates. I'll send him on his way and you can relax. Don't worry."

Just to be sure I kissed her, put her to bed, pulled on my own underpants and went to open the door. Liza was outside, flanked by her suitcases. Seeing me, she breathed a sigh of relief.

"Greetings from Novogrudok!" With a look of despair I put my finger to my lips, and she finished in an astonished whisper: "I was afraid I'd come to the wrong flat... Who's there?.."

I beckoned to her to follow me in silence, picked up the suitcases and led her into the kitchen, closing all the doors behind me and not having a clue what to say to her and how to say it, in what culinary form to serve up her sister.

"How did you get here?" I whispered.

"It's quite simple, I got out at the first stop, in some godforbidden place called Vyazma, then came back on a local train. The metro was closed, I had no money for a taxi, then some guy gave me a lift. I couldn't for the life of me explain about that cafe of yours downstairs, then I said... Who's there? Why are we whispering?"

"Guess," I said.

Liza looked at me distrustfully, shrugged her shoulders then laughed, looking past me, and said:

"What's there to guess: you've got a woman there."

"You guessed wrong," I said sitting on a stool and sitting Liza down beside me. "It's Zhenya."

Liza's jaw dropped and she looked at the door in fear.

"Zhenya?" she whispered. "That's done it... Didn't she leave Moscow?"

"The two of you don't seem to get very far with your departures. There were no tickets, she had to get one for tomorrow. But Liza, that's not everything you know. How can I break this to you... Basically I put her on the sofa and myself on the camp bed, but then everything somehow got moved around, and..."

"Jesus," said Liza after a pause. "You mean you screwed my sister?"

I nodded.

"No, I don't believe it," she said. "That straight-laced sterlet? Did you hit her? Get her drunk? Read her poetry? No, you share your experiences, the heroic city of Minsk won't forget you."

Electric Liza

"Liza," I said, turning her to face me. "Liza baby, you know very well I need no one except you."

"Now I know," she giggled, and not very pleasantly at that. "Jesus, just like Romeo and Juliet. I've only been out the door a couple of hours and already you're screwing my sister."

It's ages since I've felt such a bastard: she'd been flitting around all night from train to train like a butterfly just to end up with a piece of scum like me. Serves you right, I said to myself. Serves you right.

"I want to sleep," said Liza. "Can I crash on the camp-bed?"

I said no. I said she was sleeping with me. Liza shook her head and replied that she was very tired and wanted to sleep, if possible alone, and if not she was going back to the station.

"Okay," I said. "Sleep on the camp-bed."

"Tell Zhenya that I'm some girlfriend of yours, just lie to her, okay? Then in the morning you can introduce us," said Liza, and her eyes sparkled, she even gave me a peck on the cheek as she saw me on my way. I went back to the bedroom miffed, feeling like a robot, not a person, and got into bed with Zhenya.

"Is that you?" she grabbed my hand and pressed it to her chest; with machine-like precision I established that the first line of defence – bra and knickers – was back in place. Thus it was that our troops had been pushed back to their original positions.

"Who was it?"

I said it was some girl I knew who'd had a row with her parents and was going to sleep on the camp bed. Zhenya sighed pitifully. Soon this other girl came in, took off her dress in the dark, got onto the camp bed and fell asleep. Zhenya, having dozed off on my chest, lay quiet for about ten minutes, started pressing her whole body up against me and then straddled me – the girl had lost all sense of shame; the trembling of her flanks was enough to arouse even a robot, and my hands, quite independently of my will, helped Zhenya off with her bra and knickers.

She raged and moaned, and her intentions turned out to be quite serious, so our love game took on quite an athletic character. Finally I coughed emphatically, gave in and laid Zhenya flat out. Her groans were rich and full-bodied, and utterly drowned out the creaks of the camp bed – and before I had a chance to jump back, Liza, the crazed thing, fell on me from above, whispered hoarsely, "right then!", then bit me very painfully behind the ear, and tore me away from Zhenya onto herself.

Zhenya leapt back against the wall with a scream.

"What the hell does she think she's doing?" she retorted angrily, but there was no one to answer her: as I lay on top of Liza I fought the urge to giggle stupidly, while Liza did her best to rape me, pummelling me frustratedly with her fists.

"But this is..." Zhenya suddenly flew into a rage and with a groan launched into an attack on my insolent girlfriend. "Go away, go away!" she hissed, rocking our little pyramid from side to side. "Get out of here, you shameless creature! What are you doing? What the hell is going on?!"

I slid passively to the floor where it was easier to giggle, but Liza doggedly stood her ground – for some time there was nothing but puffing and blowing, then I felt three rapid full-blown slaps in the face, then Zhenya rose up, lunged past me, ran sobbing about the room, finally found the switch on the wall and turned on the light.

"Ha!" said Liza, spreading her arms like a circus acrobat. "Hi, Zhenya!"

Zhenya let out a shriek, clutched her head and sat down.

"Oh my God..." she groaned. "Liza!!!"

It was one of those moments which required a doffing of caps by all those present. Unfortunately none of us had anything suitable at hand.

"Zhenya, darling, let me give you a hug in this house of grief," chirped Liza (she was in fine form, it must be said).

"Liza you cow..." Zhenya began, as the appearance of her own sister somehow even calmed her at first, but then suddenly she groaned in shame and humiliation, began feverishly gathering her clothes, crumpling them up and pressing them to her chest. She howled, obviously scared to go near the sofa, where a significant part of her toilet remained and where her younger sister was making a little nest for herself.

"What homeric passions, what veneric forms – is it really you, Zhenya? – Why aren't you teaching me morals, or is it a bit awkward without your knickers on?"

"How dare you, how dare you, you bitch!" yelped Zhenya, contorting her face, shielding herself with her scrunched up dress and approaching the sofa.

"No, I won't give them to you," said Liza, rapidly hiding her knickers, and Zhenya lunged at her in a frenzy. They both shrieked, and wool flew everywhere in clumps. I ran to break them up, and immediately it felt as if forty sharp finger- and toenails, and no fewer than sixty-four fangs were stuck in me.

I cried out in pain and only just managed to fight my way out of this mincing machine, and then Liza, shaking her sister's knickers triumphantly, flitted from the sofa to the camp bed. Zhenya, in defeat, covered herself with the blanket and burst into tears.

I was starting to feel uncomfortable standing naked in the middle of the room, so I found my underpants on the sofa and pulled them on beneath Liza's mocking gaze.

"So how was my sister? I hope she didn't disappoint you?"

"Far from it," I said, moving to the camp bed.

"Well that's fine then," she said. "I don't mind the sacrifice. Anything to make her happy."

"That's enough," I said. "I think I've redeemed myself with blood," I showed her my numerous scratches.

"Serves you right," said Liza, as she breathed on and kissed one which happened to be under my right nipple. But poor Zhenya carried on sobbing, while we licked each other's wounds.

"Listen, this won't do," I said to Liza, and we moved over to the sofa to be with Zhenya.

"That's enough, Zhenya!" said Liza mournfully, as if she were reading a funeral oration. "Zhenya, stop making a fuss!"

Zhenya roared like an aleutian sea-cow.

"Oh come on, will you, Zhenya... stop it! To start blabbing at the very moment when I discover I have a sister with a human face... Zhenya, I love you, really I do!"

Zhenya sobbed bitterly. Liza and I went to her in turn, stroked her and soothed her, sometimes exchanging skeptical glances, because we knew what she was capable of.

"Don't cry, Zhenya!" Liza said. "Don't cry, darling, I'll never do anything like this again!.. (When she heard this, Zhenya sobbed with renewed anger.) Do you want me to go? For good, I mean, to the station!" Liza gave me a crafty glance. "I'll go, Zhenya darling, but just don't you cry, okay?"

"I'm the one who's leaving..." sobbed the inconsolable Zhenya.

"I'm not setting foot in here again! It's your fault, you arranged all of this, it's disgusting and inhumane! Okay, I'm bad, I'm debauched, but I've never jumped into bed with your boyfriends and... you're heartless, you're..."

Well thank God for that, I thought, at last a breakthrough has been made. The sisters had a good set-to, while I went into the kitchen, put the kettle on, then came back and sat down on the sofa beside naked Liza, whom Zhenya thereupon shielded from my eyes with a blanket; other than that, I think they must have forgotten about me, and I too climbed under my end of the blanket. Now the three of us were sitting together on the sofa – all in the same boat.

"You squander yourself right and left, for you it's like chewing gum, and you'll wear yourself out before any real feelings come!" Zhenya preached manically. "You think I envy you? Well I feel sorry for you, yes, that's right, even though you're bolder than I am, and cheekier, and younger, you won't find any real happiness, you've already lost your chance of that!.."

Liza replied in a conciliatory tone that it was all true and she'd burn in hell, while Zhenya was born for happiness like birds were for flight, to which Zhenya replied that there was no need to be sarcastic, and that debauched as she may be (but not like Liza, God forbid!), and a little on the plump side for today's skinflint fashions and boys, she was still younger, more beautiful and spiritually richer than Liza, because she had inner peace, ideals and values, which of course both Liza and I lacked.

"You're saying you're plump?" Liza reacted indignantly, extracting the kernel of rationality from all of this baloney with magnificent feminine guile. "You – plump? Just stand up and take a look at yourself!"

She yanked off the blanket, Zhenya flinched, but I intervened just in time. Liza and I grabbed Zhenya and sat her down. She was a magnificent woman, what beautiful thighs – as for me I had been truly pleased to get to know her more intimately, and I said as much – Zhenya got all upset, cringed away, clung to the blanket, and said that Liza and I were horrible and perverted, but at this point I very gentlemanly kissed Zhenya on her breast, which was heavy like a bunch of grapes. I felt Liza's sharp nails digging in my back, and we both smiled at Zhenya, though to be honest, I didn't feel much like smiling.

Then we sat on the sofa, laid the table for tea, and took to giggling inanely and spilling tepid tea on ourselves and on the sofa. It was a time of unusual lightheartedness, as happens sometimes after extreme tension, and all of us were terribly happy about something, no one quite knew what. For instance what could Zhenya be so happy about after hearing the story of how Liza and I met and of two conspiracies against her – one at the station and one in the kitchen? – God knows, anyway she was laughing hysterically. Liza laughed too as I cleared my conscience and described my nightmares. Altogether, I reckon this entire business had had a positive effect on Zhenya. We sat there wrapped up in our easy, sensuous and joyous intimacy, and our three pairs of legs touched peacefully under the blanket. And I said that physical closeness between man and woman should ideally be seen first and foremost as one of the fundamental means of achieving spiritual closeness, as the overcoming of all those physical barriers which close a person up within himself, as a mutual coming together – in the name of spiritual closeness. Zhenya backed me up with passion in her voice, but Liza – her ability to get to the heart of the matter surprised me yet again – laughed derisively and said:

"Watch out, Zhenya, he's going to suggest we make a threesome in a minute."

"Oh no..." Zhenya stopped in mid sentence, then hastily added, "you do what you like, I'm going to sleep on the camp bed."

"That's exactly what we like," Liza remarked politely, and everyone felt sad again. I added that Zhenya, it seemed, was the only one left who hadn't tried to sleep on the camp bed, and this eased the tension slightly, but only slightly. Zhenya got into the camp bed, and, to be perfectly honest she looked upset. I switched off the light – outside it was already light – and Liza and I whispered at length under the blanket. Liza told me all sorts of stories about herself, because it was time for us to get to know each other better. Zhenya tossed about on the camp bed. A couple of times I suggested to Liza that we call her over, to which Liza replied very reasonably that it wasn't worth it, because there was no way I was going to get spiritually intimate with Zhenya.

Translated by Bob Greenall.

Published in Russian in the magazine *Rodnik*, Riga 1989

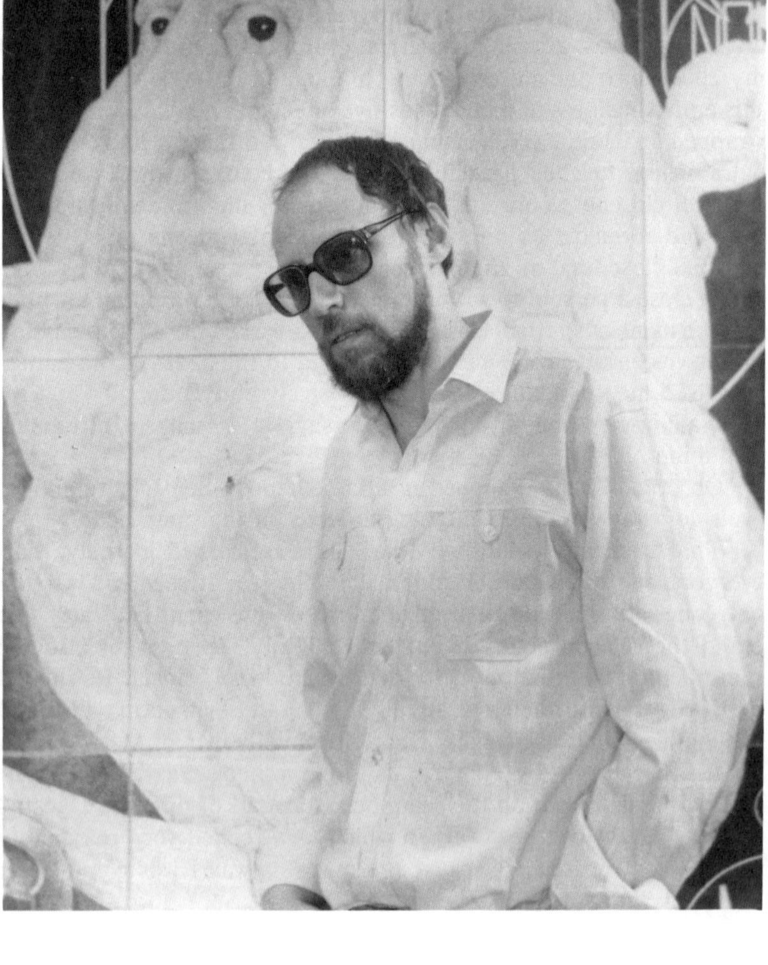

Dmitry PRIGOV
poems, drawings, thoughts

Dmitry Alexandrovich Prigov

* * *

There is no love on earth
There's tenderness and friendship
There is no friendship on earth
There's passion and desire
There is no desire on earth
There's melting and mirth, though
And melting, melting, melting, melting, melting
And weeping, weeping, weeping,
And again weeping, weeping, weeping, weeping
And mirth, mirth, and mirth!
And melting!

There is no truth on earth
There's reasoning and measure,
There is no measure on earth
There is measurement and sobriety
There's no sobriety on earth
There's decision-making, though
There is no decision on earth
There's mercy and mirth though
And mirth, mirth, mirth, and mirth, and mirth, and mirth
And mercy
And mirth

Translated by Alexander Lehrman

It's well known that you can live with many women and
    at the same time in your soul not betray that only one
How then is one to understand betrayal of the Motherland?

After all we love the Motherland not with the flesh but
    with the soul
Like we do that only one, or else we don't love her –
    and then there's no betrayal even more so

All this is just, of course, if one understands the Motherland
    to be a woman, like Blok did
But there's no justification apart from execution by firing squad,
    if she's the Mother!

* * *

When once I happened to be in Kaluga
I fell in love with a Kaluga woman

There was in her the great strength of the people
She often carried me in her arms

What about me? I come from Moscow, I'm frail and small
And here's what I said to her once in anger:

A man after all more masculine and strong
Must be, and on that I parted from her

* * *

In the bar of the Writers' Club
A policeman is drinking beer
He drinks in his usual fashion
Not even seeing the writers

They though are looking at him
Around Him it's bright and empty
And all their various arts
Mean nothing in the presence of Him

He represents Life
Manifested in the form of Duty
Life is short, but Art is long
And in their combat Life is victorious

* * *

The people after all doesn't only drink
Although not many people know that
It labors and it lives
Not like the little insects with lots of legs
And into the official press
Where they write how it works
You should read that it doesn't only drink
But that in fact it does work too.
1976

Translated by Sally Laird

Dmitry Alexandrovich Prigov

From: **Fifty Drops of Blood in an Absorbent Medium**

* * *

A frosty pattern on the glass
A drop of blood on the finger of a boy
      dressed in the elegant naval uniform
           of the Imperial Guard

A timid first-former at the blackboard:
Mummy washed the window
With her tears.

* * *

Little swastikas on the wedding sheets
A drop of blood on the forth finger.
Pure existence, like the edging
      of a rabbit-fur collar
Moscow-Berlin 1990.

* * *

A tiger's string
A bull's trunk
A drop of blood on a man's finger,
      emerging from someone else's body
Someone's future weeping.

* * *

The patter of feet running away over the roof
A drop of blood on a kitten's paw
The fate of a poet in Russia
Wondrous transformations of horror
      into triumph and back
To horror

* * *

The officer's private life
A drop of blood on the local beauty's left breast
The intense stare of invisible Mahatmas,
      translated into Russian.

* * *

The Englishman's conversation with the German
A drop of blood by the twilit monastery wall
A stone flying from the depths of Russia
    into the waters of the Atlantic
        Ocean

* * *

A drop of blood on an almost
    unmarked neck
Two hundred and fifty isomorphs
    of clearing skies
A cottage almost invisible from above
    in green Bohemia.

* * *

A head chopped off in jest
A drop of Japanese blood
    in a huge American body
The sixth day of the week and not the Sabbath –
    what is this?

* * *

Ice-cold vodka between the window frames
The faint crackle of leads
    worn bare
A lynx, turning into a girl with
    a drop of blood in the corner of her mouth.

* * *

The porcelain flaring up of pre-war
    crepe de Chine
A werewolf's drop of green blood
A lonely hunter of men's souls
    over the yellow flow
        of escaping waters

Dmitry Alexandrovich Prigov

* * *

Cigarette smoke drifting by in the mirror
An unclaimed drop of Christian blood
Huge, by all accounts, historical eons
       of other existences.

* * *

Real burning on the bends
       of a violet leather jacket
A drop of blood in an absorbent medium
Light damp breathing from an assumed
       cosmic hole between the legs

* * *

A sakura twig on the page of a Japanese calendar
A drop of blood in a teardrop on a china saucer
A thunderous hieroglyphic falling from
       a leaden storm cloud: Rome must
              be destroyed!

* * *

A bare branch outside the window
A drop of blood on a half shaved cheek
       in the mirror
The back of my head, facing the unknown
And all this is like a given fact.

* * *

A Mozart concerto
A mindless quantity of drops of blood
       sprinkled on the earth
Thus wilt thou conquer.

Translated by Alexander Lehrman
Printed by permission of the author

Self-portrait
From an interview with Dmitry Alexandrovich Prigov
poet, artist, thinker

I work with categories and symbols rather than characters and images. Traditionally, the author has something to say and his work becomes the setting for his monologue. I'm a director rather than the lead actor. I'm not present in any part of my work but at the same time I'm present in every part of it.

...Culture consists of texts, and what I try to do is manipulate these texts. I interact with these texts but only to the extent that leaves me free of them. I approach the text as close as possible while avoiding getting entangled with it too closely. My art is not confessional, as is the case with most art, the borderline between the world and me is clear-cut. I'm not a character in my works, be it poetry or pictures or installations.

...I don't deal with human emotions directly, neither am I able to identify myself with any individual feeling or idea. As soon as they become a subject of art they have to pass through certain cooling codes. The essence of my artistic activity is precisely deconstructing these feelings to show that they are basically impossible.

...Art in the medieval sense is all about bringing hidden secrets into the open. The artist plunges deep into human essence, into man's inner world and, like Orpheus, reveals this essence, this truth to the world. My "Beasts" series is a case in point.

Another trend in my work is a discourse with the dominant political context and an attempt to deconstruct it.

...Installations, in contrast to drawings, are spatial and thus can be perceived as phantoms of reality. In other words, they are simulacra or copies of nonexistent reality which are reminiscent of the existing one.

...For most artists the aim of their work is self-expression. For me it is the problematical nature of self-expression.

It may be an existential tragedy or humble submission. When all is said and done, self-expression is practically impossible, at least it is not possible on the explicit level. One can only trace a certain strategy of artistic behaviour.

...All the arts I practice are a certain poetic behaviour par excellence aiming to deconstruct various poetic behaviours. For me it is a poetic strategy to last me my whole lifetime. Writing poetry is just a part of my general artistic behaviour. My poetry should not be identified with my person. For me it is a game with images. All my various artistic pursuits collectively present my artistic credo.

...There is too wide a gap between life and art. It is far from my intention to prolong life in art or reflect life as it is. Human activity, in my view, is not an ontological phenomenon but a discourse. This is not entirely my own idea, this is the whole point of modern art today. Post-modern art is distinct from modern and avant-garde art in that the latter two are seeking to find means of self-expression among the chaos of all possible ways of self-expression, while post-modernism focuses on the problematic character of self-expression.

Like Goethe I accept the impossibility of complete self-expression as a given fact, without seeing this as a tragedy. Like him I accept life as it is without denouncing it or particularly admiring it, simply trying to classify and study its various manifestations. I'm particularly concerned with unmasking totalitarian ambitions in various discourses. One can detect the desire to rule the world in any attempt to rule the minds, particularly when the artist is being completely frank in his art. The socio-political discourse is trying to exploit a person's dissatisfaction with the state of things. The romantic-philistine discourse is trying to intensify a person's passion for self-realization. Every language has a totalitarian tendency. Each wants to be the only accepted language and thus throw a net over the world.

...My art is opposed to the mainstream, the establishment. I'm a critic and an outsider in relation to it. There is no immediate danger for me to become part of the mainstream in Russia which is still largely traditional with a preference for romantic-confessional types of art.

...Whereas visual arts everywhere in the world have made dramatic progress in their development, literature shows signs of historical fatigue. What is more, serious literature can only exist with the help of sponsors while visual arts can be self-sufficient. Literary and artistic establishments are like people belonging to different epochs. If we take prize-winning authors such as Brodsky and the classics of modern visual arts, they would be four generations apart, there is nothing to compare. This is neither good nor bad. If literature tried to overcome the times it would have to abandon the accepted forms and move in the direction of performance, talk shows, cinema. The only other alternative is a purely academic existence, book-shelf life in expectation of official recognition. I don't see any other possible role for literature. Everything that literature has attempted has already been done by visual arts before and much more effectively too.

Literature is increasingly becoming a marginal phenomenon. It no longer dominates intellectual life like in the old days when it really influenced minds. The current socio-cultural process leaves little hope for the revival of the role of literature in society. From the area where public questions were posed and solved, literature has turned into an art for art's sake solving purely literary problems.

...Love is a cultural phenomenon while sex is a natural phenomenon. Love is expressed through a set of etiquettes, of cultural behaviours, a cultural articulation of sexual behaviour. Personal communication has been disrupted everywhere in the world and the process is visibly under way in Russia as well. In the cinema, for example, a man and a woman will be shown either as sex partners or as partners in business or a certain mutual project, while their love relations as social etiquette will be completely disregarded. Literature, too, is not so much describing as deconstructing love relations as something purely conventional and belonging to previous eras.

...Socio-cultural behavior is visibly changing before our eyes. The role of art is diminishing. Readers' interpretations of art are changing as well, and each interprets a work of art in his or her own way. In a sense I see this problem much the same as Chekhov did. He was constantly aware of a chaos, over which a thin cover has been thrown with all of us carefully treading on it fearing to fall into this chaos any minute and be consumed by it. Talking incessantly about all sorts of things was a kind of a hypnotic antidote, a protection against the fear of chaos. This is how I understand Chekhov: constant expectation and fear of being consumed by chaos. Chekhovian existentialism is very close to me. I wonder if he himself would interpret it like this. But this is how I see his perception of life. Chekhov, naturally, expressed it all in terms of his own times: as an opposition of the common people and the authorites, the utter senselessness of life he witnessed. Chekhov's position of rising above the chaos is closer to me than Dostoyevsky's attempts to throw a net over the chaos and thus mentally subjugate the world. The latter tried to describe chaos but ended up realizing the impossibility of it.

...In Russia the role of the poet and writer was much too exaggerated. His creations were taken too seriously and were almost imposed on the public. The writer was seen as an ideal figure who is responsible for the vices of the world and is able to correct them. At the same time the public was also blamed for not following too diligently the mode of moral behaviour prescribed to them by literature. I have none of these ambitions. My art, my writings, the same as literature in general, are not necessary to the world. The world can do without them very well. I value the opinion of a narrow circle of like-minded friends who also need my appreciation, otherwise I'm free from public opinion. My circle of colleagues provides enough artistic space for me to be able to practice my art comfortably. Ten people or ten million is pretty much the same for me. I do not really need readers' appreciation neither do I expect it or am I interested in it. How exactly the reader reads my poems is his or her own business.

...It is quite possible that humanity is approaching the end of a cultural aeon after which all the rules of the game will be different and culture will be coded anew.

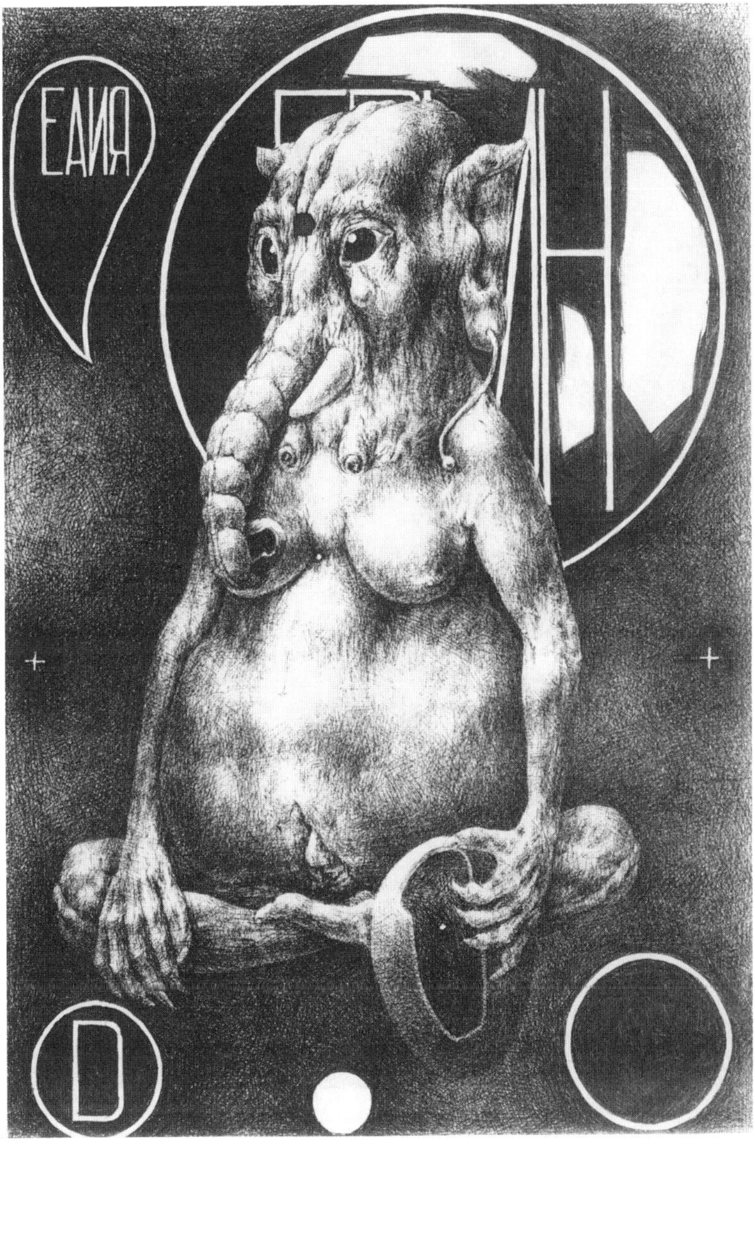
D

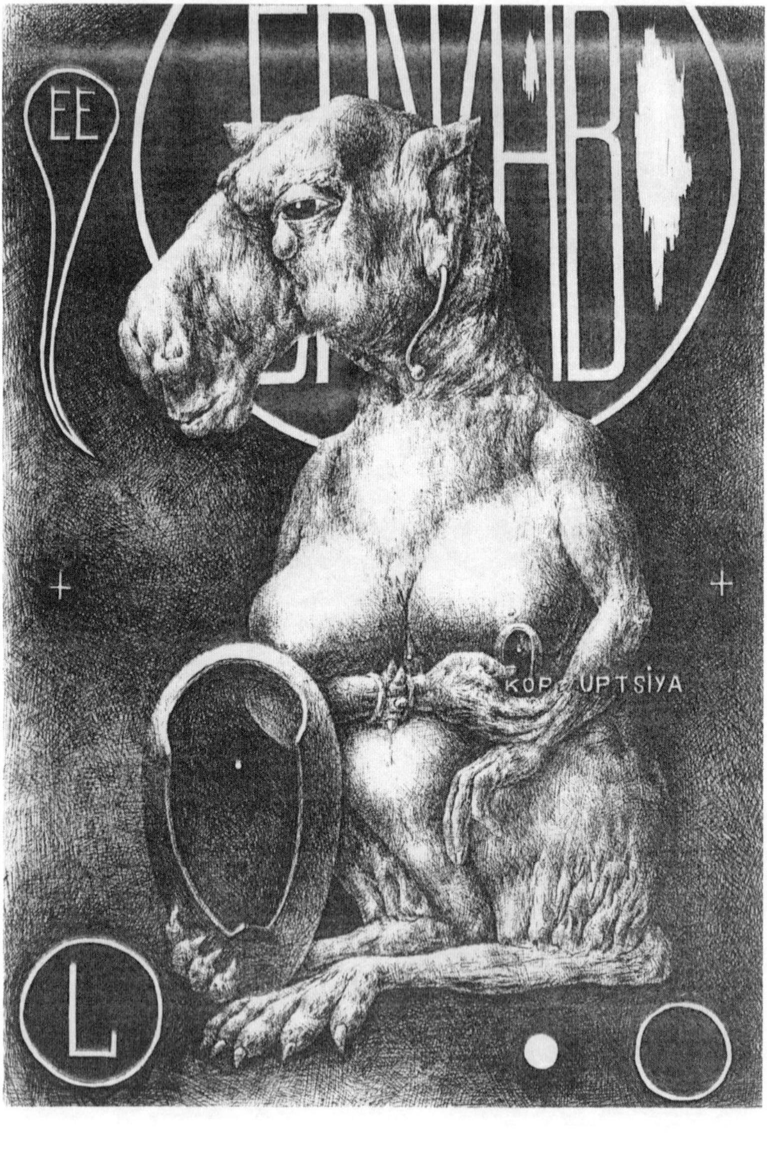
EE
KOP UPTSIYA
L

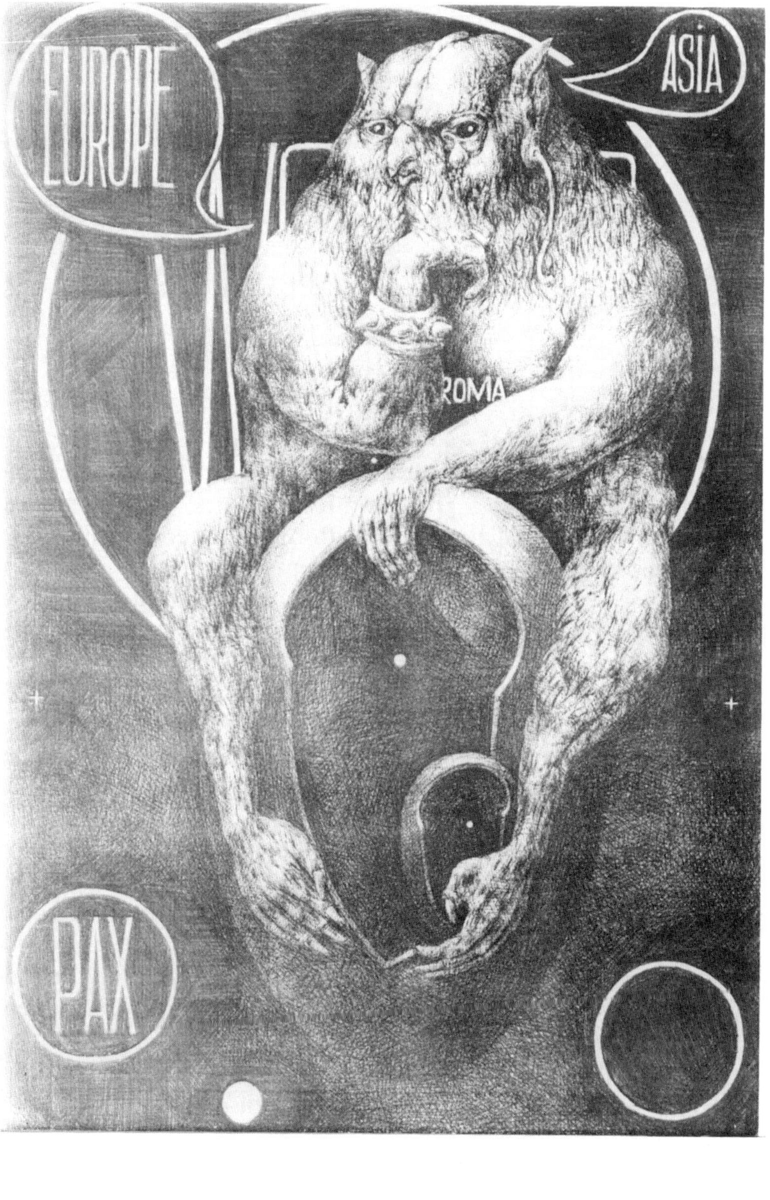
EUROPE
ASIA
ROMA
PAX

The Poet and Family Values

Vladimir Mayakovsky's great love for Lily Brik – and the extraordinary household he shared with her and her husband, Osip – continues to fascinate critics and gossips alike.

When poet Vladimir Mayakovsky met the Briks in the summer of 1915, his life was to change completely. At once she became the focal point of both his life and his poetry: every future line of his verse would be dedicated to her, and even earlier works were rededicated.

His love for her was larger than life. Characteristically, he experienced joy and sorrow in hyperbolic proportions, as Lily later described in her diary: "He did not just fall in love with me, he occupied me entirely – it was a veritable invasion. For two and a half years I didn't have a moment's peace, literally!"

History has judged the relationship between them in different ways. For some, their strange three-way affair symbolizes a decadent bourgeois morality; others saw the celebrated *menage-a-trois* as a bold experiment in human affairs – a realignment of love and friendship. Both missed the mark, reducing a unique web of commitment and intrigue to a theory of modern love.

In its first three years, their relationship remained clandestine. "It was only in 1918 that I could tell Osip about our love affair," Lily wrote. "Since 1915 my relationship with him had developed into a warm friendship, and the affair with Mayakovsky would not spoil either our friendship or Osip's friendship with Mayakovsky. We decided never to part, and indeed we remained close friends for life."

Lily's intense but platonic love for her husband did not exclude equally strong feelings for Mayakovsky. In her notes, entitled *How It Was in Reality*, she explained, "I no longer had any intimate relations with Osip, so all the talk about a 'triangle', *menage-a-trois* and the like, was far from reality. I've always loved Osip more than a brother, more than a husband or son, and I shall always love him. I've never come across descriptions of such love in any book or poem.

"My love for Osip did not interfere with my love for Mayakovsky. Quite the opposite, if it were not for Osip, I wouldn't love Vladimir so strongly. I couldn't help it, since Osip loved him so much. I don't know two people more devoted to each other."

Even after the relief of openness, their life together was stormy. The autumn of 1922 brought a breach between Lily and Mayakovsky, in a crisis which began during a trip to Berlin in October and November, and flared up in December. At Lily's prompting, the two resolved not to see each other for two months, until the end of February 1923.

Although, during that time Mayakovsky never once visited her in her flat, he hovered obsessively around the edges of her life. He roamed around, hid in staircases, listened at her door, sent messages through her maid, and flowers, books and gifts as an expression of his grief. Lily, unmoved, responded with terse notes.

Mayakovsky suffered unbearably. He oscillated between utter despair and mad joy, recording his feelings in letters to her which later were included in his long poem, *About IT*, dedicated, "To Her and Me."

Mayakovsky made an honest effort to put their relationship on a more stable basis, but ultimately this self-inflicted torture had little long-term effect on either of them. The poet wanted only one thing: to be together with his beloved, all the time.

His "incarceration" finally ended on February 28 at 3 pm. Five hours later they left by train for St. Petersburg; as soon as they had sat down on the train, Mayakovsky started reciting *About IT*. When he had finished, he burst into sobs.

The year 1924 brought a gradual turning point. In one of her notes, a disaffected Lily confessed to Mayakovsky that she was no longer so deeply in love with him: "I have the impression that you, too, love me much less and won't be suffering on my account."

Among the reasons for this change was her new affair – about which Mayakovsky knew everything – with Alexander Krasnoschekov, ex-president and Foreign Minister of the Far-Eastern Republic, then newly-returned to Moscow as deputy Finance Minister. A year later, Krasnoschekov was arrested and sentenced to several years in prison.

In autumn 1924, Mayakovsky himself left for Paris. After a week there, he was already writing to Lily, "I'm dying to know what's happening with you. I have nothing to console myself with. You are my beloved, but you're in Moscow and are probably not mine at all or you belong to another." Lily's answer was honest: "I can't help it, can't abandon A.K. while he's in prison. I feel terribly ashamed of myself as I have never felt in my life." Mayakovsky: "You speak of shame. Is that all that ties you to him and prevents you from being with me? Do what you will, but nothing will ever change my love for you." Lily had apparently underestimated Mayakovsky's fixation.

In 1925, his travels took him to America. After his return, in April 1926, the Briks and Mayakovsky moved together into a flat in Moscow's Gendrikov Lane – paradoxically only after their "married" life had ended. Their abiding friendship, not emotional fireworks, fueled and fine-tuned their experiment in communal living.

Mayakovsky was to return to France again at the end of 1928, this time to meet his American girlfriend, Elly Johns, in Nice with her daughter, whom he recognized as his own. Their reunion was a disaster and a few days later Mayakovsky went back to Paris.

The night he arrived in Paris, Mayakovsky met and fell in love with the young Tatyana Yakovleva, a Russian emigre. Mayakovsky went back to Russia in December, but in February 1929, he returned for a two-month stay and proposed to the girl. He urged her to return with him to Moscow, but Tatyana answered evasively. Their love affair continued, however, and Mayakovsky planned to visit her in Paris again in October the same year. Nothing came of this plan – perhaps because he had trouble receiving a visa.

The circumstances of this failed trip are shrouded in mystery. Some blame the Briks for somehow preventing Mayakovsky from getting his visa, because they were against Mayakovsky's marriage to Tatyana, which would effectively end their life together. The young wife would hardly agree to share him with the Briks.

A more convincing explanation lies on the wider political stage. The year 1929 proved a turning point in Russian history, with Trotsky's forced exile, and Bukharin's expulsion from the Politburo. The purges soon spread into the world of culture, with the orchestration of a press campaign against the writers Boris Pilnyak and Evgeny Zamyatin, who had both published work abroad. Mayakovsky played a rather unsavory role in that campaign and denounced his colleagues.

When a counsellor at the Soviet embassy in Paris defected in September, Stalin introduced his "Law Against Defection", with its penalty of death. Given the growing totalitarianism, the authorities had their reasons to prevent the famous Soviet poet from marrying an emigre and probably staying in France. In October Mayakovsky learned that Tatyana had married a French viscount. The news marked the beginning of the last period of his life.

The Briks themselves applied for visas in the autumn of 1929, but were refused. Ultimately, they received passports only in February 1930, after Mayakovsky's intercession on their behalf with Lazar Kaganovich, then chief of the Cheka (predecessor of the KGB).

Their last meeting was on February 18, 1930, when Mayakovsky saw them off at the station. By the date that he shot himself, April 14, 1930, they had already started their journey home.

Mayakovsky's love for Lily Brik was boundless – he could not do without her, and his all-embracing passion interfered with his relationships with other women. Even Tatyana Yakovleva recalls how he constantly talked about Lily Brik.

For Mayakovsky, Lily was the center of his life, while for her he was just one of the men she loved. They knew about each others' affairs, with an openness that left Lily cold, but caused Mayakovsky to suffer unbearably. Her relationship with her husband was much less dramatic, and they remained married until Osip's death in 1945.

History was to work its own particular spell on the story of their relationship. For those Soviet critics who claimed Mayakovsky's posthumous fame for the glory of the Party, his life with the Briks marred the image they wanted to create of the revolutionary poet.

Lily was eliminated from his biography to the point that even photographs were tampered with. Only with the publication in 1958 of Mayakovsky's *125 Letters to L.B.* did readers have any idea of the poet's real character. Lily Brik herself survived for another 20 years: she died peacefully in 1978.

The Last Emigre

by Tom Birchenough

At one of the lowest points in their life together, living in poverty in Paris in the 1930s, Nina Berberova and her companion, Vladislav Khodasevich, one of the greatest Russian poets of the century, were talking of the possibility of suicide. Berberova later remembered the incident in her autobiography, *The Italics Are Mine*.

"I always have a way out: I can return my ticket," Khodasevich confided, hinting at the option. Berberova replied, with a characteristic fortitude: "Not for anything. I want to use my ticket up to the very end, and *even try to travel some miles free of charge*."

The journey which ended with her death in Philadelphia at the end of September 1992 had been a long one indeed. Born in 1901 into a half-Russian, half-American family, she grew up within the world of the pre-Revolutionary bourgeoisie — against which she soon rebelled.

Early in her autobiography she writes about her decision — made at the age of 10 — to become a poet. A streak of impulsiveness ran throughout her life — not so much arrogance, rather an impatience, as much with herself as with others. It is a quality which gives *The Italics Are Mine* — a unique record of a whole generation, as well as testimony for the love of Berberova and Khodasevich — its particular uneven tone, which glances between intimate confidence and closely-kept privacy.

William Blake's famous words, "energy is eternal delight," became a motto. "The most horrible thing that can happen is the losing of time — that I could not bear," she said in 1991, shortly before she turned 90. "The necessity to act, to *vankish*", as she pronounced it, "the time that is my first enemy. I struggled with it day and night. Sleep, yes, but not more than seven hours..."

The upheaval in her life started at an early age, with the 1917 revolution which took her from St. Petersburg, first to Moscow, then south to Armenia, at that time under White control. Eventually, after a three-week journey in a railway freight-car, she returned to St Petersburg.

There, she witnessed the first stages of the break-up of the literary world in which she grew up – epitomized by the execution of Nikolai Gumilev in 1921 for his supposed involvement in a counterrevolutionary plot.

It was there, too, that she met and fell in love with Khodasevich. They would live together – never marrying – for the next 10 years. Their first encounter convinced them that the two important things were to be together and to survive.

"What did survive then mean?" she asks, with the benefit of hindsight, in her autobiography. "Something physical? Moral? Could we at that time foresee the death of Mandelstam on a rubbish heap, the end of Isaac Babel, the suicides of Esenin and Mayakovsky, party politics in literature aimed at destroying two if not three generations? Could we foresee 20 years of Akhmatova's silence? The destruction of Pasternak? The end of Gorky? Of course not."

But the suspicion had dawned, and within a few months they had received passports to leave Russia, and reached Berlin.

Three years of European wandering followed, during which they made their homes in 42 different transitory rooms. Finally, with the realization that a return to Russia was impossible, they settled in France. They struggled to eke out a living working for Russian-language newspapers and journals – Paris, with a Russian population numbering more than 100,000, had a whole culture of its own. The hardship of Berberova's life in the city – "the special shabbiness of emigre life," as she describes it – was to provide the setting for much of her fiction.

The years that followed were difficult but full. Struggling to survive in a variety of jobs, Berberova wrote newspaper sketches, novels, a biography of Tchaikovsky, and eventually the short stories which are her central creative achievement. She left Khodasevich, but remained close to him and to Olga, the woman he later married, whose deportation as a Jew is one of the most agonising episodes in Berberova's memoires. Khodasevich died in 1939, on the eve of the war, in the bare surroundings of a public hospital.

Starting life with a second companion, Berberova settled at Longchene, outside Paris, where she lived through the years of the war. But the relationship broke up in painful circumstances, and finally, frustrated with France, she came to America, and a life of apparently resolute solitude. "I love to be alone, of course, of course," she stressed emphatically.

Settling first in New York, she would later move to academic jobs in Harvard and Princeton.

It was only in 1989 that Berberova returned to Russia. There were meetings with two members of her family — one was a Red Army officer — and one other figure whom she had known before: the only survivors of her world. Obviously shocked by what she saw, she nevertheless refrained from public criticism, deciding "to smile at everybody" and suppress comment. She went home exhausted, and found that her blood pressure had risen dramatically.

"I am such a pessimist about Russia. You know what has changed: people have no respect for each other now, they hate and envy one another. Such jealousy, it was very painful. I can never go there again."

Three years before her death, she moved from Princeton into a new flat in central Philadelphia. The move was made on the strength of her European royalties: in France, the publication of her novels took her to the best-seller lists for more than a year. "I was a *rolling* best-seller there," she remembered with delight.

Her world in Philadelphia had an incongruous quality — it seemed strange that someone so involved all her life with Russian literature, whose 25-year stay in France coincided with many of the important events and relationships of her life, should settle here in the center of anonymous modern America, high above the city with a view over the Delaware River and of the quiet but constant flow of freeway traffic along its banks.

Her apartment had a frugality which set it apart from its surroundings: simple book-shelves, filing cabinets, a desk, single table, a bowl of cherries, most of all a working environment.

Two pictures which hung on its wall draw echoes from her autobiography. One, a group portrait from Berlin, shows Berberova — the only woman in a group of writers, including Bely, Khodasevich and others, whose names have never been widely known outside Russia. "A whole generation fell for her in that picture," the contemporary Russian poet Joseph Brodsky has said of it.

The other, an old engraving, simply framed and fading, showed the corner of St. Petersburg where Nevsky Prospect meets the Moika River. Berberova had bought it for two francs on the quays of the Seine. Later, it was one of the few things which she could save as a memory of Khodasevich, after Olga had been seized for deportation. In it, many strands of her life came together: the St Petersburg she had lost; Paris and the suffering of the war; things rescued and transplanted into another environment; the imperative of moving on; and a reluctance to draw attention to the pain of the past.

At the end of *The Italics Are Mine*, a punctilious "Who's Who" lists a huge range of Russian and European names – literary and political, personal friends or public acquaintances. The details of their lives are preserved for the future: their political allegiances, the papers for which they wrote, even the names of the cafes where they met.

On one level, it is a labor of love; on another, an act of duty to a generation practically forgotten – or, never known – outside its immediate circle. Only since perestroika, with publication of their work beginning at home, can the gaps left by years of censorship begin to be filled.

Berberova's two most recent books have already been published in Russia. They indicate the breadth of her interests – one was a history of Russian freemasonry, the second, *The Iron Lady*, a biography of Moura Budberg, secretary to Gorky, mistress of H.G. Wells, and a double agent who in her time spied for both Britain and Russia.

But it is *The Italics Are Mine* which will stand as her masterpiece. Rereading it, her autobiography appears as one of the most remarkable and moving works of its time.

Her two rules of autobiography – "The first: reveal yourself completely. The second: conceal your life for yourself alone" – catch its quality in a single sentence. She was a remarkable writer, and a remarkable woman – and with her death, a generation has finally passed into history.

First published in *The Moscow Guardian*

Alexander Shatalov, born 1957, graduated from an aviation college and worked in aviation engineering for a while. He started writing poetry early and eventually his passion for literature got the better of him. He gave up engineering in favour of a literary career. He took a job at a publishing house, published two collections of his poetry, actively engaged in literary journalism and launched a literary program on Russian television. Currently, director of Glagol, one of the few publishers in Russia that risks publishing contemporary fiction.

(fax/phone: +7 095–213 1495)

GLAGOL:
Russia's First Gay Publishing House Flourishing

by Alexander Shatalov, director

I've always been a shy person – a shy boy and then a shy young man. Now looking back on those years I'm amazed that I managed to get married at all. They say it is the woman who actually chooses her man, not the other way round as men are made to believe. Quite possibly. As for me, like most men I still believe that it was my own independent decision based on my genuine feelings.

Eventually my ingrained shyness has played a nasty trick on me: the books that I feel compelled to publish are invariably of a provocative nature. To put it more bluntly, they are often quite improper, embracing as they do sexual perversions, swear language, frank descriptions of love scenes, sharp political criticism, and much else besides.

There is little in common among the authors I fancy: the unprintable Mikhail Volokhov, a Russian emigre living in France, the outspoken and gentle James Baldwin, the fine stylist Sasha Sokolov, the enfant terrible Eduard Limonov, the passionate anti-communist Alexander Galich, the first Russian gay writer Evgeny Kharitonov, the ironical absurdist Daniil Kharms...

Book publishing is a form of creativity as much as poetry and painting. Preparation of a book requires the same passion, and the same abandon. The process of creating a book is exhilarating like wine or drugs. It is by no means a business with the sole aim of making a profit. For the publisher, the same as for the author it is a communion with other people and a way of self-expression. The second, Gorbachev, thaw of the 1990s gave rise to new literature. Most of the former taboos became obsolete – people were getting rid of their inhibitions. The need was felt for new outlets for human energy and ideas. Apart from Rybakov's *Children of the Arbat*, Igor Kon's *Introduction into Sexology* became another bestseller of the perestroika period. Russians were re-discovering not just their history but their own sexuality as well.

Russian literature has always avoided discussing sex. Western novels were often not published precisely because of their focus on sex while descriptions of love scenes were carefully crossed out from translations.

When Limonov's *It's Me Eddy* was first published in Russia it was a cultural shock. It was not at once that the public saw this work of talent as a confessional diary of great force. I offered the novel to three publishers who all turned it down. It was then that I decided to launch a publishing house of my own to be able to publish books that other publishers were afraid to touch but which I believed should be available to Russian readers.

For the first time in Russian publishing, unprintable language appeared in print. Printers refused to typeset the book, so eventually it was printed in Riga (Latvia) under the supervision of a special police force. Since then almost two million copies of the book were printed in all.

One of Glagol's greatest achievements so far was the two volume collection of Evgeny Kharitonov (1941-1981) *Teardrops on the Flowers* (see Kharitonov's story of the same title in *Glas* #4). Widely known in samizdat, the writer was persecuted in his lifetime for his homosexual inclinations. He was an innovator as a stylist as well as in subject matter. He wrote about moral tortures of one who is torn between his religiousness and his sinfulness. His literary experiments influenced a whole generation of Russian writers.

Some of the books published by Glagol, such as those by Limonov, Kharitonov, William Burrows and James Baldwin, contributed to the abolition of the law against homosexuality in Russia.

Many world famous books have been unavailable in Russia, and still are. This is why translations are still so important and craved for – they pave the way for mutual understanding. William Burrows's *Naked Lunch* is one such book which was once banned in America and then exerted a telling influence on the state of the people's minds the world over.

It has never been my intention to limit my list to homosexual books only. But this subject happens to be very topical for today's Russia. Russia still has to learn to be more tolerant towards otherness.

Provocative subjects are not limited to sex and perversions. Genuine talent is always provocative, challenging the established literary and moral canons. Igor Yarkevich's *How I Masturbated* (see Yarkevich's two other stories in *Glas* #2) openly opposes the moral principles and literary trends of the 1960s which still largely dominate the literary scene today.

Nina Sadur is another outstanding talent we are publishing this year. Like Petrushevskaya, she writes about degraded women in an exalted way. Her stories are mysterious, somewhat surrealist and very Russian (see Nina Sadur's stories in *Glas* #3 and #6).

These books are by no means reflections of my inner self. The thing is that I've been aware for some time that Russian literature badly needs some brighter colours to liven it up, so that it can take a new look at itself and be able to provide a multicolored palette and a wider choice of themes for the reader.

From: Evgeny Kharitonov,
Teardrops on the Flowers

In life love is for pigeons and pinheads.
You remember, you and I really loved.
I'm a man of feather, fire under feathers.
I know love in ice. Ice, my pigeon, forever.
I see from under the ice: yeah, wordless I loved.
Forever I love words words...

Translated by Jim Kates

Glagol's immediate plans include a new novel by the St Petersburg writer Gennady Trifonov who served a four-year sentence in the late 1970s for circulating in samizdat a series of masterfully written poems about his love for another man. At the time the case was widely publicised in the West, and that improved somewhat the poet's conditions in the Northen Urals labour camp. The persecution of homosexuals in Russia officially came to an end with the abolition of the law against them in 1992, but prejudice against them is still very strong. Below are some of Trifonov's poems which got him into prison.

Letter from Prison

I get your letters telling me
that I'm a poet, which is dazzling,
that this is why my lofty star
is not extinguished in the dark.

All of you write to me that my voice
has been absorbed by wintry groves
which are obedient to my hand,
obedient like my own handwriting.

All of you tell me: I alone
sang – as no one's allowed to sing –
of how we love without response
him who's our sole necessity,

Him who gives shape to our lives
the way the branches form a garden
when God will kiss us on our lips
the way the snowfall kisses earth.

The one for whom I long at night,
for whom I call, a wounded bird,
one who no longer haunts my dreams,
one about whom my verse is silent.

You write responding in advance,
you plead with me: "Do not give up,
endure it all and stay alive."
And I live on. And there's no life.

* * *

I'm the one who's most affectionate of all,
who falls to the ground from the heights
without breaking his neck or windpipe,
who opens his mouth wide to rhymes.
I'm music. Take me. Play me.

I am the reed flute of the steppes.
I know all there's to know of life
both when I laugh and when I moan
and that is my entire truth.

* * *

Oh Ghivi, say to me
that it's a dream, a lie.
Look, now your silver knife
is bathed in my blood.
I have not yet been killed –
it is a surface wound
from Georgian lips and cheeks
that cast a shade on me.

* * *

Everything can still come to me:
both life and death, but you – I doubt it.
This is why I long for your sworn promise
before the next winter sets in.

I want the snow of Christmas Eve
to promise me in advance
the evening meaning of your verbs –
my swoon or my delight.

* * *

Translate for me the hatred that you feel
into a language I can also speak
and which I cannot possibly give up
like water's depth cannot give up a cloud.

Surrender – it's so easy – to the words
that order roadside trees when they must bend
when to incline. These are the kind of words
that spring up suddenly, like grass, and die.

Also like grass that hasn't fully lived
Out its allotted span, because the lies
go on and will continue to exist
as long as they must justify my love.

* * *

Why must I always stay a little boy?
I've reached an age where this is really shameful.
It pains me when my words must be gulped down
and can't become a poem as they should.

My enemies? But it is really dumb
to have them when my only friends are stones
I dare not breathe, I dare not love
I grow my hatred drop by drop.

How homeless it is in my home!
How hopeless in my lover's house.
How freezing cold. How, like an illness
Our loneliness makes us unfree.

Translated by Simon Karlinsky and Peter Carleton

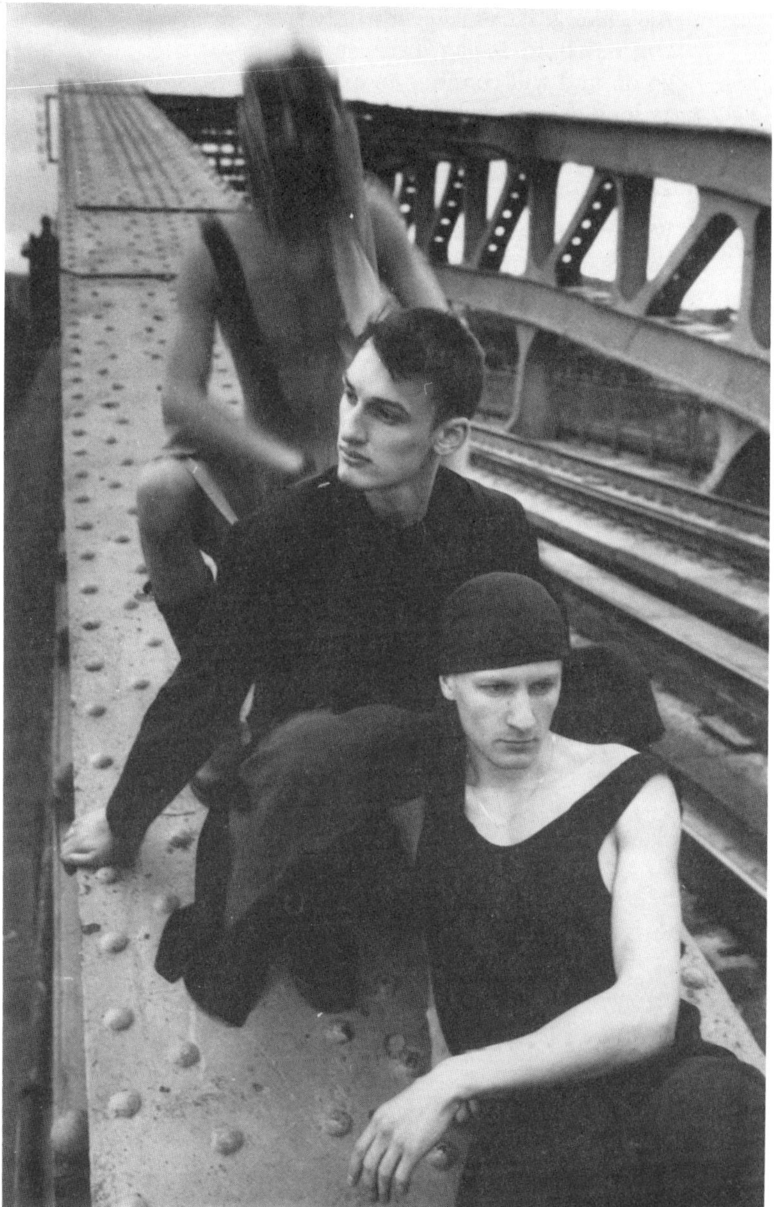

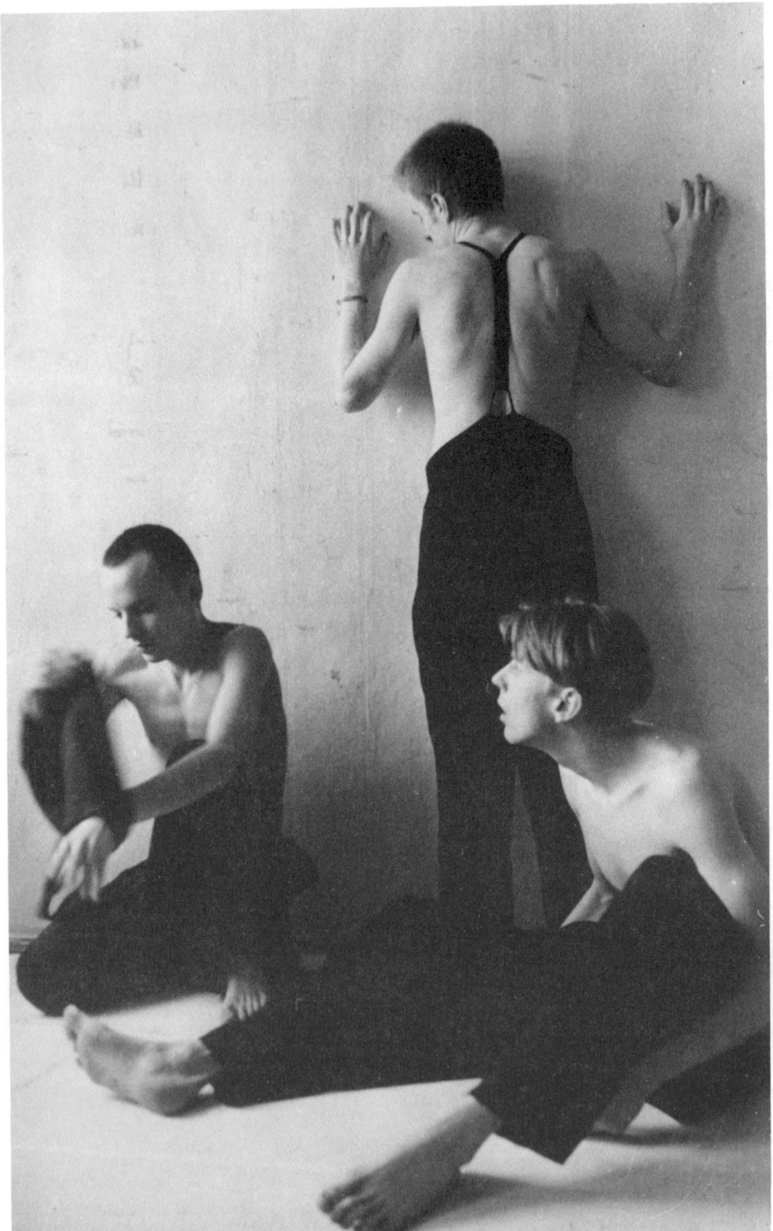

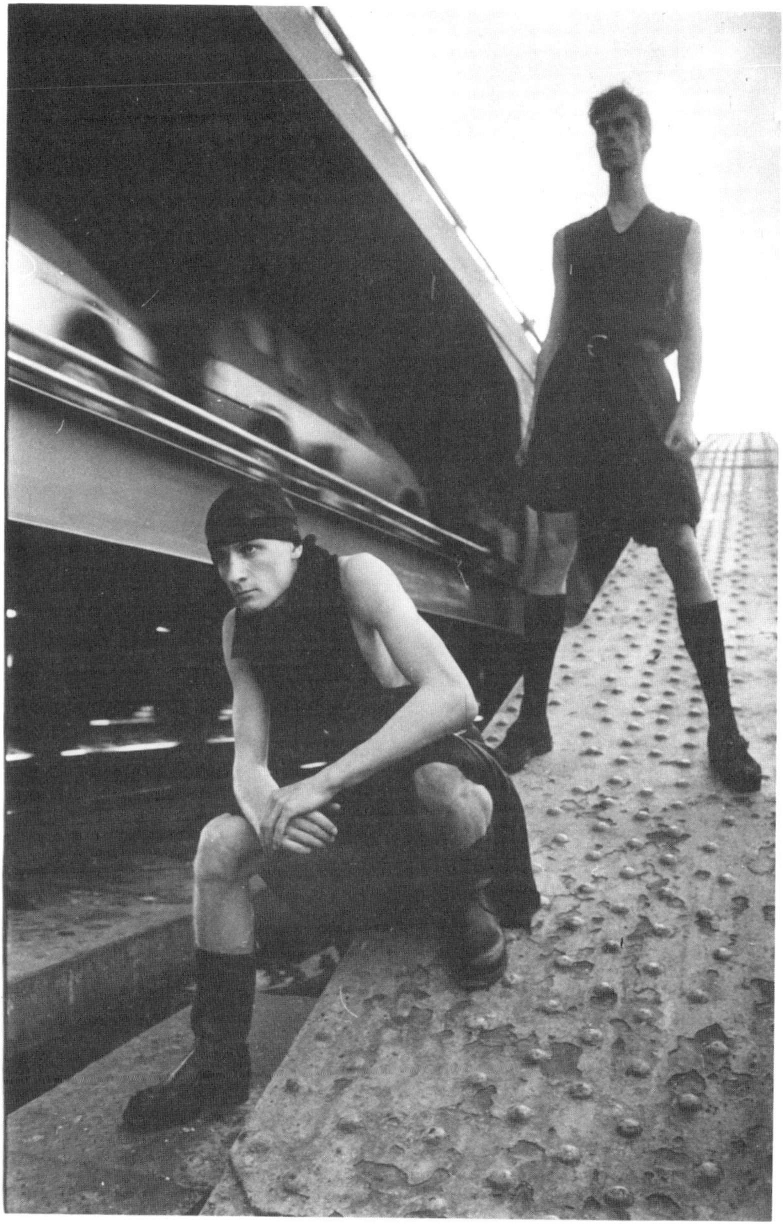

Russia's First Erotic Paper

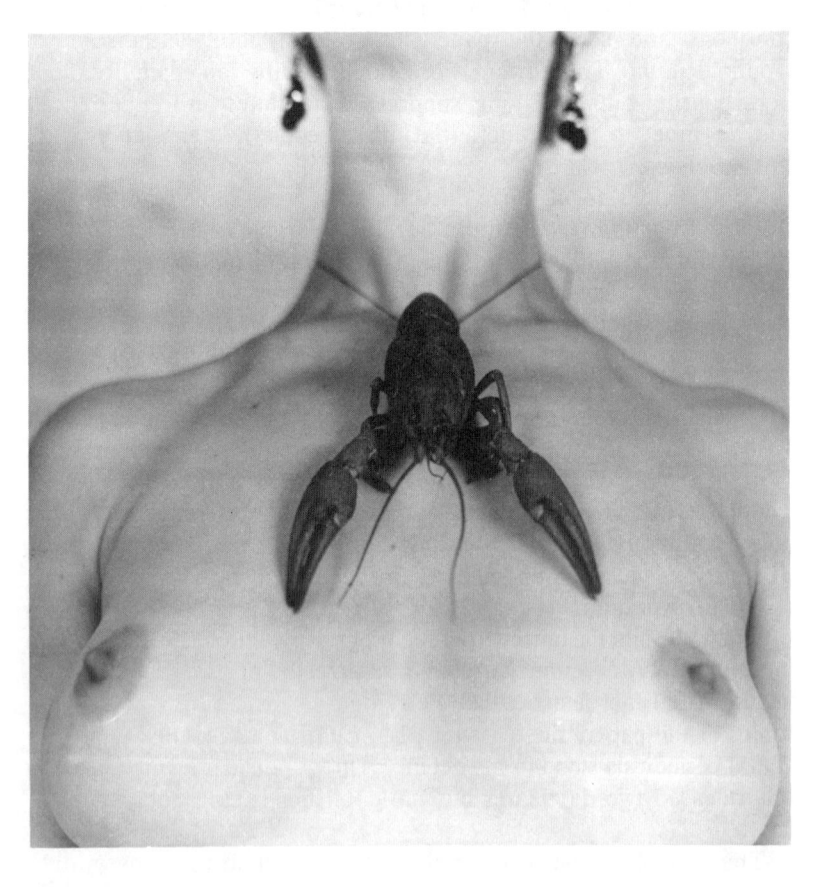

Photo by Georgy Kizevalter

Russian Perestroika brought many freedoms, some of them of rather dubious nature, creating unusual new problems on top of the usual ones. Many formerly forbidden subjects suddenly received exaggerated public attention. Eroticism versus pornography was one of them. The first erotic paper to appear almost immediately after the lifting of censorship was launched by a group of well-known writers who enjoyed their newly acquired freedom to speak frankly on formerly forbidden subjects and, in general, to call a spade a spade. The success of this new paper, called *Yeschyo* (More), was enormous and soon the paper had almost 300,000 subscribers around Russia. The editors were flooded with fan mail. Readers were pouring out their long suppressed anxieties and experiences and learning, to their relief, that other people had similar puzzles and problems.

Contributors to *Yeschyo* include such well-known authors as Evgeny Kharitonov, Vladimir Sorokin, Sergei Yurienen, Dmitry Prigov, Eduard Limonov, Natalia Medvedeva, Nikolai Klimontovich, Igor Yarkevich, Oleg Dark, Mikhail Novikov, Darya Aslamova, and some others who prefer to use pen names when they write for *Yeschyo*.

This first erotic paper was followed by others, by glossy magazines and erotic fiction series, films and videos.

Then like a bolt from the blue, disaster struck: the publisher of *Yeschyo* was arrested, ostensibly for disseminating pornography. Heated debates flared up in the press and in people's homes on whether erotic press should be allowed and where erotica ends and pornography begins. At the time when the movement "Back to Virginity" is gaining in popularity in the West, Russia is undergoing a sexual revolution.

When, despite the outcry from the progressive-minded intelligentsia, the famous writer Zufar Gareyev was arrested on the same charge, but in actual fact just because he rented a room in his flat to store copies of the paper, the Russian PEN Centre and practically all the liberal periodicals stood in his defence. Under public pressure Gareyev was released two days later but the publisher is still languishing in jail.

The rest of the porn industry is thriving while the conservative portion of the population vehemently fights what they see as a dangerous onslaught of capitalist decadence and Western influence.

Erotic Press

Sex as Drama

by Mikhail Novikov

When the first Russian-made porn video appeared I was convinced once again that in a Slavic version even such a jolly thing as sex would invariably turn into drama. The country of Tolstoy and Dostoyevsky takes a sombre look at practically all manifestations of human feelings while sex becomes a clinical experience. The emaciated bodies on the screen brought to mind thoughts about unbalanced diets, polluted water and poor medical care. You find yourself pitying the actors who try hard but their faces betray the effort, and you end up pitying yourself as well. Instead of experiencing arousal you remember that Russia takes the first place in the world in abortions.

The Russian minister of the press believes that the porn industry should be banned and that it is possible to suppress it entirely. I daresay he is wrong. In all countries at all times pornography has been one of the inevitable consequences of freedom of the press and of conscience, and to suppress what is "unacceptable in good society" is only possible together with freedom itself. In other words freedom can be had at a certain moral price and many countries are prepared to pay that price for the sake of freedom in all other areas.

The "lower" folk culture in Russia has always been quite well developed, but never allowed into the open. It is highly expressive, sophisticated and entirely sovereign, even more so than in other cultures. It is precisely for this reason that the "lower" culture has always been kept legally separate from the mainstream culture, thus creating a rather flattering myth about the exceptional morality of Russian people in general. This myth was further perpetrated in Stalinist times when a builder of Communism was supposed to concentrate entirely on the great cause with sex being furthest from his and her thoughts.

There are dozens of erotic periodicals currently published in Russia. Why is only one of them persecuted? Why are the others, which also show naked bodies in provocative positions, allowed to circulate while *Yeschyo* is pending trial for disseminating pornography? There is indeed a difference. *Yeschyo* is first and foremost a venue for parody,

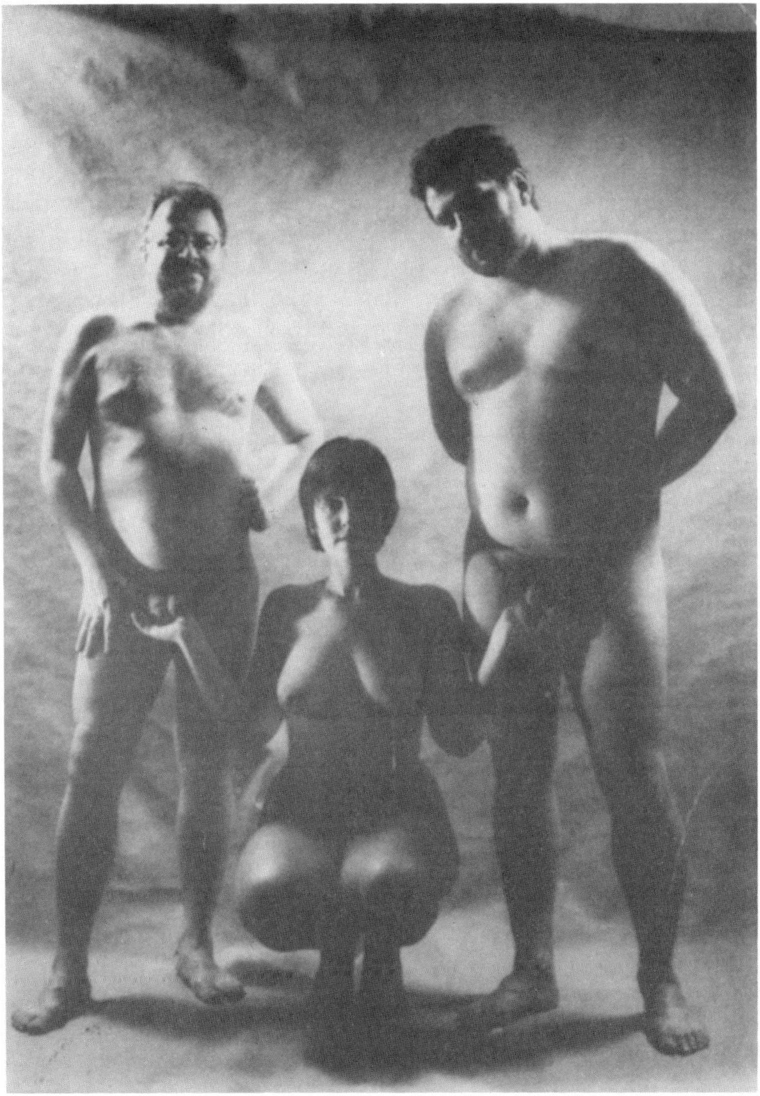

irony, game, and provocation, and aims at doing away with former taboos. The editors believe that laughter and mystification are the best ways of pulling off "wet blankets" that are invariably thrown over the arts in Slavic countries.

Yeschyo does not show top models but ordinary living people, beautiful and plain, slim and plump, intelligent and simple, lecherous and sex-hungry, pining for all kinds of love, including homosexual love. In short, it features all sorts of post-Soviet individuals getting rid of their Soviet-imposed inhibitions. This is what the authorities find unforgivable. They find the irony incomprehensible and feel uncomfortable being the object of this irony, which they often are. They haven't yet forgotten the times when they were in complete control of the press, and in their rage the one thing they know how to do is suppress and imprison.

Post-modernism and Pornography

from an interview with Zufar Gareyev

The persecuted erotic paper *Yeschyo* is simply a literary mode of post-modern behaviour or sexuality expressed in terms of literary post-modernism. Post-modernism should not be expected to be literature in the traditional sense. It is always based on scandal and parody aiming to fill in the gap while obsolete notions are being replaced by new ones and traditional roles of literature are adjusting to the changed situation in society.

...For the first time in the last few decades in Russia, literature is trying to reach the masses, and the masses happily respond. This populism of the cultural elite is for the benefit of all sides.

...Eroticism is probably the only part of human life where intellectual games, uninhibited and inspired, acquire particular pungency and excitement, giving one the special pleasure of shedding one's former inhibitions and fears.

...Many modern writers feel that in order to impress the reader it is no longer enough to challenge established political or esthetic principles, it is not enough to show the horrors of the Gulag, he or she should dig deeper and undertake something more daring, such as a sexual revolution.

...Sexual revolution in a post-totalitarian state is like an infantile disease which a society has to live through to become immune to it After all sorts of prohibitions and double values imposed on people many in this country feel tempted to try the formerly forbidden fruit. Let them have the knowledge they've been starved for. No harm will come of this new game. In a state with so many life and death problems this new interest in sexuality is the least of our problems.

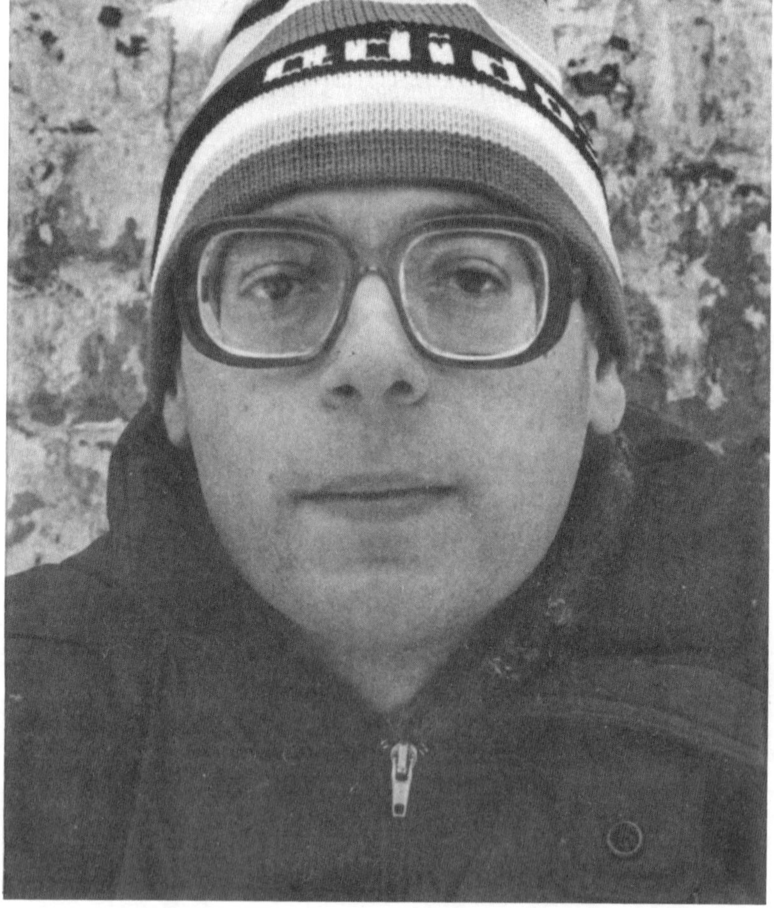

The Provisional Government

There were three positions we particularly liked: "The Long Road", "Crocodile Tears" and "Boris Pasternak".

No, it wasn't because I'm a Jew that she loved me: she loved me for my sexual sensitivity. In the first place, I never hurt her. What for? Life is enough of a trial without a woman having to suffer in bed as well! In the second place, I almost never beat her, just every so often – and then not hard... In the third place, I liked the topic of her dissertation, and she knew that I appreciated her as a creative individual, and not just a cunt!

I picked her up on the street. Things weren't going too well for her that night and she just couldn't pull anyone; I went up to her and said straight off: "You know, one should make love just for its own sake, money needn't have anything to do with it". She was astonished: "You don't say!" – but she believed me and I didn't disappoint her expectations.

From that moment on she had one constant client – me, or rather, not me, but my sexual sensitivity. She gave up working the street, went back to her post-graduate studies and picked up her old topic. But my indifference to the Russo-Jewish question used to infuriate her. She insisted that she'd feel a whole lot better if only I held to some position or other on the matter. "And if you're in the bus and they shout 'Jew' at you, won't you mind?" she used to ask me all the time. "Why should I mind the truth?" – I didn't get it. There was nothing left to say after that, so she'd get into the initial position for "Pasternak".

Afterwards, when we were tired, we'd go back to discussing her topic. She'd tell me all about the Provisional Government: Miliukov, Guchkov, Kerensky, so I could see them standing right there in front of me. "If it's a boy, we'll call him after one of them," I thought.

"Why d'you hate Jews?" I asked her once. "Why did they have to destroy my life's work, the Provisional Government?" she replied – a pure Jewish trick that, answering a question with a question. "They won't ever do it again," I interceded for my fellow-tribesmen, but it was a purely symbolic attempt.

Autumn came, bringing with it fallen leaves and grey rain, and a long period of "The Long Road" set in. I would carefully remove her tights, while I massaged her backside that was stiff from standing too long, and her slippery thighs; she checked out my main erotic zone and two subsidiaries. We usually sat down in the travelling position. I got on to the divan, she got on to me, and off we went! Where would we be without the first cosmonaut?

Half-way through "The Long Road" we'd change positions from transverse to longitudinal. We skilfully reduced each other to a state of exhaustion. When she was worn out she would whisper: "Dual Power... Kornilov..." I would come unhurriedly and artistically, and she would sigh: "October", get up, wash herself and sit down at her desk. I wanted more, it wasn't enough, I could hear the long road calling and beckoning me, but she scratched and bit when I tried to drag her back on to the divan. "People are waiting for me" – she pointed at her notes; there was nothing to be done about it, the gentlemen of February stood between us!

Cursed politics stole my love away from me! "It has to be one thing or the other," I decided, and of course I decided in favour of the other. I wanted to annihilate her topic, and all these gentlemen from the Provisional Government; I decided to burn her dissertation! Love had to be saved! But then I decided I couldn't be bothered; things could carry on as they were.

We were sitting in a cafe, drinking cup after cup of lousy Moscow coffee, and we'd poured out some cheap port, and she asked: "Would you like a group portrait of the Provisional Government with an inscription from me?" I gagged and almost choked on the plonk. Before we went for a walk I had to wipe off the table in the cafe and wash down my trousers while I was still in them – everything was covered in port. We left the empty bottle for the cleaning-woman, so she wouldn't scream at us.

We avoided the centre and went towards one of the new districts. Muscovites are such idiots – recently I've been disappointed with life in the Capital. Muscovites call regions new if they were built after 1721, even though there hasn't been a single public toilet built there in the last hundred years.

I used to love the twilight in Moscow too, it seemed romantic and somehow significant. The scent of garbage-tips and rotten meat that

The Provisional Government

issued from all the cheap canteens around the place set my heart beating fast. The sight of the old drunkards and the young imbeciles gladdened my eyes and stirred the depths of my soul. Ah yes, the Boulevard Ring... Huge trees, cracked benches, dogs of indeterminate pedigree, lonely people almost broken under the communist yoke... And what about Moscow's famous centre? About three dozen streets crammed with rotting ruins, with no trace left of their former splendour (if there ever was any, if they're not lying — there's no way to check any more)... Now all of these erstwhile charms had come to seem boring, as uninteresting as used cotton-wool. My lovely Vera's thighs and armpits, her socks and bras — these and these alone were what moved me now! "You've changed," my friends said, obviously jealous.

She was pensive. "What are you thinking about Vera? Prince Lvov?" "No, I want to pee!" Oh, my poor love, there are so many things you can do in Moscow — buy something, sell someone, get yourself a flat, catch a taxi, see the crowd at the embassy, turn schizo with a capital S, but find a toilet... My lovely Vera went into a gateway and I stood on guard and didn't let any chance passers-by get near.

We walked a bit more and then went home. Today was the day for "Crocodile Tears". The position is the old text-book classic, but at the same time you insert your finger in the anal orifice and slowly push it in further. Your partner goes through joyous torment from hypertrophied sensations of pleasure, and the tears flow as though from pain.

Then she went back to her dissertation topic.

I tried to distract her by talking about Russian boys and how they looked nowadays. Whereas before they used to gather in low bars and discuss vexed questions, nowadays the boys had taken a look at themselves and realised they were goodlooking, they'd lost interest in all those questions, and fallen in love with each other instead. For ever, till death do them part. Russian boys no longer took any interest in important questions, they were too busy screwing each other!

But she didn't care about what happened to young Russian boys, all I could see in her smiling eyes were the old men of the Provisional Government.

It was getting time to make the break. I was no longer excited by her long, trim legs or the splay of her full, high breasts, or the caress

Igor Yarkevich

of her teeth, or her fine waist... That is, of course I was excited, but it faded the instant she mentioned those names from the February and October revolutions..

She loved me, and it hurt her to do it, but she left me! Vera left me for the post-graduate Vanya! Vanya loved her, and he loved her topic and in the Russo-Jewish question he took first one side and then the other. Of course, when Vera left, I fell in love with her again, and everything about her began to excite me with a power I never felt before, but it was too late, there was no way back, and I was left languishing, like that fucker Kerensky, I suppose, when he lost Russia.

I found myself somewhere to stick it, but it was awful! What passed for her breasts only vaguely resembled breasts at all. And it was the same with all the other body parts. Fellatio was right out of the question! She only knew the one position: "A log miraculously cast up on the river-bank during the timber-rafting season and fallen asleep forever". And Vera started sending me photographs of herself naked, either alone or with Vanya. Getting her own back, I suppose!

I was finished. Wine, women and books had lost their final trace of attraction for me. Paintings, films and other works of art could no longer engage my deranged imagination, which conjured up Vera in the ready position and those ugly faces of the Provisional Government. Even the change of regime in the country scarcely roused any interest in me.

Then I fell into the hot clutches of onanism, but not for long. After that I began to hate everything Russian – Russian speech, Russian books, Russian people, Russian tears, Russian genitals and Russian hope. Less than two days after that I began to hate everything Jewish, and even the phenomenon of Jewish statehood no longer inspired me.

Then I overheard a chance comment from someone behind me:

"The Provisional Government is the ideal of democratic rule!"

Stung by the unbearable thought of my lost love I spun round and said:

"You know what, gentlemen – screw your fucking Provisional Government!"

Translated by Andrew Jefferson

First published in *The Moscow Guardian*

Centenaries

Mikhail ZOSCHENKO
(1894-1958)

Isaac BABEL
(1894-1941)

MIKHAIL ZOSCHENKO
1894-1958

It has always been believed that Zoschenko was born in 1895 -- this is what the encyclopaedias say. In his early autobiography he said: "I know precious little about myself. I don't even know where and when I was born. Was it Poltava or St Petersburg? Two different documents mention different places. Moreover, in the one the date of birth is given as 1895, in the other as 1896. One of them must be a fake, but which one is hard to say because both look like fakes."

Zoschenko was famous for his jokes and mystifications. In all probability he knew exactly where and when he was born. There are two documents mentioning the same date: the register of birth in the Church of St Martyr Queen Alexandra, and a certificate of release from regular military service issued in his name in April 1920. He was born on 9 August 1894 in St Petersburg.

Why did he change his date of birth after 1920? According to Yuri Tomashevsky, the main Russian authority on Zoschenko, it was because of his wife, Vera Kerbitz. While he was still courting her she used to say that she would never marry an older man but only someone her age (she was born in 1896). That was why, Vera insisted, he knocked off one year of his age, just in case, when they registered their marriage. This may very well be true, at least it's quite in Zoschenko's character, but then it turns out that his centenary is this year, not in 1995.

In Russia Zoschenko is mainly loved for his satirical short stories written in the vernacular of his days, and objectively painting an unsavoury portrait of the post-revolutionary boor and philistine. These stories are practically untranslatable and this is why Zoschenko is mainly known abroad for his novels investigating the secret of human vitality, such as *The Blue Book, Before Sunrise.*

He was immensely popular in the 1920s and 30s and, unlike most Russian writers, widely published in his lifetime: 130 books containing some 1,000 stories.

A humourist who made people split their sides laughing he was a retiring, even a gloomy and vulnerable person, ever preoccupied with his nervous disorders and hyper-sensitive about the glaring gap between the sombre reality and the official propaganda. He had a rare chance of observing life in the raw as he held a variety of jobs, such as a policeman, a sleuth, an accountant and a cobbler. He took part in the First World War where he suffered a severe gas poisoning, and later volunteered for the Red Army.

In his later years, he repeatedly had trouble with literary and party bureaucracy. He was reprimanded and otherwise humiliated, and finally, together with Akhmatova, expelled from the Writers' Union on the grounds of lack of party spirit. Publication of his works stopped completely and he was thus deprived of any means of subsistence.

For several decades Yuri Tomashevsky, who devoted his entire life to studying Zoschenko, has been collecting every scrap of paper relating to the great writer, every object and book Zoschenko possessed. It is on his initiative that two years ago the first Zoschenko museum was opened in Zoschenko's St Petersburg apartment (9 Griboyedov Canal) based on Tomashevsky's collection of 4,000 items.

Tomashevsky has prepared for print 25 books by Zoschenko complete with introductory essays and notes. But the greatest service he has rendered to the history of Russian literature is the painstaking textological work on Zoschenko's texts all of which had been badly mutilated by censors. In 1994 he published the book *Zoschenko: the Face and the Mask* in which he collected previously unpublished prose and letters by Zoschenko, critical articles about him written in his lifetime and contemporary studies. The book includes a corrected chronology of his life and work based on Tomashavsky's own research. His lifetime study of Zoschenko makes up the most comprehensive biography of this great Russian writer.

Mikhail Zoschenko
Youth Regained
an excerpt

Unconsoling Tableaux.

Well, until the age of thirty five or thereabouts, so far as the author could determine, people live okay. They enjoy themselves, recklessly squandering what nature has endowed them with. Afterwards, in the majority of cases, comes rapid decrepitude and the onset of old age.

They lose their taste for lots of fine things. They go grey around the gills. They turn glum eyes on many admirable things they formerly were fond of. They fall prey to all manner of odd and even incomprehensible illnesses, illnesses of the sort that put doctors into a philosophical frame of mind and cause them to fret over the impotence of their profession.

These people also fall prey to the more comprehensible and, so to speak, generally available ailments one finds described in textbooks, such as, for instance, melancholia, palsy, paralysis, diabetes, tuberculosis and the like, and so forth, etc.

Immediately they come down with something, these sick people rush off with their ailments and their baggage to various resorts and seashores in search of their squandered youth. They bathe in the sea, dive and swim, lie around for hours at a time under a murderous sun, tramp up hill and down dale and drink tonic and emetic drinks. As a result of all this they get even sicker and look with deference to their doctors, expecting miracles from them – the restoration of lost energies and the replenishment of exhausted juices.

The doctors syringe and smear their patients, soak them in special baths, administer, in the interests of science, enemas of various kinds and sizes, using salt water and mineral waters. Or they engage their patients in talk about purely nervous phenomena on the part of the organism, attempting thereby to convince the patient to stop thinking pernicious thoughts and to believe that he is as healthy as an ox and that his disorders are something imaginary, something even, as it were, on the order of phantasmagorias with no real footing in fact. This last bit utterly confounds the unsophisticated patient and reconciles him with thoughts of imminent demise. Moreover, the implacable forces of nature and the effects of normal balance gone out of whack show precious little response, for the most part, to the further machinations of science and the vivifying properties of hydrotherapy. And the invalid not infrequently ends his sojourn here on Earth without finally getting to know what it was, as a matter of fact, that did happen to him and what fatal error he had committed during his lifetime.

Even More Unconsoling Tableaux

Then, figuring that these observations were, as it might be put, purely fortuitous, that these were observations made of people whose health and nervous systems had been undermined by numerous and various shocks – war, revolution and the whole, so to speak, idiosyncrasy of our mode of life, the author, not putting his faith, therefore, in what he had seen, did an about-face and made a point of reading the biographies and accounts of the lives of all people of former epochs and centuries with any claim to notoriety.

And nope. Even more unconsoling tableaux revealed themselves to the author.

Even more tempestuous decrepitude, even more complex and incomprehensible diseases, even ghastlier melancholia, depression, disillusionment, contempt for others, hypochondria and even earlier death. Such was the scene on that, so to speak, great intellectual front.

Some of these people died having barely reached the age of maturity, others barely made it to forty. Still others, although they did manage to get beyond forty, nevertheless dragged on so pitiful an existence that they had, as it were, perished for society, anyhow.

They abandoned their glorious work. They spent whole days draped over ottomans in torn slippers, smoking pipes, moping around, quarreling with their wives, whining and whimpering. Out of boredom and in order to forget themselves, they wrote memoirs about their wonderful and heroic youth or composed theological and religious tracts, inasmuch as for that purpose they did not require the inspiration and that full-blown creative health and uplift and that sense of physical well-being which they had known in their youth.

Great People

There was one feature in the lives of these illustrious people, who had lived in ages past, which astonished the author most of all. And that was a certain what you might call resignation or submission to fate and even a certain reluctance to come to grips with their ailments.

These ailments they frequently considered manifestations of the will of God or some special malevolence of fate or their own natural aptitude for failure. And after a short course of treatment, chiefly hydrotherapy, they endured everything that happened to them without a murmur and made not even so much as a stab at peering below the surface of things so as to discover the causes and comprehend the physical origins of their maladies.

But to our great good fortune it can be said that they were not all of them alike in this respect.

There was one category of persons who distinguished themselves by particular hardiness of health and who, unlike the others, enjoyed a notably long-lasting life. These were people with a penchant for thinking and not taking, so to speak, an idealistic view of life. They were, in the main, all manner of philosophers, scholars of the natural sciences, chemists, scientific researchers and, in general, all manner of professors and sages who, each by way of his own speciality, spent their time puzzling over and pondering something or other about the various properties of nature.

In a word, these were people who not only composed odes or, say, suites or symphonies, not only painted various "Sunsets" and "Sunrises" and "Forest Glades," but also conscientiously mulled over their lives, their exquisitely complex organisms, and control of the same, and their relation to the environment.

These truly great people – materialists for the most part – practically all of them lived to a ripe old age and tranquilly, without superfluous moans, groans and lamentations, departed, as they used to say, for the "Realm of the Shades" and oblivion.

They rarely got sick and even, on the contrary, became notably healthier and healthier as they advanced towards old age.

They rarely fussed and fretted. They refrained from doing anything silly and manfully pursued their aims, unconcerned, in point of fact, even about their long-lasting lives.

It was not without a heart-throb that the author read the biography of Voltaire who, despite the vicissitudes of fate and persecution from all sides, deigned to live to the age of eighty four.

The illustrious Greek physician, Hippocrates, the "father of medicine " as they called him (in other words, the man who understood in its entirety the whole physical basis of things), lived to the age of ninety nine.

And a certain Democritus, in all likelihood the wisest man that ever lived, the Greek philosopher and founder of Materialism, rounded off a life of one hundred and two years and dropped dead with a smile, saying that he could have lived even longer if he had had a mind to do so.

The So-Called "Secret of Eternal Youth"

No, nothing in this world happens for nothing.

The author supposes – is even positive – that these professors and learned men did get to know something or other, did discover some sort of secret, perhaps, or let's not say secret but some sort of suitable, one-and-only line of behavior, and by putting it to use, they lived without a worry, regulating their lives and organisms the same way, say, your workman or your master machinist regulates his lathe.

But the secret of their personal well-being and longevity these professors – wouldn't you know it! – carried off with them to the grave.

Of course, an abstract word or two was said on this score. Some expatiated on the equilibrium of body and soul. Others expounded foggy notions about the necessity of sticking as close to nature as possible or, at any rate, of not interfering with nature and generally going barefoot.

Still others advised not letting yourself get excited and not breaking away from the masses, saying that wisdom is always tranquil.

A certain number of these people did descend from the empyrean heights and, rejecting fancy talk about the soul, laid down the rule that one ought to take the best possible care of the lesser natural particulars of one's body, adding the advice to eat yogurt, which vegetarian dish they unqualifiedly considered conducive to an especially long life inasmuch as it does not allow microbes to accumulate without rhyme or reason in our innards and in those paltry nooks and crannies of our organism that nature has assigned a lowly and second-rate function.

However, in his student days, the author knew a teacher who ate that dairy diet for several years running and who, suddenly catching a slight case of the flu, "bit the dust", as the expression has it, mourned by his relatives and his pupils, his relatives and pupils asserting, moreover, in one voice, that it was just exactly that fondness of his for sour milk that did him in, it having so undermined his strength that his debilitated organism wasn't able to cope with so, in point of fact, trivial an illness.

Why Not Talk About Things of Interest?

Without meaning even remotely to disparage or rebuke these great people in any way, the author still wishes to make the point that nothing that made any particular sense, nothing positive, above all, nothing practical and within the range of common understanding was said on this subject.

And the venerable sages who had learned something or other departed for the other world without ever having bestowed bliss on their fellow creatures.

Of course, the author has no intention of coming right up now and saying: You see, these sages dropped dead, taking their secret with them, but look here, the author, that prince of a guy and son of a gun, has discovered that secret and this very minute he's going to bestow bliss on all mankind with the revelation of his excruciating discovery.

No, the whole thing is lots simpler and maybe even something of a let-down. Everything the author has to say is in all likelihood, even positively, already known to the Department of Public Health and Medicine.

And even if it is the author's intention to speak of that sort of thing in his own limp and bumbling way, why not have a nice, plain talk about things of interest, things that arouse everybody's curiosity and hold everybody's attention?

In their leisure time, people study literature, discuss music, collect stamps, mount butterflies, gnats and all sorts of — excuse the expression — dung beetles, but the author suspects that the one real topic — after politics (which actually is the same thing in the end since the social reconstruction of society leads to new, healthy forms of life and, it goes without saying, to new forms of health, as well) — the one topic on nearly everybody's mind, the topic nearly everybody feels close to and understands about and finds as necessary as food and drink and sunlight, is our life, our youth, our vitality and our ability to make use of these precious gifts.

Loss of Health

So far as the author could tell, health, within the aforementioned intellectual stratum mostly, has taken something of a down-turn and a knocking about.

The author has the suspicion that the health, at least the nervous stamina, of all people of all categories of all countries and all classes and all stations in life has significantly decreased over recent centuries.

Why, there are times when, reading books about by-gone days in which they describe the adventures of heroes of the most diverse classes and professions, you simply go all agog and aghast.

Now, there's your fabulously stout lads and robust hearties.

There's your men of firm and even mighty character.

There's gluttons and drunkards the likes of which we've never even dreamed of.

You keep coming across passages like: "Feeling parched, he refreshed himself by downing two bottles of Anjou rose, whereupon, springing to his horse, he galloped off in pursuit of his offender..."

Well now, what happens if you put a couple of bottles of Anjou red in the hands of one of our folks, an inhabitant of this 1934 of ours? He's likely not only not to climb on his horse, he's almost certain not even to be able to say "mamma." He'll lie down next to his nag and have a snooze, moan and groan a bit, and only afterwards, finding himself some farmer's cart to hire, will he wobble off back home to tend to his own affairs, no longer giving a damn about his offender who, for his part, probably skedaddled off to the other end of the Earth the instant he noticed he was being pursued.

Fruitless Endeavors

Though no professor, no, let us say, academician or, for instance, candidate for a higher degree, the author did, nevertheless, by dint of a certain naivete and a certain amount of gumption in his character, try, to make out what was what — wherein resided the secret that the sages had discovered.

And wouldn't it be possible, once grasping that secret, to lift a corner of the curtain concealing imperishable youth and longevity?

Naturally enough, nothing that made the slightest sense came of the attempt.

Of course, the author did sort of understand that the gist of the matter lay in some kind of smooth operation of our machine, our organism, in correlation with the smooth operation of social life, of the environment and the milieu.

Yet, on the other hand, the author noticed that there were people whose lives were smooth and who died an early death on account of some trivial nasal drip, and, on the other hand, he kept coming across examples of a life of simply incredible violence and irregularity, lived in an age of violence and even cataclysm, the possessors of which, nevertheless, lived long and superbly and were noted for exemplary health and well-being.

At this point, the author, refusing to give up as yet, began to scrutinize the workings, so to speak, of the separate and distinct parts of our mechanism and, generally, of the various little thigamajigs and thigamabobs which the professors just possibly might have overlooked on account of their exalted professional and social position, finding them, let us say, too banal, too paltry and undistinguished or even simply too demeaning for the human race and the tempestuous growth of all of Christian culture which was based on idealism and a haughty sense of superiority vis-a-vis other animals who, contrary to man, originated, for all we know, from mold, water or some other repulsive chemical compound.

No, the author, – alas! – has made no new discoveries in this field. Nevertheless, he has noticed much that is instructive and worthy of genuine astonishment. And so, before taking up our tale, we wish to recount a thing or two of the sort without which you simply cannot begin to understand the whole story of the man who regained his youth.

Translated by I. R. Titunik

The above excerpt is an introduction to the main story of an aged professor of astronomy who becomes possessed with the idea of regaining his youth. He starts with the usual methods such as physical exercises and various diets, but then falls madly in love with a frivolous young girl, leaves his old wife, and for a time really regains his vitality and sexual potency untill it all ends tragically with the man having a severe stroke. Having recovered from the stroke the professor returns to his wife and, although he continues to do morning exercises and keep a diet, he is unable to experience the same feeling of the fullness of life he had known with his young mistress.

This banal story is only a pretext that Zoschenko uses to discuss the problem that was central to his life: to what degree can a person control his mental and physical health? Almost every event in the novel is supplied with a note relating a similar episode in the life of some well known personage. Zoschenko regrets the fact that common people's biographies are not written therefore he could only investigate great people's lives. The notes to the novel are even more interesting and instructive than the novel itself. First published in 1934, Youth Regained was only reprinted during the first thaw in the 1960s and is still undeservedly little known.

The translation of the complete novel has never been published and is available from the translator.

ISAAC BABEL

1894-1941

Babel was the first Soviet writer to become internationally known. His *The Red Cavalry* was translated into 20 languages and hailed by such writers as Romain Rolland, Henry Barbusse, Heinrich Mann and Maxim Gorky. Babel was first published in the magazine LEF, edited by Mayakovsky, and enjoyed Gorky's patronage.

His literary heritage is not large, and his fame rests mainly on *The Red Cavalry* and a series of stories about the Odessa criminal world featuring colourful Jewish Robin Hoods.

In the late thirties Babel was no longer published and experienced great financial difficulties. Like many active participants in the Revolution and the Civil War, he feared arrest, and after Gorky's death he expected it every day. His hunch was right – he was arrested in 1939 and shot in 1941 as a "foreign spy".

Despite his devotion to and complete acceptance of the socialist revolution he couldn't help describing the world he witnessed in its true light. His *The Red Cavalry* inspires a wide range of reactions: from the admiration of his ability to see beauty in the horrible, to the disgust and horror at his impassioned detailed descriptions of executions and tortures.

Babel's archives were arrested together with him – 24 folders containing his notes on the looting, murders, rapes and injustices he witnessed daily as he followed the *The Red Cavalry* led by General Budyonny. He was planning to supplement the 36 chapters of his *The*

Red Cavalry with 14 more using his notes. To this day the notes have not been found, neither have any documents certifying their destruction.

Most people who used to know Babel personally speak of his exceptional kindness and generosity as well as his wit and perspicacity. His wife recalls how he would give away watches, jackets, train tickets, and money to needy people.

He was a writer of enormous talent and one of the finest stylists in Russian literature. "A short story should be as succinct as a military dispatch or a bank account," said Babel, who combined great expressiveness with a rich sense of humour and the lurid landscape.

Babel as the Marquis de Sade of the Russian Revolution

by Igor Yarkevich

It is a rather baffling realisation of our time that cultural and aesthetic myths have proved to be far more durable than political and economic ones. The latter have collapsed and disappeared, but the rosy veil has yet to be torn away from the history of Russian literature.

If a book by Babel and one of the hastily produced Russian editions of the Marquis de Sade were set side by side, one might ask what parallels and associations there could possibly be. But let us loosen the grip of our habitual notions just a little, and it immediately becomes clear that these two writers are twin-brothers, their arms extended in joyous greeting to each other across the centuries and the political regimes. Both were born in revolution, both became its faithful dogs, sons and "stormy petrels", both finally became its victims.

Babel is perhaps one of the most enigmatic figures of the literary milieu of the twenties and thirties. We know astonishingly little about him, and mostly from his own fragmentary memoirs. Like de Sade,

Babel was a master of imposture. Both of their lives might be described as variations on a revolutionary-romantic theme with a prison coda.

If you compare the Marquis with his democratic populist disciple, Babel, you are sure to notice certain interesting points in common. Some, in particular, concern the body of the executioner. According to the Marquis's notions, the executioner, who carries out the will of the republic and rids the land of free France of various Marie-Antoinettes and all sorts of Louis, is the most genuine of humanists. But what does his body experience as the blade of the guillotine comes down? Is it as calm and cold-blooded as his brain? What does his body feel for the unfortunate noble-woman who pleads on the scaffold: "Wait, monsieur executioner, for just one more minute!"

Whereas the Marquis himself never got round to answering these questions, Babel was able to resolve the bloody riddles involved. In his stories, and especially in *The Red Cavalry*, we can find dozens of cheerful and impassive descriptions of such final minutes and of nobles' heads tumbling into the basket of the revolution.

"Right under my nose some Cossacks were shooting an old, silvery-bearded Jew for spying. The old man was uttering piercing screams and struggling to get away. Then Kudra, of the machine-gun detachment, took hold of his head and tucked it under his arm. The Jew stopped screaming and set his legs apart. Kudra drew out his dagger with his right hand and carefully, without splashing himself, cut the old man's throat. Then he knocked at the closed casement.

"Anyone who cares may come and fetch him," he said. "You're free to do so."

The hypnotising neutrality of the intonation somehow persuades the reader of the authority of sadism, and that nothing special is taking place, everything is going according to plan.

The appreciation of Babel's work suffers from a rather sad aberration of the mass consciousness of the intelligentsia. Resurrected in the mid-sixties, he became one of the myths of the "golden age" of the Russian avant-garde and was unconditionally enrolled in the ranks of the innocent victims of the revolution. His articles such as "Death to the Fascist Dogs" and his participation in the notorious "writers' cruise" on a river-boat from Moscow to the White Sea Canal to inspect the Gulag construction sites along its banks were regarded as no more than forced tribute to the political conformism of the thirties.

In any case, the readers of the period of Khruschev's liberal thaw raised Babel aloft on their shields as the antithesis of heartless and unfeeling socialist realism. Babel's aesthetic unexpectedly coincided with the fashionable sixties theory of socialism with a human face, according to which Bukharin and Rykov were nicer than Stalin, and Babel and Pilnyak were nicer than Sholokhov and Furmanov.

But in actual fact, Babel followed the Marquis de Sade in accepting the evil of the revolution as entirely natural and inevitable, and also beautiful in its innumerable variations. And whereas Furmanov clearly lacked talent, Babel proved himself a faithful chronicler of the feelings of the executioners. De Sade considered violence entirely natural to man. As described by Babel's pen, the bestialities of the First Red Cavalry on the Polish Front acquire the character of an exemplary moral fable.

General Budyonny was wrong to take offence at Babel – they were made for each other. Babel's tour with the cavalry around the fields of military glory was the final realisation of the utopian idea cherished by the men of the 1860s of "going to the people" – and fusing with them in the struggle for the great cause of liberation.

The executioner, observing the convulsions of his victim, cannot remain indifferent. He becomes excited and feels the desire to prolong these torments. The pages of Babel's *The Red Cavalry* contains numerous descriptions of torture and executions lasting for hours. Commissars, horses and other animals, Polish gentlemen, local Rabbis, Moldavian bandits and Tbilisi prostitutes – they are all only of interest to the writer as worthy fuel for the revolutionary cauldron. Babel follows de Sade again in raising violence to an absolute.

Yet another aberration of mass consciousness has led to Babel being unconditionally accepted as a poet of Jewish life. This would be all very fine, if not for one small detail – it is hard to be a poet of Jewish life without possessing the Jewish mentality. And if we try comparing Babel with Martin Buber, we soon discover that there aren't even any parameters for drawing a comparison. In Babel the Jewish mentality is reduced to the level of superficial folklore and feeble anecdote.

There is nothing really surprising in this: Babel is a faithful disciple of revolution, and de Sade is a total internationalist. Once all national feelings have been "blunted", all that is left is sadism, the excited description of the victim's final convulsions.

In general the "commissars' prose" of the twenties has remained a taboo area in contemporary culture. I don't believe this was done deliberately, it's simply that in recent years we've been too busy to get around to it, since we discovered that there are more important matters – inflation, defending the White House, forming the CIS... The professional level of literary criticism has also declined noticeably, and wrestling a powerful athlete like Babel, who has no pity and no complexes, requires sound and effective professional training.

In Russian literary history there have been two dismissive remarks of quite astounding pejorative force: around the beginning of the century, Leo Tolstoy dismissed Leonid Andreev with the words, "He tries to frighten me, but I'm not afraid"; thirty years later, on his return from Paris, Babel similarly disavowed the young Vladimir Nabokov – "A talented writer, but he has nothing to write about". Indeed, from Babel's point of view, Nabokov had nothing to write about: he hadn't served in the Red Cavalry, he hadn't been friends with members of the Cheka and with drug addicts...

Far be it from me to suggest that Babel be thrown overboard from the steamship of Russian literature. Of course there's no need to throw anyone overboard, but it is preferable to give them their proper place. Perhaps some day the Marquis and Babel will have monuments beside each other on neighbouring pedestals.

Translated by Andrew Bromfield

ALEX LAMONT MILLER

In memoriam

Dear Alex is no longer with us. Here, in Moscow, we have parted with him twice. The first time was last summer, when he returned to England after working for twenty three years as a literary translator for Progress and Raduga publishers. And then on 21 June, 1994, when he left for that bourn from which no traveller returns.

He was born of Scottish parents in what he liked to call jokingly "a tiny patch of Scotland in the middle of Nottinghamshire". His father was a doctor, a GP in the mining town of Hucknall Torkard. It was a great joy to Alex when his daughter, after getting a degree in mathematics at King's College, Cambridge, and working for a while at the Cavendish laboratory, decided to continue the family tradition by studying medicine. She is now a fully qualified doctor at one of the leading London hospitals.

So Alex grew up in Robin Hood country, Nottinghamshire, interestingly enough in a house which had once belonged to Dr Coates, the father of the composer Eric Coates. Music was important for Alex, too, throughout his life. He enlivened many a gathering in Moscow by turning up with his guitar and a repertoire which included some delightful songs he had learned specially in Gaelic, as well as his ever popular "Ochi Chyorniye" and "Irene, Goodnight".

He retained vivid memories of his Nottinghamshire childhood. "I would be woken up in the early morning by the tramp-tramp of hobnailed boots. I'd look out of the window, and there would be a cohort of miners, faces black, whites of eyes rolling, snap-tins dangling from their belts, all too tired to talk."

Returning to these parts in 1993 he was struck by the way life had changed there. "The Nottingham-Derbyshire Collieries are nearly all silent now. Yet when the miners' grown-up children go shopping they wheel trolleys full of goodies round the nearest Safeways, Asda, Morrison's, Marks and Sparks, or whatever. But I remember my days at primary school and the kid at the next desk opening his snap-tin to fish out bread and dripping for his lunch if he was lucky, or bread and lard if he wasn't."

From primary school he went on to Nottingham High School, which D.H.Lawrence had attended some thirty years earlier. Lawrence was still "persona non grata" in those days and Alex recalled that it was not done to even mention his name at the school.

Then came the Second World War and Alex volunteered for active service in the RAF, in spite of his young years. It was probably there that he developed a passion for taking things to pieces and finding out how they worked. Later he turned his attention to computers and became quite an expert on them, sharing his knowledge with the less initiated.

The war ended at last, and Alex was able to continue his education, which he did brilliantly, getting firsts in Russian and English at St John's College, Cambridge. It was here that he developed the special feeling for language which was to shape the course of his life, to make him a poet, writer, translator. This delicate and precise awareness of the value of words, their emotive power and slightest nuances, together with his deep and scholarly love for literature, English and Russian above all, but also Greek, Latin, you name

Alex Lamont Miller: In memoriam

it, marked him out from the moment he arrived in Moscow as a translator of the highest quality.

Alex was one of the few Westerners who came to work in Russia when it was still very much the Soviet Union. And one of even fewer who stayed on after the end of his first contract. In all, he spent one third of his life in Moscow and during that time produced the many fine translations which quickly won him a reputation for excellence. Suffice it to mention his brilliant renderings of Blok´s "The Twelve", Pushkin´s "Boris Godunov", Tvardovsky´s "Vassily Tyorkin" and "Peter the Great" by Alexei Tolstoy. His range was remarkably wide. He translated poems by Anna Akhmatova and Marina Tsvetayeva, plays by Arbuzov and Leonov, novels and stories by such different writers as Isaac Babel, Vassily Aksyonov, Vladimir Odoyevsky, Boris Pilnyak and Yuri Trifonov. His translations of Chekhov´s short stories in Raduga´s popular 5-volume pocket edition include such masterpieces as "The Steppe" and "Ward No.6".

After a successful operation for lung cancer Alex gained a new lease of life, six precious years, in which he produced some of his finest work. Perhaps the most daunting task he ever tackled was that of translating Griboyedov´s "Pains from Brains", as he decided to call it. He succeeded brilliantly in reproducing the meter and rhyming pattern of the original, something never achieved before. It is to be hoped that an opportunity will be found of publishing this work and also his translation of Avvakum´s "Life". The short stories that he wrote around this time about his life in Russia should surely also attract some enterprising publisher.

A year ago Alex returned to England to live in the house of an old friend within the bounds of Newstead Abbey estate which also has literary associations. It was the home of the Byrons until they had to sell it. Alex liked walking in the grounds and used to visit the memorial that Byron put up to his dog Boatswain. It must have reminded Alex of his own dear old Snoddy.

He missed Moscow, of course, and the people he had worked closely with for so many years. He had happy memories of skiing and walks in Izmailovo Park, swimming and sun-bathing on the beach in Sokolniki, and concerts at the Conservatoire and Chaikovsky Hall. "Not many English people had the good fortune to sit in the auditorium and hear a Schnittke symphony conducted by Rozhdestvensky, the orchestra going full blast, kitchen sink included (or tutti frutti, as the musicians say)". And on a more mundane level "It don´t half feel queer at times, I must say. No spats with control editors, no bonuses, no matryoshkas on street stalls in the Arbat..." His last letter ended with the words: "I´ll be writing again. In the meantime, always interested to know how things are at Raduga."

Reserved and modest, with a warm, wry humour and an unerring sense of fairness, Alex embodied all the best qualities of the country he came from. His sensitive translations helped to build a bridge between his homeland and the other land where he chose to spend so many years of his life. He is deeply missed and mourned by all those who had the pleasure of knowing him.

Rest in peace, dear friend.

Kate Cook

Alex Lamont Miller: In memoriam

What made me blindly hope I need no longer languish?
I rushed! I flew! I trembled! Soon joy would come to me!
To whom did I so humbly and so tenderly
  Confess my passion and my anguish?
To you! My God! Whom have you chosen in my place!
  To think that he's the person you preferred!
  Why did you lead me on, without an honest word?
    Why didn't you tell me in my face,
Making a mockery of the past right from the start,
  That to you they had lost all their attraction –
Those shared excitements and emotions of the heart
That had not been cooled down in me by wild distraction,
Or change of scene, or being so far away.
I lived and breathed by them, by them I was sustained.
Had you said that my sudden arrival here today,
My looks, words, conduct – these you heartily disdained,
I would have broken off my ties with you, of course,
    And, as we bid our last farewell,
    I wouldn't have wanted you to tell
Me any more about that man of yours....
    Yes! I'm now completely sober,
The scales have fallen from my eyes, my dreams are over.
    I could do worse now than discharge
    My pent-up bitterness and wrath
    At father and at daughter both,
At stupid lover and the whole wide world at large.
Who are these people? Where's fate cast me, on what strand?
All harass. All upbraid. A cruel tormenting band,
Faithless in love, in hate – vindictive, if not worse,
    Indomitable raconteurs,
Unbalanced clever-dicks, and half-wits, slyly cunning,
Spiteful old ladies, and old men with their minds running
    To seed on all the nonsense they've invented.
As with one's voice, you've all proclaimed that I'm demented.
You're right. He'd walk out of a blazing fire alive,
    Who could spend only one day here,
    Who could but breathe the selfsame air,
    And yet whose reason could survive.
I'm quitting Moscow! I shall not return again.
I'll flee and not look back to cavil or disparage.
Somewhere I'll find a niche where I can ease my pain.
    My carriage, quick, my carriage!

The above is a concluding monologue by Chatsky, the hero in "Woe from Wit" by Alexander Griboyedov (1795-1829), translated by Alex Miller for Griboyedov's 200 anniversary. The translation remained unpublished and is available from Raduga Publishers, Moscow.

Where Things Came From
Bear, Dandelion, Wizard, Owl and All Sorts of Other Kinds of Tales
Collected and Translated from Various Languages by Grigory Kruzhkov

40 pages, 20 colour illustrations. The text is in Russian and English.

Where Unmagical People Came From
(A Wizard Folk Tale)

In the very beginning, old people say, there weren't any unmagical people in the world. Everyone was a wizard and could do a bit of magic, turn into things, bewitch and unbewitch things and so on.

But one day it so happened that a young boy wizard fell in love with a young girl witch. Of course other wizards and witches had fallen in love before. But this young wizard fell so hopelessly in love that he just forgot everything he knew; how to bewitch things, how to cast spells, and even how to brew love potions – he basically lost all his wits.

Instead of making magic, he climbed up a tall cliff and threw himself into the sea to escape from this hopeless love. With one last pathetic cry, he jumped, and plummeted into the water like a stone!

Anyone else would at least have turned themselves into a fish if they were in his position, but he had completely lost his wits, you see. He started choking and really began to drown in earnest.

When the young girl witch saw this, she turned into a she-eagle and soared off after him. She plucked him out of the water with her sharp claws and carried him across the sea. Maybe she wanted to take him to a rugged cliff and peck him to death out of sheer rage.

But while she was flying across the sea, she suddenly turned into a heron, then into a duck, and then finally, when the shore was already in sight, she turned into a swallow with a black back. And as soon as they crash-landed on to the sand, the lovesick boy wizard woke up and the girl witch turned back into a girl.

And it's from them that unmagical people are descended, so they say. A strange breed indeed! Those of us who have spent time in their parts say that they have completely forgotten how to do magic, that they don't know any real spells, and that they can't see into a future. How can one not see into the future? Isn't it written for all to see on the clouds, the leaves and the duckweed?

Obviously these people must possess some secret unmagical strength. Something which makes them unable to predict what is going to happen or change the future. What strange wonders are these!

Translated by Rosamund Bartlett

Grigory Kruzhkov
is a famous children's
poet, translator
of English poetry,
and essayist.
The tale above
is one of the nine tales
making up
this richly illustrated
book which exists only
in camera-ready state
at the moment.

About the Authors

Sigizmund Krziszanowsky (1887-1950) was very highly regarded by his contemporaries and in his lifetime his readings and lectures attracted wide audiences. Yet he never managed to publish a single line of his prolific output. He left five novels, 100 short stories, a dozen or so plays and 400 pages of essays. "All my life I was a literary non-person" he says about himself. He was too unorthodox for his times and could only be appreciated by the chosen few.

Born in Kiev he began writing rather late in life when the liberal post-revolutionary period with its outburst of artistic creativity, now known as the Silver Age, had already been crudely crushed by the new authorities, and it was no longer possible to publish works running counter to the official ideology. He is clearly another case of a "forgotten author", of which Russia still has too many.

He was a lawyer by training but his interests embraced many fields. Philosophy was his main passion. "Your high culture is a slap in the face for all of us," an offended editor said to him rejecting his book. He was described by his admirers as an intellectual Gulliver among Lilliputians. As a writer he was compared to Edgar Poe, Swift, Hoffmann and Chesterton, but he had an unmistakable voice of his own. "I´m interested in the algebra rather than the arithmetics of life," he explained.

The hopelessness of his situation vs the literary world, the resulting poverty, and the bad luck that seemed to be his lot, drove him to alcoholism in his later years.

In the Pupil of the Eye, a story we offer you in this issue, describes his unusual relationship with his wife. They lived separately, were on visiting terms, but remained faithful to each other to the end of his life.

Nina Gabrielian, born 1953, is an active participant in the emerging feminist movement in Russia. She is the president of the creative centre "Sofia", activist in the feminist clubs "Transfiguration" and "F-1".

An Armenian by nationality she grew up in Moscow and writes in beautiful figurative Russian. She writes poetry, prose, essays on feminism and on poetry. She is widely published in literary journals and collections in Moscow, and also published two books of her poetry. She has been translating Eastern poetry into Russian for her living.

About the Authors

Vladimir Makanin, born in 1937 in the Urals, is among the best known Russian writers of the last twenty years.

"One of the most serious, powerful, and intelligent writers of his generation whose work, for almost two decades, was ignored or later vilified by critics. Today his prolific work can be seen to form an integral whole, a painstakingly assembled study of the existential dynamics of life thrown into relief by the particular circumstances and psychology of communist (and post-communist) Russia. A central theme of all his work has been the relation of the individual to the collective." Sally Laird

He became widely known with the publication in 1982 of his **Forebear**, a novel about a faith healer. Many of his novels were outstandingly successful in translation in Germany, France, Spain, Eastern Europe and elsewhere. His better known works include **Voices** (1977), **Antileader** (1980), **Blue and Red** (1981), **The Laggard** (1984). His novel **Manhole** was shortlisted for the Russian Novel Booker Prize in 1992 and the next year his novel **The Baize-Covered Table** won the Prize.

See Makanin's short story **Klyucharev and Alimushkin** in **Glas #4**, and an excerpt from **The Baize-Covered Table** in **Glas #7**.

Dmitry Alexandrovich Prigov, born 1940, is a recognised leader of the modern avant-garde movement in Russian art and literature. He earned his fame back in the dissident days when his unofficial poetry readings gathered wide crowds and his drawings and poems were circulated around the country. He graduated from the Moscow Art Institute majoring in sculpture, and since the 1980s his poetry has been widely published and his paintings exhibited in Western Europe and in North America. In recent years he published several collections of his highly original poetry and gave numerous poetry readings and lectures both at home and abroad. The TV film about Prigov "Dmitry Prigov: Poet and Rebel" was repeatedly shown on Russian television. In 1993, he was awarded, together with poet Timur Kibirov, the German Pushkin Prize for outstanding achievements in literature. Prigov's poetry and essays have been widely published in translations in many countries.

About the Authors

Sergei Task, born 1952, began his literary career as a translator into Russian of Vonnegut, Updike, Salinger, Orwell, Keats, Byron, Anouilh, and Rattigan. In 1991, he published a collection of his stories in Moscow as well as publishing short stories in literary journals both in Russia and abroad.
In the last few years he was mainly writing plays. Four of his plays were staged in the USA, where he is currently living. He teaches English literature in Vermont
See also poetry by Sergei Task in **Glas # 2.**

Ergali Ger, born 1955, spent most of his life in Vilnius but for the last few years has in Moscow.
He published most of his stories in the Riga-based literary journal **Rodnik** and other Baltic journals where they were invariably noticed by critics and readers alike. He has tried many different jobs and travelled widely. He writes one work a year but each one is an event. His latest short novel was published in the journal **Znamya** in Moscow and his collection of stories is pending publication. **Electric Liza** was included in collections of contemporary Russian writing in Germany and Spain.

Igor Yarkevich, born 1962, made a name for himself with his witty satirical stories making short work of the former idols and established notions.
Among his influences he cites names such as Dostoyevsky and Henry Miller. By the time he had a chance to acquaint himself with Freud he had already made most of the discoveries himself while writing became his own mechanism of sublimation.
His collection of stories came out in 1992 from IMA-Press in Moscow. His famous trilogy: **How I Shit my Pants, How I didn't Get Raped,** and **How I Masturbated,** a parody of Tolstoy's **Childhood, Boyhood, and Youth,** will be brought out this year by Glagol Publishers. The first two parts of the trilogy were published in English in **Glas #2.**

Glas: From # One to # Eight

#1. DEDICATED TO MICHAEL GLENNY
- Anatoly Mariengof *Cynics*
- Leonid Latynin *Sleeper at Harvest Time*
- Evgeni Popov *Pork Kebabs*
- Zufar Gareyev *When Other Birds Call*
- Vyacheslav Rybakov *Hassle*
- POETRY: Mikhail Aizenberg, Tatyana Scherbina
- Victor Yerofeev *Soviet Literature: in Memoriam*

#3. WOMEN'S VIEW
- Marina Filatova *If I Were a Man...*
- Svetlana Vasilenko *Shamara*
- Nina Sadur *Witch's Tears*
- Marina Palei *The Bloody Women's Ward*
- Galina Scherbakova *The Three Loves of Masha Peredreeva*
- Larissa Miller *A Childhood in Post-war Moscow*
- Elena Glinka *Kolyma Streetcar*
- POETRY: Nina Iskrenko, Elena Schwartz
- Julia Latynina *Waiting For The Golden Age*

#2. SOVIET GROTESQUE
- Vladimir Sorokin *A Business Proposition, Four Stout Hearts*
- Igor Yarkevich *How I Shit My Pants, How I Didn't Get Raped*
- Victor Yerofeev *De Profundis, Cheekbone, A Nose And A Gully*
- Daniil Kharms *A Letter And Other Stories*
- Yuri Miloslavsky *Urban Sketches*
- Alexander Terekhov *Charon, Buddy*
- Sergei Task *Per Somnia*

#4. LOVE & FEAR
- Victor Pelevin *The Blue Lantern, Mid-game, The View from The Window*
- Zufar Gareyev *Facsimile Summer*
- Yevgeny Kharitonov *Teardrops on the Flowers*
- Vladimir Makanin *Klyucharyov and Alimushkin*
- Friedrich Gorenstein *Bag in Hand*
- Zinovy Zinik *Mea Culpa*
- Yuri Miloslavsky *The Death of Manon, On Exile*
- Lev Razgon *The President's Wife*
- Boris Yampolsky *A Crowded Place*
- Alexander Terekhov *Communal Living, Pitch Black Void*
- Ksenia Klimova *A Marriage of Convenience*
- POETRY: Marina Tsvetaeva, Gleb Arsenyev, Olga Sedakova
- Alla Latynina *The Literary Prize and the Literary Process*

"Glas is a first-rate magazine, well planned and very well translated. Anyone interested in Russia and good writing should seek it out."
Sally Laird,
London Observer

"*Glas*, daughter of glasnost, seems likely to make a significant contribution to the restoration of readers' faith in the editorial independence of contemporary journals. If you cannot find *Glas* in the shops, ask for it. This journal deserves wide distribution."
Gerry Dukes,
Irish Times

"GLAS gives us a sense of Russian literature in motion."
Times Literary Supplement

#5. BULGAKOV & MANDELSTAM
- Mikhail Bulgakov *To a Secret Friend*
- From "*The Diaries of Elena Sergeyevna*"
- Osip Mandelstam *From "The Fourth Prose", Cold Summer*
- Evgeny Mandelstam *Excerpts from Memoirs*
- Nadezhda Volpin *Reminiscences of Mandelstam and his Wife*